ERIDANI'S CROWN

PUBLISHED BY:

UFO Publishing
1685 E 15th St.
Brooklyn, NY 11229
www.ufopub.com

Trade paperback ISBN: 978-0-9992690-1-5
Hardback ISBN: 978-0-9992690-2-2

Cover art: Tomasz Maronski

Graphics design: Tomasz Maronski and Jay O'Connell

Interior art: Tomasz Maronski

Typesetting & interior design: Melissa Neely

Copyeditor: Elektra Hammond

Visit us on the web:
www.ufopub.com

ERIDANI'S CROWN

Alex Shvartsman

UFO Publishing
Brooklyn, NY

BOOKS BY ALEX SHVARTSMAN

Explaining Cthulhu to Grandma and Other Stories

The Golem of Deneb Seven and Other Stories

H. G. Wells, Secret Agent

EDITED BY ALEX SHVARTSMAN

Unidentified Funny Objects series

The Cackle of Cthulhu

Funny Science Fiction

Funny Fantasy

Funny Horror

Humanity 2.0

Coffee: 14 Caffeinated Tales of the Fantastic

Dark Expanse: Surviving the Collapse

CONTENTS

PART 1

(Year 532 of the Council Era)

CHAPTER 1
AN INTERRUPTED LESSON

he day Eridani killed a man for the first time started out as perfectly ordinary.

She and her brother Danchu were at Gavron's house for their morning studies. The rising sun bathed the room with light through the stained glass windows of the library. The aroma of hotcakes and coffee wafted in from the kitchen; a delicious enticement for the two students to complete the lesson soon.

Eridani leaned back in her chair. She had solved her math problems and was already mentally composing an essay that she knew Gavron would have them both working on after the break.

Danchu, despite being a year her senior at sixteen, wasn't as quick a study. He hunched over his piece of parchment, his stare vacant. A drop of ink pooled at the tip of his quill.

Gavron snapped his fingers in front of Danchu's face. "Concentrate, young prince. Knowledge is the mightiest weapon you can wield in life. Must I remind you that Kalatar of Gan had conquered three of his neighboring city-states by the time he was your age?"

Jolted out of his reverie, Danchu stifled a yawn and focused on his tutor. "Sixteen-year-old Kalatar was tutored by Orodos himself, the greatest philosopher not only in the history of Gan, but in all of the North, as you keep pointing out." Danchu rested his quill at the edge of the inkwell. "All we've got is you."

Eridani suppressed a chuckle. Gavron never tired of flaunting his Gan education, even if precious few of the nobles in the city of Skond were much impressed by it. His services were mostly engaged by the newly-rich merchants who sought any opportunity to distance themselves—and especially their children—from their lowborn roots, as well as by the minor families from the outlying provinces equally desperate to elevate the status of their progeny in the de facto capital of the North.

Danchu and Eridani, the crown prince and princess of Kozhad, were his most prominent students, even if all of their royal subjects put together wouldn't be enough to populate a quarter of Skond. Their father wanted the best education he could provide for his eventual successor. Eridani, who actually enjoyed learning, found it easy enough to persuade her parents into sending her along with her older brother.

Gavron pursed his lips, and absent-mindedly caressed the university medallion he wore on a silver chain around his neck. The medallion, propped up by the bulge of his rotund belly, served as another not-so-subtle reminder of his status as a man of learning. He drew a deep breath, no doubt to administer a well-deserved and eloquent tongue lashing, when he was interrupted by a commotion downstairs.

A servant entered the library and whispered urgently in Gavron's ear. A puzzled expression on the tutor's face gradually changed to a look of concern.

"Stall them," he told the servant.

Danchu tilted his head. "What is it?"

"There are constables here," said Gavron. "They're asking after the two of you."

Eridani and Danchu exchanged glances.

"Have either of you done any mischief lately? Tell the truth, now."

Both siblings shook their heads.

"Then it may be best that the constables don't find you, not until we've had an opportunity to understand their motives."

Gavron pointed toward the hanging rug that covered the doorway to his meditation chamber, a tiny windowless room that, Eridani suspected, had begun its existence as a storage closet. With many rugs, banners, and maps covering every bit of wall space that wasn't obscured by bookshelves, the entryway wasn't easy to detect unless one knew it was there.

The siblings entered the small space, its walls covered floor to ceiling in thick, lush carpets. Gavron scrambled to put away their parchment and quills. They peeked through the crack between the hanging rug and the wall as armed men marched into the library.

Two of the men wore the gray-and-silver uniforms of the Skond militia.

Like most teenagers, the siblings had experienced an occasional run-in with such men, but Eridani could think of no offense that would cause her or her brother to be actively sought by the constables.

The third man wore the red-and-silver of the palace guard. He entered the library last and looked around, sneering at the bookshelves as though they had somehow offended him.

"The Kozhad princelings," he said, with no preamble. "Where are they?"

Gavron stood up straight and crossed his arms. "Good sir, what cause do you have for invading my home? I will make certain the patriarch hears about this."

The palace guard grinned, revealing tobacco-stained teeth; the mirth never reached his eyes. He stepped toward the tutor, towering over the pudgy man by a head-and-a-half. "Who do you think sent me? Answer my question, Foreigner, or you'll discover what else I'm empowered to do."

Gavron backed up a step. "My students missed their morning appointment today," he said. "They've been known to oversleep, on occasion. Perhaps you should try the house their family rents on the Street of Tailors."

"Search the house," the palace guard told the constables. They filed out of the library. Eridani could hear the muffled indignation of the cook as the constables worked their way through the kitchen.

The palace guard turned his attention back to Gavron. Without breaking eye contact, he slowly drew his shortsword from its scabbard.

Eridani tensed. In Skond culture, unsheathing a weapon in someone else's home was a terrible insult to the host. The palace guard might as well have relieved himself in the corner of the library.

"Lie to me again, and I'll paint these gaudy wall rugs with your blood," said the palace guard. "Where are the brats?"

Danchu clenched his fists. Eridani rested her palm on his shoulder, holding him back from rushing into the library. Her brother's heart was in the right place, but the blood it pumped often ran hot. He had learned to heed her counsel, to allow her to hold him back. It had prevented many an altercation during their stay in Skond.

"I will have your name, sir," said Gavron, "so that I may lodge a complaint with the patriarch. Whatever authority he may have invested in you surely doesn't extend to insulting the law-abiding guests of—"

The palace guard slapped Gavron with the back of his free hand. Gavron's knees buckled. His shoulder knocked into a bookcase, rattling the thick volumes within.

This time, Eridani couldn't stop her brother. He nudged her aside and stepped past the rug, revealing himself. He grabbed a rapier from the pair hanging crossed on the wall. The weapon was decorative and therefore poorly balanced, forged from wrought iron instead of steel. Danchu half turned toward the palace guard in a fencing stance and held it steady.

"It's easy to bully the unarmed," he called out. "Turn and face a real opponent."

"And what will you do with that toy?" The palace guard sneered at Danchu and advanced on him with the casual grace of a cat stalking a songbird. "It's a good thing I don't have to bring you in alive," he added. "I'm going to enjoy this."

The palace guard lunged, eliminating the reach advantage of Danchu's weapon and driving him back with a series of quick strikes. The young prince was forced to block with his much thinner sword. He managed to divert several attacks by parrying at an angle, but another swing of the shortsword cleaved the top half of the rapier's blade off.

Danchu froze for the briefest of moments, staring at the jagged stump now protruding from the elaborate hilt of his weapon. Triumphant, the palace guard lifted the sword for a killing blow. Instead of attempting a parry, Danchu grabbed the rapier's hilt with both hands, rushed his opponent as though he was trying to tackle him, and drove the remaining blade fragment into the soft spot under the palace guard's jaw.

The man's scream turned into a gurgle as he crumpled onto the carpet, the blade fragment lodged deep inside his skull.

"Years of fencing lessons, finally paying off," announced Danchu. He tapped the palace guard's body with the tip of his boot, then swaggered toward a second rapier hanging on the wall. He held his head high, like a hero from the sagas Gavron had made them read, but his voice shook a little, betraying inner turmoil.

Eridani was about to point out that her brother might be better off picking up the palace guard's shortsword, but before she had the chance to voice her suggestion, the two constables burst through the door of the library, summoned by the sounds of the struggle and the palace guard's dying scream. They drew falchions and advanced toward Danchu.

Danchu didn't repeat the mistake of allowing them to close the gap. He thrust with his much longer rapier, keeping the constables at bay and out of striking range. The two herded him into a corner and positioned themselves farther apart, making it more difficult for him to defend against both. Like the palace guard, they hacked at the rapier. It was only a matter of time until they'd manage to break or bend this weapon, too.

Eridani crept from the meditation room and toward the fallen palace guard. Even in death, he maintained a solid grip on his weapon. Eridani bit her lip as she pried the sword from his fingers.

She advanced on a constable from behind, the palace guard's shortsword in her shaking hand. He was intent on Danchu, and his back presented a large, easy target. She hesitated, until Danchu cried out in pain.

One of the constables got past his defenses and cut him, a flesh wound the length of Eridani's palm oozing blood from his forearm. Danchu cringed as he struggled to hold the rapier straight.

Eridani acted before fear and doubt could gain a greater foothold in her heart. She stabbed at the constable's back with all her strength. The sharp sword slid in with greater ease than she had imagined, until the blade lodged in the man's flesh up to its hilt.

The constable screamed. He turned slowly, dropping his falchion, until he was facing Eridani. She couldn't stand to look into the man's eyes, but he wasn't looking at her anyway; he gaped at the tip of the sword protruding from his stomach and the blood welling from the wound.

Eridani stared mesmerized at the spot where the blood stained the carpet. The thick rug absorbed the liquid nearly as fast as the man exsanguinated. A copper-brown wet stain spread slowly outward.

She had practiced fighting with various weapons from early childhood, for almost as long as she had been riding horses. Her parents didn't like this, but she insisted, and they relented. As with most things, King Malnos II found it difficult to deny his daughter her wish. Her parents had frequently hoped out loud that she would become interested in more feminine pursuits when she got older and discovered boys, but she never changed. Besides, she was a good sparring partner for Danchu, who didn't seem to mind occasionally losing to a girl so long as it wasn't in public. She was allowed to keep training, in Kozhad and then here in Skond. But, in her fifteen years, she had never before taken a life.

Left with a single opponent, Danchu advanced on the remaining constable, stabbing at him in a flurry of attacks, until the tip of the rapier found the man's heart and he went down. As if on cue, Eridani's opponent slid to the floor as well, and was still.

"Thanks," Danchu told Eridani. He leaned against a wall and tried to catch his breath.

Eridani nodded to him, took another look at the dead constables, then bent over and threw up on Gavron's expensive carpet.

ONCE THE FIGHTING had ended, Gavron crawled out from under his desk. He moved erratically across the library, collecting small items into a pile and muttering to himself. He gathered a number of scrolls and papers, and several rare books from his shelves. His fingers hovered above the spine of every other volume on the shelf, and his expression was pained, as though not pulling each of those books was a personal struggle.

"What are you doing?" asked Danchu. He'd cut the sleeve off his shirt and was clumsily wrapping it around the wound on his arm.

"We must leave Skond," said Gavron. "The sooner, the better."

"We're the ones who killed these men," said Danchu. "We will leave. You shouldn't be blamed for our crimes. You can tell them you tried to stop us."

Gavron ceased his nervous packing and faced the prince. "Three Skond officials were killed in a foreigner's house. A foreigner who has no powerful friends or patrons at court. Staying here would be suicide for me. I hope I have taught you better than to presume otherwise."

Gavron pushed a stepping stool to one of the bookcases and reached up to retrieve an expensive-looking glass bottle. He clawed at the cork with his fingers until he managed to pry it loose and took a big gulp without bothering to fetch a glass.

Gavron cleared his throat. "Forty-year-old Gannian brandy," he said. "I brought this bottle with me when I moved to Skond, and have been saving it for a special occasion ever since. My wedding day, or perhaps for when the patriarch would decide to grant me a ministry post, or some other fortuitous incident of that magnitude. I didn't expect for this bottle to remain sealed for fifteen years."

Gavron took another gulp.

"Fifteen long years, and all I have to show for that time is this house. A beautiful, spacious home with servants and expensive baubles, and no one for me to share it with. And now I must leave behind even this."

He held the bottle out toward Danchu, who reached for it, drank, and passed it back.

"Better to drink it now than to leave it behind, am I right?" Gavron laughed bitterly and drank again. "I don't know why they're looking for you two, but it can't be good news. The palace guard wouldn't have shown up to strong-arm me over a case of shoplifting or a gambling debt. Something sinister is happening."

"We should pay a visit to the sorceress," said Danchu. "She trades in information."

"The operative word is trades," said Gavron. "What can you offer her? If you come empty-handed, she won't hesitate to turn you over to the patriarch's men."

"Caer might know," croaked Eridani. Her stomach was still turning and her throat burned. She considered drinking from the bottle as well, but didn't think the alcohol would help settle her.

"Can you trust him? His loyalties may lie elsewhere." Gavron set the bottle down with a sigh.

While Gavron taught the siblings math and history, Caer instructed them in the martial arts, with or without a weapon. He was a native of Skond, and had extensive connections at the patriarch's palace. He would be able to help.

"We've trained with the man for two years," said Danchu. "He's held a blade at my throat countless times. If we can't trust him, then whom could we possibly turn to?"

"A trusting nature is a prerogative of youth, but never of kings," Gavron quoted from the teachings of Orodos. Then he went back to collecting items small and valuable enough to carry away.

While Gavron packed, Eridani went to the kitchen. She grabbed a pitcher of water with trembling fingers and rinsed out her mouth, then drank until she was running out of air. The cool water tasted sweeter than honey after the ordeal.

She eyed hotcakes and coffee with regret, but settled on fresh bread which she hoped would fill her stomach without upsetting it further. Loaf in hand, she walked through the house.

The house was empty—the servants had fled at the first sounds of fighting. She suspected it wouldn't be long until one or more of them reached out to the constables.

Even if there was no reward offered for the siblings' capture—yet—fear of retribution would incentivize the servants to report what they witnessed, and do so quickly. If any one of them alerted the authorities, the others would be questioned and punished for not doing so as well. There was very little time for the three foreigners to disappear into the busy streets of Skond.

She raided the servants' quarters for clothes, something inexpensive and drab, which would allow them to blend in; to walk unnoticed and unmolested past the constables. She found a set of clothes that fit her and changed out of her silk garments. She procured another set for Danchu, but none of the servants shared the plump tutor's height or girth.

Eridani couldn't get the image of the dying constable out of her mind. She had to keep moving, concentrate on accomplishing things, and keep her mind occupied. It was the only way she could think of to prevent herself from dwelling on how it felt to force a blade into a man's back. From recalling the brown wet stain spreading on the carpet.

She brought the clothes to Danchu, along with a clean linen sheet and some alcohol to sanitize the cut, and set out to properly bandage his wound. When she returned to the study, Danchu was rummaging through the pockets of one of the constables like a common thief.

"What are you looking for?" Eridani asked.

"Information," said Danchu, without looking up.

From across the room Gavron muttered something about it being unseemly to disturb the dead.

"One of them had this." Danchu showed his sister an oval badge with a clenched gauntlet engraved on its surface.

The two of them locked eyes. The Iron Fist were the patriarch's enforcers: assassins and strongmen he used for things too unseemly for the palace guard and murders he wanted to plausibly deny. That one or more such men would be among the people looking for them was even more disturbing news. It seemed their tutor was unaware of the badge's significance, so the siblings chose not to discuss the matter further. It didn't serve them to make the poor scholar feel any more nervous and perturbed than he already was.

Less than an hour later, the three of them departed Gavron's house.

The Gannian tutor marched down the cobbled streets of Skond, his head held high and his cheeks blushed from the recently imbibed brandy.

The two siblings, dressed in servant garb, sweated in the early afternoon sun as they hauled the heavy sacks overfilled with all the belongings Gavron couldn't bear to part with. It wasn't the most comfortable arrangement, but it worked. The trio was ignored by the few constables they passed along the way.

They made it to Caer's house without incident.

CHAPTER 2

THE UGLY UNICORN

aer was not happy to see them; Eridani could read it on his face as soon as their fencing instructor opened the door.

He was a tall, lean man dressed in a training tunic. His head was shaven clean, except for a tightly woven bun of red hair just above his forehead. Combined with a long, less than comely face and large uneven teeth, his appearance earned him the nickname of the Ugly Unicorn. However, the muscles bulging under his tunic warned all but the most foolhardy from addressing him as such. Caer was in his late forties, but he could still challenge and defeat younger men, and he often did.

"What are you doing here? We have no training arranged for today." Caer frowned at them and tried to close the door.

Danchu pushed at the door, forcing his way into the house. Not quite as tall as Caer, he was nevertheless a broad-shouldered young man, large for his age, and carried himself with the confidence of a royal scion. Wounded and fleeing, he still wouldn't accept anyone keeping him out, even if their unwilling host could have easily prevented his entry if he so chose. Caer relented and let him through. Eridani and Gavron walked in behind him.

Caer's frown deepened. He shut the door most of the way and looked outside through a small opening.

"We weren't followed," said Eridani.

Caer locked the door. "The constables came around looking for you earlier," he said. "I can ill afford to have them find you in my home."

Caer's house was in stark contrast with the opulence of Gavron's. The front door led into a small room which contained an unpolished cedar table and several chairs, a straw bed, and a large travel chest filled with clothes. The only decoration hanging on an unpainted wall was a large battle axe, its edge well-sharpened but chipped from use. In his years spent as a mercenary, Caer never acquired a taste for expensive things.

A much larger room in the back was converted into a sparring hall, where Caer trained his students with weapons both wooden and metal.

"Two constables and a palace guard with a mole on his left cheek and an attitude problem?" asked Danchu.

"The very same." The Ugly Unicorn stood by the locked door, as if he was hesitant to follow his guests into his own home.

"They came to Gavron's house," said Danchu. "There was an ... altercation." He glanced at Eridani. "I killed them."

Caer looked up sharply. "You what?"

Danchu launched into a description of the fight, and Caer's face lit up at the account of the swordplay. He frequently interrupted with questions. Danchu, infected with his instructor's enthusiasm, described each parry and thrust in loving detail. He stumbled only when the story reached the point of Eridani's involvement.

Eridani didn't like her brother taking the blame, but she didn't want to throw his chivalry in his face by contradicting him, either.

"These details aren't important," she interjected. "What matters is that your training allowed Danchu to defeat several more-experienced adversaries."

Caer nodded. "The constables are usually nothing but hoodlums, raised far above the station they deserve. The palace guard, on the other hand, must've been a dangerous opponent. I'm impressed."

"The patriarch's men won't share your enthusiasm for the prince's skill when they discover the bloody corpses in my home," said Gavron.

Caer nodded. "They'll kill you for this, if they catch you."

"During the fight, the guard said he didn't have to bring us in alive," said Eridani. "They already wanted to kill us. The question is, why? Have you heard anything, Caer?"

"It's not like the patriarch consults me on his decisions." Caer crossed his arms. "Whatever their reasons were before, you'll certainly be wanted for murder now. As a loyal citizen of Skond, I must go to the palace and report that you came to see me. The old war wounds have been bothering me lately, so I'll have to walk very slowly. By the time I get there, you might have already left the city, eh?"

Danchu looked at Eridani and she nodded slightly.

"Come with us, instead," said Danchu. "Given all this uncertainty, we can use a friend with a big axe."

Gavron's eyes widened. He shot Danchu a venomous stare, but said nothing.

"Where? Why?" The Ugly Unicorn appeared to be as surprised by the prince's plea as the Gannian scholar.

"Back to Kozhad, to our family," said Danchu. "We can continue our training, and there will always be a place for you at my father's court." He rested his palm gently on the old mercenary's arm.

"I noticed how your expression changed when we talked about the fight. I know you miss it terribly, but you're getting older; too old to re-enlist as a mercenary. This is another chance at adventure and glory; a chance you won't get while teaching children in Skond how to hold a wooden sword."

Caer chewed his lip and glanced longingly at his axe.

"We'll pay you to be our bodyguard," said Eridani. "A handsome sum, to get us home safely."

Danchu frowned at his sister. "This isn't about the money for Caer, don't you see?"

"A man's skill should always be properly rewarded. If Caer agrees to come with us, he should be reimbursed." She turned to Gavron. "Give me your purse."

The scholar hesitated.

"We're going to need money to see us safely to Kozhad, and it's not like we can stop by our apartment to get some," said Eridani. "You'll be paid back double for anything we borrow."

Gavron's expression remained sour, as though he'd taken a bite of raw onion. He reached under his jacket and retrieved a coin purse.

Eridani untied the string and plucked out four thick gold triangles with the patriarch's crest etched onto each side. Because of their shape, the coins were called dragon scales, and were the highest denomination circulated in the north. She estimated the value of the four coins to be roughly equal to what Caer might earn in a month. She proffered them to the Ugly Unicorn.

Caer studied her appraisingly for several seconds, in the way he sometimes did when planning out the next exercise for her and her brother. Then he nodded. "I accept your coin."

Having decided, Caer wasted no more time. "We must leave the city immediately," he said. "All gates will be watched, but there are ways around that. I will arrange for our travel. Stay here until I return. It is best that none of you are seen on the streets."

Gavron stroked his university medallion and shuffled from foot to foot.

As soon as the door closed behind Caer, he said, "Are you mad? He is a man of Skond, with deep roots here. More likely than not, he will head straight for the palace and turn us in while we wait here like hogs being fattened in a pen. It's best to leave now, while there is still time."

"Caer is an honorable man," said Danchu. "He won't betray us. You shouldn't have turned this into a financial transaction, Eridani." He pointed at the cheap furniture and bare walls. "The man is clearly not motivated by money. What if your offer had insulted him into refusing to help us?"

Eridani held up her palms. "Be calm, both of you. Caer's honor is a complicated thing. There is loyalty to us as students and friends, and there's loyalty to Skond. Couldn't you see the hesitation in his eyes? But his greatest loyalty, the code of honor he lives by, is that of the elite mercenary units he spent his youth serving in. A mercenary that accepts your coin is honor-bound to fight for you. This supersedes his loyalty to Skond and allows him to help us without the doubt and guilt of conflicting allegiances."

The two men chewed on that for a time.

Danchu nodded curtly. "Well done, sister."

Gavron winced. "I should have stayed in bed this morning." He balanced his girth on a three-legged wooden stool. "I've been reduced to placing my life and well-being in the hands of a sellsword, and it's barely midday. I shudder to guess at what the evening might bring."

WHEN DANCHU REMOVED his makeshift bandages they discovered that the bleeding had slowed, but did not stop completely. Red viscous liquid seeped slowly from the cut. Eridani filled a pitcher with water and rinsed Danchu's flesh wound, then applied the special ointment Caer kept around to treat the cuts and bruises that occasionally resulted from overly rigorous training. Her brother winced and hissed when the alcohol-based salve touched his skin, but didn't turn away. Fresh strips of cloth Eridani used as bandages were quickly becoming blotted with dark-red stains.

Eridani packed the flagon of ointment and whatever clean linen she could find. There wasn't an overabundance of it in the Ugly Unicorn's house, but she knew the cut needed frequent attention to avoid an infection and so she searched thoroughly.

"Travel by caravan may be a foolhardy idea," said Gavron. "There are too many people, each one a possible informant for the patriarch. Someone is bound to recognize us."

"Would you rather brave the bandits and the wild animals on horseback, ill-equipped and reliant on one of us to keep watch each night? Would you even find the way to Kozhad once we deviate from the paved roads?" Eridani unrolled the scroll they brought along from Gavron's home.

Depicted on it was the map of the Heart—the world's sole continent— named for its shape's rough resemblance to an ideograph of a human heart. Rivers and mountain ranges were drawn in blue and black ink, roads and trade routes marked in red. Major cities were indicated with small, elaborate drawings of castle-like structures. The North was the peninsula at the top right of the map. Its curved shoreline and the bay that cut into the continent to the west contributed to the heart shape which was further stylized by the mapmakers. Skond was indicated by a sketch of the patriarch's palace drawn by an artist who likely never saw it with his own eyes. Gan was marked with the silhouette of its famous university building, farther southeast, near the border with Haldova. Kozhad was not on the map at all.

"Here." Eridani pointed to a blank spot on the map, about halfway due east and a bit to the north of Skond. "Kozhad may seem nearby on this bit of parchment, but the distance is great and the journey can be perilous," she said.

Danchu nodded. "The caravan isn't entirely safe, and neither is attempting to travel on our own. We must ponder the relative advantages of both, but we need Caer's contacts to get us past the city walls in either case."

There was a commotion outside. Gavron tensed up and Danchu rested his hand on the hilt of his training sword, which he had retrieved from the sparring hall. Eridani kept her expression neutral and hoped desperately that her assessment of Caer's state of mind was accurate. She cracked the front door open and peeked out. A large carriage pulled by a pair of horses approached the house. The carriage was wide and unwieldy, not designed for the narrow streets of Skond. The driver shouted at the passersby, urging them out of the way.

The two horses were gray with patches of white, and looked to be past their prime. Tattered green cloth covered the walls of the wagon. The material was bleached by the sun and threadbare enough around the edges for Eridani to make out the wooden frame underneath. The wagon was meant to transport goods rather than people. Certainly not people of royal blood. She nodded in approval.

The coachman pulled on the reins and the carriage stopped. Caer and another man climbed out of the wagon and entered the house.

"Meet Master Turo," said Caer. "We will be traveling with his caravan for the next several days."

Turo was a shorter man, the fact made especially noticeable when he stood next to Caer. He was broad-shouldered and steady, wisps of brown hair reaching the base of his thick neck. Tattoos covered his arms, their designs partially obscured by his short sleeves. He sized up the group in silence.

"He will need payment," said Caer. "Five scales."

"That's quite steep," complained Gavron. "We can buy our own horses for less."

"There's a premium on transporting wanted men," said Turo. "Two scales for each of you, and one for the girl." He pointed at Caer. "My friend rides free, if he pledges to help guard the caravan."

"I'm a trained swordsman, too," said Danchu. "I can be one of the guards."

Turo sized him up and chuckled. "You've been listening to too many sagas, boy. You pay, like the rest of 'em.'

Eridani rested her palm on Danchu's shoulder to prevent him from further argument. She nudged Gavron, who sighed theatrically and reached for his purse.

It took Caer only a few minutes to pack some clothes and essentials into a sack. He then retrieved the giant axe from its place on the wall. The aging mercenary's lips stretched into a thin smile when he gripped the well-worn handle.

Eridani and her brother exchanged meaningful glances. Caer seemed eager to leave behind the monotonous life of a trainer to privileged children and teenagers, most of whom would never test the skills they were learning in mortal combat. He stood straighter and appeared more focused when holding his weapon.

"Wait," said Gavron, as they were getting ready to leave the house.

He poured some water into a cup, whispered a few words over it, then dipped his index and middle fingers into the clear liquid and touched the wet fingertips between his eyebrows. "An ancient Gannian ritual for those about to undertake a journey," he said.

"I thought you weren't a religious man," said Eridani.

"Orodos wrote that even an unbeliever will pray for shelter when caught in a thunderstorm," said Gavron. "If there are any gods out there pulling the strings of fate, we could use their favor."

TURO'S CARRIAGE WAS designed for smuggling goods into Skond. A secret compartment three hands deep was built into the bottom of the wagon. An ingenious design obscured its true depth. The wagon was so filthy that only the most thorough of guards would consider digging underneath the layer of rotten straw that covered its floor.

There was no shortage of merchants and farmers willing to pay men like Turo to bring their wares into the city, in order to avoid the high import tariff. Even accounting for the smuggler's fee and the risk of occasionally having the entire shipment discovered and confiscated by the constables, it was still cheaper for the merchants to operate in this manner.

Gavron had used this example when teaching the siblings economics a few months prior. Eridani suggested that a reduced tariff would generate more income for the patriarch, but Danchu dismissed the idea, arguing that this would only cause the smugglers to lower their fees accordingly. He argued that smugglers and merchants engaging in these black market activities were disloyal to the patriarch and that lowering the tariff wouldn't turn them into law-abiding citizens.

Eridani found it ironic that they were now relying on such a smuggler to get them out of Skond. She whispered as much to her companions, but they weren't amused. The trio was lying flat on their backs, forced to breathe in the rancid stench of the wagon. The carriage shook as its wooden wheels rolled over the cobblestones. Eridani's muscles were sore, her back and sides bruised as the much thinner layer of fresh straw at the bottom of the secret compartment didn't offer enough protection to cushion the impacts.

Their discomfort should have been relatively short; the city walls were only a few minutes' ride from Caer's home, and no one bothered to inspect the outgoing traffic since the tariff was charged only on incoming goods. However, Caer instructed Turo to head across town. "We'll have an easier time passing through the East gate," was all the explanation he offered. And so their suffering was prolonged.

"Remain quiet," said Caer, when the carriage came to a stop. He was seated in the wagon above them. Turo rode in the front, next to the coachman. "They're searching the outgoing carts."

"They must've already found the bodies," said Gavron. "What are we going to do?"

"Quiet," hissed Eridani.

They waited in uncomfortable silence. They could eventually hear the muffled sounds of constables interrogating a family of peasants leaving Skond on foot ahead of them. Then it was their turn.

The constables sounded on edge as they interviewed Turo and the coach-man. Neither of the two men fit the description of the fugitives they sought, but losing two of their own motivated them to be thorough. The constables pulled back the drape and checked inside the wagon. Likewise, Caer didn't arouse their suspicion as the sole passenger. Not until they saw the enormous battle axe by his side.

"What's this?" asked one of the constables.

"If you don't know what this is, you're in the wrong line of work, friend," said Caer.

Eridani heard another constable guffaw, but the target of Caer's ridicule wasn't amused. "I know what an axe is, you idiot. Why are you bringing it?"

"I've been hired to guard a caravan," said Caer. "Because I'm not as young as I used to be, it's become strenuous to fend off bandits with my bare hands."

Someone chuckled, but the constable who was the target of Caer's mocking sounded even angrier. "This weapon is worth more than the wagon you ride in. How could these bottom-scrapers afford a guard? No, something is off about this. Perhaps you stole this axe on your way out of town? Wait here, I will get the sergeant. He can decide what to do with you."

"You shouldn't have antagonized him," Turo whispered, once the guards walked away.

"I know what I'm doing," said Caer. "If they focus on me, they won't focus on the wagon."

Eridani's heart raced as she listened to the approaching footsteps. From the sound of it, an officer arrived with several more constables for backup.

"That's the thief," said the angry constable.

"That's no thief, you simpleton!" spoke the new voice. "Caer and I fought together in the Haldova campaigns over a decade ago. How are you doing, old friend?"

The wagon creaked as Caer jumped out. "Veld? It has been too long!" Caer laughed. "Had I known you came back to Skond, I would have found you sooner and dragged you to a tavern!"

"Of course you would have," said Veld. "As I recall, you stood the drinks last time, so it would be my turn to buy."

"I will have to take advantage of that when I return," said Caer. "Besides, you need some drinks if you have to deal with subordinates like that one all day long."

"Get out of my sight," Veld told the guards. "This coach is cleared to go through."

"Why is so much effort being wasted on this checkpoint?" asked Caer.

"Shouldn't you rather concern yourself with who's coming into the city?"

"Orders," said Veld. "We're looking for the King of Kozhad and his sister. They've been living in Skond for some time."

"I know the two," said Caer. "But don't you mean the Prince of Kozhad?"

"Nah," said Veld. "Not since the Duke of Buzzards' army took Kozhad last week. They say the duke personally gutted the old king and his wife."

It took all of Eridani's self-control not to cry out. She bit her lip and her hand reached toward Danchu. Her brother was tense and shaking, his fists gripping handfuls of straw. Tears rolled down Eridani's cheeks as her hand found Danchu's, gently unclenched his fist, and they clasped each other in silent mourning.

She felt utterly helpless, trapped in that foul-smelling box. Her parents gone, her homeland conquered, her comfortable existence in Skond up-turned like a table in a tavern brawl. And she couldn't react, couldn't properly grieve, couldn't even hug her brother. She had to remain silent and motionless as though she, too, were already dead. She bit harder into her lip until she could taste blood.

"The duke, he's the kind of aristocracy I wouldn't mind working for, the kind who aren't afraid to get their hands dirty," said Veld. "Anyway, these two kids are the only legitimate heirs. Once they're gone, the duke can claim Kozhad for his own, with the patriarch's blessing."

"Politics aren't my game," said Caer. "Why would the patriarch care to take sides in such a minor skirmish?"

Eridani thought that he managed to keep his voice casual, almost bored. Perhaps he wasn't acting. He never met her parents. War was merely a business transaction for men like him and the sergeant.

"They say the duke is going to marry some minor relative of the patri-arch's," said Veld. "Kozhad isn't a major power, but its rulers are among the oldest bloodlines in the North. They predate the patriarch's own line, and are guaranteed a seat on the council. I'm sure he won't be sorry to see them gone once and for all."

"Too bad I didn't know about this," said Caer. "I might have signed on with the duke. I bet he pays better than these pissant traders."

"He probably does," said Veld. "Let's talk more of it over a flagon of good wine when you get back. The line behind your employer's carriage is growing long."

The wagon creaked again as Caer climbed on.

Even after they cleared the city gates, no one spoke. Eridani mourned her parents in darkness. She pictured their faces, the way they looked when the two of them had stood together and waved, seeing their children off to Skond. Eridani willed herself to etch every detail into memory, to protect the image against becoming blurred by the passage of time.

CHAPTER 3

THE TWO BARGAINS

n the evening, the four of them sat around the campfire, each lost in their thoughts. It had taken nearly two hours for the wagon to navigate the dirt roads outside Skond and reach the campsite of Turo's caravan. Dozens of wagons clustered together there, with tents put up nearby. The merchants, traders, and other travelers were due to depart in the morning.

Danchu watched the setting sun. Even among the bustle of the encampment he seemed alone, as if shut off from the rest of the world by his bubble of grief. His gaze was unfocused. Ever since they'd been able to escape the confines of the secret compartment, he'd ignored the others when they awkwardly tried to express their condolences, even ignored Eridani when she tried to talk to him.

Eridani bristled. She needed his support as much as he needed hers, perhaps more, but he just sat there, brooding. She had no choice but to give him some time to process what had occurred.

Gavron examined the map he had borrowed from Turo, with the caravan path marked on the parchment. "I'll stay with the group until we reach Ernholm," he said. "From there it should be easy to find transportation to Gan."

No one spoke. Gavron rolled up the map. "Have you given any thought to what you are going to do?"

Eridani realized that she hadn't. The pain of the loss still blinded her. "We have to put some distance between us and Skond," she said hesitantly. "There may not be any place in the North where we will be safe."

The North was a patchwork of independent kingdoms and city-states, but the true power was concentrated in Skond, whence the patriarch and his council controlled the entire northern peninsula. Centuries ago, the council was set up to mediate disputes between the nomadic tribes of the far north and their settled neighbors, but it gradually came under the control of the line of Skond's rulers who asserted more and more authority with each passing decade. Her father always said that, the way things looked, in another two or three generations all of the North would become united under the patriarch's rule.

Father... Eridani forced the thought out of her mind. "We'll make our way south. There may be courts in Haldova or even the Quadi Empire willing to offer refuge to a pair of exiled royals."

"I'll see you safely as far as Haldova's borders," said Caer. "Then I'll head back. Skond is still my home."

"No," said Danchu. He spoke softly, his voice barely heard over the crackling fire. Everyone turned toward him.

"No," he said again, louder this time. "I'm the rightful King of Kozhad. I must return home, gather my subjects, then march on Woodcastle and exact justice upon the Duke of Buzzards."

"We have no army, no supporters," said Eridani. "Even if you manage to rally the citizens, they are no match for the duke's soldiers. How many of our people are you willing to see suffer and die for a remote chance at revenge?"

Danchu stood up and glanced at each of his three companions in turn, then concentrated on his sister, his gaze now focused. "Would you rather live out your days in exile, Eridani, never to see home again? Knowing that the murderer of our parents is laughing and drinking wine, the crown of Kozhad collecting dust among the trophies on his mantle? I can't bear that." He winced and stroked the bandage on his arm.

Eridani wasn't sure what she wanted to do. Should she follow her brother on his dangerous quest for revenge? Could she even consider abandoning him, the only family she had left, and striking out on her own? The idea did not appeal, but she also didn't think she could convince Danchu to reconsider this course of action.

Before she could formulate an argument, there was a commotion at the edge of the camp.

The coachman sidled up to their fire. "A patrol is looking for you," he said. "Head for one of the tents, but don't rush so as not to draw attention to yourselves."

Eridani and the others wasted no time. They unobtrusively moved toward a tent, heading farther away from the fires, allowing dusk to hide them in plain sight. Eridani watched the detachment of soldiers ride into the center of the camp.

There were a total of eight uniformed men. Their weapons were sheathed. There were twice that many armed men in the encampment, but some of them likely weren't trained soldiers, and the outcome of a fight—should it come to that—was far from certain. Eridani suspected that few, if any, of the caravan guards would be willing to take up arms against a Skond military unit on behalf of a pair of fugitives, regardless of the odds.

The soldiers rode up to the largest fire and stopped, but didn't dismount. They showed no fear of the mismatched band of shady characters surrounding them. In the shadow of Skond, their uniforms provided an even better protection than their weapons.

A young man, who wore a red armband identifying him as a corporal, nudged his horse forward. "Who is the caravan master?" he asked. There was a sense of authority to his voice, even if he didn't speak all that loudly— Eridani could barely hear him from where she stood.

Turo was having dinner by the fire. He set down his slice of roasted meat, wiped his greasy hands on a rag, and grunted as he rose to his feet.

"Me," he said, without bothering to introduce himself or offer any additional courtesy to the corporal. The two men stared at each other for several seconds.

The young man spoke first. "I am Corporal Pel," he said. "I'm looking for a pair of young nobles from the far north and a portly Gannian. Does that sound like anyone among those traveling under your protection?"

"There are no noblemen here." Turo placed his hands on his hips. "And if there were, I wouldn't know it. This is a free land and I ask those who seek my help crossing it only for coin; their lineage is their own business."

"The land may be free, but the roads belong to the patriarch," said Pel. "I see that you have many wheeled wagons here that won't do well traveling through the brush. It would be very inconvenient for you to fail to recognize our authority."

Pel let his horse advance until he was precariously close to Turo. The caravan master stood his ground and glared up at the corporal.

"My men are going to search every tent, every wagon, and every traveler under your charge," said Pel. "They'll make the merchants unload all of their wares and then confiscate any illicit goods they happen to find. It may take a while."

Although Turo didn't react, other men around the fire grumbled, and several cast unkind glances in the direction of Danchu and Eridani.

Pel raised his voice, so more people in the camp could hear him. "If, on the other hand, anyone has seen the fugitives we're after and reports to us their whereabouts, they can claim a handsome reward offered by the patriarch. Twenty-five dragon scales total if all three are captured alive."

Turo twitched. Others murmured among themselves. Eridani shivered; even if Turo's stubbornness and strict control over his people could have won out against the corporal's threats, she didn't expect him to resist the allure of such a princely sum.

"We have them," Turo said simply, dropping all pretenses at subterfuge. He waved to his men, and several of them surrounded Danchu and Caer like a pack of jackals. Eridani and Gavron were at their flank, but the guards didn't concern themselves with these two as they were unarmed.

"There are four," said Turo. He turned to Caer. "Sorry, old friend. I'd rather not have someone as lethal as you here and upset with me, after the soldiers leave." He turned back to Pel. "For what it's worth, that one is only a sellsword."

Pel examined the four travelers surrounded by Turo's men and nodded with satisfaction. "We'll take him off your hands," he said. "The sellsword's fate in Skond is not for me to determine."

Vastly outnumbered, Caer and Danchu surrendered their weapons. Pel's soldiers herded the four of them away, forcing them to abandon Caer's axe and Gavron's luggage.

"What about my reward?" called out Turo.

Pel smiled, then produced a bit of parchment, ink, and a quill from his saddlebag. He scribbled a note and signed it with a flourish.

"Present this at the palace," he said, "and the reward will be yours."

ONCE PEL'S MEN and their prisoners traveled sufficiently far from Turo's camp, the corporal leaned in toward the four pedestrians surrounded by armed riders and said, "Don't worry. We're not taking you back to Skond."

Eridani exhaled softly. She was uncertain of these men's intentions, but a glimmer of hope was something for her to cling to.

Danchu was equally surprised. "You wear the patriarch's colors," he said.

"You wear a servant's clothes," said Pel, "and yet, you are a king."

Pel smirked and half-bowed to Danchu in a mocking fashion, which looked even more ridiculous on horseback than it might have if the corporal was standing on his own two feet. "Your Majesty."

Danchu gritted his teeth but made no reply.

"Where are you taking us?" asked Caer.

"Lady Voriana kindly begs an audience with the newly minted King of Kozhad." Pel's smile widened. "She insists, actually."

Eridani allowed herself to relax a little. Lady Voriana was one of the richest people in Skond, having inherited her late husband's holdings and his seat on the council. She was highborn, from a prominent family that had fallen on hard times. Her husband, Bael Caveron, had made his vast fortune as a merchant and banker, and needed the legitimacy of her lineage to acquire a seat on the council.

Their marriage had seemed to work surprisingly well, far beyond the alliance of convenience everyone expected it to be. They appeared to genuinely like each other, so much so that Caveron—once a great womanizer—was not known to seek out a single mistress.

Elevated to the rank of Lord, Bael Caveron wielded political power on the council, while Lady Voriana spent lavishly from his fortune on charitable causes and on sponsoring feasts and holidays for the citizenry.

After Lord Caveron's untimely death, Lady Voriana seamlessly took control of his enterprises, and even his council seat, earning her the nickname of the Dowager Councilor from her political opponents. Far from becoming upset, Lady Voriana adopted the moniker and wore it as a badge of honor, as a way to remind the people of Skond of all the goodwill her late husband's fortune helped generate.

To say that the masses liked her more than the rest of the council would be akin to claiming that children liked the candy maker more than the barber who specialized in pulling rotting teeth.

"We are honored to accept Lady Voriana's invitation," said Eridani, as though she was given a choice in the matter.

Gavron chuckled.

"What's so funny?" asked Caer.

"I'm picturing your friend Turo's face, when he tries to claim his reward from the patriarch," said Gavron.

"He's probably not that foolish," said Pel. "The promise of a reward was a face-saving way for him to turn you over without a fight."

"He betrayed me, and let me live," said Caer. "I question his wisdom."

"If he is dense enough to show up at the patriarch's palace and wave that parchment, he deserves the reward such an action will earn him," said Pel. "Come, we have horses for you farther ahead. Lady Voriana is eager to speak with you."

PEL'S SOLDIERS DELIVERED them to a sweeping, luxurious estate. The grand house built of imported limestone stood on a hill an hour's ride from the city; the walls of Skond could've been seen through the house's wide windows had the view not been obstructed by stained glass depicting the North's legends and history.

The house's opulence rivaled that of the patriarch's palace. There were halls decorated with hanging carpets and paintings from across the known world. Spacious rooms were well appointed with tastefully selected furniture. Side tables and wardrobes made of rare woods and veneered with ebony and tortoiseshell stood along the walls, topped with statuettes and vases made of marble and jade. Armchairs and divans stuffed with goose feathers and upholstered with gold brocade trim stood within an arm's reach of small round tables that held bowls of fresh fruit and crystal decanters of liquor. All of this was kept pristine by an army of servants who expertly blended into the background as they went about their chores.

Such wealth placed outside the city walls had to be protected, and sentries from the private militia were posted everywhere. Unlike Pel's men, they didn't wear the patriarch's colors, but rather the black-and-orange of the house of Caveron.

Once Danchu and his entourage were given sufficient time to take in the grandeur of the estate, Lady Voriana arrived to greet them personally.

Their host was in her fifties. It was easy to see that she had been very beautiful, once. She walked with her spine straight, and the easy grace of a noblewoman. But her hair was graying, her wrinkles slowly gaining a foothold upon her brow despite the well-applied makeup, her eyes tired. Eridani wondered if the power and responsibility of managing her late husband's vast holdings were taking their toll on their host.

She embraced Danchu and then Eridani lightly, and spoke with great eloquence of how sorry she was for their loss and their ordeal. She offered the hospitality of her home and suggested they rest and eat and bathe, and that they would speak again tomorrow.

On the following day, clean clothes more befitting their station than the commoner garb they had traveled in were laid out for Danchu and Eridani when they awoke. The two were ushered into the study, where Lady Voriana sat with a number of scrolls and sheets of paper scattered on the desk in front of her. She rose, a warm smile lighting her face.

"My dear children, it is so good to see you again. I only wish we had met under happier circumstances." She stepped from behind the desk and embraced each of them. The smell of her perfume lingered in the air.

She listened politely as they took turns thanking her.

"There is much more I can do for you, young King of Kozhad," she told Danchu. "You will need an army to lay siege to Woodcastle. I can help you hire the finest mercenaries in the North, enough swords to defeat the duke and reclaim your crown. That is, if we can reach an understanding, of course."

Danchu appeared flushed, visions of victory undoubtedly floating in his head. Before he could pledge undying loyalty to their unexpected benefactor, Eridani spoke. "A campaign like this would cost tens of thousands of dragon scales. Kozhad is a small, relatively poor kingdom. What could we possibly offer in return that would justify such an expense?"

Lady Voriana smiled at Eridani. "Very good, child. You should always beware the motives of anyone offering a deal that is seemingly tilted in your favor. Fear not. I shall expect a considerable return on my investment." She turned to Danchu. "Do you know why your parents were killed?"

Danchu scowled. "The accursed Duke of Buzzards must've been jealous of our lands and our station. Woodcastle had been loyal to Kozhad in better days when it was governed by honorable men. The duke attacked like a rabid dog turning on its master."

"That is the how, not the why," said the Dowager Councilor. "With utmost respect to your lineage, Kozhad has fallen on harder times over the course of the last few generations. There is little there for the duke to covet. In fact, he has already returned to Woodcastle, having barely bothered to install an administrator in Kozhad."

Lady Voriana twisted a braid of her graying hair as she spoke. "The Council of the North is a vicious place, where factions are locked in a quiet battle over the fate of thousands, and more people are killed with the stroke of a quill than any one warrior could slay in a lifetime. Your bloodline is among the few ancient enough to guarantee a seat on the council, even if your father was wise enough to avoid exercising that privilege.

"There are certain individuals on the council who would benefit greatly from filling that vacant seat with a loyalist. So much so, that they would encourage the duke to break his oaths and march on Kozhad."

"Who ordered my parents killed?" Danchu's hands formed into fists.

"Who has the power to order you hunted down in the streets of Skond?" asked Lady Voriana.

Danchu's eyes narrowed and he banged his fist on the table. "The patriarch!"

"Indeed," said Lady Voriana. "The patriarch has been usurping more and more power from the council. My husband was one of his greatest opponents, but then he died—possibly poisoned, though no malicious act was ever proven nor any such accusation leveled in public. My own seat is no longer secure as it is not guaranteed by birthright as is yours. Once you and Eridani are gone and the patriarch fills your seat with a loyalist, he will have even more power. I suspect it won't take him long to throw me out."

"That murderous schemer will not get away with this!" shouted Danchu.

"He very well might," said Lady Voriana. "And to think, two decades ago when his rise to prominence was only beginning, his connection to the ruling bloodline of Skond was so tenuous that he had more trouble getting onto the council than my late husband did." She sighed. "In another decade he will hold enough power to dissolve the council and declare himself emperor."

The council had been established over five hundred years ago, predating the first unification of the North by Kalatar of Gan. The founders bickered over where to house it, each worrying that their rival might gain an advantage if they were to become its host. Gan, known for its neutrality, seemed a natural choice, but it was too far south and too near the Haldovan border. They selected Skond because it was centrally located, small, and relatively powerless. Over the centuries, the council's presence elevated the city and the status of its mayor who was guaranteed one of the seats. The North's elite now spent their time in Skond and that drew traders, barristers, and sycophants like fruit flies to a rotting apple.

Officially, the council wasn't a government but merely a safe place for the royal and the powerful to meet, to forge treaties and work out their grievances. Eridani recalled a number of lessons Gavron taught them about its history. Like any institution given a little power, over the years its primary function seemed to be to gain more power for itself at the expense of the formally independent member kingdoms. Eridani's father's opinion of the council closely matched Voriana's and he steered clear of it whenever possible.

"So you want to keep Danchu alive and in charge of Kozhad in order to stop the patriarch from becoming emperor?" asked Eridani.

"To stall him. It will take a lot more than that to stop him," said Lady Voriana.

Despite the democratic-sounding title, the mayorship of Skond was controlled by its own ruling bloodline. The current Mayor of Skond was only a distant blood relative to the previous mayor. There were whispers claiming that his lineage was a forgery and he was in fact a commoner, but one didn't voice such theories too loudly for fear of drawing the attention of the Iron Fist. Although the sitting Mayor of Skond did not always hold the title of the Patriarch of the North, the two roles coinciding was so frequent as to often be used interchangeably in the common vernacular. The current patriarch's enemies called him the Spider, for he expertly spun the web of political machination to control his underlings and entrap his political opponents.

The lady's expression grew somber and she leaned forward. "I don't merely strive for the status quo. I want your proxy, King Danchu. For as long as you remain on the council, I want to control your vote."

Danchu looked to Eridani. She thought back on the history of the North, but could not recall such a thing.

"Is that possible?" she asked.

"There are precedents," said Lady Voriana. "They don't usually become a matter of public record, nor make it into the history books." She scrutinized the siblings. "There are other things I will want as part of the deal, but none of as great an import. You're angry and rightly so, Danchu. Take your time, think about my proposal, consult your advisors. We will discuss the details tomorrow."

She nodded, indicating that the meeting was over.

Danchu held private council with Eridani, Gavron, and Caer afterward. He summarized the conversation for his advisors, then rattled off a dozen military stratagems to use against the duke. He talked of weapons and supplies the lady's funding could provide.

Caer held up his hand. "The fishermen have a saying: don't spend the profits before you reel in the tuna."

Gavron nodded. "These negotiations are tricky and may take some time. You must balance your need for revenge against all but handing away your kingdom to another master."

Eridani saw how exhausted her brother was, how weak he seemed. The grief and his wound were both sapping his stamina. She let Danchu and the others have their say, and before the discussion became repetitive she chimed in, "I'm still tired after yesterday's ordeal. Could we hold off on further discussion until our host lays out her terms?"

She bought her brother the respite she judged him to need at the expense of several hours of boredom while pretending to take a midafternoon nap.

On the following day they met for the third time, in a much larger room, where the Dowager Councilor's various advisors crowded behind her, while Eridani and Gavron stood behind Danchu.

Upon Danchu's confirmation that he was indeed willing to hand over the proxy of his family's council vote, the lady's attorneys presented a heap of treaties for the King of Kozhad to sign.

The meeting went on for hours. Eridani did her best to pay close attention to the details of each concession her brother was agreeing to, but she had a difficult time parsing the flowery language of trade agreements, grants of assarting land in the Pine Forest north of Kozhad, and preferential terms and tariffs for the Caveron Trading Company.

Danchu struggled to stifle yawns and accepted the proposals one by one, without much thought. Eridani shifted her weight, seeking some relief for her aching feet. She wished her brother had a better head for negotiating treaties, but she couldn't really blame him. Without the lady's support none of those things would be within Danchu's power to grant anyway, and it wasn't like anybody else was offering to help put him on the throne.

"This next item concerns your sister," said Lady Voriana.

She had Danchu and Eridani's undivided attention with that.

"My nephew Auwinn is only three years her junior. I suggest a betrothal to tighten the connection between our families. They can wed in two year's time, when he is of age."

Danchu glanced over his shoulder at Eridani, who struggled to keep her emotions from showing on her face. Was she about to be sold off, like a parcel of land or a tax break, another bargaining chip for the fate of her family's crown?

Danchu hesitated, turning from Eridani to Lady Voriana, even looking to Gavron for support. Everyone waited for his answer.

"This is not my decision to make," he finally said. "My father did not believe in forcing an arranged marriage upon his daughter, and neither shall I." He asked Eridani, "What do you think?"

Eridani hesitated. She thought she'd rather die than be engaged to some child she had never met. And yet, how could she refuse? If she said no, would she be ruining the treaty? What sort of fate would she be consigning herself, her brother, and their friends to if she dared refuse?

Before she could speak, Danchu gestured. "Look at the hesitation in her face, Lady Voriana. It is answer enough. I am prepared to give up much, but I don't barter my family."

Eridani held her breath as she searched the Dowager Councilor's placid face for a reaction. Was there the subtlest hint of surprise at Danchu's categorical refusal in the older woman's eyes? She couldn't be certain.

The lady merely moved on to the next item on her long list of demands, and the conversation turned to the hunting rights in the Pine Forest.

AFTER THE ROUND of negotiations was finally over, the Kozhad royals were ushered back to their rooms, to rest before the afternoon meal.

Danchu looked pale and almost stumbled in the corridor.

"This took a lot out of me," he said. "I'm going to lie down." He shambled toward his room.

Eridani's jaw tightened. This was unlike Danchu, who was a strong young man, possessed of stamina enough not to need afternoon naps. She was concerned and made to follow him, but Gavron rested his hand on her shoulder.

"That was a foolish thing he did," he said, once Danchu was out of earshot.

Eridani kept her voice neutral. "The arranged marriage?"

"Indeed."

"I was concerned as well, but the lady didn't seem to mind the refusal."

"You mean she didn't show her disappointment, which isn't the same thing. I'll wager a pouch of dragon scales against a stale loaf of bread the marriage is what the Dowager Councilor was really after. The proxy vote is valuable, but it will last for only as long as Danchu upholds his word. The bloodline merge, on the other hand, is permanent."

"Danchu isn't the sort of man to renege on his word," said Eridani.

"That's part of the problem. Danchu is a perfect figurehead. A young, handsome king, honest and brave, the sort of ruler men won't hesitate to follow into battle. But he is a lousy politician. He is too trusting, and not nearly devious enough. He will need your counsel at every turn, if he's to ever reclaim his crown."

Much as she wanted to, Eridani couldn't argue with her tutor's assessment. "All the more reason not to marry me off to some child," she said. Uncomfortable with the direction this conversation was taking she added, "Excuse me. I'd like to check on my brother."

Eridani tapped lightly on Danchu's door. He grunted assent and she entered.

Danchu of Kozhad sat on the wide, soft bed, his coat and shirt lying in a heap by his feet, and clumsily struggled to remove the bandages from his right arm. The bleeding had stopped, but the cloth was saturated in black pus that smelled of rot. When the last layer of cloth was removed, it revealed the area surrounding the wound had turned black, and a patchwork of black strands extended from it in all directions like a great spiderweb that covered half of his arm.

Eridani gasped. "It's infected!"

"It's worse than that," said Danchu. "This is poison."

"Are you certain? Would a mere constable wield a poisoned blade on a mission to capture a pair of youths?"

"The patriarch wanted us dead badly. I think he might have preferred it if his men brought us in dead rather than alive. It would have been more convenient and less embarrassing for him that way. Besides, the man who wounded me was a member of the Iron Fist and not merely a constable. They've been known to poison their blades."

Eridani said nothing. She stared at her brother's arm, willing him to be wrong.

"I saw this once, at father's court," he said. "A young duke got into a scrape with a southern mercenary from somewhere within the domain of the Quadi. The duke won the duel and paid only with a shallow cut on his calf. The cut wouldn't stop bleeding for hours, and when it finally did it turned black, with tendrils of rot extending from it in the same fashion as they do on my arm."

"What is this poison? How is it treated?"

Danchu paused, his face pale, and took several deep breaths. "A healer was summoned, who recognized the affliction. It is caused by the venom of the red scorpion from the deserts of the far south. He said that the duke's only chance at survival was to have his leg removed as quickly as possible. The duke wanted to live, so he let the healer ply him with poppy extract and bring on the bone saw."

Eridani focused on the black tendril that reached almost as high as the elbow. The chirurgeon might have to cut near the shoulder. "Did it work?"

"No. The duke died a week later, in terrible agony. The venom spreads much faster than the rot."

This couldn't be happening, Eridani thought. She had already lost so much. She couldn't lose her brother, too. "Perhaps Lady Voriana's healers know more than the one back home."

Danchu shook his head. "In all of the North, only the Sorceress of Skond is said to possess the cure. No, there's nothing to be done, and we mustn't let our host suspect a thing. I will hold out until we're marching on Woodcastle and the mercenaries are paid; that way she will have no choice but to support your claim to the crown."

"Oh, Danchu, this is not what I want." She hugged her brother, so he couldn't see the tears welling in her eyes. Gavron was wrong; Danchu was capable of subterfuge. But he was also right: the young king was rash and too eager to heroically throw away his life.

"Rest now," said Eridani. She helped him settle onto the pillows and stayed there until he fell asleep. While she sat vigil over her brother, she kept eying the ornate knives and swords that decorated the walls of his room.

CHAPTER 4

THE OMINOUS PROPHECY

rmed only with the dagger hidden within the folds of her baggy cloak, Eridani returned to the city that wanted her dead.

The constables barely glanced at her when she passed through the city gates. No one expected the renegade princess to walk into the patriarch's stronghold. All the constables saw was another peasant seeking her fortune in Skond.

Eridani proceeded with caution, avoiding patrols and maintaining a brisk but steady pace that helped her blend in with the young messengers and apprentices running errands for their employers. As she walked toward the Street of Tailors, she was immersed in the laughter of children and singsong patter of merchants trying to entice the passersby to their stalls. The smells of cured meats, fresh flowers, and exotic spices permeated the air. Horseshoes clanked against the sun-drenched cobblestones. This was the Skond she had grown used to, the city she almost considered home. Not the brutal, nightmarish side of it she had been exposed to in the last few days. She would have given almost anything to regain the sense of security and the carefree existence she used to enjoy. She pulled the cloak tighter around her shoulders and pressed on.

She slowed to a leisurely stroll within a hundred paces of the house her family rented, looking for any signs of it being watched. She turned back and walked by a second time. There was nothing obvious, but she couldn't be certain. She had to rely on luck and the element of surprise—the patriarch's men would surely not think either Danchu or her foolish enough to return.

On the third pass she ducked into the shadow of the servants' entrance and rushed to the second floor, skipping steps. Thinly carpeted wooden planks groaned under her weight. She reached the top of the staircase and found the doors to the upstairs rooms ajar. The apartments had been ransacked, picked clean of anything valuable.

Eridani winced as she walked through the rooms. Did the patriarch's men loot the place? More likely it was her own servants, people she had trusted to cook her food and sweep her floors, people who—she would have sworn only a week ago—were loyal to her and her brother. She reached Danchu's bedroom. There, on the oak four-square bed which likely remained in place because it was too heavy to be moved, slept Dewynn, one of the house staff. He was dressed in clothes from Danchu's wardrobe and stank of cheap wine.

Eridani remained still and listened to Dewynn snore lightly for a few heartbeats, then advanced quietly toward the far corner of the room. There, Danchu had hidden their coins under the floorboard. The bulky wardrobe normally positioned above the hiding place was gone, but the flooring appeared undisturbed.

She crouched over the floorboard and drew her dagger. She wedged the blade between the two boards and tried to gently pry them apart. The flooring wouldn't give. She applied more force, until the board cracked with a loud crunch.

Dewynn rolled off the bed and growled like a startled cat. He blinked sleep out of his eyes and squinted at the intruder. Their gazes locked, with Eridani still on her knees, crouched over the broken floorboard.

"What an unexpected surprise." Dewynn slurred his words slightly. He advanced on Eridani and she stood up, until they were facing each other. He was a head taller than her. Muscles played under Danchu's tunic, which was barely large enough to fit Dewynn. "You came back just in time. I ran out of wine and out of things to sell for more, but you'll fetch your weight in decent brandy, won't you?"

"Have you no loyalty? No shame?" Eridani looked up into Dewynn's bloodshot eyes. "My family treated you well."

"Loyalty? Ha!" Dewynn closed the distance between them, forcing Eridani to retreat a step. "What has a stuck-up bitch like you, or your pompous fool of a brother, ever done to earn my loyalty? Don't flatter yourself. You've never been anything but a meal ticket."

Eridani was on him in a flash. Had he been sober and alert, she might not have risked an attack. As it was, she surprised him. Dewynn stumbled back as he tried to keep away from the blade she wielded. Eridani used his own momentum, pushing him, causing the servant to fall over backward and hit the wooden floor hard. Before he could gather his wits, she was on top of him. Her dagger pressed against the flesh of his neck below the chin, while her left hand pulled his head back by the strands of his tangled blond hair.

"How dare you threaten me?" She spoke through clenched teeth, hoping that her anxiety would sound like anger. "I'm the Princess of Kozhad, born of the ancient bloodline of warrior kings. On a bad day, I could cut down ten lowborn brutes like you without breaking a sweat." She pulled harder on his hair. "Do you know what I'm taught to do with traitors?"

The servant shivered in her hands. "Mercy," he whispered. There was no hint of bravado left in his voice. He looked like a large, scared child.

Eridani stared at the beads of sweat forming on Dewynn's forehead. It would take almost no effort to let the blade dig deeper. She had already killed once; she remembered being surprised at how little resistance the sword encountered as it entered a man's back. Is that what she was now—a ruthless killer? Could she afford to be anything else? If she spared Dewynn's life, how long would it take him to run to the constables?

She pressed the blade deeper into his flesh and drew blood. Dewynn whimpered.

She showed him the cheap dagger she had pilfered from Lady Voriana's estate. A few drops of his blood stained its blade. "This is a poisoned dagger," she said, thinking of Danchu. "The blade was dipped in the venom of desert scorpions from the far south."

Dewynn sat up and clutched at the cut on his neck. He shook like a toddler in winter.

"Betray me again, and you will die a slow, painful death," said Eridani. "Prove yourself loyal, and I'll give you the cure." She was risking her life to save Danchu—would this creature do any less to protect his own?

"What must I do?" asked the servant.

She crossed her arms and waited.

"What must I do, Mistress?" he said, and offered an awkward bow, his hand still clutching his neck.

"There is another traitor. A caravan master named Turo. Today you will have your cut tended and sleep off your wine. Tomorrow, you will kill him for me." She pointed at the door. "Go. If you succeed, return for your cure at sundown, the day after tomorrow."

Eridani had no illusions about the fumbling drunk's chances of killing

Turo. Most likely, he would meet his end at the hands of the caravan master's sellswords. If so, it was the death he deserved, delivered a day late. But then, there was some remote chance of him ambushing Turo and getting away alive. And if he somehow succeeded, by the time he learned there was no poison in his body, Eridani would be long gone from Skond.

She watched Dewynn leave and turned her attention to the damaged floorboard, but couldn't retrieve the coins until her hands stopped trembling.

NO ONE STOOD guard at the entrance to the sorceress's estate. Her reputation, combined with the superstitious nature of most people, was protection enough.

Eridani pushed open the metal gate and walked into the wild garden. Twisted, malformed trees surrounded the sorceress's home. Bushes and grass grew wild, seemingly untended for decades. She picked her way through the undergrowth, careful not to twist an ankle. Such a large plot of land inside the city walls must've cost a fortune, but Skond's only practitioner of the arcane could afford it.

Eridani didn't fear magic, because she didn't believe in it. Her father had always cautioned that everything in the world could be explained in a rational manner. Only the ignorant attributed what they couldn't understand to the meddling of gods, demons, or sorcerers. The old witch had the cure for the poison that was killing her brother, and Eridani would bargain for it as she might with any healer or alchemist.

Ivy crawled up the castle-like walls of the large house. Eridani tried the heavy front door. It creaked as it opened. The cavernous hall was not lit. Eridani took a few steps inward, and stopped to let her eyes adjust to the dark.

"Hello?" she called out, but no one replied. The house seemed abandoned.

Eridani walked around the hall. The house was three stories high but she could find no ascending staircase. The only path she found led in the opposite direction. She felt her way down the steep incline, resting her hand on the wall for support. The long corridor continued to descend. Deeper down, she could see no light at all. She advanced slowly, feeling ahead with her toes before taking each step.

A dim candle flared up on the wall next to her. Startled, Eridani looked around, but the candle gave off more smoke than light and revealed nothing but a small area of bare corridor.

"Hello?" Eridani tried again. When no one answered, she pressed on. A new candle lit up every dozen steps. Eventually, the floor leveled out but the walls extended outward in both directions. She was standing at the entrance into another large hall.

She took a few tentative steps forward and a dozen candles positioned in an oval formation flickered to life. Even so many of them together provided little illumination; shadows swirled in the center of the hall. Eridani squinted. She could make out a shape hidden in the shadows.

She took several more steps toward the center. The shadows shifted right in front of her like a tangle of ethereal snakes. Someone moved within, cloaked in darkness.

"Hello," she said, for the third time.

The shadows parted and an enormous ogre stepped through. The monster bent down until it was face to face with Eridani, less than an arm's reach away. It was gray or dark green, she couldn't quite tell in the dark. Its face was a caricature of a man, seemingly too large for its form, misshapen like an unfinished clay molding. She could smell decay on its breath. It bared its fangs, each pointed canine the size of her fist, and roared a deafening challenge full of primeval rage.

Eridani stood her ground.

"Show yourself, Sorceress!" she said. "Save your illusions for others. I know there are no mythical monsters in the world."

The ogre stared at her for a moment, then its visage melted and dropped to the ground in a cascade of sand.

Magic tricks, thought Eridani. Better magic tricks than what she'd seen at carnivals, but magic tricks nonetheless.

The candles flared up, illuminating more of the oval hall, and revealed a woman in a flowing green gown standing at the far end of it. Her hair was white, and her face full of wrinkles, but she stood straight and carried herself with apparent ease. She was smiling.

"That is precious," she said, stepping forward. "Well done on seeing past the mirage, but to assume there are no monsters? Ha! Oh, to be so young and foolhardy again."

Eridani thought it best to swallow the insult. She pressed her palm to the center of her chest, a respectful greeting among equals. "I'm Eridani of Kozhad."

The old woman offered a mocking bow. "The name is Oshekzhothep the Seer. It's a little exotic for your tongue, so feel free to call me Sorceress."

"I need your help, Oshekzhothep." Eridani was sure she mangled the pronunciation. "I seek the cure for the poison of the red desert scorpion."

"Straight to the point, eh? And why should I bother to help you?"

Eridani held up a purse of coins she had retrieved from under the floorboard. "I can pay."

"Gold is meaningless to me," said the sorceress. "I can transmute as much as I need from the base elements."

Eridani wasn't deterred. "There are many tales of you accepting coin in exchange for your services."

"Those tales are told by people who are either too ashamed or too afraid to disclose the real bargains they'd struck."

Eridani suspected the witch was merely trying to up her price. But then, she really could have all the gold she needed, whether she came by it via supernatural means or not. "What bargain would you strike with me, then?"

The sorceress walked around Eridani, studying her as one might a statue. "Can you offer me power? Influence? Secrets? Those are the true commodities, not some metal or stones that glint prettily in sunlight."

"The cure is for my brother," said Eridani. "He is the King of Kozhad. Surely it would benefit you to be in the good graces of a king?"

The sorceress continued to circle her. "My bargain is with you, not your brother. He may be a king, but it's you who dared to enter my abode on his behalf." She stopped in front of Eridani. "Permit me to read your future."

Eridani looked at the sorceress with suspicion. "You want to study my palm, or cast bones?"

The old woman chuckled. "True divination isn't a parlor trick. All that's required is your consent. Then I shall know whether you'll ever possess anything I might want."

Eridani sighed. "Go on, then."

The sorceress stood still and stared straight at Eridani, but her eyes seemed focused elsewhere, as though she were looking somewhere far away. A rustling sound came from the dark corners of the hall and the red flames took on an orange hue. They flickered as if caressed by the wind, even though Eridani felt no breeze.

The candles flared up and the sorceress refocused on Eridani. The smirk was gone from her face. Her pupils were wide, and she regarded Eridani as though she saw her for the first time. "You have a complex and ambiguous destiny," she said. "Much of your future is a mystery, even to an adept like me. There is potential for both greatness in you and great evil, and your path is lined with many difficult choices."

Eridani had visited a seer at a carnival once. There, a fat woman stirred coffee grounds and delivered vague prophecies. Hers were about the promise of future happiness and requited love rather than difficult choices and destiny, but Eridani couldn't shake the feeling of similarity. She put no stock in the empty predictions of either fortuneteller. "Will you help me, Sorceress?"

"I will take a chance on you, yes," said the sorceress. "After all, the investment is small enough. You might prove to be of great value to the Invisible God someday."

Eridani hadn't heard of an invisible deity, but with so many pantheons of gods being worshiped across the Heart, she wasn't surprised. She waited for the witch to name her price.

"I will give you the antidote for the poison to deliver to your brother. In return, I will ask a favor of you sometime in the future, and you must grant it no matter what, if it is within your power. Do you accept?"

Eridani thought back to the fairy tales and legends where the hero was suckered into what he or she felt was an easy bargain. They were meant as cautionary tales, but those characters were usually in a position where they had something to lose, whereas she thought she was paying a smaller price than the value of the coins in her purse. What favor could she possibly grant this witch? She was going to leave Skond and their paths would most likely never cross again. And besides, fairy-tale heroes always found ways to outsmart the devils they bartered with.

"I swear it," Eridani said.

The sorceress plucked a small blown-glass vial out of thin air. It was filled with a viscous liquid the color of ash. "Have your brother drink this."

Eridani accepted the vial. Her hand brushed up against the hand of the sorceress, which felt leathery and cold.

"Make haste," said the sorceress. "Save your brother, if you can. He is the only one you can rely upon. Beside him, everyone you know and trust will come to betray you."

It may have been the chill of the underground hall, but Eridani shivered.

Those words stayed with her as she left the sorceress's home, clutching the vial in her hand underneath the cloak. Only after the afternoon sun warmed her skin was she able to shrug off the ominous prophecy.

CHAPTER 5

WOODCASTLE UNDER SIEGE

fter Danchu drank the elixir provided by the sorceress, the tendrils of black rot withered away, the pus dried, and the area covered in black receded to the size of an apple and resembled little more than a fading bruise. By the time Lady Voriana's agents hired the mercenaries, his recovery was near complete, and Danchu rode triumphantly at the head of a mercenary army two-thousand-men strong.

There was one last meeting held at the lady's home before they set out. Danchu and Eridani were joined by Pel, who was assigned to accompany the group by the lady to look out for her interests, and Shikot, the commander of the mercenary company she had hired. Caer and Gavron weren't invited, prompting Eridani to reflect on this prior to the meeting. She cautioned Danchu against allowing their benefactor to surround him with advisors loyal to her rather than his own people, and Danchu agreed.

"We will take Woodcastle first," said Shikot. He was a wiry man of medium height, with curly brown hair and a bushy mustache. His complexion and cheekbones hinted at the Western Peaks being his homeland. "Strike at the duke before he learns of our plans and has time to mount a significant defense." He pointed a calloused finger at the map unrolled in front of them. "We're told the duke left only a token presence in Kozhad after he ..." Shikot glanced at Danchu, "... accomplished his goals there. Retaking it should present no challenge, after Woodcastle has fallen."

"Woodcastle is well fortified and its master, for all his flaws, is a competent commander," said Pel. "What is your siege strategy?"

"Element of surprise," said Shikot. "We outnumber the duke's men four to one, and many of them aren't stationed at the castle. If we move swiftly, we can capture the stronghold before he's had the chance to prepare for the siege. They won't hold out a week."

He was wrong.

Either the Duke of Buzzards employed competent spies or, more likely, it was the patriarch's agents that learned of the mercenary company gathering near Skond, investigated, and tipped off their ally. Regardless, the duke knew they were coming.

Bahel Elkwire—better known as the Duke of Buzzards for the great number of the predatory birds nested in the hills surrounding his stronghold—gathered his men and ample supplies behind the imposing stone walls of his keep and prepared for the siege. He couldn't hope to match the military strength of Shikot's company in open combat, so he holed up instead, and watched his enemies struggle with logistics and the mounting expense of feeding and upkeeping their army.

Shikot seemed content to draw his pay from the Dowager Councilor while maintaining the status quo. He refused to launch a direct assault on Woodcastle: too many of his men would perish.

Caer and Danchu both argued that this was poor strategy. Gavron cited examples from books he had read on siege tactics. Shikot was adamant, unmoved by their increasingly frustrated rhetoric.

A courier dispatched to Lady Voriana returned empty-handed—she refused to add the enormous expense of procuring siege engines and approved of Shikot's strategy of starving the defenders out.

THREE WEEKS LATER, Eridani marched past the multitude of tents erected by the mercenaries and past the guards stationed around the largest tent at the center of the camp. Inside, Shikot lounged with several of his officers, smoking pipes filled with dried aromatic grass, drinking wine, and playing dice. Pel sat alone to the side, reading a thick leather-bound volume. He brought the book with him and studied it dutifully; he said it was among the greatest treatises on warfare ever written.

Eridani stood in front of Shikot, hands on her hips. "The behavior of your men is unacceptable," she told the mercenary captain.

Shikot put down his cup. "What seems to be the trouble?"

"I was approached by a woman named Darla, whose family has a small farm not far from here. She claims your men came and took everything from her stores, slaughtered her dairy cow for meat, and left them destitute and unable to survive the next winter."

Shikot shrugged. "Where do you think the meat and grains for your dinner come from? We take what we must from the duke's subjects whom he has cowardly abandoned outside his keep's walls. It is the way of war."

"They're the future subjects of Kozhad," said Eridani. "What will they think of us? How can we demand their loyalty if we start off by robbing them blind? I want all the farmers reimbursed for everything taken, and from now on I want us to take only what they're willing to sell." She looked over at Pel, who'd put down his book and was listening. "If Lady Voriana won't cover the extra expense, then I will pay for it from the Woodcastle treasury, once we take it."

"I can't approve the expense on my own, but I will dispatch a messenger," said Pel. "Lady Voriana has invested heavily in your success. I think she will see the wisdom in your thinking."

Shikot grimaced, then shrugged again. "It's your money. Inform the men," he told his officers, before turning back to Eridani. "We'll set it up, but handling reparations is your headache."

WORD HAD SPREAD quickly among the peasants. On the designated day, a long line of haggard-looking men and women formed at the outskirts of the camp. Eridani sat at the makeshift table, with Gavron at her side. Caer stood a step behind her acting as a bodyguard, in charge of several of the mercenaries assigned by Shikot to keep an eye on things. Pel also showed up, presumably to oversee the proceedings for his employer.

One after another, the peasants approached her and told their tales. She asked them what was taken by the mercenaries, and listened patiently at the outpouring of hurt and grief each person seemed to desperately need to get off their chests.

She expected an accounting of cattle and bushels of grain and vegetables, but in addition the peasants spoke of beatings and rape and other sins committed against them by armed men, most not even of this mercenary company. She had no illusions about the hardship of the peasants' lives, even those in Kozhad where her father had ruled fairly, but their stories were worse than any difficulties she had previously imagined. Each tale was enough to break her heart.

Eridani bore it with all the grace she could muster. On behalf of her brother, she offered kind words and generous amounts of silver to each seeker, even those whose tales of woe had nothing to do with Shikot's men. She talked to each of them of how life would be different once they became subjects of Kozhad, how brutality and bullying would not be tolerated. They accepted her silver eagerly and her promises with caution.

As she dispensed her largesse, the mood in the crowd lightened and some of the peasants became overly bold in their claims. An urge to take advantage of this situation was only human nature and to be expected, and Eridani was ready for it. When a man claimed that the mercenaries robbed him of his herd of eight goats, she asked his name and his village, then opened a thick ledger and flipped through the pages.

She looked up from the ledger. "There's no record here of you paying a tithe on the money earned selling milk, or cheese, or wool, not to mention meat." She rose and leveled her gaze at the peasant. "Were you cheating your lord then, or are you trying to take advantage of my generosity now?"

The man's face turned pale as he grasped for a response. He couldn't have known that the real tithe ledgers were stored somewhere behind the walls of Woodcastle, that the one she was browsing belonged to Pel. Few commoners could read and Eridani didn't hesitate to attempt such a bluff. The man's lip trembled as he stood there, failing to come up with a convincing lie.

"Be gone," Eridani said. "I have neither patience nor charity for liars."

The man left without argument, as fast as his feet would carry him. The word spread quickly among the rest. Although some may have still embellished their losses, the sight of the ledger in front of Eridani kept their greed in check.

Several dozen encounters later, she recognized Darla, who bowed deeply, her eyes moist. "Thank you, Your Highness. Without me husband, I can barely handle the farm. If it weren't for ya, me children would surely starve."

"I'm sorry for your loss, Darla. When did your husband pass?"

"Oh, he's not dead, Your Highness. He's been took, my Cheve, took for corvée when we couldn't scrape enough coin to pay the duke."

Eridani winced. Corvée was an ugly practice: all men owed several days of unpaid labor per year to their lords. Additionally, those who couldn't pay the taxes, or rent to their landlord, were conscripted into forced labor and treated little better than slaves, forced to work off their debt for months and sometimes even years at a time.

"When my brother reclaims his crown, he will have all men like your husband released," promised Eridani. "It will not be long, now."

Tears flowed freely down Darla's cheeks. "Thank you, Your Highness, and may ya namesake star ever watch over ya from the heavens."

Eridani handed her a larger-than-average purse of silver coins, and Darla backed away, bowing. There were many more people in line behind her and Eridani kept at it until she had spoken to every single one. By then it was dark outside, and all their faces had become a blur.

Eridani was exhausted, her throat raw, and her back aching. She stretched, bid thanks to Gavron and Caer, and set out in search of a quick meal. That's when Pel, who spent the entire day quietly observing, approached.

"You did well," he said. "You seem to have a gift for dealing with people, much like the lady herself. It's an important skill for a leader."

"Thanks," Eridani replied. "But I'm no leader. I wanted to help those poor souls, and help Danchu as well."

"Don't be so modest. A true leader shows up. Where was your brother today?"

"He trusts me to handle this," Eridani said, with a little more edge to her voice than she had intended.

Although she wouldn't admit it, she knew Pel was right. Danchu should have at least made an appearance. He was a good man, but he paid as little mind to the commoners as did most of his highborn peers.

Despite her arguments and those of their advisors, Danchu seemed to accept Shikot's flawed strategy too easily. She wondered what Pel's book might say about engaging in a prolonged siege of a castle while in such a weak strategic position. She was sure Pel disapproved of Shikot's strategy as well, but did not voice his concerns since his employer supported it. Voriana was no general, but she held the purse strings.

Eridani thanked Pel again for his compliment and headed toward the fires, where the smell of roasted meat beckoned.

ON THE FOLLOWING morning, a young man showed up at Eridani's tent. He stood at a respectful distance, well away from the guards posted at the entrance, nervously kneading his knit cap with both hands.

When Eridani emerged, she approached him. "Are you here for reparations? That was yesterday, but I'll see what I can do."

"No, ma'am... I mean, Your Highness." He shifted his weight from foot to foot. "I'm here to enlist."

Eridani regarded the man. He was perhaps a year or two her senior, broad-shouldered and seemingly fit. Probably one of the younger sons of a local farmer for whom life as a soldier offered more promise than staying put and working the land for the eldest brother who'd inherit it. A fine potential recruit.

"Enlist? You'll want to speak to Shikot, then. He's in charge of this company."

"I don't want to become a mercenary, Your Highness. I want to enlist in the army of Kozhad."

She was caught by surprise. Danchu and she hadn't discussed recruiting, but surely they would need their own soldiers once they recaptured Kozhad and the mercenaries left. And if so, why not start now rather than scramble to build a viable fighting force later on? They could spread the word, gather a small number of recruits, and have Shikot's men work for their gold and do some training while they idled at Woodcastle's walls. Of course, it wasn't her decision to make unilaterally.

"Wait here," she told him. "Let me speak to my brother about this."

DANCHU TOOK TO the idea of commanding his own army like a fish to water. In short order, he and Eridani recruited a force of fifty young men and women from the nearby farms and villages, and began training them in earnest.

Her brother had been reluctant to recruit women at first, but Eridani had insisted. She wanted Danchu to do things differently; to treat his subjects with respect, and to offer them opportunities not granted by other monarchs. If his subjects love him, Eridani argued, they will fight for him, making it more difficult for some enemy to unseat Danchu the way the Duke of Buzzards had routed their father. As was usually the case, Danchu allowed his sister to persuade him.

Caer and Danchu, bored out of their minds until then, had fresh recruits to whip into shape. They taught them the basics, under the observation and good-natured jeers of the mercenaries.

"These peasants have no learning," Danchu said, exasperated. "Several of them can't seem to grasp the concept of left and right. They stumble, the entire formation stumbles. We've been at it for two days now and I'm starting to think they'll never get it."

"They don't need to know how to march. They need to know how to fight." Caer was especially pleased to be training recruits for real warfare instead of teaching privileged children to fence with flimsy, ceremonial blades.

"That they do," said Danchu. "But I want them to learn all of it: marching, taking orders, standing at attention. These things teach discipline. They help turn a bunch of farmers into a cohesive unit."

"All right," said Caer. "You want them to march? Give me until sundown and I will have them marching."

At the evening meal, the normally reserved and gloomy Caer was cheerfully recounting the exploits of the day.

"I got this problem licked in short order, I did," said Caer.

Danchu drank from his cup. "You taught them right from left, then?"

"Better." The Ugly Unicorn beamed a self-satisfied smile. "I had small patches of hay and straw attached to their trousers. Hay to the right leg, straw to the left. No farmer would mistake the two. During drills I shout 'straw, hay, straw.' They're marching like veterans!"

"We're making real progress," said Danchu, as he swatted a mosquito on the side of his neck. "Which is a good thing. I'm sure the troops will get their first taste of battle soon. The cowardly duke can't hold out much longer. They must be reduced to eating rats and birds by now, if they can catch them." He grinned and bit into his steak.

The siege was in its sixth week.

CHAPTER 6

CHE COLD,
DARK NIGHT

n the dead of night, someone entered Eridani's tent. She woke
with a start, rolled to the side of the thick fur that served as
her bed, reached for her dagger.

"Peace! It's me, Pel. I'm not here to attack you." He held
up his palms.

Eridani rubbed her eyes and pulled the blanket up to her neck. "What
do you want?"

"I have some bad news. Please listen, there's very little time."

Pel looked upset. He didn't seem threatening, nor did he appear to be there
seeking some sort of ill-considered romantic encounter.

"What is it?" Eridani asked.

"The mercenaries are leaving. They received orders from Lady Voriana
and have already pulled up camp. If the duke's men don't know this already,
they'll notice soon. You and your brother need to put as much distance as
possible between yourselves and Woodcastle before that happens."

Eridani shook off the last vestiges of sleep. "Why would the lady betray
us? She has invested a fortune into this campaign. Why give up now?"

"I don't know," said Pel. "My guess is that she got a better offer. With the
duke under siege, the patriarch must've given her some concession, perhaps
a permanent seat on the council, in exchange for withdrawing her support
of Danchu."

Eridani motioned for Pel to avert his eyes. He turned around and she
scrambled to get dressed.

"Why are you telling me this?" she asked, while struggling to put on her
boots.

"I grew up poor in a small village a day's journey away from Skond. Even when harvests were good, the tithes and tariffs had bled us dry. In a bad year..." He trailed off for a moment. "I had no choice but to seek employment in the city because my parents couldn't afford to feed all their children. I owe Lady Voriana a debt; I rose higher in her service than most lowborn boys can aspire to. Even so, for all the good she has done for the people of Skond, I've never seen her demonstrate the kind of compassion you showed to the duke's subjects."

Pel still faced away from Eridani. For all the weeks they had spent together in camp, he'd remained a private man, speaking few words and never before opening up like this. Perhaps not looking her in the eye helped him speak freely.

"The world needs monarchs like you, and while you and your brother may never get the chance to rule in Kozhad, the least I can do is deliver a warning that might yet save your lives."

Eridani put on her cloak and tapped Pel on the shoulder so he'd know he could turn around. "Thank you, Pel. I hope this won't get you in trouble with your mistress."

Pel smiled ruefully. "She never explicitly ordered me *not* to warn you. And she knows my heart well."

Eridani hugged him. Pel let her, but didn't return the embrace, perhaps uncertain as to how to respond to such a gesture from a royal. When she let go, he nodded to her, his face crimson red.

"I must go now. Best of luck, and be safe."

AFTER PEL HAD left, Eridani stepped out of the tent. The mercenaries were gone, their tents rolled up and packed with quiet haste in the night. Mercenaries always knew how to retreat expeditiously. Only a handful of tents remained: those occupied by the Kozhad army-in-training.

Eridani burst into one of the tents, woke up the two soldiers inside, and ordered them to gather everyone else. She then headed for Danchu's tent.

Ten minutes later, Eridani, Danchu, Caer, and Gavron held an impromptu private council.

Danchu stomped his foot in frustration. "We have no horses, no supplies, and the duke's men outnumber us nearly ten to one. Our only option is to retreat before they realize the bulk of the siege force has gone."

"We have to split up," said Caer. "A party of fifty-four souls is too slow, too easy to track, especially since the enemy knows this land well. Disperse through the woods. We can gather again at a safe location farther from Woodcastle in the morning."

"Darla's farm," said Eridani. "It's far enough from here, and she'll be loyal to our cause."

"The same is not necessarily true of your recruits," said Gavron. "Many of them may shift loyalties now that they're not on the winning side."

"Let's minimize the risk," said Caer. "Take a few of the soldiers you judge most loyal with you and head straight for the farm. Gavron and I will each lead a group away, and join up with you tomorrow, but they won't know the rendezvous point in case they're captured or choose to defect."

"I'm no military commander," Gavron protested.

"All you have to do is hide out in the woods for a night, protected by soldiers. You don't have to lead them into battle," said Caer. He looked at the tutor with distaste. "You've proven yourself good at cowering, so go and cower."

"Your opinion means little to me, Sellsword." Gavron crossed his arms.

"Please, now is not the time for bickering," said Eridani. She pointed at Woodcastle. "There are torches lit, more than there should be at this time of night. They know something is happening here."

"Let's go," said Danchu.

Outside, he addressed the troops.

"We have been betrayed. The mercenary force will no longer help us in our struggle against the villainous duke and his henchmen. This means we must retreat. Our future is uncertain and fraught with danger. Those of you who wish to leave and return to your families should go now. I'll understand."

The recruits buzzed with conversation. Gradually over a dozen men and women headed off into the woods in groups of two or three. The rest stayed, even though concern and fear plainly showed on their faces.

Danchu handpicked five soldiers and let Caer and Gavron split the rest into two groups. As they sped away from Woodcastle, they could see the defenders raising the gates.

The journey was exhausting. Traveling through the forest on foot in the middle of the night left many of their group with scratches and bruises. Over three hours passed before they saw the outline of Darla's farmhouse in the distance.

Eridani ignored the pain and discomfort. She focused only on one thought: *everyone you know and trust will come to betray you.* Was the old sorceress right? Were her words more than a mere parting sting, an attempt to punish Eridani for her insolent attitude toward the arcane arts?

Lady Voriana, the paragon of virtue and patron of the disadvantaged, was the last person Eridani would have expected to betray her and Danchu. If the Dowager Councilor was capable of such treachery, then who was next? Would Caer consider joining forces with the Duke of Buzzards now that Danchu's cause was nearly hopeless? Would Gavron risk being tortured or give up her location as soon as the duke's men threatened him, should he become captured?

She glanced at Danchu, walking in the lead of their group, his back straight and his shoulders wide. A true warrior, he refused to let betrayal and circumstance bring him down. He was someone Eridani could always rely on. Even the sorceress did not dare question their bond.

They approached the log house and one of the soldiers knocked on the front door. There was a brief commotion inside, then Darla cracked the door open, a lantern in hand. Her eyes widened when she saw Eridani and Danchu. She seemed uncertain whether she should step outside or welcome them in.

"May we seek shelter for the night, my lady?" asked Danchu.

The young king's words got Darla moving. She swung the door open and ushered them into her home.

The house had no inner walls. It was a single room, barely larger than Danchu's master bedroom back in Skond.

Darla and her three children shared the space. A large brick oven dominated the room. There was a small fire in the hearth built into it; even in the summer, the nights in the north tended to be chilly. A chimney conducted most of the smoke outside, but the smell of bitter ash still permeated the room. The hearth fire and the lantern were the only sources of light.

There was no bed as such. Instead, there was a layer of fresh straw on top of the oven's flat brick surface, where the fire could keep the occupant warm in the winter. Darla's children, ranging in age from teenager to a toddler, used the straw mats at the base of the oven as their bedding.

An unpolished pine table and some stools were the only furniture; a handful of shelves lined the walls, with cooking utensils and wooden bowls placed on them. A few gardening tools hung on hooks. There was no wardrobe—the clothes Darla and her children wore were what they owned.

Eridani took in the sights and smells of the log house. This was true poverty: not the kind of simple, carefree pastoral existence imagined by the storytellers, but a difficult and unglamorous life of drudgery.

After one of the soldiers explained to Darla what was wanted of her, the peasant woman sprang into action. She ordered her two older kids out of the cramped house. "The wee ones are used to sleeping in the barn, they are," she said, brushing off concerns. "Some of ya men may be more comfortable there as well, glad for the soft hay to rest their heads on."

Indeed, there wasn't enough space for the seven of them to sleep, but Danchu wanted everyone indoors and out of sight. Darla offered Eridani her oven-top bed, she and the baby took one of the mats, Danchu took another, and he offered the remaining mat arbitrarily to one of the soldiers. The rest had to make do on the cold hard floor.

Despite an exhausting trek across the nighttime forest, despite being warm and comfortable now, Eridani kept tossing and turning, unable to fall asleep for a long time. She was thinking of Gavron and Caer, and their troops. The uncertain future for all of them weighed heavily on her.

Perhaps now that the circumstances had changed for the worse, Danchu would assent to leaving the north, to finding a friendly court far from Kozhad and Skond that might be willing to offer succor to a deposed king.

She managed to fall asleep, but her slumber was restless and filled with troubling dreams.

CHAPTER 7

THE ROYAL BLOODLINE

 commotion woke Eridani from uneasy sleep. There was the sound of horses neighing outside, armor clinking, and men dismounting. Whoever had arrived weren't being inconspicuous about it. Had Caer managed to find horses for them?

Danchu and the others were waking up, too. A soldier stumbled toward the log house's sole glass window while rubbing sleep from his eyes. The other window holes were covered with sheepskin; even a single pane of glass was a luxury for a family like Darla's.

The soldier shrunk back from the window. "The duke's men! They found us!"

Armed men kicked the door open and marched in. They had their swords at the necks of the three nearest soldiers before anyone could react. Danchu, Eridani, and their two remaining followers drew their own blades, their backs to the brick oven.

"Your turn to be outnumbered and trapped," said one of the attackers with glee. "Lay down your weapons and come outside, or we'll lock the doors and burn down this hovel and you with it."

The man wasn't bluffing about them being outnumbered. Through the open door, Eridani could see no less than thirty men on horseback outside.

Darla huddled in the far corner of the cabin with her baby. Several more soldiers walked in, and with them Darla's eldest son. He pointed at Danchu. "That one! That one is the king, he is," as though Danchu's fine clothes didn't set him apart from the others anyway.

Eridani almost cried out. *Everyone you know and trust will come to betray you.* Darla must have sent her son to fetch the duke's men; that explained how they were discovered so quickly. Eridani shot a look full of pain at Darla.

"I'm sorry," the older woman said. "You shouldn't have come here. What ya think would happen to my babies when the duke found out we sheltered ya?" She scowled at Eridani, her eyes seeming tired and sad, and turned away.

More enemy soldiers entered. The cabin was crowded now, swords pointed at Danchu and his people from all directions. One of Danchu's men tentatively put his own weapon on the floor. Others followed suit, and soon even Danchu lowered his blade with a sigh of resignation. Eridani was the last to let go of her dagger. They were escorted outside.

In the shade of the barn, surrounded by his lieutenants, stood Bahel Elkwire, the Duke of Buzzards himself. He was a tall, wiry man in his early forties, sporting a thick mustache but no beard. His jet-black curls popped from under a steel helm. He wore light armor, leather with thin strips of steel patched on to offer a bit of extra protection in a melee. A scabbard hung at his hip. His feet were planted wide on the ground, but he shifted his head constantly, in brief and somewhat jerky motions reminiscent of his avian namesake. Despite her desperate situation, Eridani couldn't help wondering whether he was naturally filled with nervous energy or drank an overabundance of coffee.

He spotted the prisoners and grinned. The duke's men ushered the captives toward him until he was face to face with Danchu.

"You've caused me a lot more trouble than I'd expected, Princeling," he said, with an undertone of malice in his even, almost cheerful voice.

Danchu tried to lunge toward the duke, but was restrained by two men, each holding his shoulders and twisting his arms behind his back.

"Hold your tongue, traitorous scum," roared Danchu. "I'm your liege!"

The duke laughed in his face. "You've got fight in you, child. I like that. You're perhaps a better man than your father, who whimpered and begged for his life at my feet."

"You speak of the man you swore a loyalty oath to! You have less honor than a camp-follower whore. You—"

The duke punched Danchu hard in the solar plexus and he doubled over.

"You may speak brave and pretty words, but you're soft and weak, like your father. You're no leader, no worthy king, and neither was he. Your ancestors were great men once, but recent generations did nothing but drive their once-thriving kingdom to insignificance and poverty. Kozhad is better off with the mayor I appointed."

Danchu gasped for breath and struggled to stand straight, the Duke's soldiers still restraining him.

"A real man fights his own battles, followed by his loyal troops," said the duke, "and doesn't beg some rich bitch to buy him a bushel of mercenaries."

"Is that why you have henchmen holding me back?" managed Danchu between gasps. "Afraid to fight me yourself?"

The duke laughed again and motioned to his men. "Release him. Give him his sword. Make room." He turned to Danchu. "You may be soft, but you tried to stand up to me, and you deserve a better death than your father." He drew his sword and sliced the air a few times, stretching his arm. "My old man didn't believe in coddling his brood like yours did. He sent me off to the army and I fought for eight years in the Haldova campaigns. I've got scars and the experience that goes with them. So raise your blade against me, if you dare."

Eridani wanted to talk Danchu down, to stop him, but she understood that any such attempt would be futile. The duke knew what he was doing—he'd announced his intentions loudly, and made sure plenty of his men were present to witness the fight. He wanted the word to spread that he had defeated the rightful king of Kozhad in honorable combat, and he'd done a fine job of goading Danchu into a challenge. Not that he had to try very hard: Danchu would risk nearly anything for a chance to kill the man who'd slaughtered their parents. Eridani watched as her brother was released and given his sword. She dreaded what would come next, but it was perhaps slightly better than the alternative. Danchu might stand a sliver of a chance with his sword and none as a disarmed captive.

A wide circle of men formed around the duke and the king. They shouted insults at Danchu. Weeks spent under siege, hungry and bored, didn't predispose them toward the deposed monarch.

Danchu flexed his shoulders and pointed the tip of his sword toward the duke. Bahel Elkwire ignored his opponent but raised his sword in salute to the soldiers. His men cheered. He stood with his legs wide and firmly planted in the dirt, and waited for Danchu to make the first move.

Danchu lunged at the duke, his attack fast and ferocious, his movements fluid and precise. Vengeance must've really focused him; Eridani knew Caer would be proud of his student, were he watching.

The duke stood his ground and parried the attacks, but was no longer smiling. Perhaps he was realizing that his opponent wasn't the pushover he'd expected. Bahel parried and swung, matching his years of experience against the king's youthful vigor.

The duelists seemed evenly matched, Danchu's anger and desperation forcing him to fight like he never had before. He managed to slip past the duke's defenses, but the tip of his sword glanced off the metal plates sewn into his opponent's leather armor.

Before Danchu could disengage, the duke kicked at his ankle. Between the momentum of the thrust and being tripped, Danchu lost his balance and tumbled into the mud. The duke swung at Danchu's exposed back, but the King of Kozhad was faster. He rolled to the side and the saber scraped the ground he'd occupied moments before.

Eridani gasped, the same feeling of helplessness she experienced when learning of her parents' deaths while stuck in the hidden compartment of a wagon overtaking her. Here she was, forced to be a passive observer again while her brother fought for his life.

Danchu scrambled up to his feet and the two men circled each other, breathing heavily.

"This is how you die, Princeling," said the duke. "Far from home, devoid of friends, and caked in mud."

Danchu held his temper in check and searched for an opening.

The duke switched tactics. "The patriarch thinks he can pay me off by arranging a marriage to some thrice-removed niece, but I've got a better idea. I will have both a legitimate claim to the throne and the seat on the council, once I wed your sister."

Eridani felt as though an icy hand clutched her heart. She would never let this monster touch her, no matter what. She'd sneak a knife or a shard of glass—anything sharp—and try to take him out given half a chance. Of course, the duke might simply let her rot in the dungeon and still claim the spoils he spoke of. The thought of that was almost as unbearable as the idea of physical contact with him.

Danchu gritted his teeth but remained focused, not letting the duke's taunts get to him. He moved warily, searching for an opening.

The duke licked his lips. "I hope she's a better lay than her mother."

Danchu roared and came at the duke, their blades clashing again and again. The young king's attack was ferocious, forcing the duke to retreat several steps this time, but even with Danchu's onslaught fueled by his fury, the two remained evenly matched.

The guard at Eridani's left gurgled. She turned and saw an arrow protruding from his neck. Her gaze followed the path of the arrow and she saw a handful of soldiers led by Caer advancing toward the farm. With everyone intent on the duel they'd managed to get close, but were still greatly out-numbered by the duke's men. She saw Gavron, looking miserable, hanging back at the edge of the clearing. A self-admitted coward, he still chose to come to their rescue rather than run away from a dangerous situation. The witch was wrong after all: she and Danchu had loyal friends.

It took her a second to assess the situation. As the guard crumpled face first onto the ground and the enemy troops around him took notice, she turned to the guard on her right and kneed him as hard as she could in the groin.

"Follow me!" she shouted to the rest of the captives and bolted toward Caer.

The duke's men may not have expected a sneak attack, but their weapons were at the ready and they turned to face Caer and his soldiers.

Caer's two archers took out several opponents from their position at the edge of the clearing. As Eridani ran, she watched them send arrow after arrow into the midst of the enemy. A group of a dozen men and women led by Caer advanced toward where the prisoners were held, while several more engaged the sentries who were guarding the horses.

Oblivious to the attack, Danchu and the Duke of Buzzards fought furi-ously. Danchu was faster and his blade made it past the duke's defenses several times, but they were glancing blows easily thwarted by the helm and the armor. The duke managed a shallow cut on the king's shoulder, but it was barely worse than a scratch and didn't slow the younger man down.

Eridani made it to the relative safety of the soldiers loyal to her and her brother. The other prisoners were a few steps behind her. Two of them weren't fast enough and got cut down by the enemy, but the remaining three were far enough ahead of the duke's men to reach safety. This left only Danchu.

She didn't call out for fear of distracting him at an inopportune moment. Instead, she followed Caer's charge, seeking a sword she could liberate from one of her fallen enemies.

She watched as Danchu pressed his attack, and the duke continued to retreat until his boot caught on a stone and he lost his balance. He landed on his posterior with an *oomph,* and although he retained the grip on his saber, his chest was left wide open. Danchu did not hesitate, closing what little distance remained between them.

With his lord in trouble, one of the duke's lieutenants took a step forward and threw a knife at Danchu's exposed back.

Danchu grunted in pain as the knife connected just below his right shoulder blade. He wouldn't let the treacherous attack stop him and raised his sword for the killing blow, but the wound made his strike slower and less precise. The duke managed to recover enough balance to block with his saber from the sitting position and then, as Danchu's momentum drove him forward, bury the point of the saber in the king's belly.

Eridani screamed. The world spun around her. Danchu dropped his sword and clutched at his stomach with both hands. He fell to his knees.

The Duke of Buzzards took notice of the chaos surrounding him. "Don't let her escape!" he shouted.

With Danchu mortally wounded, there was no reason to press forward. Caer changed tactics, ordering his men to retreat toward the horses. Eridani felt Caer and the others drag her away, but all she could do was watch her brother.

The Duke of Buzzards stood over the king of Kozhad, saber in hand. Danchu looked past him at Caer and Eridani and the others and registered the fact that they were escaping. A thin pained smile spread on his face. He looked up at the duke and said something, perhaps a curse or an insult—Eridani couldn't hear from the distance.

The duke raised his saber and swung it at Danchu's neck.

Something snapped within Eridani as she watched the curved blade connect with her brother's flesh.

CHAPTER 8
LIBERATOR

ridani couldn't remember most of the details of the rest of the fight. Some detached sliver of her mind noted that Caer's men took all the horses so the duke's soldiers couldn't mount a pursuit. It was a daring, well-executed, and nearly perfect attack against a superior force, except it failed in its ultimate goal. The last King of Kozhad was dead.

They rode for several hours, and Eridani spoke to no one. She ignored Caer's clumsy attempts to console her and Gavron's flowery condolences. The tutor and the Ugly Unicorn eventually gave her space, pulling their horses away. No one else dared approach. Somehow, as the distance between them and Woodcastle grew, her tears dried and her despair turned to determination.

She was the last of her bloodline, alone in the world, with no relatives and few friends. Danchu's noble ambition, his quest to reclaim the crown, and his lust for revenge had earned him an untimely death. She was free to follow her original plan: to flee south, to seek the anonymity of some distant court that might be sympathetic to her plight. Nothing was stopping her now. Nothing was holding her back.

Except revenge.

It seethed within her like a toothache, always there in the background when she tried to keep her mind occupied, worried about something else. But when her mind turned to it, it was like touching an ailing tooth with her tongue—the pain and anger and despair flared up, swelled within her until they became all-consuming.

She'd felt hatred and betrayal before, when her parents died and her world got turned upside down. But it was never quite like *this*. Now she finally understood how her brother had felt, and for the briefest of moments her instincts were to tell him, followed immediately by the realization that she never could, and the anger bubbled up to the surface once more.

No, she would not flee south. Eridani brought her horse to an abrupt stop. She waited for others to gather around her. A small band of men and women, tired and bloody, grim expressions on their faces, waited to see what she would do.

"We're going the wrong way," said Eridani. "Our future, the only destiny worth pursuing, lies in Kozhad."

"My queen, we don't have the numbers to retake Kozhad. It is said the duke has only a few men stationed there, but we have fewer still," said a young man with a fresh cut on his cheek.

Queen. She'd have to get used to that.

"We will get more men," said Eridani. "Darla told me the Woodcastle corvée labor gangs are strip-mining a quarry not far from here. I will take the duke's indentured servants and arm them against their tormentor."

Caer peered at Eridani, his expression inscrutable. "You wish to rouse and arm the serfs?"

Eridani waved toward her soldiers. "Who are they, if not children of serfs brave enough to risk life and limb in order to better their lot in life? Were the men recruited into your mercenary company any different? Were you?"

"The difference is months, sometimes years of training," said Caer. "The training officers beat the subservient serf spirit out of the men. Little by little, the officers distill their souls and fortify them into warriors." He pointed at the band of soldiers that followed them. "This is the process we have barely begun with them. What you propose is to herd an unruly mob toward the duke's trained fighters, and hope for the best."

Eridani considered this. "The way I see it, our options are limited. I will lead the serfs, or anyone else who will follow me. If I have to, I will take Kozhad by myself, armed with nothing more than a stick. We will reclaim my home quickly, while the duke expects us to run or hide."

"Why the hurry?" asked Gavron. "Why not take the time to recruit a stronger force? Surely it would benefit us to be methodical about this."

"The duke has every advantage," said Eridani. "He has more men, more money, and, if he were to run out of either, support from Skond. We failed to surprise him when we had the superior force. Now, surprise remains our only advantage. I must eliminate the duke so the patriarch won't have a proxy to make trouble in Kozhad. That's the only way we can buy any sort of respite and perhaps survive."

"I must be insane," said Gavron. "Any rational man would have ridden for Gan with great haste already. What sort of madness makes me follow people who are so clearly possessed of a death wish?"

Caer thought it over. "This is a lunatic plan born of desperation." He stroked his chin. "I like it."

ERIDANI STOOD IN front of the crowd of nearly two hundred men. They were not a pretty sight: the serfs were dressed in dirty rags, their hair disheveled, their skins covered in scabs and sweat. And the smell ... Eridani struggled to keep herself from wincing every time a gust of wind blew in her direction.

"Men of Woodcastle," she said, projecting her voice. "You have suffered greatly under the tyranny of your duke. But, no more! I'm Eridani of Kozhad, your rightful queen, and I grant you freedom and the chance to earn wealth and glory."

There had been only seven overseers in charge of these serfs. The site was a granite quarry. Extracting the stone from the shallow pit was back-breaking labor, and yet so few of the duke's men were required to keep them working. Eridani knew it was the fear of the duke, fear of retribution, that kept the serfs in line, rather than the overseers' blades.

Eridani's troops surprised the overseers and captured them without a fight. She ordered them killed: she couldn't risk them reporting to the duke on what she was up to, before she was ready to face him. Also, she felt watching their oppressors get what they deserved—their corpses thrown into the pit—would further predispose the serfs to her side.

She was surprised at how easy she found it to order the prisoners killed. There was no hesitation, no remorse. With Danchu's death fresh on her mind, anyone serving her enemy was an obstacle to be removed rather than a person.

"Together we shall dispatch the duke, like my men have dispatched his lapdogs today," she said. "Every man who joins my army will be given ownership of the land they work. Under my rule, veterans will not be required to forfeit any portion of their harvest to the crown!"

She went on, extolling the virtues of joining her side, and ignoring the fact that she could deliver on none of those promises without first succeeding against long odds. It was a rousing speech, which she capped with: "Those of you who wish to join my army, step forward and pledge your loyalty. Destiny awaits!"

Not a single serf moved toward her. They stood there, shifting weight uncomfortably on their feet.

Eridani glanced at Gavron who stood at her side. He shrugged.

"What's the matter?" Eridani asked. No one responded.

Eridani walked toward them. "You." She stopped in front of a broad-shouldered man who was a head taller than she. Surely he'd make a good soldier, given the proper training. "What's your name?"

The man seemed confused, as though the question she had asked were a puzzle. "Ian, Your Majesty," he finally said.

"Do you desire riches and glory?"

He thought even longer at that. "I just want to go home."

"Home?"

"Yah."

"Do you have a family, Ian?"

"I do, your grace. Wife and two daughters."

"Don't you wish to improve their lot in life? Lift them up from poverty and squalor?"

"We do all right working the land, Your Majesty." Ian paused again. "I can't improve their lot if I go off to war and get myself killed."

Eridani looked past him at the other serfs, who were nodding in agreement. This was definitely not how she'd imagined things would develop.

"Run along, then, coward. I require brave men, those willing to recognize the opportunity before them! Anyone?"

Eridani walked from one serf to the next, but none would look her straight in the eye.

"I've freed you," she shouted, her voice cracking. The events of the day had once again intruded upon her thoughts. She tried to stay busy, to avoid dwelling on her brother's death, but it wasn't working.

"We owe our lord but three days of service every season," said one of the serfs. "We'd get to go home tomorrow anyway."

"What of those of you forced to work off your debts?" She thought of Cheve, Darla's husband. She wondered if he was one of the wretched creatures standing before her.

"Begging you pardon, Majesty, but we'd rather work than fight," spoke out one of the serfs from the back.

"Any of them who possess a fighting spirit would have gone off to become soldiers, mercenaries, or bandits, when they were younger," Gavron said, in a low voice. "These men have no backbones."

"Go, then." Eridani crossed her arms. "Run to your hovels and your lives of mediocrity."

The serfs didn't need to be asked twice. They dispersed quickly and quietly.

"That did not go well," Eridani said to Caer as she watched them leave. Gavron wisely made no comment.

Eridani had thought the corvée laborers would be desperate enough to fight for a better life, but she had overestimated them. They were content to merely exist, no matter how difficult or unfair their lot.

She stared past the dispersing men. There was a small camp in the distance, with a handful of tents set up and fires burning. The smell of boiled vegetables was detectable in the air when the wind blew from that direction. "What's that?"

"Camp followers," said a young woman in her army. "Whores and cooks and seamstresses, eking out a living. Women aren't allowed to rent and work the land on their own, so sonless widows and girls who couldn't or didn't want to marry men often have nowhere else to go." She paused, seemingly lost in her memories. "I would have ended up in a place like this, had you not permitted women to join your army, my queen."

Eridani stood straighter. There existed a group of people even more disadvantaged, more desperate than the corvée laborers. People with nothing to lose. How did she not think of it sooner?

Eridani marched toward the camp.

ERIDANI'S ARMY ENTERED the village, a mismatched band of forty men and women, on horseback and on foot. The villagers hid in their homes, wary of armed strangers. Her followers knocked on doors, reassured the locals that they weren't bandits, weren't there with ill intent. "Your queen has come to speak to you all. Gather in front of the elder's house. Tell the others."

Like all the other villages they had visited over the last few days, the elder's house was easy to find. It was the largest and best-kept of the dwellings. The elder was charged with collecting taxes, passing along decrees, and otherwise acting as the representative of the noble who owned the land to the people who worked it. Without fail, such individuals found ways to leverage this position and enrich themselves.

A man in his late forties named Tomish was the elder in this village. He bowed to Eridani warily.

"How many families live in this place?" asked Gavron. Having spent most of his life in academia, he quickly took to what little authority the band of armed volunteers had provided him.

"Seventeen, honored visitor."

The elder showed both learning and some good sense. He couldn't determine Gavron's position or rank, so he selected the form of address least likely to offend.

"Your queen commands that all adults present themselves to her forthwith. I charge you with ensuring that all comply."

Tomish sent several of the gawking children running off in different directions, to gather anyone working in the fields or perhaps hiding away from the village when the group of strangers was spotted approaching their homes.

Eridani waited patiently for the serfs to gather. By the time each family was accounted for, over fifty people, including children and the elderly, were present. Gavron spoke briefly, introducing Eridani as their queen and the rightful ruler of Kozhad. Then it was her turn.

"I'm on my way home to reclaim my birthright," she told them. Then she proceeded to explain how things would be different once she took her rightful place as the ruler of Kozhad. Some listened indifferently, but others appeared excited that this royal chose to speak to the common folk almost as though they were equals. Some said they remembered her parents fondly. And while she had learned her lesson with the corvée laborers and didn't expect many of them to die or fight for her, Eridani was confident that she could rule these people; that they would take eagerly to her reforms once she had the power to institute them.

"Women are permitted to join my army same as men," she went on to say. "If any of you are unhappy with your lot, if you seek freedom and respect, step forward and you may come with us."

They recruited a handful of men along the way, but in every village several women chose to join her ranks: daughters with poor marriage prospects and childless widows, those who preferred the companionship of fellow women, and even some married women who saw this as an opportunity to escape their wedding vows.

These were strong, tough women who'd grown up used to the daily routine of hard physical labor. They may not have been trained with a sword, but they could competently wield a sickle or a large knife, and some of them could brawl as well as any man.

Caer armed the women with what he could. Some wielded cutting tools looted from the quarry; others carried pikes and farming tools. A few had cheaply made swords, left over from their fathers or husbands. It was a motley, undisciplined, untrained band, but they were willing to fight and they were all Eridani had.

The villagers shuffled on their feet, but no one stepped forward. Eridani didn't expect to recruit many here; this village seemed relatively prosperous and few would likely wish to leave.

A tall young woman dressed better than most villagers approached Eridani. She wore a sleeveless shirt and her arms were well toned. Her shoulder-length brown hair was styled in ringlets. "Who are your officers?" she asked.

Eridani pointed at the Ugly Unicorn. "Caer is an experienced fighter. He is my general."

"Interesting," said the young woman. "You speak of equality, but your one officer is a man." She shook her head in mock disapproval.

Eridani was taken aback by this peasant's gall, but she was also intrigued. "My army is small yet, and I will advance anyone who distinguishes themselves as it grows, regardless of gender."

"I'm Sana," said the woman. "I'm skilled with many kinds of weapons and have read several books. I can outfight any of your soldiers, and outwit your advisors. Make me an officer, and I will join you."

Before Eridani could reply, Tomish intervened. "You're not going anywhere, foolish child. I forbid it!"

Sana turned to him. "There's nothing here for me, father. You've known this all along. You accepted this when you allowed me to train with the old-timers returned from war, and to learn reading. I must go out into the world and make my own way. This is exactly the chance I've been waiting for."

Anger turned to sadness in Tomish's face. The man seemed like he knew his daughter's heart well, knew he was not going to stop her from leaving once she set her mind to it. His shoulders slumped. "If you go with them, you will die." He turned to Eridani and her people, concern for his daughter overriding caution. "You will all die! Even if you manage to take Kozhad by surprise, the duke and his men will come, and what chance does your skirt army stand against his well-trained killers?"

There had been other detractors. Most didn't dare voice their dissent in front of Eridani's soldiers, but a few were brave or foolish enough to mock her openly. Eridani had gained some experience in debating such people. Having recalled the example of the Dowager Councilor, Eridani chose to appropriate the name.

"Why should the skirt army be an insult?" she asked her followers. "Women can work and fight—and rule—as well as any man." There were nods and some cheering. The women liked her rhetoric. They were genuinely excited to be valued, ready to fight to the death not so much for her as an individual, but for the idea of their self-worth.

"I like your initiative and boldness, Sana. You're welcome to join us, and I hope that you do. But you have to prove yourself to become an officer. I won't hand out honors for the asking. Prove your loyalty, your bravery, your intelligence. Distinguish yourself, and you stand as good a chance to advance through the ranks as anyone else. What say you?"

Sana smiled. "You're no pushover. I like that."

After that, one more woman and one man volunteered as well. Despite his reservations, Tomish gave his daughter a horse and the best weapons he owned. He donated several more weapons for the other volunteers to use.

Eridani thanked him, and made note of his name as a possible administrator. She met all kinds of elders, some so bad she had deposed them on the spot and used their wealth and possessions to outfit her army and to distribute the rest among their villagers. She appropriated horses and food from others, claiming it as an advance against future taxes they would collect on her behalf. But those few who seemed like good people she left alone; her kingdom would need such men if it were to prosper in the long term.

They moved on to the next village.

By the time Eridani reached Kozhad, her skirt army numbered well over a hundred recruits.

CHAPTER 9

TO REIGN IN KOZHAD

ozhad was a small kingdom: a town of only a few thousand residents and a few thousand more living in the surrounding area. Although the ruling family hadn't been wealthy in generations, they had governed well. The town was relatively prosperous, the narrow streets were clean, and the buildings changed gradually from basic log structures on the outskirts of town to comfortable brick dwellings as one approached the palace.

The palace of Kozhad stood at the center, overseeing the town square. It was a two-story mansion that featured a throne hall and a handful of rooms; in Skond, even relatively minor nobles possessed homes of such size and scope. Eridani's entire ancestral home could fit within the patriarch's grand ballroom.

There were no walls around the palace, just as there weren't city walls surrounding Kozhad. There was only a decorative gate, one a child could climb with ease. It was why the Duke of Buzzards had been able to depose her father with so little effort. This time, it worked to Eridani's advantage. She sent some of her more experienced troops ahead as scouts, to surround the town and prevent any of the duke's men from escaping and delivering a message to him. Then the skirt army marched right in to the town square.

The spy she had sent ahead reported that only two dozen of the duke's men were stationed in town. The duke relied on the mayor he had appointed to keep the peace, and a few trusted tax collectors to ensure a steady trickle of funds from Kozhad to Woodcastle. Otherwise, the duke seemed to have little interest in the fate of the town or its people.

The lieutenant in charge of the duke's soldiers rallied his men, but seemed uncertain of what to make of his enemies. They were outnumbered three

71

to one, but they were outnumbered by *women*. Eridani and her army advanced on them near the center of town, where the duke's soldiers had taken over several of the houses, booted the original residents, and turned them into barracks.

"Surrender, and you shall be spared," Sana shouted.

The enemy soldiers looked in bewilderment at each other and at the serf women facing them.

Sana stepped forward, closing the distance between herself and the enemy troops. She wore her grandfather's splint armor—narrow strips of bronze sewed into a cloth foundation—over a long skirt. A cheap iron skull cap unadorned with any decorations covered her head.

"If you hesitate because you're embarrassed, because you don't wish to surrender to women, ask yourself this question," she said as she stopped in front of the lieutenant. "How much more embarrassing will it be if you choose to fight and are defeated by us?"

The lieutenant seemed to consider this.

"You could save face," said Sana. "You could say it was ignoble of you to fight women, and so you chose to lay down your arms instead."

The lieutenant thought about it some more and seemed to have reached a decision.

"Never! These peasants will scatter at the sight of our steel. Attack at—"

Sana was quick. Her dagger found the lieutenant's neck. The man fell to the ground and moaned, his command cut off mid-sentence.

"Which one of you is in charge now?" Sana asked.

The soldiers muttered and nudged one among their number forward.

"Do you wish to offer your surrender and to recognize the authority of Queen Eridani?" asked Sana.

The soldier nodded reluctantly. He lay his sword on the ground, careful to move slowly as he kept a wary eye on Sana. Then the rest of the duke's soldiers proceeded to surrender their arms as well.

ERIDANI LED THE men and women of her tiny army toward the front gates of the palace. A crowd of citizens had formed quickly once it became clear that there would be no violence in the streets. Eridani had imagined a much more exuberant reception, but the crowd was rather muted. In a way, she couldn't blame them. They were uncertain of what would come next. She was uncertain herself. Still, if she was to rule them, if she was to have her revenge, she would need to gain their loyalty and devotion. She did her best to project confidence and smiled at her subjects as she walked.

The palace gates opened and Pieter Hingen walked out with several of her father's advisors and enfeoffed nobles following. Hingen was a brute of a man, his shaven head towering above those in his retinue. He started out as a leather merchant and rose to the rank of advisor in her father's court because he was pragmatic and thorough. It wasn't so much his advice the king valued, but rather his ability to carry out orders with single-minded efficiency.

Eridani had never liked him.

When Eridani was younger, her mother had taught her to judge the value of a person by how they treated those beneath their station. Eridani heeded the lesson and quickly realized how wise it was: men and women who were charismatic at court, all smiles and flattery in front of the royal family, sometimes showed their true faces by being consistently rude to the servants. None were worse than Hingen. Out of earshot of his betters and equals, the man seemed to revel in causing misery to the cooks and the stablemen and any of the other servants he encountered in the palace.

Having observed several such incidents, eight-year-old Eridani had reported them to her father. King Malnos II had listened patiently to his daughter's findings.

"A sovereign presides over all kinds of subjects: kind-hearted and nasty, smart and foolish, obedient and unruly," her father had told her. "I can't hope to make them all into better people. After all, I'm their liege, not their priest. But I can use their talents and skills for the benefit of the realm. Pieter may have an unpleasant demeanor, but he is a capable administrator. I wield him as a tool, and ensure that his talents are used to do enough good to outweigh the small sins you've witnessed."

It was meant to be a lesson on government and use of power, but young Eridani was too idealistic to accept such compromises back then. She remembered the conversation so well because it was the first time she came to believe it was possible for her father to be wrong.

Pieter Hingen and his retinue met Eridani and her people a handful of steps from the gates. The big man projected his voice, so that the amassed citizens could hear him.

"Approach no farther! We have vowed to our lord Duke Elkwire that no spawn of Malnos the Feeble will again darken the palace of Kozhad."

Eridani had only to give the order and her soldiers would cut down the arrogant upstart along with his flunkies. But that wouldn't do; she needed to win over the hearts of her people. The position of ruling by the strength of her sword was unacceptable and untenable in the long term.

She raised her voice to match Hingen's. "Step aside, traitor. I'm the daughter of King Malnos II. The throne of Kozhad belongs to my bloodline, and I've returned to claim it and to punish those who collaborated with the mutinous Duke of Buzzards."

"His grace the Duke of Woodcastle has freed the good people of Kozhad from the yoke of your bloodline. He has left the town intact and punished only those who resisted him." Hingen gave up the pretense of speaking to Eridani and addressed the crowd directly. "If you support his enemies and force his army to return and to purge our town of these women playing at soldiers, do you imagine he will be so restrained the second time? For the good of your families, you must turn your backs on these rebels and ask them to leave peaceably."

The crowd murmured, citizens of Kozhad divided between the loyalty to the crown and the fear of reprisals from the much more powerful Duke of Buzzards.

Eridani calculated her options. She had to have more volunteers, able-bodied men and women of Kozhad joining her army, if she was to have any chance against the duke. Slaughtering Hingen might serve only to set more of the people against her. She had to continue debating, playing his game.

"What right do you have to speak on behalf of Kozhad? You were but a minor official at my father's court. Why should anyone listen to your words?"

"His Grace the Duke has bestowed unto me the title of Mayor," said Hingen. "When the nobles of Kozhad knelt and swore loyalty to Duke Elkwire, they became honor-bound to follow my orders, for so long as His Grace, in his voluminous wisdom, allows me to serve him."

Eridani's gaze sought out an older man standing behind Hingen, a noble who had always been kind to her and her brother before they left for Skond. "Is it true, Feodor? Did you forsake your honor and swear fealty to a traitor?"

Feodor didn't look her in the eye as he responded. "The duke's men gathered all the nobles and forced us to kneel, right here in the square. Each of us had to publicly swear loyalty to him. They ... cut the throats of any who refused."

"Before you question the honor of these men, consider that your own father begged for his life and cried like a *girl*." Hingen undoubtedly made the comparison to remind the crowd that Eridani was herself of the wrong gender to assume power. "No nobleman is honor-bound to remain loyal to a monarch who would display such cowardice."

Eridani was sure Gavron could debate the leather merchant into a corner, but it wouldn't do for her to pause and consult her advisors. She pressed on. "No matter the lies you spread of my father, he was a kind and caring monarch who looked after the interests of his people, and I intend to do the same. It is not for you, or for a mutinous duke, to question the royal bloodline."

"Even if you were right, I see no legitimate heir here," said Hingen. "Where is your brother Danchu? He is the only one with any possible claim to the throne. All I see before me is a daughter who should've been married off to some other kingdom years ago, speaking above her station."

Blood rushed to Eridani's face. "Seize them!" she ordered her troops. They drew their swords and moved to surround Hingen and his handful of nobles.

"Wait," said Feodor. "It is true that only a man has ever reigned in Kozhad. But there is historical precedent whereby a woman might ascend to the throne."

The crowd susurrated louder, eager to witness more of the drama unfolding in front of them.

"The princess may designate a champion to fight for her claim. If he were to win, she may rule Kozhad as Queen Regent, with the champion by her side as an advisor, until such time as a male heir comes of age."

Hingen's lips curled into a humorless grin. "I will personally fight such a challenger."

Eridani hated the idea. Hingen had nothing to lose, but having someone else fight her battles would only serve to make her appear weak, even if her champion won. And she was certain she couldn't defeat the brute in one-on-one combat herself, even if acting as her own champion were acceptable. Feodor may have been trying to help, or he may have been trying to save his own skin. Either way, it put her in an awkward position. If she ignored the suggestion she would likely lose any chance at the support of the citizenry.

"I accept the challenge." She turned to Caer. "Will you be my champion?"

Caer looked Hingen up and down. "I'll fight him," he said, his voice devoid of concern.

Eridani didn't think the Ugly Unicorn was bluffing; he knew well that his foe's size was a poor substitute for experience.

"I'm afraid that's not acceptable," said Feodor. His voice was subservient, but he stopped short of calling her "my queen." The man was clearly trying to keep his options open, to see who might come out on top. "The champion must be a born citizen of Kozhad."

This complicated things further. Many of her soldiers were from the fiefs that swore loyalty to Kozhad, but none were citizens of the town itself.

There was a commotion. A wiry young man, nearly as tall as Hingen, shoved his way through the crowd. "I'll be your champion, My Queen."

Eridani's eyes widened as she recognized Toval. He was a childhood friend, a son of a soldier in her father's palace guard. They were the same age and had often played together, until they grew older and it became inappropriate for them to spend time together unsupervised.

Toval had always been fast and strong, but he was no warrior. The thought of risking the life of this one-time friend to further her cause sickened her. Her father's words came unbidden to her mind: *I wield him as a tool.* Perhaps he was not wrong after all. If she were to reign in Kozhad, she must wield her subjects as tools, and sometimes as weapons, even when that put friends at risk, even when the decision to do so was a difficult one.

She surveyed the crowd, making certain there were no better options. Then she turned to the young man. "Kneel."

Toval approached, bowed to Eridani, then kneeled awkwardly in front of her.

Eridani drew her sword and rested the flat side of the blade on his right shoulder.

"In front of the citizens of Kozhad I knight you, and declare you to be my champion," she said. "Rise, Sir Toval the Valiant."

The crowd cheered, and Eridani smiled. She was in control of the narrative now—whatever happened next, the crowd loved the tale of a gallant lowborn risen high. They would root for him to win, and therefore for her.

"The duel will take place in the square, in two hour's time," said Eridani. "Prepare yourselves." She nodded to her troops. "Make certain the so-called Mayor doesn't...change his mind."

She believed Hingen was the favorite in the upcoming duel and likely had no intention of running away from this challenge. But, once again, the narrative her suggestion created for her subjects was more important than the truth of things.

"Thank you," she told Toval. "Follow me, so we can get you prepared."

CAER USHERED TOVAL away when they returned to where the bulk of Eridani's soldiers were camped. They occupied the blocks around the makeshift barracks, which now served as the prison for the duke's men.

They found a good blade for Toval and Caer gave him a crash course in swordplay.

Toval was strong and fast, and he knew the basics as well as any son of a soldier might. But he wasn't a trained soldier and stood no chance when sparring with Caer. They hoped that Hingen wasn't trained in the art of the sword, either. Caer concentrated on teaching Toval how to use his opponent's greater mass and height against him.

"It's not a joust, boy," the Ugly Unicorn said. "Cut at his knees. Kick at his groin when your swords are locked. Do what you would in a street brawl. Have you been in any?"

"I've brawled enough," said Toval. "Don't worry. I won't let the princess... I mean, Queen Eridani, down. I won't let my father down. He fought to his last breath when the duke's men came. I will honor his memory today!"

"All right, then. Watch me." Caer kicked low, tripping Toval.

The young man got up without protest and resumed his stance.

"Good," said Caer. "Now, you try it."

Eridani left them to it and went to issue orders to her troops.

TWO HOURS LATER, it seemed as though the entire population of Kozhad was gathered to watch the upcoming spectacle. Street vendors were peddling food at the edges of the town square, and the crowd grew denser the closer one got to the center. Some people carried crates they could stand upon to get a better view of the action. Eridani's soldiers cordoned off a rectangular area in the center of the square. The cobblestones were swept and mopped. They glinted in the late afternoon sun as they dried.

A throne-like maple armchair facing the makeshift arena was set up for Eridani. On both sides of it were a handful of seats. Eridani's people had raided the two nearby taverns for stools.

A line of soldiers was formed beyond the stools, keeping the spectators separated from the action. The town's elite were allowed in front of this live barrier of warrior women.

There were too few of these stools, and soon a heated argument ensued among the nobles and advisors over who would get to sit on them. Although many of these powerful men had initially hidden in the crowd, uncertain of what Eridani might do to them should she regain power, they were emboldened by this sign of respect from the queen. More and more of them trickled in toward the front. All of them wished to be seen seated by her side, in case her champion won the challenge.

The attendants then explained that the seats were reserved for the enfeoffed nobles, and the advisors grudgingly relented, allowing all of the richest landowners in Kozhad to assume the honored positions. The nobles' mood lightened considerably; the Skond-educated princess was showing them proper respect. Perhaps they could work with her, after all. Eridani watched them stone-faced as they smiled and ordered their servants to bring wine, as though they were about to watch a performance by a traveling carnival.

At the designated time the crowd parted, allowing Toval through. He was wearing light leather armor that fit him almost right, and carried the sword he had been practicing with. The crowd cheered loudly when he raised the sword in greeting and turned slowly, so that all could see him.

Pieter Hingen entered the square wearing a breastplate, a helmet that covered his face with the wolf-like steel snout and had only a thin slit open for his eyes, and metal greaves over thick leather trousers. He carried a two-handed battle axe and moved with a fluid grace of a man unencumbered by so much metal.

Toval seemed dejected. His sword would glance off the metal plate while the bigger man would not be sufficiently slowed by his own armor. He looked questioningly at Caer, who stepped forward and whispered into the younger man's ear. Toval nodded solemnly and Caer went back to stand behind Eridani's maple throne.

When Hingen reached the center of the square there was some cheering, far more muted than that for Toval, and some outright booing. Even the nobles and the advisors restrained themselves from cheering too loudly for their mayor, keenly aware of the armed soldiers behind them.

"He's a brave, foolish boy," Gavron muttered.

"He's willing to die for his queen," replied Caer. "That only makes him a fool if the queen is not worth dying for."

The two opponents faced off. Without a preamble, Hingen roared and rushed at Toval. The younger man, unencumbered by heavy armor, ducked out of the way, letting the mayor's momentum carry him past. Toval swung at Hingen's back. His sword screeched against the plate but caused no damage. Hingen turned and elbowed Toval in the face. The younger man stumbled and then retreated, blood trickling from his nose. He wiped it off with his sleeve and faced the mayor.

Hingen used his body mass and his armor as weapons, bruising Toval several times, but failed to inflict any major damage. Each time he attacked, Toval was nimble enough to get out of the way, turning the weight of his opponent's mail into a liability.

After unsuccessfully rushing his opponent several more times, Hingen changed tactics. He moved more slowly, forcing Toval to retreat, herding him toward a corner of the rectangular arena in order to restrict his movement.

Toval was forced to make a move—he feinted right which got Hingen to shift that way as well, lifting his axe. Instead of trying to get past his opponent, Toval ducked and kicked as hard as he could at the mayor's feet, like Caer had shown him.

Hingen stumbled, landing on his knee, but he did not fall. He pushed with his left hand against the cobblestones to prop himself up, but before he had a chance to rise Toval closed in and banged the pommel of his sword against the side of the mayor's helm with all his strength.

The bell-like sound reverberated across the square. Hingen dropped the axe, instinctively trying to cover his ears. Toval wrapped both hands around the grip and hit the helm with the pommel again and again. Despite his arming cap, the force of the blows was enough to stun and disorient Hingen, who writhed face down on the ground, clawing at his head until his hands managed to find the edge of the helmet and he ripped it off his head.

Toval buried the tip of his sword in the soft spot at the back of Hingen's neck before the mayor had the chance to recover.

The crowd erupted. None cheered louder than the nobles and advisors in the front, who were now certain of Eridani's victory.

Eridani rose from her chair and walked into the center of the square. She stood over Hingen's body, ignoring his blood which pooled at the edge of her boot.

Toval, who panted with exertion as he leaned on his sword, its tip still buried in the mayor's neck, let go of the weapon. He sidestepped the corpse and kneeled to Eridani, both his knees resting on the cobblestones. "My Queen."

Eridani smiled at him and rested her hand on his shoulder. The crowd cheered again.

Feodor rose from his stool and approached the two of them, pausing to bow every few steps. "The challenge is over and settled," he shouted. "On behalf of Kozhad, we welcome our queen."

Eridani raised her hand, silencing the onlookers. "The matter is not settled," she said.

Toval looked up at her in confusion. Hundreds of men and women throughout the square waited for her to explain her meaning.

"There are still traitors among us, those who swore fealty to a regicide instead of defending their liege to their last breath." She stared directly at the nobles seated on the stools. Like moths to a candle, they had helpfully gathered themselves in one place at the merest hint of the chance to ingratiate themselves to the ones in power. Her kingdom deserved better. She gave the signal to her soldiers.

"The penalty for treason is death."

The line of women soldiers positioned behind the seats came forward as one, swords and daggers skewering the nobles. Some of them never even had the chance to rise from their stools.

Feodor shrunk back from Eridani, his eyes wide. "Mercy!" he bleated, his voice high and cracking, loud enough to be heard over the screams and moans of his dying peers.

Eridani ignored the old man. Instead, she gave Toval a meaningful look. He stared back for a second, comprehension dawning on his face. He rose slowly, dusted off his knees, then gripped the hilt of his sword and removed it from the head of his vanquished opponent. He advanced on Feodor, the bloody tip of his blade pointing toward the old man.

Feodor screamed as he scrambled away from Toval, his words no longer distinguishable. He reached the edge of the makeshift arena, where Eridani's soldiers blocked him and shoved him back toward Toval.

Feodor fell, prostrated himself in front of the young knight and made no further attempt to flee. He whimpered as Toval stood over him with a raised sword. Toval glanced at Eridani.

Surely, the old man harbored no ill will toward her family. He must have begged the duke for his life as he was doing now. Eridani thought back to the times she and Danchu had played with Feodor's grandchildren. *Danchu.* The plan to avenge her brother's death required her to be strong.

"There is no leniency for traitors," she said, keeping her voice even. If she were to rule in Kozhad without constantly having to watch her flank, she had to set an example. She couldn't make exceptions, couldn't allow herself the luxury of mercy.

Toval thrust the tip of his sword's blade into Feodor's heart.

Eridani faced the bulk of the crowd, partly so she wouldn't have to see Feodor's corpse. "Listen well, citizens of Kozhad. When these men swore loyalty to my enemy, they forfeited more than their lives. They forfeited their bloodlines."

The crowd was hanging on her every word, and her voice carried across the square.

"As vassals they were permitted to own land, and so they owned nine out of every ten houses in Kozhad. They owned the farmland and the forests. The workshops you toil in, the gardens you tend, they owned most of that. But, no more!"

Eridani climbed the seat of her chair so her subjects could see her better. "While my champion defended my honor in the square, my soldiers were dispatched to the homes of these traitors. Their estates have been expropriated, their families have until dusk to leave Kozhad and never return."

The treasury had been looted by Elkwire; she needed the nobles' wealth to run her kingdom. Banishing the families may have been harsh, but she couldn't afford to take chances. She had just made a mortal enemy of every one of the nobles' heirs. A more ruthless monarch would have simply had them all killed.

"There is a new day in Kozhad. Men shall no longer be required to provide corvée labor, and women will be afforded the same rights as men, as they already are in my army."

The lowborn men and women in the crowd were quiet, trying to work out what all of this meant for them. In the everyday lives of these people, change rarely brought good tidings. Yet, the queen seemed to be offering them enormous concessions.

Eridani wasn't finished. "Any of you who paid rent or tithe to the traitors will now be paying it directly to the royal treasury, and all of these bills henceforth will be reduced by half." She paused, letting the words sink in.

Over eighty percent of Kozhad citizens paid the enfeoffed nobles for the privilege to live, work, or farm on their land. Eridani was cutting out the middlemen, still collecting the dues she needed to run the kingdom and pay her soldiers, but everyone among those eighty percent now had a potent reason to want her to stay in power.

As the citizens worked the implications out for themselves, the crowd erupted in cheers, applause, and laughter. Their celebration lasted late into the night.

CHAPTER 10

THE SUMMER NIGHT AT WOODCASTLE

ahel Elkwire couldn't sleep. He tossed and turned, his blanket cast aside. The balmy summer evening had turned into a muggy, uncomfortable night. Beads of sweat pooled on his neck and stung his skin. He listened to the breathing of the girl he'd taken to bed that night—he couldn't recall her name. He watched her chest rise and fall rhythmically as she slept at the far edge of his bed, illuminated by moonlight.

He considered waking her up: perhaps another round would tire him out and let him finally fall asleep. But it was too hot, and the bruises on her face from earlier that evening were beginning to swell. He had lost control again, and he hated when that happened. He decided that, in the morning, he would give her a gold coin and send her away for a couple of weeks. By then her face would heal, and the next time he fancied her, he'd try to only hit below the neck.

Bahel grunted and turned away from the girl, his ear grinding into the down pillow. She wasn't the problem; it was that other girl, the thrice-damned spawn of King Malnos, who had been a thorn in his side ever since he had conquered Kozhad.

Malnos was a decent sort, as inbred scions of the ancient bloodlines went. Bahel had no animosity toward the man, but the patriarch's offer was too good to pass up. Money and power were his for the taking. He didn't owe the king any true loyalty beyond the meaningless sounds of an oath.

The patriarch's gold bought weapons and men, well beyond what the complacent militia of Kozhad was capable of defending against. Bahel's army swept through the town, killing only those foolish enough to resist. Most people had the good sense to take one look at the invading force and surrender. He gained control of Kozhad in less than an hour.

Malnos and his wife had been trapped in their own so-called palace. Everyone else was ordered to leave the building, then Bahel came to see them in private, with only a few of his loyal bodyguards present. He had hoped to convince Malnos to publicly abdicate in his favor. He couldn't spare the man's life, of course, but there were all kinds of promises he could dangle in front of the deposed monarch and, in his experience, desperate men were prone to grasp at the flimsiest of straws.

Malnos had proven himself to be surprisingly difficult. He refused to yield, refused to verbally acknowledge Bahel. While the queen cried and thrashed on the polished floor of the throne hall, the king stared at him with utter contempt of the sort that only the highborn seem to know how to convey. After Bahel had his men kill the queen—mostly to end her hysterics—the king gritted his teeth and still wouldn't say a single word, even though tears rolled down his cheeks.

Frustrated, Bahel drove his sword through the king's stomach. It was the most painful way he knew of to kill a man without the effort of torture. He sat on the throne of Kozhad and watched Malnos gasp like a fish out of water and finally die. Then he instructed his men to spread the word of how the royal couple both debased themselves as they begged for their lives. He knew that the townsfolk would believe this account. His own father had taught him that history was written by the winners, and that an oft-repeated lie would eventually become accepted as truth.

Bahel had no intention of staying in the ill-defensible house of a palace, surrounded by people he didn't trust. He cleared out the treasury, forced the nobles to pledge loyalty to him in front of the peasants, installed Pieter Hingen as mayor, and instructed him to forward a small percentage of the collected taxes to Woodcastle. He could have demanded more, but why slaughter a cow and eat steak once, when he could enjoy its milk for years to come.

That's when his good fortune seemed to have run out.

He delivered a perfect victory for the patriarch, and yet his patron bungled the one part of the plan he was responsible for and let Malnos's off-spring slip through his fingers. Worse yet, they managed to ally themselves with the one old crone who could afford to hire an even bigger mercenary army than the patriarch himself.

Bahel was smart enough to know how fortunate he was. Had the patriarch's messenger not arrived early enough with a warning, his people couldn't have stocked Woodcastle with provisions necessary to survive a siege. Had the Dowager Councilor not secretly stayed the hand of her mercenaries while she and the patriarch butted heads and negotiated a deal, he would long be a corpse rotting under the dirt in the shade of Woodcastle's walls.

Instead, he suffered a few weeks of boredom and hunger, but he lived. What's more, he seized initiative and eliminated Malnos's sole male heir. All that remained was the girl. She was resilient and managed to stay a step ahead of his soldiers. Last he heard, she'd surrounded herself with several dozen whores and peasant clodhoppers. As if those serfs could protect her for even five minutes against trained warriors.

Over half his men were out searching the countryside, dozens of raiding parties everywhere. It was only a matter of time. His luck was changing for the better again.

Bahel turned toward the sleeping girl. He decided to wake her after all, and take her from behind so he wouldn't have to see her bruised face. Instead, he could picture the face of the princess, and imagine all the things he would soon do to her.

As he reached for the girl, the tranquility of the night was pierced by shouting.

ERIDANI'S MORTAL ENEMY may have been the Duke of Buzzards, but her immediate foe and the Duke's greatest ally was time itself.

With Kozhad's coffers refilled from the wealth of the eradicated nobles, she was able to pay her soldiers, and there was no shortage of new volunteers. Even so, her untested irregulars were no match for the duke's battle-hardened men. She had to act quickly, before the duke learned of what had transpired in Kozhad, before he could recall the search parties and gather a fighting force she couldn't hope to match.

"This is a foolhardy venture," Caer said, upon hearing her plan. "There's no telling if the duke is at Woodcastle. He could be riding with some of his men searching for you, or he could be attending his master in Skond." He drank from an ornate stein and rested it on the long table in the throne room. "Even if you find the bastard holed up in his lair, he's got enough troops there to defend the castle from the likes of us."

"This course of action is preferable to the alternatives," said Gavron. "It is only a matter of time until this brute learns of our whereabouts. We can gamble now, or wait for him to gather his army and come for us at his leisure. And he has already proven that Kozhad is not defensible against his forces."

Eridani smiled inwardly at the reversal of the usual roles. She could hardly believe Caer preaching caution while Gavron spoke in favor of bold action.

"Elkwire must be dealt with," the tutor said. "It's not merely a matter of vendetta; he is the proxy through which the patriarch can funnel any number of troops, until they grind us to dust. With him gone, we may win a reprieve while our enemies search for another suitable puppet."

Caer slammed the empty stein against the table and wiped foam from his lips with the back of his hand. "So be it. I've taken greater risks in my day."

Eridani laughed. There was no better proof of the validity of her plan than it prompting Caer to agree on anything with Gavron.

And so, she gambled everything yet again. She gathered every horse in Kozhad and most of her soldiers, selecting the most experienced among her fighters and, when she ran out of experienced ones, the largest and the strongest. Sana, whom Eridani had promoted to lieutenant shortly after recapturing Kozhad, was left in charge of a token troop to guard the town.

They rode day and night, alternating between horses. They stopped to sleep on the ground for only a few hours a night and ate from the meager supplies they brought along, avoiding towns and villages. No courier or spy would be likely to outpace them.

When they reached Darla's farm two and a half days later it was early afternoon. It was not a happy reunion, and Eridani ordered Darla and her family tied up and kept in the barn. She would ponder on an appropriate punishment for her betrayer later. Then her troops rested and ate, devouring Darla's meager supplies of grain and preserves like so many locusts.

Eridani questioned the peasant in hopes of finding Danchu's grave, but was told the duke's men had carted the corpse away. Her brother's body had likely been sent to Skond as proof of Elkwire's accomplishment.

She lay on the straw bedding in Darla's house but couldn't sleep. Best she could do was allowing her body to rest; her mind and heart both raced faster than a pair of foxes pursued by the hounds.

They waited until dark. The sky was devoid of clouds and the full moon shone brightly enough to let them navigate through the woods without lanterns. Eridani had hoped for rain or at least cloud cover, but the weather was what it was, and her army was too numerous to remain undiscovered for much longer. They rode for Woodcastle.

Two hundred warriors dismounted in the woods and advanced on foot until they could see Woodcastle's walls. A pair of archers took out a lookout who was nodding off on the battlements. A team of five scouts led by Caer sneaked up on the pair of sentries at the front gate.

Eridani couldn't help but reflect on the fact that she had followed Shikot's initial plan of a surprise attack. Although she didn't have an overwhelming advantage in numbers this time—with so many of the duke's soldiers out looking for her, the numbers were about even—she gambled that the Duke's men would surrender once he was dead.

The scouts climbed the wall and unlocked the gates, and her troops invaded the enemy stronghold. It was only then that a sentry positioned at the entrance to the duke's barracks noticed the intruders. "Ambush! Ambush!" he shouted, until his cries were cut off by an arrow to the heart.

Eridani's soldiers flooded the barracks and fell upon the duke's men, slaughtering them before they had the chance to ready themselves. The element of surprise swung the advantage in Eridani's favor.

Even so, she knew the experienced fighters would rally soon, and then the farmers with mere weeks or days of sword training would be in terrible trouble. She and a small group of fighters stormed the castle proper, where she hoped her sworn enemy would be found.

ON THE GROUND floor of the castle, they found a servant girl who was too overtaken with fear to speak, but nodded vigorously when Eridani asked if her master was in the castle. She pointed a shaking hand at the stairs.

Six of her most experienced fighters led the charge, dispatching what few defenders they encountered in the building. Eridani climbed the second flight of stairs two steps at a time, with the clanging of steel against steel and the moans of dying men as her battle hymn. She could hear sounds of fighting coming from the third—top—floor of the castle, which Caer and others had reached moments earlier.

At the apex of the staircase she found a bedchamber. Two of her people, a farmer's son who was among the first to join her army and a middle-aged woman she had recruited from among the camp followers at the quarry site, lay dead on the floor. A girl wrapped in a blanket cowered on the far side of the bed. And by the window, the Duke of Buzzards himself fought against Caer, Toval, and two other warriors like a cornered animal.

Bahel Elkwire was barefoot and shirtless, and wore only a pair of leggings. He bled from several shallow cuts on his arms and chest. He swung a saber with his right hand while using a long dagger to deflect sword thrusts with his left. His hair was tangled and drenched in sweat.

The saber connected, biting deep into the shoulder of one of the fighters. The duke deflected a thrust of Toval's sword with his dagger, but it left him open to Caer's blade. Its tip punctured clean through the meat and muscle on the anterior of the duke's left forearm. The Duke of Buzzards cried out in pain and dropped the dagger. He took another step back, his shoulder blades touching the massive stones of the wall. The attackers advanced for a killing blow.

"I yield!" the duke shouted. He tossed his saber at Caer's feet and leaned against the wall, trying to stem the flow of blood from his left arm with his right hand.

Caer and Toval kept the tips of their swords pressed against the duke's neck and heart. Eridani picked up the dagger the Duke had dropped and stepped forward until she was face to face with her nemesis. She pressed the blade to his neck, its sharp edge drawing a thin trickle of blood. She focused on this small wound, recalling a moment from several months ago when she'd held a dagger to the neck of another man, back in Skond.

"You murdered my family," she said, her voice cracking. This was the revenge she wanted, the scene she had played out in her head countless times since she learned of the duke's betrayal. Yet, it felt wrong somehow. It wasn't the same as driving a sword into a man's back in the heat of combat. She hesitated.

The duke must have sensed her doubt. He slouched, taking care to move slowly, until his gaze met hers. "There are things I know that you can use," he said, his voice hoarse. "The patriarch's secrets. He was the one who ordered your family's demise. Schemes and machinations of the council. I can help you blackmail them into leaving Kozhad be."

The pressure against his neck eased by a tiny fraction as Eridani considered his words. Despite the pain of multiple wounds his lips twisted into a semblance of a wolfish grin.

"There is only one thing I want from you," said Eridani.

The second time Eridani killed a man, she stared her victim in the eye.

PART 2

(Year 536 of the Council Era)

CHAPTER 11
THE GAME OF BATO

aer and Gavron hunched over a table filled with blue and yellow beads. In the years since the two men had met they hadn't exactly become friends, but they'd grown closer by necessity. They were both foreigners in Kozhad. They both shared the harrowing experiences of fleeing Skond and subsequent adventures with their queen. Now, they both served as her top advisors. But it wasn't until they discovered mutual interest for the game of bato that they began spending time together.

"I believe I have you cornered, Sellsword," Gavron gloated, as he placed two more yellow beads onto the table from his dwindling stack.

Caer grunted noncommittally and leaned even closer to the tabletop, studying the board.

Bato was an ancient game of skill and tactics. Much praised by Orodos and other classical philosophers, the abstract game was a required subject of study among the learned men of Gan. Gavron utilized a deliberate style, seeking to patiently build an advantage over time and attempting to duplicate stratagems of the game's top champions, whose matches were painstakingly recorded move-by-move in special books.

Caer, on the other hand, had learned the game from his fellow mercenaries during the Haldova campaigns. Military commanders respected the game because, when played under the constraints of a flowing hourglass, it was widely believed to train one's mind to make snap decisions in the chaos of combat. Also, the game was a favorite of Kalatar, the most successful military commander in the Heart's recorded history. Among mercenaries the game was often played with limiting each player to as little as fifty heartbeats per move, thereby increasing the game's difficulty.

91

Because of this experience, Caer's plays were daring, surprising, and occasionally brilliant. He was willing to take big chances that could swing the game in either player's favor instead of seeking incremental gains through cautious, safe moves.

Despite their different approaches, they were evenly matched; this fact amused Caer and sometimes frustrated Gavron.

Caer had been conserving his pieces early in the game, sacrificing board position for a possible late-game advantage. He placed four beads onto the board and moved two others forcing a confrontation between some of his blue units and Gavron's yellows.

"You're gambling again, hoping fortune will favor you instead of trying to set up a position where victory is inevitable," Gavron complained, as he reached for a pair of dice. "I hope you're more risk averse on the actual field of battle."

"Real battles are not won by the timid. There is much skill in taking advantage of the lucky breaks you get in war. And in life." Caer's expression turned solemn, worry lines forming on his aging face. "But yes, I am more cautious with real lives at stake. I don't relish the thought of leading Kozhad's army against my homeland."

Gavron looked away from the board. "After three years, I've allowed myself to believe that the war might never come."

"It has always been a matter of time," said Caer. "We have to hope that all of us are ready when the war begins. And when it does, we shall need ample supplies of both luck and skill."

ERIDANI LISTENED STONE-FACED to the spy's report. The young woman, recently returned from Skond, confirmed the ominous news. A larger-than-usual force of mercenaries and soldiers was gathering in camps north of that city. Eridani could think of no other reason for the build-up, no other kingdom the patriarch might have wanted to pacify.

It had been a little over three years since Eridani ascended to the throne of Kozhad. She ruled her small kingdom with a steady hand, writing laws, and adjudicating disputes. It could have been a pleasant, almost boring existence if not for the looming shadow of her enemies. With his pawn—the duke—gone, the patriarch seemed to have given up on eradicating her bloodline, pointedly ignoring her existence instead. Even so, living in the shadow of Skond always felt like trying to nap while locked inside a hungry bear's cage. And now that bear appeared to be rising to its hind legs, baring its teeth.

"Why now?" asked Toval, after the spy was dismissed. He paced across the throne hall. "It's been years, and I believed he would never make his move. Something must've changed."

The way her other advisors—Gavron, Caer, and Sana—exchanged glances did not escape Eridani's notice. The patriarch's motives were obvious to them, as they were to the queen, but lowborn Toval lacked their education and tactical skill. The others had questioned Eridani's wisdom for including him in her private council, but Eridani had her reasons. He was a Kozhad local, a hero in the eyes of most of her subjects. Besides, he was utterly loyal. The others may not have given her cause to doubt them, but the sorceress's prophecy weighed heavily upon her. Did it apply only to those who joined her and Danchu's side back then? Even if not, Toval was plainspoken and as far from devious as a person could be. His emotions and thoughts were written on his face. With him, she could always be sure.

"It is no secret the patriarch has been moving toward declaring himself Emperor of the North. He can't do that while Kozhad remains a thorn in his side," Gavron explained. Her tutor had been glad enough to stay in Kozhad, his dream of gaining a ministry position and the respect that came with it finally realized.

"This was true three years ago, and will probably still be true in three years' time," said Sana. "He has powerful opponents on the council. The kings of the north are not so subdued yet as to allow the patriarch to raise a large army and have it trample over their lands on the way to Kozhad."

"The political infighting on the council is what has kept us safe thus far," said Gavron. "But it is possible the kings have gradually come to realize we are an even greater threat to them than the patriarch, who is already their overlord in everything but name."

Toval ceased his pacing and stared at Gavron. "How is that? The queen gave them no cause, made no moves to menace any of them."

"My policies and my very existence menace them," said Eridani.

Toval waited for an explanation, but she remained silent, lost in thought.

Gavron spoke instead. "Eliminating corvée, lowering taxes, cracking down on graft and corruption inherent in the bureaucracy of every kingdom. She makes other monarchs look bad by comparison. Most of them were willing to ignore her at first, amused at the young girl's naïveté and expecting her to quickly fail." He raised his palms. "Their words, not mine. Our spies have reported such sentiments expressed freely among the elite of Skond.

"But now, years have passed and she hasn't failed. Every day peasants and craftsmen migrate to Kozhad. Soldiers and mercenaries sign on with our army. We've upset the status quo, and the other monarchs appear willing to let the patriarch gain even more power if that will rid them of us."

"The patriarch's army is larger and better equipped, but his advantage is not overwhelming," said Caer. He spoke slowly, almost reluctantly. Like Gavron, he'd chosen to remain at Eridani's side. He continued to train her and to act as a military advisor, but it was Sana who was named general and given command of Kozhad's army. "The day he feels certain of an easy victory, the war will come."

Eridani was concerned as to whether the old sellsword's loyalty might erode once the conflict with his home city of Skond began. Would his advice remain at its ruthless and calculating best when it might be wielded to murder his countrymen? Outwardly he seemed content with his position, but the Ugly Unicorn wasn't one to keep others' council on such matters.

Sana, on the other hand, had proven to be both loyal and ambitious. She was a bit inexperienced and hasty, but she channeled her recklessness well, leading troops by example, fearlessly confronting Kozhad's enemies.

There was a small part of Eridani that welcomed the possibility of a head-on conflict, but she knew that to be a bad idea, a desire borne of her heart and not her mind. She had become restless over time, the wanderlust she would never have suspected in herself tugging at her heart. She came to regard the life of a queen as boring, a self-imposed confinement within the gilded cage of responsibility.

Eridani had taken to sneaking out of the palace, out of Kozhad, for a few hours at a time. Dressed in the cloak of a lieutenant she would ride to the nearby villages to observe the reforms she had implemented firsthand. With so many women from her skirt army elevated to positions of leadership in the constantly growing army of Kozhad, the cloak offered her a perfect disguise and allowed her to feed the niggling, constant need for action and danger that had been simmering within her.

After a handful of such adventures, the afternoon-long excursions were no longer enough. Despite the protestations and the gnashing of teeth from her advisors, Eridani would ride in charge of a detachment of soldiers to clear out bandits in the Pine Forest or join her constables on a hunt for an escaped murderer. Her outings grew longer and more dangerous, and seemed the only way to satisfy that persistent itch in her heart.

Toval was her constant companion during these trips. He acted as her bodyguard and confidant. It was clear to Eridani—and anyone who saw them together—that he wanted their relationship to be something more. But Toval never allowed himself to act on his feelings, and Eridani—who did not reciprocate his infatuation—felt it was kindest to pretend not to notice.

"We must redouble our recruitment efforts, and hire mercenaries as well. So long as there is doubt in his mind, or he believes victory would come at too high a price, the patriarch will stay his hand," said Sana.

"I've been negotiating with one of the largest mercenary companies in Gan," said Caer. "We've been putting off hiring more fighters because the treasury can only bear the expense for a short while, but it may be time to exercise that option. The caravan arrived from Gan yesterday and will be heading back the day after tomorrow. If you so command, I will travel there myself and finalize the contract."

Gavron's face lit up at the mention of his home. "If anyone travels to Gan, it should be me. Who better to navigate the intricacies of a Gannian negotiation?"

"Send either, or both," said Sana. "I have plenty of work to do here."

Gavron glanced at Sana, somewhat deflated. Unlike Toval, he wasn't shy and had made his romantic interest quite clear to her. But his feelings for Sana were also unrequited. She barely tolerated the Gannian, restricting any contact with him to the business of running Kozhad. She certainly didn't consider him as a possible romantic partner, of which she had quite a few. Eridani, whose position made it unseemly for her to engage in casual courtship, was a little jealous of Sana, though she'd never admit it out loud.

"Toval and I are joining a hunt early tomorrow morning. I will make a decision when I return." Eridani thought best under the open sky, away from cramped rooms and competing egos.

"Respectfully, is this truly the best use of your time?" asked Gavron. "Regardless of this specific decision, there is still much to learn, much to prepare—"

"Is three hours a day not enough?" countered Eridani. "I spend that much time on our grand plan, and still run the kingdom. I deserve some time to myself." She rose to her feet. "We'll reconvene tomorrow."

GAVRON CHECKED THE mirror for what must've been the tenth time and adjusted his cravat. He wore his finest clothes, his hair coiffed and jelled. Everything had to be perfect for the professor's visit.

The letter had arrived the day before, written in perfect calligraphy on the finest heavy paper, sealed with an elaborate wax stamp from the University of Gan. It even smelled refined.

Master Sovio was a professor from the esteemed University of Gan where Gavron himself had studied two decades prior. Having recently arrived in Kozhad with a trade caravan, he requested an audience.

Gavron swelled with pride as he read the letter. Three years ago, he had led an unremarkable existence as a private tutor of mostly unremarkable students. Even that was taken away from him, his routine shattered in a matter of heartbeats. He was forced to flee, his life was endangered, and on several occasions he even had to sleep on the hard ground outside, when their small band fled across the countryside one step ahead of the duke's men. How his fortunes had changed!

Although he did not know this Master Sovio, the string of accolades in the professor's signature suggested that he was a scholar of the highest order. The sort who would not have deigned to talk to someone like Gavron even back when the latter was a student there; if a student needed something, he could talk to a docent. And now, this esteemed scholar was begging an audience.

In the twenty-four hours since receiving the letter and sending the messenger back with a proper response, Gavron had driven his servants mad. Every inch of the house he rented a block from the palace was cleaned, and cleaned again. Gavron spent lavishly at the market, buying new hanging rugs and fresh flowers, exotic delicacies to serve during the visit and the finest brandy money could buy this far away from Gan—which actually turned out to be pretty decent. Trade was flourishing and the variety and quality of wares now available in the market of Kozhad had grown acceptable in his estimation.

Gavron almost tripped over himself when the clang of the front door's brass knocker announced his visitor's arrival. The professor was here! He swung the door open to greet his esteemed visitor personally, and worked hard to keep the expression of surprise from his face.

Master Sovio was a woman.

She was perhaps ten or fifteen years his senior, and a head shorter than him. Her pronounced cheekbones and thick eyebrows made her appear stern, but her eyes darted inquisitively and her mouth curved upward ever so slightly, as though she were laughing on the inside but didn't quite allow the smile to escape onto her lips.

"Minister Gavron, I presume?"

"Yes, Professor Sovio, please do come in." He had been staring at her, prompting her to speak first. So much for a great first impression. "Welcome! Welcome to Kozhad."

He stepped aside and Professor Sovio walked in. The university medal hung from a thick golden chain around her neck. Gavron's own medal had been lost during the journey from Skond to Kozhad, and he felt a momentary pang of regret for not yet acquiring a replacement.

He shook it off and felt irritated at himself for stumbling mentally. Female professors weren't unheard of in Gan, but the title of Master was never altered. The oldest university in the Heart was stubbornly resistant to change where its traditions and practices were concerned.

They settled in at the table and exchanged pleasantries. Gavron made up for his initial blunder, playing the perfect host. He waited as long as was polite before getting to business. "What brings you to Kozhad?"

"We're captivated by the events unfolding here," said Sovio. "The university sent me to examine these new societal structures your queen has been experimenting with and to report back. It should make for a fascinating case study."

"Yes, the queen has instituted some rather unorthodox policies. Under my guidance, of course." Gavron watched the professor intently for a reaction but her face betrayed nothing. "Our reforms have led to a reinvigorated Kozhad where trade flourishes and citizens prosper. The population of Kozhad and nearby villages has increased by at least a quarter already."

"Therein lies the challenge," said Sovio. "Some of the things your queen has done, such as granting equal rights to female citizens, are indeed remarkable. However, her economic policies are bound to become unsustainable as the population grows."

"I'm saddened to hear you think so," said Gavron. He had hoped for praise, not frank criticism. "Please elaborate?"

"It's all about the taxes," said Sovio. "Kozhad cut the taxes on its citizens in half, and remains solvent because it cut out the layer of nobles and maintains a bare-bones government structure."

"That's true," said Gavron. "With less of their money taken away, our citizens prosper, and there's an influx of skilled laborers and merchants which in turn grows our economy and generates additional tax revenues."

"Which is perfectly manageable on such small scale," said Sovio. "As your kingdom grows, it will require more administrators to function. More guards. More tax collectors. These people have to be paid. A certain level of graft has to be accepted, or additional auditors and enforcers must be hired to try and prevent it. The margins upon which your court operates now cannot sustain this layer of bureaucracy, not even with the extra funds these policies generate in the short-term.

"Additionally, your queen has been overly generous in rewarding her followers with land. More farmland is promised to her veterans down the line. But, with so much land given away, its value is diminished, and the value of crops grown by so many is diminished along with it. Over time, farmers will earn less money, and pay less in taxes.

"And then there's the matter of the military. You must maintain a standing army because of the external threats to your kingdom, and because you no longer have the nobility to rely upon for armed men. Armies are expensive. Each time Skond increases the size of their army—I understand they have done so again quite recently—they pressure you to do the same. As such, there exists a state of a bloodless war of economies between your two governments, to see who can bear the expenses associated with such a conflict longer. A healthier, larger economy that collects a higher tax, tariffs on imports, and tolls to use its roads is bound to win such a war every time."

"That is a depressing prediction," said Gavron. "You seem convinced of the outcome. Why then travel here to observe us fail?"

"Theory is one thing. But here, you're providing scholars with proof, an actual experiment the size of an entire small kingdom. Much will be written about what happens here, and observing firsthand will allow my account to be the most prominent." She smiled. "I coined the phrase 'the war of economies,' you know. I intend for it to be the title of my treatise."

Gavron frowned. "Don't write your book yet. We may surprise you."

"Ah yes, I am sure there is a plan. Eridani is quite clever, after all. Does it have anything to do with the rumor that she disappears, along with some of her tutors, for three hours daily? Some speculate she's studying sorcery so that she can curse her enemies into oblivion."

"I'm afraid I cannot comment on the private affairs of Her Majesty, Master Sovio."

"Come, Gavron. You must surely realize your position—and your queen's—won't remain secure for much longer. Help me, and I can promise you a lifetime appointment at the university. You'll be welcomed home with open arms."

Gavron rose from his seat. "That's *Minister* Gavron. You're asking me to spy on my liege."

"We're not your enemies. I merely want information so I can write—"

"I think it's best we end this meeting. Now."

Gavron glared at Sovio as she left his home, her head held high, her medal glinting in sunlight.

"I AGREE THAT it's time to engage a mercenary company," said Eridani the following morning. "I'll go myself."

There was a chorus of protests from her three advisors. Only Toval seemed excited. "I'm happy to come along. Never been that far."

Eridani hadn't traveled that far, either. Gan was located quite a distance to the northeast.

"It's two week's journey each way!" Gavron rose from his seat. "What about the plan? What about your training? If hiring mercenaries is to buy us time, then you should stay here and take full advantage of that time. Let one of us go."

"You once taught me that there are different kinds of learning, and that I can't truly know the world by reading about it in books. Visiting Gan, seeing the land on the way there firsthand, it will be good for me."

Eridani pondered the merits of bringing each of her advisors. "All of you have work to do in Kozhad. I will travel incognito with a trade caravan."

She waved off the protests. She didn't say how much she wanted to be away from them all, away from the crushing responsibility of running a kingdom. Sooner or later she would have to confront the patriarch, fight a war, lead her people. She wanted some time to be a regular person, even if it was only for a few weeks. She deserved it.

"We already have the second-largest standing army in the North. Let's see if we can swell the ranks and dissuade the patriarch." Eridani rested both fists on the table and eyed each of her advisors in turn. "I'm not ready to make my move yet. Our plan can only work if we buy sufficient time for me to prepare."

CAER AND GAVRON played bato again.

"You're distracted," said Caer, setting up a new game after trouncing his opponent twice in a row. "Are you worried about Eridani? She can handle herself for a few weeks. She's young and full of wanderlust. Time away from the palace may do her some good."

"All that is true," said Gavron. "It is perfectly reasonable for her to go—but why not take one of us along?"

Caer made no reply, but he paused, several game beads in hand.

"She doesn't trust us," said Gavron. He wasn't usually so open with Caer, but he needed to talk to *someone*, and this seemed like the wisest route. "She doubts your loyalty because we are on a course toward war with your homeland, and me..." He trailed off, staring into the game board, then refocused. "I had an opportunity to fulfill a lifelong dream, but I chose to be loyal to her instead. And yet, she doesn't trust me."

"She has lost much for one so young," said Caer. "She has been betrayed by those she trusted, too. Trust does not come easily after that."

"What are we to do, then? How do we get through to her? Convince her of our loyalty?"

"We give her time," said Caer. "She's playing a high-stakes game of bato against the patriarch. We help her win it, regardless of what she thinks, what suspicions she might harbor. That's true loyalty. And in time, she will come to recognize it."

CHAPTER 12
A STRANGER IN GAN

ridani sat alone at the edge of a long communal table, taking in the sights and sounds of Gan's open-air market.

Food merchants set up their carts in several long rows, surrounding an area where dozens of tables stood with benches affixed on their sides, each long enough to seat twenty people. Smells of exotic spices and grilling meat wafted through the hot mid-afternoon air. The market wasn't busy: only a handful of people sat here and there along the tables in small groups, eating and drinking.

Eridani's view of the nearest carts was unobstructed, and she studied each in turn, leisurely considering her options.

"Try the chicken strips over there."

She turned to see a slender man about her age. He wore a plain but clean shirt and trousers, smiling at her and pointing toward one of the carts.

"They marinade cuts of white meat for a day using a special family recipe before they grill them. The outcome is to die for."

"Thanks," said Eridani. "I'll keep that in mind."

"I'm Arnis. Welcome to Gan."

Eridani stared at him appraisingly. "Who says I'm not from Gan?"

Arnis cocked his head. "An attractive northern woman, wearing a military cloak and sitting alone at a communal table? I'm guessing you're from Kozhad because of the uniform, but I'm certain you're no local, or you would have already purchased those chicken strips instead of wasting time considering the other options." His smile widened. "Have I guessed correctly? If I managed to amuse you, perhaps you could repay that small favor by telling me your name."

Arnis spoke with a hint of the local accent, but his patter was a bit too polished. There were always men like him in larger towns. Men who knew everything and everyone, and would ingratiate themselves to foreigners, eager to help visitors procure whatever they desired, for a price. Such men could sometimes be useful.

"Sana," she said, picking the name of her general on a whim. "You've guessed well. I'm an officer in the army of Kozhad." She was stuck waiting in this place anyhow. Cultivating a local contact could be useful, and hearing his thoughts on Kozhad might be interesting. And besides, he was rather cute.

Her interlocutor slid onto the bench across from her without waiting for an invitation. "That is simply marvelous, Officer Sana. We hear such interesting things about your kingdom here in Gan. It is self-evident that women serve in your army on equal footing with men, but what of the other tales the storytellers spin for their supper? Were you there when your queen slaughtered the nobles in the town square?" His eyes grew wider, his cheeks flushed. "Did your own blade taste their blue blood?"

Eridani felt both flattered and vaguely uncomfortable. It was good that the word of her deeds had spread as far as Gan. Storytellers rarely chose to tell of current events, focusing instead on tales whose truth was hidden under the weight of decades and centuries. And yet, Arnis seemed a little too eager, almost aroused by the violence in her past.

She shook her head. "I wasn't among the executioners, but the nobles were traitors and got what they deserved." She thought of old Feodor lying on his back, his face a mask of horror as Toval stepped toward him, following her command. She forced herself to focus on the present. "Queen Eridani purged her domain of the old nobles so she could rebuild it into something better. Her people no longer suffer under the boots of these evil men, and the kingdom is prospering. Have you heard that a steady trickle of lowborn, from serfs to tradesmen to merchants, have been moving to Kozhad along with their families?"

Arnis nodded at her, rapt. "There are many tales of your queen. Storytellers say she rules fairly and is wise for one so young. They say she throws no lavish feasts, nor extravagant hunts, but spends much of her time on the affairs of state." He flashed a fetching smile. "And if she has the loyalty of someone like you, then I believe those stories without question."

Eridani couldn't help but smile. His flattery was rather obvious, but no less pleasant for that.

"They also say Queen Eridani disappears for three hours every morning into the heart of her palace and none but her closest advisors know what she does. Most Gannians believe she trains, learning to fight with all manner of weapons in order to become a great warrior and one day lead her army and conquer the North the way Kalatar once did." He paused, the question unstated but implied.

"The queen does not share such secrets with me," said Eridani.

"And if she did, you would not tell a handsome stranger you've met at a market, eh?"

Eridani giggled. It was behavior unbecoming of royalty and she was glad no one who knew her was here to witness it.

Arnis leaned in across the pine table. "Do you want to know what I think?" He lowered his voice, like a conspirator plotting insurrection.

"What's that?" Eridani asked.

"I think your queen has found herself a lover, or perhaps several," said Arnis. "It sounds like she works hard, and is not a spendthrift when it comes to palace luxuries. But she must be wise enough to know that some of the finest pleasures in life are free."

Eridani's first instinct was to punch the boor in the nose. How dare he talk about her in that way! She wouldn't even have to get up—he'd leaned forward, presenting such an easy target. But she controlled herself, kept her expression neutral. It slowly dawned on her that this fast-talking grifter wasn't trying to turn a profit. He was trying to flirt with her.

In Kozhad, where everyone knew her and everyone was below her station, young men didn't dare to try sweeping her off her feet so blatantly. This was a novel experience, and not altogether unpleasant. She would let it slide. She was certain Arnis would mistake the anger that had rushed blood to her face for excitement.

"It is not appropriate to speak this way of my queen," she said.

Arnis offered an ironic bow, his eyes twinkling. "It won't happen again, Officer Sana."

Eridani spied a group of men approaching the common area.

"I'm afraid the people I am here to meet have arrived. It was nice talking with you, Arnis."

He turned, glanced in the direction she was looking, and whistled. "You're no ordinary officer if you're meeting with Commander Remi." His eyes widened. "A general, perhaps? A noblewoman?"

"You really must go now," she said, a touch of steel in her voice.

He sighed as he rose from the bench. "Perhaps we shall meet again. Good luck with your meeting, Lady Sana." He offered what looked like a sincere bow this time and headed in the opposite direction from the mercenaries.

Eridani studied his fit, well-proportioned form as he went.

COMMANDER REMI WAS a squat, stocky man in his fifties. His bull-like neck supported a balding head, his sparse blond hair failing to fully cover scar tissue from what must've been a nearly fatal wound above his left ear. He walked with a slight limp. He couldn't have been much older than Caer, but whereas her trainer remained in excellent shape thanks to a rigorous regime, the mercenary commander seemed less coordinated and slower, his form flabby with fat.

Remi reached the tables and looked around. He was followed by six armed men of varying ages, his officers and bodyguards. The two youngest stayed a pair of steps back. Their eyes ceaselessly scanned their surroundings.

It was at the mercenary's insistence and counter to Eridani's instincts that their meeting would take place in public. When Caer learned of the terms, he explained that many mercenary leaders chose to conduct business this way: whether or not they reached an accord, it was beneficial for the leaders of even the largest mercenary companies to be seen courted by the envoys of dukes and kings. It allowed them to drive up their price when negotiating with other clients.

Eridani got up from her seat and raised her hand, catching the older man's attention. He saw her, nodded, and walked over, his men in tow.

"Well met, Commander Remi," Eridani said. "I'm Sana, the envoy of Queen Eridani of Kozhad, empowered to negotiate a contract on her behalf."

Remi squeezed his portly form between the bench and the table across from her, where Arnis had sat minutes earlier. Two of the older men in his retinue stood behind him while the others dispersed around the table, ensuring a modicum of privacy but also drawing attention to the meeting taking place.

"Thank you for coming, Sana," said Remi. He did not comment on her age or her gender. There were some benefits to the position of the one holding the purse strings. "How large a force is your queen looking to retain?"

"A thousand fighters," said Eridani. "At least three quarters must be veterans of no less than three battles. Kozhad is prepared to offer a two-year contract, provided your men will help train our standing army during that time."

Caer had spent hours imparting upon her the minutia she'd have to negotiate. This was but the broadest opening offer.

Remi scratched his chin, fingers tracing over gray stubble. "There's much demand for well-trained companies in Haldova of late. Still, we could manage a thousand men, at six scales a month per head."

"Six dragon scales?" Eridani raised her voice in outrage. "The going rate is two!"

Remi shrugged. "Perhaps in times of peace, when men-at-arms are plentiful, some of the less experienced companies could be retained on the cheap. Prime fighters, well-armed and well-trained, require premium pay."

"There's a difference between premium pay and highway robbery," said Eridani. Even at two thousand scales per month, a two-year commitment would clean out her treasury. She couldn't afford to come even close to the mercenary's asking price. "We'll pay for the barracks and feed the men. Those who wish to retire in Kozhad will be given free plots of farmland."

The mercenary exchanged glances with his lieutenants. "Let me be honest with you, Sana. At another time, your offer might've been quite reasonable. But there's turmoil in Haldova again and they are ever in need of fighting men. Those who weren't hired to shed blood in the southwest have better options here in the North." He sighed. "The patriarch is willing to pay four scales per fighting man, and hire as many as fifteen hundred. You'll have to beat his offer if we're to reach any sort of accord."

Eridani gritted her teeth. Had the patriarch anticipated her move and used his deeper pockets to counter, or was he merely beefing up his army, willing to spend a fortune so he'd have sellswords to throw into the meat grinder while troops loyal to him remained in reserve? Either way, she had no hope of matching his bid, and even if she was willing to pay the usurious price, a much smaller band of sellswords she could afford at those rates would not make enough of a difference in the coming war.

She tried another tactic. "You seem reluctant to work for the patriarch. Perhaps that is reason enough to accept our coin?"

"You're perceptive, for one so young," said Remi. He scratched his chin, as if trying to choose his words. "It's no secret that the patriarch has designs on uniting the North. If and when he does, it will put an end to all infighting between the small kingdoms and city-states. There will be fewer opportunities for men like me." He sighed again. "Still, business is business. No one, short of Kalatar himself rising from the grave, could hire a mercenary company in Gan for less than four scales per head."

Dejected, Eridani stalled. "I'm not authorized to offer such a sum. I will bring your offer back to the queen."

The older man nodded. "Don't think on this for too long. The way things are looking, there may soon be no unemployed sellswords left in Gan."

AFTER THE MERCENARIES had gone, Eridani remained in her seat, trying to come up with an alternate plan. She had to find a way to increase the size of her army. The moment her enemies had a significant advantage in numbers they would no longer be content with an impasse, and she'd lose.

"Here." Arnis slid onto the bench next to her, and placed a clay plate filled with steaming chicken strips in front of her. "I'm sorry your meeting went poorly, but I hope the food will make you feel better."

She stared at him, then at the plate. She was in no mood to eat and was about to say so, but the enticing smell from the freshly cooked meat changed her mind. She picked up a strip of chicken and chewed it. It was every bit as good as Arnis had said.

"Why do you assume my meeting has gone poorly?" she asked between bites.

"It barely lasted long enough for me to buy the food," said Arnis. "Were it going well, you would be at it for hours, ironing out the details. Remi is a tough and meticulous negotiator. I'm sorry, Sana." Arnis grabbed a strip of meat off the plate and took a small bite. "I wish I could help."

Eridani eyed the rapidly diminishing stack of chicken strips. "Happen to know where I can find hundreds of sellswords on the cheap?"

Arnis looked like he was about to say something else but instead he resumed chewing.

"What?" Eridani asked.

He looked up from his food.

"You were going to say something, and then changed your mind."

"It's nothing," he said, as he wiped his lips with a small handkerchief. "You wouldn't take it seriously."

Eridani pushed the plate away from both of them. "You won't know if you don't try. Come on. Talk now, eat after."

Arnis looked around until he was satisfied no one was near enough to overhear him. "Gan is called the City of a Thousand Gods because everyone is permitted to worship freely here, and so one can find shrines and temples to every deity known in the Heart, including a few long-forgotten elsewhere."

Eridani wasn't a believer. She had seen no evidence of gods in the world. Any stories she had heard or read that weren't obvious fables could be explained rationally. Besides, if such beings existed anywhere, the affairs of men were of no more interest to them than the goings-on inside an anthill concerned Eridani. And if Arnis was about to suggest that she pray for divine help, she was going to give him a piece of her mind.

Arnis continued, "No matter which god the people may worship, they all hold the memory of a man, Gan's greatest son, in nearly as high esteem."

"Kalatar of Gan," said Eridani.

"The greatest conqueror the world has ever known, yes."

"How does that help? Should I dress up in ancient garb and pretend to be Kalatar to rally fighters to the banner of Kozhad? I think some of them might figure out I'm not him. It's the breasts, you see."

Arnis chuckled, but Eridani thought she detected the smallest hint of a blush in his cheeks. "Look, do you want to hear me out or not?"

Eridani held up her hands, palms out. "Sorry. I shouldn't be taking my irritation out on you. Please, continue."

"Kalatar may be dead, but many in Gan would follow the man," Arnis glanced at her, "or the woman armed with his sword, the Reaper."

"The Bloodsword is just one of many legends surrounding Kalatar and Orodos," said Eridani. "It doesn't exist."

Arnis looked her in the eye. "It exists, and I know where to find it."

CHAPTER 13

GOD UNDER THE FLOORBOARDS

 very child in the North and many beyond knew the legend of the sword of Kalatar. It was called by many names: most commonly the Bloodsword, but also the Reaper, Peacemaker, the Crimson Blade. No matter the name, its origin story remained consistent.

Kalatar lived four hundred years ago. He inherited the throne of Gan at a young age and spent decades in various campaigns. His territories extended as far as the Bela Mountains, the range that separated the lands of the Quadi to the south from the rest of the Heart. When Kalatar reached the Bela Mountains, he inexplicably ordered his troops to turn back. Accounts differed widely as to why he lost his taste for conquest, but returning to the North undefeated and with the treasure of half the world looted from palaces and banks along the way further advanced his iconic status.

Early on in his reign, Kalatar had conquered six of the neighboring kingdoms before his twentieth birthday. He laid siege to the castle of the seventh, one ruled by the most powerful of the North's ancient kings. Kalatar wanted the king to abdicate and open the castle gates, but the king demanded a trial by combat—his champion against Kalatar's. The young warlord would not designate a champion. His teacher, Orodos, considered by many to be the greatest philosopher in history, had always counseled him to fight his own battles. In this case, he took the advice literally.

The king's champion was an enormous man, broad-shouldered and two heads taller than Kalatar. It was rumored he had giants' blood in his veins. Yet, Kalatar did not fear him. They crossed blades and fought for hours, neither willing to take a single step back.

In the course of such a prolonged duel, the giant's blade could take no more abuse and snapped in half. Instead of delivering the killing blow, Kalatar waited for his opponent to be given another weapon. He wanted his victory to be absolute. After a time, it was Kalatar's sword that broke. The giant was a fierce and honorable warrior and he, too, waited for Kalatar to fetch another sword.

It is said they dueled from sunup til sundown and each of them had replaced their weapons many times over. It was almost dark when the giant finally dropped to his knees with exhaustion.

"I can fight no longer," he said, and exposed his neck for Kalatar to deliver a killing blow. But Kalatar did not strike.

"You have fought me gallantly and well. Swear loyalty to me and I will not only spare your life, but offer you my friendship."

The giant wept as he prostrated himself in front of Kalatar of Gan and swore loyalty to his new master.

The king had watched the fight from the walls of his castle. "Betrayer!" he shouted when he saw his giant kneel before Kalatar. He gave the order and his archers let loose one hundred arrows.

Out in the open there was no place for the duelists to hide. The giant shielded his new master with his own outsized body.

Kalatar held his dead opponent, arrows protruding from the giant's flesh, and cried. He then ordered his army to attack. Soon many of the defenders were slaughtered and the king and his remaining soldiers were captured.

"I had sworn friendship to the giant," Kalatar told Orodos. "It would be easy to kill the treacherous king, but I want you to come up with an execution that would honor the memory of a friend."

Orodos did not disappoint his young master.

He ordered the soldiers to kill the king's men, one by one, and drain the blood from their bodies. Then the royal alchemists extracted the minute traces of iron from the blood. By the time they'd collected enough to meld it with carbon and forge a fine steel blade, three hundred and sixty-five warriors had been executed and exsanguinated.

As the sword was forged, the blacksmiths quenched the red-hot blade in the chilled blood of the king's four children. When it was complete, the jewelers adorned the tip of its pommel with the finest gem from the necklace taken from the corpse of the king's favorite wife.

By the time the Reaper was complete, everything was taken from the king—his lands, his castle, his armies, his children, and his wives. Kalatar then used the sword to end the king's misery and considered the giant to have been avenged.

Kalatar carried the Reaper in many a battle. He crossed blades with some of the finest swordsmen in the world, but the blood-forged, vengeance-born blade never broke; it didn't even chip.

When Kalatar lay dying, many decades later, he ordered the lands he had conquered to be split peaceably among his three sons. He carefully divided his territories, his wealth, and his armies among them. But he also knew that bequeathing the Reaper to any one of his children would allow that son to gather enough support to challenge and defeat the others. Not wanting his descendants to turn against one another, Kalatar ordered the sword destroyed.

It was said the gods themselves would reforge the Reaper once another warrior worthy to wield it was born.

Eridani stared at Arnis dubiously. "You just happen to know where the greatest treasure in Gan is hidden?"

"I do," said Arnis. "It's in the temple I serve at."

His voice was even. His eyes stared straight at her. Eridani had met her share of liars, and she felt certain this boy believed he was telling the truth.

"Temple? You? I'm more confused than ever."

Arnis smiled. "Of course, as a foreigner you didn't realize. Anyone from Gan would have known at a glance that I serve at one of the valley temples. It's the cut of my clothes."

"The Valley of the Gods?"

Eridani knew about the area on the outskirts of Gan that housed a great many temples, shrines, and altars. Those who sought divine guidance could find almost any flavor of it in the valley.

"Which god do you worship?" Eridani asked, concerned. She wanted to like Arnis, but there were cults and sects Gavron had taught her about whose practices and beliefs would have made that impossible.

"I serve the God Under the Floorboards," said Arnis.

"Sorry, I haven't heard of that one. Does he have a name?"

"To speak his name is anathema. In fact, only the high priests know it. Everyone else refers to him as I do." Arnis considered his words. "I admit, ours is not among the most influential or popular of temples. But it's old. Our faith was already ancient and forgotten by many when Kalatar was alive. That was why he chose to entrust the sword to us. Those who didn't believe the ruse of it being destroyed would've never thought to look for it in my temple."

Eridani's eyes narrowed. "Why would you tell me this centuries-old secret?"

"Kalatar charged us with more than merely hiding the Bloodsword. A seeker must be chosen once every season, one brave and strong enough to retrieve it. By finding a willing candidate, I'm doing my god's work." Arnis's eyes twinkled when he spoke of these matters. "The God Under the Floorboards watches over the sword in the secret chamber under the temple. Only the warrior worthy of Kalatar's legacy is destined to retrieve it. The time for the next seeker is upon us: should you choose to seek the sword of Kalatar, I can present you to the high priests and they might grant you the chance to prove yourself worthy."

"You mean to tell me that every three months some poor soul goes looking for the Reaper, yet none have succeeded? Is the treasure guarded by men and booby traps as well?"

"My god is the only sentinel of the sword," said Arnis, "for no mortal can match his power." He made a sign of obeisance with his left hand. "Many seekers lose their courage and run without ever having descended to the chamber. Others are frightened away by the god's mere visage. Few manage to reach the sword, but they aren't destined to wield it and so, no matter how hard they try, they cannot lift it from its resting place."

Eridani tried to figure out Arnis's game. Was he lying to lure her into a trap? If so, a less fantastical story would have surely served him better. Could he be telling the truth—or at least some variant of it he himself believed?

Eridani considered her options, weighing caution against the lust for adventure that stirred within her. Without a way to recruit men to her cause her future was grim. Perhaps these other seekers had failed, but many of them must've been religious fanatics, men conditioned from childhood to fear gods. In this she had a considerable advantage. Perhaps she would fail and find nothing. Perhaps it was merely a replica, a chunk of steel welded into a slab of stone, so the priests could claim anyone who got that far wasn't worthy enough to draw it. But then, perhaps she could find a way to gain whatever treasure the temple guarded. Her father had taught her to wield men as tools; what better way to do so than through their faith? Was she not intelligent enough to reap the benefits of the worshipers' delusions, much as their prophets and high priests had always done?

"All right," she told Arnis. "Take me to your temple."

"Tonight," Arnis said, his face shining with the ardor of faith. "We must go at dusk."

THE AFTERNOON HAD been wonderful. Arnis sent a boy to let the priests know they were coming but insisted the seeker should not arrive at the temple until after dark. He spent the day showing her the wonders of his city. Gan was even larger than Skond, and had a very different character. Northern architecture and sensibilities mixed with styles from Haldova and beyond created a unique and vibrant city. Eridani gawked at its many wonders like a country girl, and was glad that she was traveling incognito. Unlike the queen, her Sana persona was allowed to be curious, excited, and to generally have a bit of fun away from the responsibilities of the palace.

She admitted to herself that she might not have enjoyed the tour as much were it not for Arnis acting as her guide.

As the shadows lengthened with the setting sun, Eridani and Arnis set out toward the Valley of the Gods. By the time they reached the temple of the God Under the Floorboards, they could barely see the path ahead of them. The squat one-story building evoked the barracks: it was long and relatively narrow, its once-yellow walls bleached by the sun and the passage of time. The entrance was at the short side of the rectangle. Wide redwood doors adorned with a carving of a flight of dragons against the background of a starry night sky creaked when Arnis pushed them apart.

Dozens of lit torches hung in heavy bronze sconces, and many candles burned on tall, thin tables that ran alongside the two longer walls, which were painted with more scenes of majestic dragons in flight. The ceiling was painted black with hundreds of specks representing the stars, and a small sliver of the moon standing out prominently among them. Eridani recognized several of the constellations.

A trio of older men dressed in white-and-gray robes stood in the spacious foyer of the temple, facing the door.

"Welcome, seeker," spoke the one in the middle. "Why have you come tonight?"

Arnis had explained the ritual. Eridani copied the sign of obeisance he had shown her earlier. "I'm Sana. I have come to pay my respects to the God Under the Floorboards and to prove myself worthy of the inheritance he is guarding."

The priest on the left spoke, "Only the strong of body and pure of spirit may enter the inner sanctum. Have you come here of your own free will and have you prepared for the challenge?"

"I have," said Eridani.

"The quest you pursue is fraught with mortal danger. If you wish to reconsider, you're free to leave," said the priest on the right.

"I'm ready," said Eridani.

"Very well," the priest in the middle spoke again. "May the God Under the Floorboards bestow his blessings upon you."

The other priests and Arnis all repeated the phrase. Eridani bowed again. Then they stepped aside and allowed Eridani to proceed with Arnis in tow.

They walked through a corridor past several smaller rooms until they reached a round metal door built into the wall several feet above ground.

"This is it," said Arnis. "The path below."

He had to apply some force to pull the door open. Eridani peered into the opening. Inside was a metal sliding tube that led into darkness. The air in it smelled stale.

"How do I get back out?" she asked.

"There's a staircase," said Arnis. "But the ritual requires the seeker to enter this way."

Eridani reached over to the nearest sconce and grabbed the torch. It was made of light wood, its tip soaked in sulfur and lime.

Arnis raised an eyebrow. "This isn't part of the ritual."

"I'm not going down there without a light," said Eridani. When Arnis hesitated, she added: "I'm allowed to bring my weapon and whatever supplies I wish, right?"

"Well, yes," said Arnis.

"Then the torch shouldn't be a problem. I will put it back afterward."

"I suppose..." Arnis held the round door open wide.

Eridani put one foot into the chute. She held the torch in one hand and her scabbard with the other, making the maneuver awkward.

"Do you want me to help you in?"

Eridani sat on the edge of the tube facing toward it, her feet resting against the steeply-angled chute inside. Was she imagining an edge to Arnis's voice? She was feeling apprehensive, far less confident now that she faced the ominous-looking portal to who-knew-where.

She wondered about the past seekers. Four per year, making their total number well over a thousand. She was willing to believe that they all failed, but it was difficult to accept that none of them talked afterward. The location of the sword was valuable; surely more than one of them would have been tempted—

She heard Arnis move and as she half-turned to see what he was up to, she felt his hands on her shoulders and back, and then he shoved, pushing her into the chute.

Eridani cried out in surprise as her body slid downward. The chute was made of slick polished steel so there was nothing to hang on to. She resisted the urge to grab for its sides, holding on tight to her sword and her torch instead. The trip down a steep incline lasted for only a few heartbeats. She hit the hard floor with a grunt, landing on her posterior. Her tough military clothing mostly saved the skin on her arms and legs, but she was sure there would be some scrapes and bruising.

The chamber was dark, the only illumination provided by her torch. There was a large window high above her but the night was cloudy, and it offered virtually no additional light. Her eyes had not yet adjusted from the brightly-lit temple upstairs, but she could make out an enormous shape rising, moving toward her from the other end of the room.

Instinctively, Eridani extended her arm, pointing the torch toward the shape. It shrunk from the torch's fire, growling. Eridani took a step back as well, until she was pressed flat against the wall. What sort of an animal did these lunatics keep in their basement?

The single torch could only illuminate a small portion of the chamber she was in. It was a vast space, nearly half as large as the building above it. The window at the top suggested that the chamber extended all the way to the ceiling of the first floor, in the back of the temple.

As her sight adjusted, she could see more of the shape that paced back and forth in the center of the chamber. It was nearly twice the size of Eridani. A pair of tough, leathery wings extended from its back, connected to diminutive arms with sharp blade-like talons on them.

Eridani thought back to the images upstairs. Could they have an actual *dragon* down here? Impossible!

She recalled the monster made of fog and sand the sorceress of Skond used to try and cow her. This must have been an illusion, too, a convincing one. No wonder the other seekers didn't make it far.

Emboldened, she took a couple of steps toward the creature. She could see it better now. It wasn't a dragon. It was an enormous bat. Instead of hanging upside down from the perch near the ceiling the way that the bats do, it stood upright on skeletal, clawed feet. Its fur was gray and threadbare. There was a collar around its neck and two smaller ones around its legs. Thick, long metal chains connected the collars to the metal spikes buried into the ground by the wall.

As Eridani approached, the bat raised its wing, partially covering its face from the torchlight.

"Put that away!" Its voice sounded like a loud whisper, ancient and inhuman.

Could illusions speak?

Eridani had been a skeptic her entire life. She did not believe in gods or magic. Although the sorceress's prophecy did manage to rattle her, years had passed since and her advisors had remained loyal. She was certain the creature in front of her was no god, but it was no illusion, either. It appeared to be made of flesh and blood. A monster that spoke and therefore was able to think! Her long-held assumptions about the world devoid of magic and legendary creatures were wrong. What else might she be wrong about?

Eridani held the torch away from the creature. "What are you?"

The bat slouched even more and whispered a response. Eridani couldn't make out the words.

"Speak up."

"Come closer." Its strange-sounding voice was barely audible.

Eridani took a step forward, but then she looked again at the large window set in the wall high above them. There were no curtains, just metal bars. There was nothing to prevent the sun from bathing the chamber during the day. And if the creature could tolerate that, why would it be so afraid of a single torch? She hesitated, stopped.

The bat pounced faster than Eridani would have expected. Its talons slashed at her right hand in an attempt to knock away the torch. The chains rattled and screeched as it used its body to try and pin her to the ground.

Eridani threw herself out of the way, the talons leaving long shallow cuts in the sleeve of her jacket. Momentum carried the bat past her. It landed on its belly, then rose quickly, but not before Eridani dashed out of its way. She backed into a corner and shifted the torch into her left hand. She drew her sword with her right hand and pointed both toward the bat.

The bat rose and resumed pacing in the center of the chamber, like a duelist waiting for an opening. Its eyes never left Eridani.

"I mean you no harm," Eridani said.

The bat paced, its only response the jingling of its chains.

Eridani inspected the chamber. There was a heavy door to the left of where the creature's chains were affixed to the ground. To the right of the door was a small alcove and in it, atop a slab of stone, laid an old sword with a large ruby embedded in its pommel.

So, whatever underhanded thing Arnis and his masters were up to, perhaps they weren't lying about the Reaper after all.

She tried again. "Why did you attack me? Are you trying to protect the Bloodsword?"

The bat emitted a sound akin to several sneezes. Was it *laughing?*

"This chunk of metal means nothing to me beyond its purpose." It spoke clearly now that it wasn't trying to lure her closer. Its voice grated, like the sound of a knife against a whetstone.

"What purpose is that?"

The bat drew itself upright, towering over her, its wings spread wide.

"Bait."

Eridani shrank deeper into the corner. She didn't think she could defeat the much larger creature. She cursed herself for her arrogance and pride, for choosing to undertake this mad scheme, for coming here alone. She forced those feelings out of her mind. For now, she needed to focus on surviving.

"You're no god. What manner of creature are you?" she asked.

"I am what you see," said the bat.

"The priests upstairs may call you their god, but based on their décor they think you a dragon."

"My kind hunted yours for centuries before your recorded history began; before you discovered fire or iron." It eyed her sword and her torch. "When I was young, your ancestors scared their offspring with stories of such hunts. Human memory is a flawed, fragile thing," said the bat bitterly. "In a handful of generations, glorious creatures of the night became diurnal fire-breathing snakes."

"You're very old." Eridani counted her blessings. Had this creature been in its prime, she probably wouldn't have been fast enough to survive its attack.

"I am the last." It spoke the words evenly, as though it had come to terms with its fate long ago.

"I'm sorry," said Eridani.

"Don't pity me!" The bat hissed. "I was here before this structure was erected and I'll be here long after your bones crumble to dust."

"You've been a prisoner here for centuries. Let me go, and I will help free you."

The sneeze-laughter echoed through the chamber again. "There is no place for me to go. Do you think you're the first to offer this bargain?"

"I'm the queen of my people. I command an army," said Eridani. On a whim she added, "The sorceress of Skond has foretold great things in my future. Perhaps freeing you is one of them."

"All you humans think there's a stink of destiny about you." The bat flapped its great leathery wings, agitated. "You're nothing special. You're only dinner."

Eridani shivered. The creature wasn't trying to kill her out of an obligation to guard the sword, nor some other grand design. She was merely a mouse dropped into the cage of a snake. When she got her hands on Arnis...

Eridani forced herself to focus again. Dreams of revenge were as useless as second-guessing her bad decisions. She studied both the bat and the room, searching for a way to escape.

The priests must've interpreted their deal with Kalatar very differently from what he intended. Instead of trying to find a worthy successor to his legacy to claim the sword, acolytes like Arnis scoured the city for anyone foolish enough to voluntarily enter their god's lair.

But, if they fed the monster human flesh every three months, where were the bones? Where was the creature's excrement? The floors were clean, freshly swept up and washed. This meant the priests were able to enter the chamber, presumably through the one door she could see rather than the chute, to tidy up.

She looked at the window again. The sun rising in the east would force the nocturnal beast away from the door. She imagined the rays of sunshine through the bars on the window. In the morning, the beast would have to move to the corner she currently occupied to remain in the shade. Perhaps it was less dangerous then—that would explain why the priests insisted on having seekers arrive at night.

She focused on the bat's chains. When she was growing up, her father had kept dogs. Some were nice and friendly, but one in particular was an evil, angry creature that would attack anyone careless enough to approach it. The dog was chained in the yard, and foolhardy children—she among them—made a game of taunting him. Winning at that game meant avoiding a nasty bite and involved learning precisely how far its rope would allow it to reach.

The chains that held the bat gave it plenty of leeway but, as best Eridani could figure, they weren't long enough to cover the entire chamber. The farthest corner away from where she stood seemed out of the monster's reach.

The torch might have lasted another hour or two at most before it burned out. The bat could probably overpower her even now, but it had no reason to rush. Waiting until it had the advantage of darkness was the superior stratagem.

She had to find a way to get across—but how? The bat prowled in the center, muttering something in the language that couldn't have rolled off a human tongue.

Fear grudgingly made room for disdain in Eridani's mind. This monster *chose* to live as a captive merely because it couldn't conceive of a better circumstance for itself. There was nothing more pitiful than a willing slave. After so many centuries, its spirit must have been broken. Or perhaps it was insane, or merely stupid and complacent by human standards. Either way, Eridani thought, she should be able to outsmart such a creature.

Eridani considered a number of plans, each more desperate than the next. She knew she would only get one chance at this, and she was gambling with her life. Finally, she settled on a strategy she thought might succeed.

Never taking her eyes off the bat or lowering the torch, she used her sword hand to reach into a side pocket above the knee. The bat ceased its pacing and watched her intently, but made no move to attack.

Eridani fished a small flask from her pocket. As the bat watched she awkwardly brought the flask to her mouth, holding both it and the sword in her right hand and used her teeth to pull the cork.

The bat took a tentative step forward and sniffed.

"Brandy," said Eridani, after she spit out the cork. "I'm thirsty."

She had no idea how good the bat's sense of smell was, but it could probably smell the alcohol. It seemed satisfied with her explanation and relaxed a little. The contents of the flask weren't for drinking: it was rubbing alcohol, good for cleaning wounds to stave off infection. But the bat couldn't have known that. It must've figured that a drunk human would make for an easier prey and retreated a couple of steps, far enough that Eridani could swallow a few sips and still be ready to defend herself if attacked.

Eridani poured the contents of the flask onto the shoulders and back of her leather cloak.

The bat froze, momentarily confused, then rushed at Eridani, its fangs bared. Rather than defending her position, Eridani stepped forward and touched the flame of the torch to her shoulder. As the alcohol soaking her cloak caught fire, she rushed at the bat, a burst of bright flame in her wake.

The creature shrieked and covered its eyes with a wing. The flame burned out as quickly as it started, but the pair of heartbeats it won Eridani allowed her to rush past the bat. The monster rallied and gave chase. Eridani threw the torch at its snout and dove for the corner.

The bat swatted away the torch, which barely stalled it, but the miniscule delay was all Eridani needed. The bat lunged and was yanked back by the collar around its neck. It strained against the collar, the chain connecting it to the spike stretched in a straight line. It swiped at Eridani with its talons, but as she was now squeezed into the chamber's farthest corner from the door, the bat's talons could reach no closer than an arm's length away from her face.

Eridani panted as she leaned against the wall. She loosened the grip on her sword and made a conscious effort to slow down her breathing. The unpleasant smell of burned leather and singed hair permeated the chamber. The bat retreated toward the center, still muttering. It cautiously approached the torch on the floor and kicked it with a taloned foot. The torch rolled toward the corner where Eridani had previously stood. Its flame flickered a few times and went out.

Eridani stood in darkness, unable to sit down or shift her position in any significant way. Without the benefit of light she couldn't estimate where the safe zone ended, so she remained still. She could barely make out the shape of the bat as it moved around the chamber, cursing her in a litany of dead languages.

It was going to be a long night.

ARNIS PRAYED TO the God Under the Floorboards. He prostrated himself on the bare floor of his small, sparse room at the temple and asked the Great Dragon for the usual things: health and safety for him and his fellow priests, prosperity for Gan, and respite for the souls of his parents who had already moved on to the next realm.

Serving at the temple was a heavy burden on one's soul. The blessed forefathers had done the unthinkable, chaining their own god. Generations of priests spent their lives in service to the enslaved dragon, taking care of its needs and wants, all while knowing that their souls would suffer terribly in the next realm for the sin of failing to release their deity. It was the sacrifice they accepted willingly; the suffering of their souls was the price paid by the select few for the benefit of all mankind.

Having finished the prayer he headed toward the Sacred Lair. It was his duty to clean up after the previous night's meal. He was to mop the floors, remove the bones, and wipe down any blood splatter from the walls. He was also to collect the Great Dragon's excrement, which the priests would later use to make salves and ointments to be sold to the faithful.

Even when the sun shone brightly, one risked their life when stepping into the Sacred Lair. It was yet another burden of priesthood: the God Under the Floorboards would occasionally pounce and devour a priest he did not deem worthy. It had been over a decade since an incident like that happened last; the Great Dragon knew that any time he ate one of his attendants, the priests would not provide him with another sacrifice for a long time, forcing him to fast and suffer.

Arnis didn't expect a problem this time: the Great Dragon would be satiated, pleased with last night's sacrifice. Arnis liked Sana. He was glad that he got to meet her and spend time with her, and convince her to enter the Sacred Lair. Having served as a sacrifice, her soul would experience blissful joy in the next realm.

Arnis carried the bucket of water, broom, and rags to the heavy door at the lower level of the temple. He set the supplies down, made the sign of obeisance three times, unlocked the door with a bronze key that hung on his belt, stepped through and gasped.

The body of the God Under the Floorboards was sprawled face-down on the floor, its wings shredded to strips, its torso bleeding from many cuts. There was a sword driven into the back of its neck, the blade buried in the god's flesh deep enough that only a few inches of steel stood out, its tip sticking out through its throat.

Sana sat on the floor next to it. She was covered in the Great Dragon's blood, her hair tangled, her leather cloak covered in scorch marks. She held the Bloodsword in her lap.

She looked up at Arnis with bloodshot eyes. Then she climbed to her feet, leaning on the Bloodsword like a cane, and growled, "You!"

WHEN MORNING CAME, Eridani was half-dead with exhaustion. Her entire body ached, her calf muscles felt like they were on fire, and her temples throbbed with a headache. The sun was rising and as its rays flooded the chamber, the bat had retreated into the shade of the opposite corner. Its movements changed in daylight. It seemed lethargic, slow, as though it was struggling to remain awake. Eridani stretched her arms and legs for several minutes, regaining her own mobility. She gripped her sword and advanced on the monster.

Eridani knew what it felt like to hate. She hated the Duke of Buzzards, even now that he was dead by her hand. She hated the patriarch, and Lady Voriana, and any number of lesser enemies complicit in the deaths of her parents and brother. But at this moment, there was nothing she hated more than the disgusting ancient thing cowering in front of her.

She marched up to it and stabbed at it with her sword. Even with its life threatened, the creature seemed not to be able to resist effectively in daylight. It moved sluggishly, trying to block the thrust with its wing. The sword cut through the plagiopatagium with some difficulty, as though it was an extra-thick blanket.

The bat howled as Eridani slashed repeatedly, shredding its wings, wounding its forearms. It lashed out using its claws to swipe back, but it was too slow and its aim was no better than that of a drunken brawler.

After a few minutes the damage to its wings and limbs was so extensive the monster could no longer use them to protect itself. Eridani stabbed its body repeatedly, piercing the mousy gray fur.

The wounded beast summoned up the last vestiges of its strength and surged from the corner. It made it only a few steps, tripping over its chains, collapsing in the center of the chamber. Eridani followed and kept stabbing and cutting at it for as long as its great thin body continued to twitch. When it was finally still, she drove her sword deep into its neck and collapsed next to it, sweating profusely, her heart pounding. She lay there for a time. It took all her strength to get back up.

Eridani walked to the slab of stone upon which the Reaper rested. What was it Arnis had said? Only the worthy could lift it? Perhaps it was another lie, an excuse for why other seekers did not succeed in retrieving the precious sword. Still, having faced a creature of myth she could no longer discount things supernatural and magical out of hand.

She grasped the grip of the Bloodsword. It offered no resistance as she lifted it.

The weapon was heavier and longer than the sword she was used to, but not uncomfortable. She took a few practice swings with it. It was well-balanced and felt right in her hand. The grip was large enough to use it two-handed but the weapon felt sufficiently light to wield with one hand. The ruby in its pommel glinted in sunlight.

She sat on the floor next to the corpse of the last dragon, the Reaper in her lap, and waited for someone to come through the door.

WHEN ARNIS ARRIVED an hour later, her first instinct was to do to him what she had done to the bat. In fact, had he arrived much sooner, his fate would have been sealed. But she'd had time to calm down, time to think and to plan while she waited for the door to be unlocked.

Her father taught her to wield men as tools. One did not discard a hammer because one managed to injure their finger with it while driving a nail into the wall. Arnis and his fellow priests were religious fanatics; that made them easy to manipulate, to bend to her will.

"You!" she growled, as she climbed to her feet. "Kneel to me as your new master."

Arnis stared at her and at the bat wide-eyed. His entire body shook. Hot tears rolled down his cheeks.

"My true name is Eridani, Queen of Kozhad. I have proven myself worthy. I killed your god, and I hold the sword of Kalatar." She raised the longsword above her head.

Arnis seemed frozen, unable to act.

"I fought the God Under the Floorboards and emerged victorious. I'm stronger than it was. Swear fealty to me and perhaps I'll forgive your treachery."

Slowly, Arnis lowered himself to his knees. "I'm yours to command, Eridani the Deicide. In this realm, and the next."

"Listen well. Here's what I want you to do."

THAT AFTERNOON THE priests of the God Under the Floorboards paraded across the Valley of the Gods carrying the head of a giant bat on a spike.

Crowds gathered, for no one had ever seen such a beast. Passersby shouted questions at the priests, and they explained that Eridani of Kozhad—who was the reincarnation of Kalatar and wielded his legendary sword—had killed their god in one-on-one combat.

Eridani the Deicide was the next great ruler, her ascent prophesized by Orodos himself, the priests said. It was a great honor to serve her, and greater still to fight at her side. Eridani would accept brave men and women into her army and reward them richly with land and coin. Anyone who ever dreamed of serving under the banner of Kalatar must hurry to the temple of the God Under the Floorboards and sign up, or at least witness with their own eyes the great Bloodsword, returned to the mortal realm by the heroes and gods that inhabit the next.

The word spread quickly across the Valley of the Gods and beyond. Soon people began to trickle toward the temple.

There were a great many admirers of Kalatar in his home city of Gan.

CHAPTER 14

CHE DOG AND
CHE VIPER

The servants found the body at dawn. They arrived at the lodge, bundled against the shiver of early winter, to tidy up after the partygoers.

The Birch Lodge was a one-story house on the shore of a small lake, set up much in the same fashion as an average tavern, but with aspirations and prices that soared high above the custom of such establishments. It was available to rent by the night to those prosperous enough to host private soirees and wise enough to do so outside of their own homes. The visiting soldiers and diplomats from Haldova who arrived with the delegation the day before were the most recent clients to have rented the lodge. Their purses heavy with coin, they were indiscriminate with their invitations and many a local eagerly accepted free food and drink.

The cleaning staff surveyed the main room: tables and stools shifted or upturned, puddles of spilled beer and piss, chicken bones and empty mugs littering the floor, a faint smell of vomit permeating the room. They assessed the mess with experienced eyes. There was no structural damage to the building, nothing was burned or singed, and the night staff managed to usher all the drunks out before they locked up, leaving no disgruntled, hungover patrons to deal with. All in all, they'd seen a lot worse.

It wasn't until later, when they scrubbed and mopped their way past the kitchen, they noticed that the lock on one of the pantry rooms was broken. The bronze ring hung on a single hinge attached to the frame, the other hinge ripped from the wood of the door.

Inside, a body lay lifeless atop the sacks of potatoes and grain.

"I'm sorry to bother you with this," said the constable, for what must've been the tenth time as they walked toward the Birch Lodge. "My commander thought you'd want to be informed, seeing as how she's one of your own."

Sana blinked sleep out of her eyes while the kid—he looked barely fifteen—stammered on. He'd introduced himself after he showed up at her doorstep and demanded she be woken up, but Sana promptly forgot his name.

"You did the right thing," she said, as amicably as she could at such an early hour. "Please relay my thanks to your commander."

The kid seemed nervous around her and kept on talking. She mostly ignored him, grunting assent or nodding occasionally to be polite. Even though he said the woman they found was wearing the insignia of the skirt army, she caught herself hoping it wasn't one of hers but a misunderstanding; a local who came by the uniform jacket in some roundabout way. Would that really be better? Either way, a woman was dead. She wondered whether wishing for it to be a stranger rather than a subordinate made her a bad person. She tried to force the fog out of her mind. The morning chill helped somewhat with that, but she wasn't at her best and she knew it. Her constable companion wouldn't shut up the entire way.

There was a small group of constables and civilians coming in and out of the Birch Lodge. She shouldered past them. "Out," she ordered the constables crowding the entrance to a coffin-sized storage space. She hoped whoever was in charge had the good sense not to disturb the body.

Any possibility of this being a stranger evaporated the moment Sana saw the victim. It was Genna, a woman in her mid-twenties who had joined the army of Kozhad shortly after Eridani recaptured the city. She had been a quiet sort, unassuming and diligent, perhaps not the best fighter but a good and reliable regular. A daughter of destitute farmers, she had sent much of her pay back home to support her parents and siblings.

The two of them were friends, as much as their respective stations would allow.

Sana gritted her teeth. Genna lay on her back, her army jacket crumpled in the corner, her clothes torn to shreds under the belt. That made the motive clear. Sana silently vowed she'd find whoever did this and make them suffer.

She procured a lantern and inspected the body more closely. There were no stab wounds but a lot of bruising on the neck; it seemed the assailant had strangled his victim. She examined the body thoroughly and zeroed in on the hands. There was blood caked under the dead woman's fingernails. Sana was fairly certain the blood wasn't Genna's.

She covered the body gently with the jacket, then turned to the officer who was hovering in the corridor behind her. "Have the owners of this establishment provide the list of everyone who worked here last night. Have *them* identify every guest they can. Round everyone up, question the guests and have each one name anyone else who might have been at the party. Then round them up, too."

The officer saluted. "What are we looking for?" he asked.

"Any men that have been recently cut or scratched."

GAVRON WATCHED THE Haldovan delegation enter the throne hall. The southerners wore colorful shirts of expensive silk and exotic cut, shoes cobbled for style rather than comfort, their bodies soaked in cologne so thoroughly he could smell its saccharine fragrance from halfway across the room. They reminded him of the paintings of peacocks he'd seen in travel books, fanning their plumage to attract a mate. Who were all these men? The guards were left outside, and surely the envoy did not require so many advisors. Likely as not, they served no function at all other than to underscore the importance of their liege. He had never traveled to the Haldova plains, but the opulence and shallowness of their royal courts were the stuff of legend.

A short, wiry man stepped forward and bowed deeply toward the throne. "Your Majesty, may I present His Excellence the Ambassador Extraordinary and Plenipotentiary of the Haldova Monarchy, Duke Cragnew of Sefeda."

Eridani sat atop her throne, her short brown hair unadorned—the crown of Kozhad had never been recovered from the Duke of Buzzard's treasury and was believed destroyed, but the queen did not seem in a hurry to replace it. There were only four advisors at her side, dressed plainly when compared to the Haldovans. The one symbol of status was the sword of Kalatar, an emblem of power worth the weight of a thousand silver crowns. It rested within a special contrivance by Eridani's right hand where its distinct blade could be seen by all.

The queen nodded, and the gaggle of peacocks parted. A man in his forties stepped forward. He was dressed extravagantly like the rest, but there was also an air to him of someone born to power. He stood straighter, his sharp clean-shaven chin held high. He held up a large scroll sealed with wax.

"It is an honor to meet you, Your Majesty. I carry credentials from my sovereign, Crown Prince Ajelogn of Haldova. If you would care to examine the document, it will asseverate the authority vested in me by the Crown."

"Thank you for braving the early winter to visit us, Ambassador." Eridani smiled, her casual tone a contrast to the envoy's practiced greeting. "I accept your credentials. Negotiations such as ours are about building trust. What trust is to be grown from cold formalities and fancy legal terms strewn throughout letters and contracts? Let us speak to each other plainly, and build a friendship upon the strong foundation of honestly declared intentions and mutual benefit."

If the queen's failure to adhere to protocol threw the envoy off balance at all, he hid it remarkably well. Without turning away from the throne he handed the sealed scroll to one of his men. "Your approach is as refreshing as it is unorthodox, Your Majesty. I look forward to building rapport."

Gavron chewed the inner side of his lip as Eridani outlined her proposal to the Haldovans. It was a bold move, but one that was necessary to break the dangerous stalemate between Kozhad and Skond.

A year and a half had passed since Eridani's triumphant return from Gan where she had managed to recruit an army of fanatical followers. Gavron remembered holding the Heart's most famous artifact for the first time. "Do you think it's real?" he asked her, his fingers running reverently along the scabbard. "Does it matter?" she replied. "So long as there are multitudes prepared to follow its bearer. Their faith gives the sword power, not the other way around."

Eridani cobbled her army from the regulars and mercenaries, and those so enamored with the idea of the second coming of Kalatar they would hardly hesitate to fight and die for the wielder of his blade in a foreign land. Pawns in a conflict that was otherwise meaningless to their lives.

Kozhad's ranks swelled, and the perpetual state of almost-war between the two cities continued. Although the fervent followers of Kalatar didn't demand mercenary-grade wages, they still had to be housed and clothed and fed, and the treasury was running out of money. As Master Sovio had predicted, the same policies that made Eridani such a popular ruler weren't proving economically feasible with a larger army to upkeep. In another year or two the Kozhad treasury would be completely exhausted, and the patriarch would win without his troops loosing a single arrow.

After Eridani laid out her proposal, the envoy appeared pleased as a fox that had got into a chicken coop.

"I must say, despite all the tumultuous history between our lands, I can't recall the sovereign of Haldova ever being so cordially invited to invade the North before."

"Let me be clear, Ambassador. We seek an *appearance* of an invasion rather than an actual conflict at our southern borders. I'm convinced we can negotiate concessions and treaties that would reward your monarchy handsomely for the trouble. A war would benefit neither of us, sapping our respective strengths to the delight of enemies within and without."

"But, of course! Let us talk more of these concessions."

Gavron thought the plan to be madness. The North and the Haldovans had invaded each other countless times over the centuries. How could Eridani trust them so? On the other hand, having an army amassed along the border would at least force many of the northern rulers loyal to the patriarch to withdraw their troops. They might possibly even pressure him into negotiating a truce with Kozhad under the guise of uniting against a common enemy.

At least it was going well, so far. The envoy had shown great interest in Eridani's plan. They spent two hours discussing the details. It was then that one of Sana's adjutants entered the hall and whispered urgently into the queen's ear.

Eridani's expression hardened as she listened to the report. "We may have a problem," she told the envoy. "There was a murder committed last night. It appears one of your men is a suspect."

The envoy cocked his head. "I'm deeply sorry if this is the case. My men are disciplined and law-abiding. I trust them, but I shall also endeavor to trust you. Please have your people look into this matter further. If you find a Haldovan guilty of a crime, punish him as per the laws of your land. Surely neither of us would want some misunderstanding to sabotage our treaty."

Eridani issued her instructions to the adjutant and the negotiations resumed.

AFTER THE HALDOVAN delegation retired for a mid-afternoon break, a smaller council was held by Eridani, Gavron, and Sana discussing the matter of the Birch Lodge murder.

"We are holding two men," said Sana. "Either could be guilty, or perhaps both. They're the only ones who attended the party and have fresh scratches and bruises of the sort Genna might have inflicted during the struggle."

"The situation is fraught," said Gavron. "We risk undoing the alliance we've only began to build over this arrest."

"The ambassador has given us leave to punish the guilty," said Eridani.

"Yes, but he didn't know the suspect was his son," said Gavron. "Soon he will return, singing a different tune. Traditionally, diplomatic immunity may be invoked in such cases and we should consider our options carefully—"

"Do you think I care?" Eridani's hand grasped the arm of her throne and she leaned forward, staring at her advisor. "Am I the sort of ruler who'd let rapists and murderers get away with their crimes in the name of political expediency? The guilty will be sentenced to the Traitor's Dive, no matter who they happen to be. Do you understand?"

Sana and Gavron both nodded.

"Gavron, I want you to personally interrogate these men," said Eridani. "Figure out who was responsible. I want a prompt and public execution, lest others come to believe they can get away with such crimes in Kozhad."

THE KOZHAD JAIL was adjacent to the militia barracks; a building that contained a half-dozen cells with reinforced doors and iron bars over the narrow windows placed high near the ceiling. The jail was most often occupied by drunks or brawlers, a brief stay until the unruly individual would cool off and face whatever admonishment the civil judge appointed by Eridani chose to prescribe. It was occasionally a fine, rarely a demotion in rank, and most often simply a strongly-worded warning. All of such minor offenders were cleared from the jail that afternoon. Only a pair of men occupied cells on the opposite ends of the building.

The ambassador's son lay on a bench in his cell. He stretched lazily as he appraised Gavron's bespoke clothes. "Are you here to release me?"

"Young man, you're addressing a minister of Her Majesty. Stand up!"

The boy blanched but did not argue. He slid off the bench and stood in front of Gavron. He must've been eighteen or nineteen, but he looked even younger; his blond curls framed a slightly chubby face, his hands were soft and manicured. Having met the victim, Gavron wondered if someone like this could have overpowered her.

"What's your name?"

"Rene Cragnew of Sefeda, my lord."

"Do you know what you stand accused of, Rene?"

Gavron studied the youngster's expression, but his face betrayed nothing.

"I do, my lord. I'm innocent."

"Were you at the Birch Lodge last night?"

"I was for a time, yes. In fact, I was one of the hosts. We wanted to meet some of our future allies. Come to know them in friendship rather than in battle. We invited dozens of people and any of them could have done this."

Gavron didn't like the Haldovan's smarmy tone and his seeming lack of concern over being arrested. Having spent years tutoring the scions of Skond, he nevertheless recognized Rene's behavior to be fairly typical of a young noble who grew up accustomed to power and wanting for nothing. His attitude was hardly an admission of guilt.

"They found bruises and scratches on you that those other guests do not have. Show me."

Rene nodded, stripped off his shirt and half-turned. There were several freshly-scabbed gashes below his right shoulder blade.

"How do you explain these?"

"As the party was ending, some of my companions and I sought out an establishment which was recommended by our newfound local friends called the Lush Garden. Perhaps you've heard of it?"

When Gavron made no reply, Rene continued. "We were told the girls there would be both pretty and enthusiastic. They were. And they can confirm that I was there, and received these little scratches in ... due course."

"I see." Gavron said. "What was the name of the enthusiastic, pretty companion who scratched you?"

"I never ask their names," said Rene. "Besides," he smiled ruefully, "who said there was only one?"

Gavron frowned. If this man-child was lying, there would have been enough time by now for his friends to drop off a few purses full of coin at the whorehouse. He would send a constable, but he was certain the witnesses there would corroborate the version of events Rene was presenting.

"Please speak to my father. He will vouch for my character, and I'm certain he would find it easier to focus on the particulars of the treaty if his son wasn't incarcerated."

"Your father and Queen Eridani have already spoken. He pledged to accept whatever finding and punishment we deem appropriate."

For the first time, Rene seemed at least somewhat worried. He still hid it well, but Gavron's experience with teenagers was extensive. "Don't you see, my lord? I do not need to force myself on strange women when there are plenty of willing ones at the Lush Garden." He began putting his shirt back on. "I do, however, feel terrible that something so untoward took place at our party. If there are some reparations my family could offer to help resolve this matter, I'm sure that can be arranged."

"I'll keep that in mind," said Gavron through his teeth. "For now, I shall investigate further. And while I do, you'll have to remain here." He opened the door and added over his shoulder, "It's not the accommodations you're accustomed to, but it is said hardship builds character."

THE INHABITANT OF the other cell was a man named Kip. He rose off the bench the moment the door opened and stood at attention. He was lanky and nearly a head taller than Gavron. He was dressed in the trousers and shirt issued by the Kozhad army.

When Kip realized who it was that entered his cell, he bowed deeply. "Your Excellence!"

"Hello, Kip. My aide tells me you're from Gan, and you signed on with us a bit over a year ago?"

"Yes, Minister Gavron. Gan born and raised. Like yourself, your excellence." Kip's regional dialect was as much an answer as his words. He was a Gan commoner, all right. "What they say I did, I didn't do it, Minister. Honestly. I would never! My mum raised me better than that."

"Slow down, Kip. Tell me what happened yesterday."

"The Haldovans stood us free drinks and food; that's an invitation no honest soldier can resist. I ate and I drank too much, and then I left. That's all, I swear!"

"Then how do you explain that?" Gavron pointed at Kip's face.

He didn't have to ask about the scratches this time: they were on the soldier's left cheek, paired with a swollen purple bruise under his eye.

Kip shuffled from foot to foot. "I was mighty drunk. On my way back, I tripped over a rock and fell face first into some bushes."

"Was there anyone with you who saw you fall?"

"I was by myself, but I swear that is what happened. I never touched that lady, I swear by my oath to Eridani and by Kalatar's spirit."

Gavron sighed. Kip was one of the fanatics, useful idiots who filled voids in their own lives with the worship of Kalatar and, by association, Eridani. But did his fervor and loyalty make him any less likely to be guilty of this crime? Or did the Haldovan's pompous self-assurance mark him as a rapist? Further interviews might uncover a witness who saw Kip leave the Birch Lodge with his face intact—a fact the soldier was not clever enough to suggest on his own—but could such testimony be really trusted? Someone might choose to lie because the unlikable Rene made for a better villain in their mind. And then the treaty, Gavron's own comfort and station, his life, and everything Eridani had worked toward would be in grave jeopardy.

"No witnesses, alone at the party, and the only suspect strong enough to overpower poor Genna. Facts do not add up in your favor, Kip. They do not add up at all."

Kip's lip trembled. He stared at the minister pleadingly.

"I believe you," said Gavron. "But I have no proof with which to argue your case. The queen wants someone to take the Traitor's Dive tomorrow." He watched a range of emotions on Kip's face— relief and hope quickly displaced by despair as he spoke. "Do you know what a Traitor's Dive is?"

"No," Kip half-whispered, half-squeaked.

"In the far north it is considered the harshest of punishments, reserved for the worst of crimes," said Gavron. "Treason, parricide, rape." He paused to let that sink in. "They tie your hands and feet and place you naked in a large burlap sack along with several heavy stones, a dog, and a viper. Then they sew the sack shut and throw it in the river."

Kip stared at him in horror, his eyes large as saucers.

"As the sack fills with water, the terrified animals begin to bite your unprotected flesh, rending and tearing at you until all three of you drown together."

The tall soldier was on the verge of a breakdown. "I'm innocent, Your Excellence! Please, you can't let them drown me like an unwanted litter of kittens!"

"As I said, I believe you, but my options are limited," said Gavron. "When I leave here, I will forget to lock the door to your cell. Wait for one hundred breaths—can you count? Good—then run and do not stop until you are beyond Kozhad's walls. Do not return until and unless the real killer has been found." He dismissed the soldier's gratitude.

"But ... If I am to leave and be branded a murderer, how will I serve the will of Eridani the Fierce?" Kip lowered his voice. "I heard it said she spends three hours every day communing with the spirit of Kalatar, who instructs her in the ways of warfare."

Gavron smiled. Eridani's secretive sessions each morning had become the stuff of legend; this suited their plans fine. "Trust me. You will serve your queen in this manner far better than you would sewn up in a burlap sack."

After he left the cell, Gavron motioned for the two guards stationed outside the door to follow him. "Clear the building and post the guards outside, archers on the roof," he said.

"Minister?" The lieutenant in charge of the guards raised an eyebrow at the unorthodox request.

"A test of loyalty," said Gavron. "If either prisoner tries to leave the building, it will be an admission of guilt."

"Ah!" The lieutenant's face brightened. "That is a clever way to identify the murderer. We shall recapture whoever runs, to be sure."

"Listen well," said Gavron, "here's what I want your people to do ..."

"YOU DON'T LOOK well rested, tutor." Caer set up the pieces for their weekly bato game.

"You're right, Sellsword. I didn't sleep much last night. I had to make a difficult decision for the sake of us all." Gavron wasn't planning on sharing what he had done with anyone, but he had learned to trust Caer's discretion and expected many more sleepless nights in his future if he didn't find a way to unburden. He began telling the story, his observations of the two prisoners, and ultimately his decision. Halfway through the telling he began having second thoughts about revealing so much, and for what—his acquaintance's understanding? Absolution?

"They cut him down as soon as he stepped outside the jail," Gavron finished. "The poor bastard never stood a chance."

The two men sat in silence across the bato board.

"He may have been guilty," Caer finally said.

"Or, I may have sent an innocent man to slaughter and spared a murderer. I fear I shall never know the truth. What I do know is that the treaty with Haldova must succeed at any cost. If our plan does not bear fruit, thousands will die. And if that means sacrificing the loyal dog so that the viper may live another day to be unleashed upon our enemies, that is what I must do."

The Ugly Unicorn leaned back from the board. "When you command men in battle, a time invariably comes when you must knowingly send them to their deaths. Being a minister is no different." He fiddled with the game pieces. "This Kip sounds like he was a good soldier. Had he known your plan, he may have volunteered for the slaughter."

Gavron felt relieved at the Unicorn's somewhat clumsy attempt to console him. He didn't want to admit it to himself, but he secretly feared that the aging mercenary would call him a coward and a villain. It was how Gavron himself felt, tossing and turning in those sleepless hours during the night.

"Eridani must never know," Gavron said. "As far as she's concerned, the murderer was executed when he tried to flee. I wish to spare her the moral ambiguity of my choices."

They were silent for a time again.

"I wonder which it is you fear more," said Caer, "Eridani's reprimand if she finds out the truth, or the possibility that she might approve of your actions."

Caer resumed setting up the blue and yellow beads, the game pieces, many of which would be destroyed or sacrificed in gambits and machinations as the two men matched wits.

They never spoke of Kip again.

CHAPTER 15

THREE HOURS
A DAY

ix months after the Haldovan delegation left Kozhad, reports of troop movements at the southern border began trickling into Skond. The council had dispatched dozens of spies, and the information they returned was troubling. By all accounts, Prince Ajelogn was assembling an invasion force.

The de facto leader of the Haldova Plains located to the immediate south of the territories overseen by the council, Prince Ajelogn commanded the loyalty of dozens of monarchs. His grip on the vast territory at the heart of the Heart was far firmer than the patriarch's own control over the north. His aging father had wrested control over the Plains in a series of bloody conflicts that went on for decades. Many a mercenary from the north had lined their pockets with dragon scales from those wars. But enough time had passed and the Haldovan war machine was rebuilt. The son was ready to continue the grand works of his father.

Prince Ajelogn acted with subtlety. He transplanted blacksmiths and builders and herds of pigs, farmers to plant and harvest the fields, and workers to build barracks and wagons. He carefully laid groundwork for supplying an army along the border long before a single company of soldiers was moved into place there. The workers toiled in the winter and the farmers planted in the spring. By late spring tens of thousands of men were assembled near the border and more were arriving each day. By early summer, the reports from the spies alerted the Council of the North to the prince's movements. The spies reported vast warehouses being built, wide roads paved, and other expensive works undertaken that suggested the size of the Haldovan army would be the largest the region had seen, even greater perhaps than the number of men Kalatar commanded in his prime.

135

Envoys were dispatched to the court of Prince Ajelogn. He welcomed the envoys, plied them with the best food and wine, and assured them that he would not dream of attacking his friends in the north. Then he sent them back with lavish gifts of art and spices for the patriarch. On their return journey they caught glimpses of miles-long caravans of supplies moving northward.

The envoys delivered the bad news to the patriarch. They couldn't have known that the caravans they encountered were mostly packed with empty crates, and that barracks being built in many towns near the border were to house military units that didn't exist. As far as the spies and the envoys could tell, war was coming.

The patriarch ordered the envoys not to share what they had learned with the nobles, but several of them were bound by stronger oaths or could be bought; the word quickly spread among the North's elite.

By mid-summer several envoys from across the North arrived in Kozhad and secret negotiations were held. Each noble wanted to know: would the queen with the second-largest army in the North stand with them against the southern invaders? Eridani personally met with the envoys and made assurances. She proposed trade pacts and strengthened alliances that were outside the purview of Skond. The deals she struck made the North stronger, but the patriarch weaker. Even if the patriarch knew of these backroom agreements, it was poor timing for him to confront the renegade members of the council—not with the war looming. He had to open the coffers of Skond and pay for ever more troops, increasing the northern presence at the borders while still maintaining a standing army against Kozhad and its queen.

Free of such constraints, Eridani pledged a small number of her soldiers to patrol roads and rout bandits across the north while the local nobles' own men were sent south to strengthen the border troops. The banners and uniforms of Kozhad became a welcome sight across the land. The common folk knew those soldiers to be disciplined. They would not loot, would not misbehave. Eridani's name was on the lips of the commoners, and every day more of them wished for her to enter Skond as a conqueror rather than a prisoner.

In August, Pel arrived in Kozhad, contrite and respectful, begging on behalf of his mistress, Lady Voriana, for Eridani to forgive her rash actions earlier. The lady had been wise to send Pel. Although the queen held no love for traitors, she also remembered that it was Pel's warning that saved her life.

Eridani didn't make it easy for her betrayer, extracting promises and concessions that were far less generous than her treaties with other leaders. But she was secretly pleased. She knew that if the Dowager Councilor, the most astute politician in the north save perhaps the patriarch himself, was prepared to treat with her again, her fortunes had truly turned.

Pel's presence in Kozhad may have begun as that of a supplicant for a former enemy, but their negotiating sessions soon grew longer than they needed to be. Eridani was surprised at the strange bond she felt toward him, a bond that originated from their brief exchange that night back at Woodcastle. She felt she could talk to him, be open with him, let down her guard in ways she couldn't even with Sana or Toval. Before long, Pel and Eridani were spending quite a bit of time together, outside of the throne room. And although they tried to be discreet about their budding relationship, she could see by the approval in Sana's eyes, discomfort on Gavron's face, and jealousy in Toval's body language that her closest friends and advisors understood the changing dynamic of the relationship between the queen and the envoy.

When Pel returned to Skond, he carried a letter with an official seal of Kozhad, informing the council that Queen Eridani would arrive forthwith to take her place on the council and discuss the plans for repelling or forestalling the impending invasion.

Between the increasingly panicked citizenry and the will of those on the council he did not yet control, the patriarch had no choice but to welcome her.

Like a complex game of bato, the match between Eridani and the patriarch was coming to a climax. The pieces were carefully and patiently placed in a manner that would not reveal her strategy until it was too late.

EVERY NORTHERNER HAD different expectations as to how Eridani might return to Skond. Most thought her decapitated head on a spike would be paraded through the streets as warning to anyone who might challenge the patriarch's consolidated power. A smaller group argued that she would be captured alive and brought to Skond to stand trial. In either case, it was thought that Kalatar's sword would find its way into the patriarch's palace to be displayed prominently among the many other treasures and relics. A much smaller group believed that Eridani would somehow prevail, that her catapults would demolish the walls of Skond and that she would ride triumphant through the burning streets as her mercenaries pillaged the homes and shops of the North's greatest city.

They were all wrong.

Eridani arrived with a retinue of only one hundred guards and advisors, and the gates of the city were opened for her. Crowds gawked, and the patriarch's elite red-and-silver clad guards watched in reluctant inaction as her delegation rode through the streets toward the palace.

The patriarch's palace was enormous. It reminded Eridani of Lady Voriana's estate, except larger and less tastefully decorated. Servants collected their horses and gear with practiced efficiency, then ushered them inside. The imposing archway led directly into the grand hall, a chamber where walls were lined with marble and columns reached twenty paces high to the ceiling decorated with a fresco depicting a map of the city.

She recalled the one time she visited the grand hall before, when she first visited Skond with her parents as a child. Her father had told her that the ceiling used to depict a map of the North, but the patriarch ordered it redone. He wanted the visitors to understand the importance of Skond, to accept its dominance over the affairs of the North's many kingdoms.

Her parents often spoke of how the patriarch had become too powerful, how in years past the council would have been able to check him; to chastise him and prevent the desecration of a two-hundred-year-old fresco by a well-known artist. She recalled those conversations vividly, all these years later. Over the course of her life, the patriarch had been a malevolent force, a spider in the center of the web of deceit and betrayal which had destroyed her family. She had grown to hate him, of course, but she knew him only as an idea, an abstraction. To face the man, to look him in the eye, was an entirely different exercise in hate.

The Kozhad delegation shed its members as it progressed deeper into the palace. Most stayed behind in the grand hall. Others remained behind the checkpoint where palace guards closed ranks against anyone wearing a weapon. They didn't dare ask Eridani to surrender the sword of Kalatar. And as she advanced through endless rooms and chambers and corridors, everywhere people stole glances at her and at the Bloodsword she wore at her hip.

Eridani wasn't comfortable with the progression of events. It was as though she was losing power, losing influence while the patriarch was gaining it as she ventured deeper into his home. But it was only a standard security procedure and not an elaborate death trap. They needed her too much. She set everything up for this moment, spent several years preparing for this confrontation, and now that it was happening, fear gripped her soul with an icy gauntlet. It was too late to change the plan, too late to retreat.

The only viable path was to push forward, and to win.

By the time they reached the gilded doors of the council chamber it was only Eridani, Toval, and Sana. She nodded to the two people she trusted most in the world—her two closest confidants who had joined her after her encounter with the sorceress of Skond, thus possibly unaffected by the accursed prophecy. Then the heavy doors opened and she stepped forward into the chamber alone.

Twenty-three pairs of eyes stared at her as she entered the room. The North's most powerful men and women sat along the sides of a long rectangular table. It was rare for all those entitled to a seat on the council to be in attendance. Only a dozen or so members were generally present for any given meeting, but this time every single seat save her own was occupied. Kings and dukes, those born to power and those who claimed it by the strength of their blades, lifelong friends and deadly foes, all bound to rule together by tradition and treaty. They were like the bato pieces on a board, interconnected by an invisible web of ever-shifting alliances.

Eridani had learned the skill of slowly and deliberately setting up her bato plays from Gavron, and the value of making aggressive, daring moves from Caer. Her current stratagem combined the elements of both. Years in the making, all her beads were committed to the board and the outcome of the endgame came down to a single power play.

At the head of the table, under the red-and-silver banner of Skond, sat the patriarch himself. He was a clean-shaven, middle-aged man of slight built and medium height. The sort of person one was unlikely to notice in a crowd, a mousy bureaucrat with ink-stained fingers and a weak chin. He stared at her impassively as did everyone else, his face betraying nothing. And although his appearance seemed non-threatening, Eridani could sense his murderous resolve. The same resolve she had learned to recognize in herself ever since Danchu's death.

Eridani marched toward the sole empty chair and took a seat. She leaned back and looked around the table, refusing to break the silence first, even as the rest of the council stared at her expectedly.

As the silence grew uncomfortable, Lady Voriana spoke.

"Eridani of Kozhad, it is good to see you again."

The two women locked eyes across the table. Despite whatever arrangements Pel and the other envoys had worked out, Eridani hadn't forgiven the Dowager Councilor's betrayal, but she was willing to spare her if it meant accomplishing greater goals. As for the Councilor, she was too jaded and politically savvy to let a little thing like a past betrayal get in the way of forging a new alliance.

"You look ... different," said Lady Voriana. "Wielding power seems to agree with you." There was mirth in the old woman's voice, but it didn't extend to her eyes.

Eridani offered nothing but a barely perceivable nod in return and the chamber felt silent again.

"Enough small talk." The patriarch spoke, his voice surprisingly deep for his middling frame. "Queen Eridani"—he managed to pour just the right around of sarcasm into his words—"you've been neglecting your ancestral council seat. Now that you've deigned to attend, have you come to pledge your troops to defense of the North against the Haldovan aggressors?"

Eridani rose from her seat, all those present waiting to see what she'd do. She addressed the council at large, pointedly ignoring the patriarch. "I'm not here to pledge my army to the lowborn usurper who sits at the head of this table."

Everyone spoke at once, or tried to. Eridani raised her voice and plowed on, forcing others to listen. "He consolidates power by dividing you, turning you against one another, sapping your strength and bleeding your lands of wealth. The web of politics he spins is choking all of the North. His machinations are ultimately responsible for emboldening our enemies and creating a threat that looms over us all." She turned to the patriarch for the first time and looked him in the eye. "I'm here to rid us of his poisonous presence and to unite the North."

The patriarch regarded her with the sort of disdain a man might feel toward a puppy who chewed up his favorite pair of shoes. "You wish to rid the council of its leader, do you? And replace me with what, a petulant girl who stumbled upon a relic and decided it made her special?"

Eridani patted her scabbard. "It isn't the sword that makes me special. Five years ago, I was forced to flee this city because the spider at the center of its web coveted this council seat. He wanted it badly enough to murder my family, encourage a traitorous vassal to take over a sovereign city, and put a bounty on the heads of the last remaining scions of Kozhad." She paused and looked around the table. "He did all that not to strengthen the North, but merely to gain more influence. He has done similar things before as he clawed his way to power, and he would not hesitate to do it to any of you in the future.

"But I digress. Five years ago, I was powerless and destitute. Today, I sit on my ancestral throne and control the second-largest standing army in the North. *That* is what makes me special."

Eridani projected her voice as she spoke. Several times the patriarch tried to cut her off, but she would not yield, would not allow her foe to interrupt.

"Many of you have heard that I spend three hours of each day training. I have done so every day for over four years, preparing for this moment. There were abundant rumors: was I learning warcraft or sorcery, the stealthy art of assassins or the alchemy of poisoners?"

All those present were familiar with such rumors. Even the patriarch temporarily ceased his attempts to silence her. They hung on her every word.

"I studied for years, but it wasn't to learn new ways to kill the enemy standing in front of me. The world does not lack men and women willing to kill. Instead, I learned how to rule."

The room buzzed with reactions, councilors turning to each other incredulously. Eridani pushed on. "I studied accounting and philosophy and law. I read everything Orodos and other thinkers had to say about the art of wielding power. And, most importantly, I studied history because virtually every predicament we might find ourselves in today has played itself out, time and again, in annals of history, somewhere within the Heart."

She pointed at the patriarch. "There is a reason an insignificant bureaucrat like him rose to power. Those of noble birth take their power for granted. They rule as best they can, relying on advisors and on their own wit. But a learned ruler can achieve so much more!

"The Spider is right. The North must unite if it is to survive and prosper, and it can do so only with a practiced hand steering its reins. You can rely on a lowborn upstart who has shown his willingness to betray and kill any of you for his own gain, or you can invest your trust in me."

This gamble could not have worked were her words not true. Everyone on the council either feared the patriarch, mistrusted him, or outright hated him. He was like bitter medicine: unpleasant but necessary in troubled times. There was too much history, too many animosities among the councilors for any one of them to rise as the possible new patriarch, and the Spider knew this well, played the others against each other to ensure no significant faction could rise to oppose him. The new queen with her own base of power, not beholden to anyone, nor weighed down by the legacy of having to choose sides in many of the past schemes or negotiations, presented a way out.

Eridani watched as they tried to get the measure of her, struggled to see past the façade she presented, but she knew them all; every name, every tract of their land, their every river and forest, every dark secret that could be uncovered with a handful of well-placed dragon scales.

"For over a century, the families of Clive and Bask feuded over disputed farmland. Pride and tradition would not allow either clan to back down, and so countless treasure and lives were expended over a patch of dirt neither family truly needed. Land where neither clan could plant seeds for fear of their opponents burning the fields and murdering the peasants.

"I brokered a truce by having Lady Voriana, who is rich in treasure but not in territory, lease the land long-term and pay both clans equally for the privilege. Now their coffers are fuller and they can both save face as well as resume trade and travel between their neighboring realms."

Clive and Bask, scions of warring families, smiled at each other and nodded to confirm Eridani's words.

"Duchess Costa, accept my leadership and I will help you hire the clever engineers from the far east who use networks of small canals to irrigate parched lands like yours.

"Baron Halish, pledge your loyalty to me and I will underwrite a loan on far more reasonable terms than the usurious rates the Skond banks are charging you now.

"King Pallas, join the fray and I'll ensure the crippling tariffs Skond charges your merchants to import cattle are considerably reduced.

"Follow me, lords and ladies of the North, and we shall all prosper together!"

The patriarch was on his feet. "How dare you question my love and commitment to the North! It's easy to show up and seem benevolent by offering handouts and tax reductions, but those funds are paying for the paving of roads and the repair of dams, and the army that is protecting all of us from the Haldovan battalions at the border.

"You are the worst kind of populist, spouting platitudes and telling everyone what they want to hear while you have no viable long-term plan to fund the largesse you're promising.

"My title isn't a meaningless word. I'm the father figure, stern but fair. I make difficult decisions that are meant to benefit us all, even if each of us must pay taxes and tariffs, pledge men and land to the cause. I've done a competent job at it for decades, and you think you can do better because you've read some books?"

"Yes," Eridani said. "I know I can. I learned many useful things from those books. For example, I learned there are two ways to depose the sitting leader of the council. I hereby call for the Opprobrium Rite."

The chamber erupted in chaos, some cheering, some booing, a few looking confused as to what Eridani had proposed.

"That is an antiquated notion. The Opprobrium Rite hasn't been invoked for over a century," said the patriarch.

"It may be an old law, but it's a law of the council nevertheless," said Eridani. "Only a councilor of Old Blood may invoke it, which is part of the reason you wanted to eradicate my family's seat, isn't it? Not many among the original families who formed the council still exist." She addressed the others. "It takes two-thirds of the council to vote the Spider out of power. Side with me, and he will leave this room in chains. He will never be able to retaliate against you for casting your vote."

"Be sensible," the patriarch addressed the room. "We aren't going to let her walk in here and upend the power structure of the council. That way lies anarchy and madness, an inner discord that will benefit no one but the Haldovans. I say we send this upstart child back to her insignificant keep. The council must stand united against threats internal and external alike."

"The Opprobrium Rite has been called," said the Dowager Councilor. "Our votes shall decide which one of you is to be sent away."

"I veto this madness," said the patriarch.

"There is a second way to recall the leader of the council," said Eridani, as she drew her sword two inches from its scabbard. "An even more ancient rite. Do you wish to engage in one-on-one combat, right here and now?"

The patriarch blanched visibly. He quickly regained control and stood with his shoulders square, but his initial reaction did not escape those seated around the long table. "That is barbaric and ludicrous," he said. "I will not condone—"

"Opprobrium!" Eridani roared, cutting him off. She picked up the intricately carved cedar goblet that was placed on the table in front of her, turned it upside down, and slammed its lip against the tabletop.

Her vote was cast. This was the crucial moment. Between the councilors she courted in advance and those loyal to the Dowager Councilor's faction, she had ten votes, but she would need sixteen for this to work. According to the Rite, the leader being deposed did not get to cast a vote. As per Lady Voriana's advice, the others would need to act quickly, to show momentum in Eridani's favor and sway undecided councilors who might be hesitant to cast their votes for her in fear of retaliation from the Spider.

For two excruciatingly long seconds the chamber was still. *Has the Dowager Councilor betrayed me again?* Eridani wondered. *Everyone you know and trust will come to betray you.* The prophecy that haunted her dreams came unbidden into her mind. She didn't trust anyone in this room, but she did place her faith in people voting their own interest. The bato pieces were on the board and the endgame had commenced.

King Pallas, another of the few remaining Old Blood councilors grunted as he leaned forward and picked up his goblet. "Opprobrium," he announced, his deep voice reverberating through the room. He, too, turned the cup upside down.

Pallas's move seemed to break the spell of indecision. A chorus of voices joined in the call for opprobrium. Cups slammed against the table. Soon there were thirteen cups upturned, while the remaining eleven stood upright.

Eridani's heart skipped, but she saw indecision in the faces of many of the holdouts. It wasn't over yet.

A hint of a smirk returned to the patriarch's face. "You don't have the votes," he said.

"They have two hundred heartbeats to decide," Lady Voriana reminded him.

"Fine." The patriarch shot her a venomous glance. "I will not forget those steadfast in their loyalty." He stared pointedly at King Pallas. "Nor those who opted to betray me."

"You see how the Spider attempts to rule by fear?" said Pallas. "However you vote, you're only safe as long as you fall in line. Perhaps not even then."

King Uran, also of the Old Blood, who sat at the right hand of the patriarch and was often considered his staunchest supporter rose from his seat.

"We cannot be divided today," he said. "My lands are farthest south among us. The armies of Haldova are poised on my doorstep. I stand to lose the most if they sense our weakness and cross the border.

"We all know the patriarch. He speaks the truth. Those of you who vote against him will be punished, in due course. He will scheme and maneuver until you're replaced on the council by those loyal to him."

The councilors listened well. King Uran was a respected elder, most likely next to become patriarch should he outlive the Spider. If anyone could keep the wavering councilors in line, it was him.

"Now is not the time for internal squabbles. We can't afford to focus on vengeance and posturing. We must stand together, and it is clear to me that the mayor of Skond has lost the ability to unite us." He placed his goblet upside down and slid it toward the shocked Spider. "Opprobrium."

This broke the stalemate; five of King Uran's friends and loyalists joined him in the opprobrium vote, one after another. The patriarch looked pale and clammy despite the cool air in the council chamber.

"It is decided," said Lady Voriana. "The Spider is hereby banished from the Council of the North."

Two of the younger men from among her faction rose from their seats and grabbed the patriarch, twisting his arms behind his back.

"Do not let him escape," Lady Voriana said. "I would not put it past him to defy our will and try to rally the guards."

"My men will take him to the dungeon and ensure he's guarded by those loyal to the council and not to Skond," said King Uran. He turned to the Spider. "I'm sorry, old friend. You're not the leader we need in time of war."

"You're all mad," the ex-patriarch shouted as he strained against the men dragging him out of the room, "to place your lives and fortunes in the hands of an inexperienced girl. You will all rue your choice before long. Traitors!"

The heavy wooden doors slammed behind him, muffling the Spider's curses.

Lady Voriana picked up her goblet and raised it toward Eridani. "All hail the matriarch!" A chorus of other voices joined her.

Eridani made her way to the big chair placed at the head of the table. She raised her hand to silence the cheering.

"Please," she said, "I prefer Queen Eridani. The title of matriarch—or patriarch—is soaked in too much blood for my liking."

Baron Halish from the far north said, "There is an ancient title among the free tribes who roam the frozen lands under the aurora. They used to call their overall leader 'king father' long before the title of 'patriarch' came to prominence. We've resurrected one ancient rite today. Perhaps let this be another?"

Eridani lowered herself onto the most powerful seat in the North. "Queen mother. I like the sound of that." She thought there was no practical difference between that and the matriarch, but the change to the title was a statement unto itself, and the word "queen" was so much stronger in conveying who was in charge.

Twenty-three pairs of eyes watched her as she eased back in the chair and allowed herself a few seconds to enjoy her victory.

"Ladies and lords of the council," she said. "We have much work to do."

AFTER THE MEETING had run its course, the councilors left the chamber in small groups, to discuss the events over food and drink, to negotiate new alliances and test existing ones, to issue orders that would earn them a profit before the news spread, and to send written instructions to their realms. None stayed behind to try and win favor from the newly minted queen mother.

She was their figurehead, but she was not their leader. They saw her only as a tool to further their own ambitions. For now. She would assert power; prove to them her worth over time. But not today. She had had enough for today. The entire ordeal had lasted three hours—almost exactly as long as she spent daily preparing for this moment, learning to be a ruler rather than merely a royal. But these three hours felt longer than her overnight ordeal in the company of the monstrous bat. She was bone-weary and wanted a soft bed more than she desired any throne.

She took one last look around the empty chamber, most of the goblets still overturned on the wooden table in silent salute to her victory. Then she stepped outside.

Lady Voriana was waiting in the corridor, wearing her grandmotherly smile. Eridani hardly believed she had once been young enough to even consider the meaning of that smile to be kindness.

"Don't get comfortable, child," the Lady cautioned. "For most on the council, the Opprobrium Rite wasn't about handing you power. Theirs wasn't a vote for you but rather a vote against the Spider. You were quite clever in presenting yourself as a viable alternative to him. But now that he's gone, there will be any number of them wondering if the seat at the head of the table is a better fit for their posterior than it is for yours."

Eridani listened to the older woman impassively. "Don't patronize me," she said, leaning in close. "You've said nothing I don't already know. And don't presume that your treason is so easily forgotten."

The Dowager Councilor shifted from foot to foot uncomfortably at the intensity of Eridani's words. "Come now," she said. "Don't dwell on the past. Have I not redeemed myself by helping you today? Am I not providing men to patrol the streets and money to ply the citizenry with diversions and beer as we go about the business of replacing their beloved leader, even as we speak? What more can I do to prove my allegiance?"

"Absolution does not come easily for me." Eridani leaned against the wall, feeling as though the palace itself was weighing her down. "Neither does trust."

"If you're to rule the North, you will have to delegate, and you will have to trust," said Lady Voriana. "The task is much too big for anyone to tackle alone, even for a remarkable young woman like you."

"You're patronizing again," Eridani said, but her voice had lost some of its severity. Now that the danger had passed, she felt utterly drained. "I shall endeavor to forgive you, even if I may never come to fully trust you again, if you dispense with the verbal acrobatics and speak the truth plainly to me from now on."

Lady Voriana smiled. "Speaking plainly comes no easier to me than forgiveness does to you. Still, I will make an effort."

Eridani nodded. "There's one more thing I want from you."

The Dowager Councilor arched her eyebrow.

"Pel. I'd like to appoint him Captain of the Guard," said Eridani

"You wish to steal away my most capable and valued officer?"

"Absolution can't be painless."

Lady Voriana sighed. "So be it. He's yours."

PART 3

(Year 538 of the Council Era)

CHAPTER 16

ḢAPPILY EVER AFTER

el yawned and stretched. His palms touched the headboard. "I have terrible news to report, Your Majesty."

Eridani rubbed her eyes and wrapped the warm, soft linen sheets tighter around her. After years of training, years of waiting for the enemy troops to lay siege to Kozhad at any moment, it felt almost surreal not to have the imminent threat of death looming over her. "What news is that?"

Pel turned on his side, facing her. "It's almost dawn and we must leave the comfort of this bed for an unpleasantly long stretch of many hours."

Eridani ran her hand through Pel's hair. "I shall forgive the messenger for delivering such terrible news, this once. But only if he gets himself dressed and ready. We have a lot of work waiting for us this morning."

"Work, work, work." Pel stretched again, then leaned over and reached for the table next to the bed that contained a bowl of fruit, two cups, and a nearly empty bottle of wine from the previous night. He picked out an apple from the bowl. "Who knew happily ever after would be so boring?"

"What do you mean by that?" Eridani pointed toward the bowl and Pel passed her another apple.

"You've avenged your family and are now queen. Your enemies have fallen. And you have me." He beamed. "If that isn't a fairy-tale ending, I don't know what is."

Eridani bit into her apple. She could see Pel's point: everyone had seemingly gotten what they wanted. Gavron had become a minister in the court of Skond, the position he'd dreamed of since the day he arrived in the city. She'd appointed Caer the interim mayor. The old mercenary was

151

befuddled by the honor but rose to the responsibility and the challenge like he always had.

"A lowborn bedding a queen. That sure sounds like a fairy-tale ending for *you*. But that's not what I was asking. I meant, which part of being my consort do you find boring?"

"Ha!" Pel pulled himself up and swung his feet off the side of the bed. "I have no complaints there. But the endless meetings, audiences, and politicking, I don't know how one doesn't run screaming from the throne room after an hour, let alone a full day's worth."

"This is where you and I differ, soldier boy. These meetings, the process of exercising power, of bringing all of the North under my control step by step so I can shape its future according to my vision—nothing could be more exciting to me." The past month had been a whirlwind of activity. Eridani had little time for self-reflection, but as she spoke the words she knew them to be true: "When I solidify control of the North, I will finally have everything I want. It'll be the happily ever after you speak of."

"Everything you ever wanted? That'll make finding suitable gifts for you quite a chore."

Eridani laughed. "Now that you mention it, I could use a nice crown. The Duke of Buzzards might have melted down the ancestral crown of Kozhad. At least, we never found it in his treasury. I should commission a silversmith to design a replica when I find the time."

"Let me take care of this for you," said Pel. "My past employer was partial to trinkets and I happen to know some of the best jewelers in town. It shouldn't be difficult to find someone from Kozhad with the talent to draw a sketch of the crown you lost, and it'll be a lot more fun than watching you meet with the representatives from Shallowpond."

"You have my leave," said Eridani, as she set down the half-eaten apple. "It's time for us to get up. I mustn't keep the esteemed nobles from the backwater corner of nowhere waiting."

ERIDANI SAT ON the throne in the grand hall and read from a thick tome containing some of the more obscure treatises by Orodos. The delegation from Shallowpond was late and she was feeling annoyed. Despite finally finding a sliver of time to read the rare volume—the palace library contained innumerable treasures—she was concerned that the image of her having to wait for *anyone* sent the wrong message. Shallowpond was many days journey from Skond and the road presented any number of challenges, but one simply didn't keep their queen mother waiting.

She beckoned for Sana to approach the throne. "Anything?"

"The delegation from Shallowpond never arrived in the city. I'm afraid we won't know more until further news comes from outside our walls."

Eridani sighed. "Perhaps we should make them wait a few days to see me when the tardy envoys finally show up."

"You do have an unanticipated visitor who could fill in the time you allotted for the envoys," said Sana. "The Sorceress of Skond is at the palace gates, asking for an audience."

"Her." Eridani thought back to the shadow-filled underground hall in the witch's home. "Come to collect on the promise I made to her years ago." The sorceress's prophecy was fulfilled, at least with some of the people Eridani knew and trusted. It could yet come true with others despite the queen's best efforts. Eridani thought her foolish to ask for a favor to be named later, but the sorceress's long-term investment seemed to be paying off. The queen mother was in a better position to grant an exorbitant wish than an orphan hunted by palace guards. But what favor could she possibly want? "I should see her in private."

Gavron, who stood near enough to the throne to hear them, leaned in. "Perhaps you should receive her here. It is unheard of for the Sorceress of Skond to come calling. Princes and kings and the patriarch himself must come to her when they need her magic. Let the people witness her bowing to you in the grand hall."

"I see the wisdom in that." Eridani leaned back on the throne. "Send her in."

OSHEKZHOTHEP THE SEER strode across the grand hall in an elegant white gown, its fur-trimmed hems sweeping the polished stones. The nobles, clerks, and other visitors of high enough stature to be admitted to the hall whispered to each other excitedly. Many of them had never met the seer, or would claim to never have, yet all seemed to know her on sight. She stopped before Eridani's throne and bowed slightly, black onyx beads jingling softly in her elaborate necklace.

"Queen Mother."

"Sorceress," Eridani replied, with cold politeness.

"The last time we met, we struck a bargain," said the sorceress, without preamble. "I'm pleased to see that the Invisible God has granted you fortune and has raised you to this high position, so that you can fulfill my request."

"Fortune, nothing," Eridani said. "It was hard work and wise planning that got me where I am today."

"Perhaps." The seer's lips stretched into a semblance of a smile. "Perhaps."

Eridani glowered. "Ask your price, sorceress, but do not forget: your aid was for naught. My brother perished at the hands of our enemies."

"I grieve your loss. And yet, the elixir worked as promised. Did it not?"

Eridani nodded reluctantly. She had grown used to dominating the conversation through either intelligence or status. But she didn't feel in control when talking to this old witch.

"Then I have delivered on my end of the bargain and will expect the same of you, Queen Mother."

There was something to the way she spoke that title. A hint of mockery subtle enough to make Eridani doubt whether it was intended or whether she had imagined it.

"What is it you want?" she asked, irritation barely masked in her voice.

"Pel Ashen, the Captain of the Guard."

Eridani's eyes narrowed. Could the crone possibly know of their relationship? She thought they had managed to keep it private thus far.

"And what exactly do you want with him?"

The sorceress's back straightened and her voice deepened as she stared Eridani directly in the eye. "I want his dead body delivered to my home tomorrow morning."

Anger swelled within Eridani's chest. She gripped the throne's handles forcing her expression to remain calm. Fearing that her voice might betray her emotions, she merely asked, "Why?"

The seer stared past Eridani as though she was watching something in an empty corner of the hall. "The future is a mighty river filling an empty basin, its path driven by events and decisions like the flow of water is driven by its tributaries. The path is what makes the future easy to see and predict; once a mass of water gains sufficient momentum it does not stray from its course easily. Even so, there are elements that can occasionally alter the path. The smallest of pebbles can start an avalanche that will block the roaring tide and send it off in an unpredictable direction." She refocused on Eridani. "Pel is such a pebble. A small, sharp stone, insignificant overall, but bothersome enough to stop and clear out of one's shoe."

As the crone delivered her rambling speech, Eridani regained control of her senses. She half-rose from her throne. "How dare you assume that I would murder a loyal subject on your whim?"

Oshekzhothep pointed toward the length of the room where courtiers listened intently to the exchange. "Will you deny me and prove yourself an oath breaker in front of your subjects?"

"Better an oath breaker than a tyrant," said Eridani. She thought fast. "Our agreement was for me to grant you a favor that was within my power. I don't consider executing the innocent to be lawful. Therefore it's not within my power at all."

The crone grinned, displaying white teeth that were unnaturally perfect for her age. "You have the power. You must only choose to wield it." She took several steps toward the queen, causing Eridani's bodyguards to tense up, but stopped short of reaching the throne. "I see darkness and death closing in," she said. "Sooner than you can imagine, you will be desperate for allies and you will need my help again. Do not make the mistake of denying me, *Queen Mother.*" The mockery in her voice was less subtle this time.

Eridani rose to her feet. She was furious at herself for feeling intimidated by the old woman. Yet, after the pain and grief the previous prophecy had caused her, she was finding it difficult to dismiss the seer's words out of hand. Still, there was no way she would murder her lover—murder anyone, over some gloomy words delivered in a stage whisper. "Get out," she said. "Leave now or my guards will cut you down."

"I shall expect Pel Ashen's body delivered to my home no later than by midday tomorrow," said the seer.

She turned and walked away without waiting for a response.

As she watched her go, Eridani clasped the high back of her throne and squeezed until her knuckles turned white. She felt angry, not only at the crone's mad request but at her own inability to shake the weight of her new prophecy. The original—*everyone you know and trust will come to betray you*—still haunted her. It was why she limited Gavron's and Caer's responsibility and power in favor of newer allies. She hoped that the prophecy did not extend to friends and followers who joined her after the seer uttered the unclean words.

She retired from the hall and into a tiny secret garden in the middle of the palace. It was walled off on all sides, with not even a window facing it, and was accessible via a single door. She found that she could think best when she sat by its small artificial pond and watched the multi-colored carp imported from the south swim in the clear water.

She was only beginning to calm down when Sana pushed open the door, her expression somber. "You must come right away," she said. "The Haldovans have invaded."

SHE AND SANA joined Caer, Gavron, and Toval in the council chamber.

"Here's what we know," Caer said, as soon as the two women took their seats. "The Haldovan troops have crossed the border en masse. But first, Prince Ajelogn sent copies of a damning letter to every noble in the North, timed to arrive ahead of the foreign troops."

"A letter?" Eridani felt a knot in her stomach. She had offered the Haldovans generous terms but it appeared they wanted even more. "Oh, no…"

Toval looked confused. He was loyal and competent with a sword but, as was often the case, not as sharp as the others among Eridani's inner circle.

"The Haldovans revealed our bargain," said Sana.

"Yes," said Caer. "They bided their time well. They waited for the chaos they knew would follow your taking over in Skond, then revealed the details of your collaboration with them to the northern nobles. We hear they offered everyone who would surrender to the Haldovans the mercy of retaining their lands and titles, and governing those lands in the name of the Haldovan Empire."

"I wish to see this letter," Eridani said.

"We should procure a copy soon from some of the loyalists," said Caer. "But more than a handful will take the accursed prince up on his offer."

"It explains why the Shallowpond delegation never showed up," said Gavron.

"They either switched sides or were overrun," said Sana. "Shallowpond is the nearest major northern city to the border."

"We'll know soon enough," said Eridani. "We must send messengers everywhere and demand the loyalty the others have pledged. Summon the Council of the North as well; seeing which of them show up will give us a good idea of who remains on our side." She was so close to the happily ever after she'd discussed with Pel that morning, if not for the Haldovans' betrayal. She thought back to the seer's words that rang through the hall less than an hour ago. "The damn sorceress was right again."

"What do you intend to do about her?" asked Gavron.

Eridani winced. "What? She can rot in the pit before I turn one of ours to her, as though she was some sort of a godling with a thirst for human sacrifice."

"That may not be wise," said Gavron. "The people of Skond will soon learn of our subterfuge with the Haldovans. Do we really want this news to be compounded by you breaking the bargain with their Sorceress?"

Sana looked at Gavron in disgust. "I can't believe what I'm hearing. Are you really advocating for us to kill Pel? That's low, even for you."

Gavron recoiled at Sana's words as though he was slapped. He would have taken them better if they came from anyone else, but his feelings toward her were an open secret.

Eridani closed her eyes. *Everyone you know and trust will come to betray you.* She never trusted the Haldovans, but she thought she could rely on their self-interest. She had misjudged their ambition. Was she cursed to be betrayed over and over again? She looked at the people surrounding her. Who would be next? Gavron the social climber? Caer the mercenary? The reckless Sana? None of them were perfect. How could she trust anyone?

"The damage has been done," she finally said. "People will rally behind me, or they will not. We'll know soon. Meanwhile, a public response to the sorceress's challenge is required."

Caer nodded. "What do you have in mind?"

"Since she wants Pel so bad, I will have him lead a squadron of our troops to the witch's home and burn it—and her—to the ground."

Gavron cleared his throat, stole a glance at Sana, and spoke anyway. "But is that wi—"

"I will hear no more on the matter," said Eridani. She thought of Pel, blissful in his ignorance of the threat for a short while longer, out there bargaining with some jeweler. "Find Pel and relay my orders. It may not be good politics for me to break my oath, but the definitive response will at least be useful as an object lesson for hesitant nobles."

Eridani was busy planning and issuing orders until it was dark. Pel still hadn't returned. It wasn't until late in the evening that a messenger dispatched to his home near the palace reported that it was empty and that a note with Eridani's name was left on the table along with a small cherry wood chest.

She opened the letter and read Pel's neat, precise cursive.

> *I heard about the choice forced upon you by the sorceress. I'd like to believe you'd protect me above all else, but I know you better than most. I know you to be a realist who is quite capable of making difficult sacrifices when they seem necessary. Never before have I considered myself to be a coward, but with news of invasion and turmoil in the city, and given that my life is at stake, I find that I'm not brave enough to meekly await your decision.*

The letter within the chest was intended for my former employer, sent by the Haldovans before news of my recent position must've reached them. I leave it for you as a parting gift. May the knowledge of your enemy's intentions help you persevere.

I'm sorry we won't share that happily ever after together.

Pel.

Oh, Pel, she thought. If only you trusted me. She focused on *happily ever after* until the words appeared blurred to her. She blinked the moisture from her eyes. Pel had betrayed her—again—as the sorceress had prophesized. She really shouldn't have been surprised.

Her heart could not be permitted to ache. Her mind could not be permitted to wander. She had a war to win.

Eridani opened the chest. The wax seal of the Haldovan Empire that once held it shut was already broken. She pulled out the perfumed pages written by an expert scribe on expensive paper and began to read.

CHAPTER 17
TEA AND BRANDY

avron was sitting down to breakfast when Sana arrived at his house.

He ordered his two servants to show her in and to leave for a few hours. He had been obsessed with her for years now, but she made it quite clear she did not reciprocate his feelings. He could hardly believe that she of all people would come visit his home on Lighting of the Hearth day.

As he waited, he glanced around the house nervously. It had been looted and damaged in the years since he had been forced to abandon it. But now it was filled with antique rugs and expensive artwork, decorated to the exacting standards of Gannian nobility. Surely, the lowborn Sana would be impressed.

She entered the dining room with a wooden box in her hands; a tall, broad-shouldered brunette whose curled hair cascaded down to her shoulder blades. Gavron thought she was perfect.

"Welcome, welcome," he said. "I must say, I'm a little surprised that you came, and knew to bring wood. You're quite early, but that's all right."

"Wood?" Sana seemed a little thrown off.

"It is a Gannian tradition," said Gavron, slightly deflated. "Each guest brings a log of wood to the Lightning of the Hearth celebration. They are used to warm the house and cook a meal, though finer food is offered to the guests throughout the evening, of course."

159

"Oh." Sana glanced at the box she was holding. "There's a gift from Queen Eridani inside, though I suppose the box can be used for kindling."

"She remembered!" Gavron was beyond pleased.

"I'm a little surprised, too," said Sana. "Surprised that you're having your Hearth party despite learning only yesterday that we're at war."

"I know the timing is terrible," Gavron said. "But I couldn't bring myself to cancel. I worked so hard to reclaim my home, to gain the position and wealth that I have today." He stared lovingly at the paintings adorning his walls. "Power is dangerous. Today we rule Skond. Tomorrow we might all hang from the parapets. I simply couldn't cancel the celebration I've looked forward to for so long." He refocused on Sana. "I'm thankful for Eridani's understanding. And yours."

Sana nodded. "Here." She offered the wooden box to Gavron. He opened it, revealing an ornate glass bottle.

"It's fancy Gannian brandy," said Sana.

"Fancy indeed." Gavron gently stroked the marking on the wax seal. "The best Gannian brandy money can buy. Very strong." He looked into Sana's gorgeous brown eyes and almost drowned in them. "Will you do me the honor of sharing a glass with me?"

Sana shook her head. "I need my mind clear. You drink. I'd appreciate some tea."

"Of course." He poured from a pot of herbal tea into a cup. The blend smelled of blueberry and flowers. "Please, sit."

They sat at the table and Gavron poured himself a generous shot of amber liquid. He took a sip. He knew this brand of brandy only by reputation and it tasted every bit as smooth as people said it was. It was much better than the bottle he drank from on the day they fled Skond.

"The brandy isn't the only thing I brought," said Sana.

"Oh?" Gavron rested the glass on the table. "Did you bring me a Hearth gift, too?"

"Hardly one you would like," said Sana. She drew several sheets of paper from her sleeve and handed them over. "It's a copy of the Haldovan letter. It mentions you."

"Oh?" Gavron said again. "Me? Why would…" He spread the sheets on the table.

"Read," said Sana. "It speaks for itself." She lifted the porcelain cup to her lips and drank.

To the esteemed nobles of the North:

I am Prince Ajelogn, First Scion, rightful heir to the throne of Haldova, Archduke of Cherville, Lion of the Plains, and Grand General of the Haldovan Armies. As you read these words, my troops have crossed the border into the North. By midwinter, I shall gain the title of Patriarch of the North and sit on the throne of Skond as the lifeless bodies of my enemies hang from its walls.

My victory is inevitable. I've hired every available mercenary in the Heart, built supply lines, trained soldiers, and amassed my forces at your borders, all with the knowing consent of your so-called ruler, the Upstart Queen, Eridani.

A year and a half ago, the court of my father received an emissary from Eridani of Kozhad, proposing an alliance and offering many concessions that were not within her power to grant. She wanted our help to rise to her current position. She wanted a pretense of an invasion to force the old patriarch to commit his troops to the border, thereby sparing her neck from an executioner's axe for a few more months.

My father thought her proposal beneath our notice. "The hurricane does not treat with a hut in its path," he told me. But I was intrigued. Who was this traitorous creature, cunning enough to reclaim her ancestral home with nothing but a gaggle of peasant women, yet eager to conspire with us against the interests of her own homeland? Who was this hare, bold and foolish enough to negotiate with a fox?

Stories have reached us of the Upstart Queen traveling far and wide dressed as a commoner. It is said this is how she came to possess what she claims to be a relic of Kalatar, though the truth of that claim remains suspect. It amused me to use the same tactic against her. I traveled under an assumed name as part of the delegation to Kozhad so I could surreptitiously take a measure of her.

I was not impressed.

Eridani surrounds herself with sycophants of low birth. Among her top advisors are an ex-mercenary, her one-time tutor, a dim-witted childhood friend, and a farmer's daughter. Kozhad lacks the dignity and structure of a true court; its tiny palace feels rather like a home to the council of elders of some medium-sized village.

Despite the populist rhetoric they espouse, her advisors predictably lack the principles and nobility of true aristocracy. During my stay at Kozhad, I wished to test their constant claims about the skirt army being a viable fighting force. I personally killed one of their woman-soldiers, someone of low-enough rank not to be missed. She did not put up the sort of resistance I would expect from anyone who might be admitted into the Haldovan army. The Upstart Queen's advisors were clever enough to detain me, yet her tutor was so eager not to upset the negotiations that he blamed the killing on a simpleton soldier and set me free.

Although I found Eridani and her court wanting, her traitorous plan was to my liking. Eridani provided us with information about the patriarch's troops, and kept his forces split up while we prepared for what she thought was a fake invasion unharassed. I never expected her plan to work and for her to depose the patriarch, but I was pleased to hear of further turmoil which would only make it easier for me to expand the Haldovan Empire all the way to the frozen coast.

As my forces sweep across your ancestral lands, know that the Upstart Queen is to blame.

You need not be among those who perish this winter. I have dispatched messengers with copies of this letter only to select nobles whom my advisors have judged worthy. Any of you who open their gates to my troops, who pledge their loyalty and their soldiers to my cause, will be given leave to retain your titles and govern your regions as vassals of the Haldovan Empire. So long as you pay annual tribute, your cities will not be burned; your treasuries will not be raided. This I swear in accordance to the Forty-seven Dictums of Warfare, a code of honor from our southern borders recently made popular at our court. An honor system that would've never permitted one such as the Upstart Queen to betray her homeland. You owe this traitor no loyalty. Choose to side with the inevitable victor instead, but choose soon.

I am coming.

GAVRON FINISHED READING and stared at the facsimile of the Prince's elaborate signature replicated by a scribe at the bottom of the letter. His hands trembled. Raising his gaze from the pages to Sana felt like lifting a large stone. Sana was watching him intently.

"He was fiendishly clever. I never saw the prince behind the veneer of a spoiled son of a minor noble."

"Her name was Genna," she said. "She was with the skirt army since before we took Kozhad, since almost the beginning. She deserved better than for her murderer to be set free. I didn't know that other soldier, but I'm certain he deserved better, too."

Gavron's stomach churned. His face was flushed red. The whole world learning of his mistake was not as bad as the disgust with which the woman he loved stared at him at that moment. "I'm sorry. I acted only to help our queen, to help all of us survive against Skond."

"She would have never approved. Not this."

"Perhaps." Gavron coughed several times. Each time his muscles contracted it sent a spasm of pain through his body. "I bore the weight of this decision. For her. For all of you."

"You decided," said Sana. "And now the murderer you set free returns at the head of the largest invasion force in the history of our homeland. Eridani has no choice but to make an example of you. It will play well in the streets: a pompous foreigner, not well-liked in Skond or Kozhad, is to blame for the enemy prince slipping through our fingers. To appease the mob, you must hang for your crimes."

"No! I am loyal, I have been her close confidant all these years—"

Sana cut him off. "Were you not the one advocating that we give Pel to the sorceress? Doesn't feel quite so logical when you're the scapegoat, does it?"

Gavron doubled over and puked onto the floor. Through the pain and the bitter taste in his mouth he managed, "She couldn't. We've shared too much."

"She offered the only mercy she could," said Sana. "The brandy is poisoned. Your body will hang, but you will die here, in the privacy of your home."

Gavron was on his hands and knees beside the table, his vision blurring. "It was cruel," he said, his voice barely a whisper. Sana rose from her chair to stand over him, still holding her teacup. "Cruel to send you."

"The queen mother felt obligated to do this herself," said Sana. "I talked her out of it. I volunteered." She leaned closer. "I argued for a hanging, but when she wouldn't budge I realized this might be nearly as unpleasant for you."

Gavron wanted to respond, to use his last moments to make Sana understand him. He wanted desperately for her to see his side of things, even as the unfairness of the situation smothered his soul like a heavy wool blanket, but he could no longer control his voice.

"I wonder what words will be carved on your tombstone," said Sana. "Perhaps it will be: *Here lies a once-decent man, corrupted by his overwhelming need of validation.*" She toasted Gavron with her teacup. "For Genna."

Gavron's body spasmed on the ground, his elbow smearing the puddle of vomit. After a handful more heartbeats, it was still.

ERIDANI BRUSHED RAINDROPS out of her hair in the big, empty vestibule of the sorceress's house. The garden was as wild as she remembered it; the mansion sitting at the center of the property as unwelcoming.

At least this time she was not a fugitive; she arrived with two dozen soldiers in tow, all loyal Kozhad troops. There were angry crowds in the streets. People gathered in ever-growing groups on street corners and in the squares. The rain kept the mob from swelling, but their mood was ugly. They stayed clear of the well-armed soldiers on horseback who surrounded Eridani's stagecoach, but she could see through the veiled window the animosity and disrespect in the eyes of her recently acquired subjects. The city was a volcano ready to erupt at any moment and there was little she could do other than to watch with apprehension and hope that the billowing smoke would not be followed by an outpouring of lava.

Her bodyguards entered the mansion first, and found no sign of the sorceress. Eridani shrugged off their report; she knew the witch would be lurking there, ready to present herself to the right visitor. She recalled her people and entered the mansion alone, struggling to cast off the same anxiety and fear her fifteen-year-old self suffered during the previous visit.

"Come, Sorceress. I'm in no mood to play your games today."

Eridani planted her feet firmly in the middle of the vestibule, refusing to descend to the murky underground level of the mansion which hosted their previous encounter. That is where the terrible prophecy was thrust upon her: *everyone you know and trust will come to betray you.* She tried to push thoughts of Gavron out of her mind. She was sad and angry—sad to lose one of the few people she had known and trusted for years, angry that he would overreach and fail in such a spectacular fashion. He had always been too eager to prove his value, too desirous of respect from friends and enemies alike. He was unprepared to match wits with the likes of the Haldovan prince.

Despite his good intentions, he ended up betraying her, and it cost him everything. She had to placate the angry mobs, to offer them someone other than herself to suffer the brunt of the blame. The contents of the prince's letter—which she had no doubt would disseminate quickly among her citizens—made it nearly impossible to choose anyone but Gavron. It made it impossible *not* to choose him.

Was it already done? Eridani recalled Caer's face as he witnessed the tutor's fate become sealed early that morning. He didn't speak out against the plan, but she saw the muscle in his jaw twitch, his silent anguish in stark contrast to Sana's glee. Sana seemed overly eager to accept the burden of delivering the poison.

Eridani stood there for several hundred heartbeats. She was trying to make up her mind as to whether to abandon this pitiful attempt at displaying dominance and to descend, or to turn around and leave, when the sorceress appeared without fanfare, simply walking through one of the doors. She wore another elaborate gown, yellow this time, complemented by a small sunflower woven into her gray hair.

"You're here, yet my prize is not."

"Pel learned that you were after his head and fled the city. But I'm sure you already know that, don't you? Perhaps this is what you intended all along?"

The sorceress looked at her with the exhausted patience of a mother observing an unruly toddler. "Fled, you say? Pity for you. Did you fall for a weak-bellied coward? Or was him absconding your idea, a misguided attempt to save his hide?"

Eridani stared at the older woman defiantly. Her right fist clenched out of sight in her pocket. "You knew, then? You demanded his life because he shared my bed?"

The sorceress stared past Eridani the way she did at the palace. "His influence made the future uncertain, more muddled than I would like."

"Well, he is gone now. Surely, he can't meddle in your fortunetelling from afar."

"Perhaps not." The witch shrugged. "Yet our bargain remains unfulfilled. Still, here you are, come to beg for another miracle."

"I won't deny it," said Eridani. "I'm besieged by enemies from without and within. I don't know who to trust. You predicted this. You said I'd need your help, so here I am. What magic do you possess that can aid me?"

"Ah, so you've come to believe in magic?" The sorceress smiled. "They grow up so fast."

Eridani thought back to her encounter with the God Under the Floorboards. "I've seen things out in the world," she said. "Enough to convince me. What powers do you possess? Can you curse the enemy armies? Erect a wall of fire in their path?"

"You may have come to believe in the arcane, but you do not understand it. Magic is a delicate instrument rather than a blunt tool. One wields it expertly, like a chirurgeon. A bit of prophecy whispered in the right ear can incite a riot. An enchantment can inspire a poet to write a saga that convinces the masses to love their lord and despise his foes." She refocused on Eridani. "A healing potion for a prince can unseat a patriarch."

"I see," said Eridani. "Your magic is weak, and you resort to manipulating people to get your way."

The sorceress stiffened. "Weak and subtle are not the same thing."

"Then prove it and help me. Help your city. I doubt you want the Haldovans to overrun Skond."

"You still owe me," said the sorceress. "If you wish to strike another bargain, I will offer you only the smallest nudge in the right direction. Advice that won't be palatable but might save you, if you choose to heed it. In exchange, I will ask a steep price."

Eridani crossed her arms. "Whose head will it be this time?"

"Your firstborn child."

Eridani stared at the witch, trying to process the ridiculousness of the situation. Did she somehow find herself in a sort of tall tale peasants would tell around the campfire at night? Who did this crone think she was, making a demand like that? Her first instinct was to draw the Bloodsword, to cut down this conceited, egotistical, crazy bitch. After all, did she not admit that her magic was only as good as an experienced politician's scheming?

Oshekzhothep the Seer observed the queen closely. After both were silent for a few heartbeats, she added, "If you survive this war, there will come another time, in another land, when you will need my help. I swear by the grace of the Invisible God that I will come to you and offer it freely, and it will be much more potent than a mere suggestion whispered in your ear. I will show you a path to gain what you want most."

Eridani yearned to pull the sword, to run it through the witch's yellow-clad flesh, but she stayed herself. It would be impetuous to act on emotion. She never gave much thought to having children, but she hadn't ruled the idea out, either. And if she ever gave birth, she would murder half the world before giving up her child to this freak. Yet, why not promise the sorceress what she wanted, like last time? The old woman had no power over her, even if her prophecies were eerily accurate. Eridani had failed to deliver Pel, and yet here the witch was, proposing another bargain.

She didn't want to seem overeager. "What if I bear no children?" she asked.

The witch smiled. Her mirth seemed as unnerving as the entire Council of the North staring at her when she first entered their chamber. "Then you shall owe me no payment at all."

"I accept your bargain," Eridani said. "What advice do you have for me? How can I defeat the invaders' superior force?"

"You won't like this," the sorceress warned.

"There's nothing I like about our bargains. Speak."

"You must seek the aid of your worst enemy," said the sorceress.

Eridani's eyes narrowed. "The patriarch? He's rotting in the dungeon. What can he possibly do to help me? And even if he could, why would he?"

"Because not everyone values victory above all else," said the sorceress. She fiddled with the sunflower in her hair. "You paid dearly for this suggestion. Don't discard it. Ask for his help."

ERIDANI DESCENDED INTO the dungeon, dismissed the guards, and headed down the dank, poorly lit corridor. Her steps echoed across the empty cells. She reached the farthest cell and unlocked the reinforced door. Inside, sat the dungeon's only prisoner.

The patriarch looked gaunt, his hair unkempt, a month's growth of beard covered his face. He still wore the same clothes from the council meeting, which were now rumpled and dirty. Had it only been a month? The thought surprised her. Her reign as queen mother already seemed so much longer.

"Is it time?" he asked, when he saw Eridani.

"Time for what?" she asked.

"Time for me to die, of course," he said. "You're only keeping me alive until you've consolidated sufficient power that killing me won't ruffle too many feathers in Skond." He scratched vigorously at his leg. "Damn fleas. I must say, I didn't expect you to have things well enough in hand so soon. Perhaps, I've underestimated you again."

"I'm not here to kill you," said Eridani.

"Oh?" The patriarch didn't seem as relieved by the news as she would have expected. "Then things are going so badly you actually need something from me?" He slowly rose from the straw mat he was sitting on. "Don't be surprised at my deductions. You and I are essentially the same. Enlightened rulers who attempt to govern through economics and good policy instead of squeezing the serfs for every last bit of grain. Ambitious, forward-thinking, yet ruthless enough to make difficult choices when necessary."

Eridani flinched. She didn't relish the comparison. Didn't the sorceress characterize him as someone who was motivated by things other than dominance over his foes? No matter. She was already here. "I've come to ask for your counsel," she said.

She expected her foe to mock her, to enjoy her predicament. Instead, he merely listened and nodded as she described events as they came to pass in the recent days.

"We're gathering the loyal troops at several rallying points midway between Skond and Shallowpond," she said. "Their goal is to slow down the advance of the Haldovans as much as possible, to harass their supply lines. They will burn bridges, cut down trees to block roads, anything to delay the enemy. We don't have the numbers to defeat them. Our only hope is to buy time until the impending winter storms bog them down through spring."

"I'm impressed," said the patriarch. "Your stratagem of working with the Haldovans against me would have been brilliant had they not double-crossed you. As it is, your present situation is precarious at best. Many of the nobles will go with whoever they perceive as the eventual victor and, at this point, that's most likely to be Prince Ajelogn. Even if you stall his forces long enough for the weather to aid you, that will only buy a few months. Then what?"

He walked the length of the cell back and forth, four steps in each direction, as he talked.

"I do believe I may have a way to help you," he said, "but I'd like certain concessions."

"Such as?" Eridani asked.

"A clean, dry cell. Decent food and wine instead of water and gruel. A change of clothes. Some books to read as well as paper and quill to write." He stopped pacing and stared at Eridani who still stood in the doorway. "I won't ask you to release or to spare me. Even if you were to make such a promise, we would both know those words to be meaningless. But it will cost you nothing to allow me some comforts for as long as you must keep me alive."

Eridani wanted to say *This cell is too good for you.* She wanted to shout, *You murdered my family. You deserve far worse.* But the Spider was being pragmatic and reasonable in his demands, and she could afford to be gracious in her victory. In fact, she couldn't afford to refuse him if the sorceress was right and he held a key to her victory.

"You can have the comforts you want if your suggestion proves useful," she said.

The broken, thin man before her nodded regally, as though he were still in charge. "You need more fighting men," he said. "You must unite the nomadic tribes of the far north. They have the numbers, the horses, and the fierce savagery to tilt the scales of this war in your favor."

Eridani sighed. "You might as well have suggested that I plant magic beans and have warrior golems grow by spring. The northern tribes have no interest in our affairs. The only outsider they ever followed into battle was Kalatar himself, and they thought him a demigod!"

"When reading historical accounts one must not forget that they were written by biased men," said the patriarch. "Kalatar subjugated the tribes. They hated him at first, yet grew to respect him when he led them to victory and plunder. But in the beginning, he forced them to ride under his banner by conquering Glimmerholm and capturing their sacred totems. He made hostages of their gods."

"I never knew this," said Eridani.

"Few do," said the patriarch. "Even after Kalatar earned the respect of the nomads, he never returned the totems. They've been stored in the vaults deep underneath this palace ever since, as an insurance against the nomad war bands venturing beyond the lands under the aurora." The patriarch resumed pacing across the cell. "Shortly before you managed to unseat me, I sent an emissary to the tribal elders at Glimmerholm. I offered to return their gods in exchange for their war bands assisting my troops in..." He glanced at Eridani. "...Uniting the North and repelling the invasion if necessary. As you say, they do not care about our politics. If anything, they'll be happier making the same deal with you, once you wave that prop around." He pointed at her scabbard.

The patriarch explained to Eridani the details of his proposal to the elders. He agreed to pen a letter to his envoy ordering him to help Eridani's people complete the negotiations. Treating with the nomads was no guarantee of victory, but it was a possible way for her to defeat the Haldovans.

As Eridani was leaving the dungeon she looked at the patriarch quizzically. "Why did you help me?" she asked. "I know it wasn't for a loaf of bread and a warm blanket."

"I'm a patriot," he said. "You may not be the successor I chose, but you can unify and lead the North, much like I've always envisioned doing. I hate to admit it, but the North is better off with you in charge than under the heel of the invaders."

Eridani nodded, wondering if she could ever bring herself to do what he did, were their roles reversed. She didn't think so.

On the way out of the dungeon, she ordered the guards to have the prisoner's cell cleaned and for the food and drink and books and anything else he requested within reason to be delivered to him until further notice. Against her instinct for vengeance she accepted that it was worthwhile to keep him comfortable — there was a chance she might need his counsel again.

CHAPTER 18

THE ICHETHI

"This isn't a good time for you to leave," said Sana. "The enemy troops are advancing, nearly half the council has defected, and Skond is on the verge of an uprising. You go adventuring now and we're done for. People will assume you've run away. There will be chaos."

Eridani nodded. Her top general was never afraid to contradict Eridani, unlike some of the bootlickers and yes-men among the bureaucrats she'd inherited from the patriarch. "You're right. Yet we can't hope to defeat the Haldovans as things stand now. Our only chance is for the snowfall to stall their advance until spring, and to gather a fighting force that can match theirs by the time the snow melts and the roads leading to Skond become passable again."

Eridani followed Sana's gaze out the window. The sky was blue and cloudless. To their misfortune, the early winter was warmer than usual with no portent of snow.

"Perhaps, I should go to the gathering of the tribes in your stead. It's ten day's journey each way. You can't afford to be gone that long," said Sana.

"I must go," said Eridani. "I'm told the elders won't finalize the agreement with an underling. Still, you're right. The people shouldn't know I'm gone."

Sana's eyes widened. "What? You think no one will notice if you disappear for a month?"

"It's not like I gallivant around town these days," said Eridani. "We'll tell only the most trusted people. To an outside observer it will seem like business as usual: decrees will come from the palace, envoys and generals will arrive and receive their orders from my right-hand woman." She smiled. "We may not be able to keep up the charade for an entire month, but every day we buy is another day we avoid the chaos you speak of."

ERIDANI LEFT AT the last possible minute, leading a company of two dozen handpicked soldiers from Gan. She chose from among the fanatics who would allow an enemy to flay their skin before they betrayed the secret of Eridani's mission to anyone. They used the strongest horses and made the journey across the pine forests and the frost-covered tundra in only nine days.

Five days in, Eridani first saw the aurora. She'd read about this phenomenon in books, but letters on a page could not do it justice. It was a spectacle: fire in the heavens that came closest of all her life experiences to convincing her of the existence of the gods.

She wrapped her furs tighter around her and looked around. Technically all of the North was the domain of the queen mother; by ancient compact, lands under the aurora belonged to the barbarian tribes. They paid no tribute to Skond, nor would any sane tax collector willingly enter their lands.

Despite her concerns, Eridani and her entourage rode unchallenged until they were less than a day's journey from Glimmerholm. At that point, they were met by a group of fur-clad men riding small, muscular horses—the breed known throughout the Heart for their endurance and resistance to the cold. The men were armed with short, curved swords that were greatly feared by those who lived at the edges of the territory claimed by the tribes.

The honor guard, as Eridani thought it wise to view them, ensured that the queen and her people reached Glimmerholm without incident.

THE MEETING PLACE of the tribal elders wasn't a city but a wide patch of tundra with yurts extending from its center in an ever-widening series of concentric circles. There must've been thousands—from the humble tents on the outer reaches of the encampment to large structures near the center that appeared permanent and could each house dozens of people within their animal-hide walls.

"This is the Ichetai," said her guide. When they first met, he proudly declared himself to be a member of a tribe whose name she couldn't pronounce, but never offered his own name. "Elders of every tribe meet here at the start of winter. They discuss all important matters." He pointed toward the horse stables and vendor stalls set up beyond the widest circle. "Tribes exchange horses, medicine, brides." Eridani winced at the last one but she held her comment. "Competitions are held to see which tribe has the best fighters and the best songs."

"My Queen!" A kind-faced man dressed in the Skond fashion approached on foot from the direction of the tents.

"You must be my envoy," said Eridani.

"I'm the Skond ambassador to the northern tribes," he replied. Eridani noted the verbal acrobatics there. Could he be trusted? He approached. "My name is Chezan," he said quietly. "But please keep addressing me as your envoy. It is improper to use personal names here except in intimate settings, among family and close friends." He smiled apologetically. "You're Queen Mother of Skond. Not of the North. To them, we're all southerners."

"I'm their queen as well," said Eridani. "If they won't acknowledge as much, then our cause is already lost."

THROUGHOUT THE ICHETAI, Eridani felt eager to get to her business with the elders, but she had long learned the virtue of patience in politics.

As an honored guest she wasn't required to pitch her own tent. One was provided to her in the second circle, among tribal elders and their families. Her soldiers were given drafty tents on the outskirts of Glimmerholm, barely better than their own traveling gear and uncomfortable enough that even the hardened zealots muttered complaints under their breath.

At the center of the tent city a large area was set aside for food and entertainment, such as it was. She watched barbarians struggle to outwrestle and out-dance each other. They competed in simple sporting events and displays of skill with tribal honor at stake. She listened to mostly bad music and ate mostly bad food, and labored to appear both gracious and above it all at the same time.

Chezan was at her side, filling her in on the tribal lore, suggesting exotic delicacies for her to try, and warning her away from some of the dishes being placed on the rug-covered benches in stone bowls.

"That's fermented horse meat," he cautioned when Eridani sized up the latest offering. "To say it's an acquired taste would be an understatement."

Eridani blanched as the smell of the dish assaulted her nose. Horse wasn't considered a meat animal in most regions of the Heart. Out here, in the frigid north, the diet was far more limited. The tribes had little in the way of grains and even less of fruits or vegetables. What few fish their nets caught in the rivers and ocean waters, and an occasional hare or squirrel they snared couldn't provide the protein their people needed to survive. Each tribe possessed vast herds of horses tough enough to survive by grazing on the short, sparse grass in the warmer months and on bales of hay in the winter. Those horses were the backbone of each tribe. They provided milk in lieu of cows and hair in lieu of sheep. Older and lame animals were slaughtered and every part was used: their flesh for meat, their hides for sewing, their bones for carving everything from hair brushes to short two-pronged forks, to amulets. Carved amulets were everywhere, larger ones hanging at the entrance to each yurt and smaller ones worn by the tribesmen. They represented the pantheon of deities whose totems the patriarch and his predecessors had held hostage for generations.

"When will I speak to the elders?" Eridani asked, for what must've been the fourth time, feeling like an impatient child pestering her parents on a long, boring journey.

"Soon now," said Chezan. "When they've run out of contests and food and wine." He followed her gaze toward the fire pit where several whole carcasses were roasting. More food was being prepared nearby. "It's tradition."

"The winter months seem like a poor time to hold a gathering," Eridani said.

"Life is rough this far north," said Chezan. "Spring and summer are short, and there isn't any free time for wrestling and horse races. This late in the year they're ready to hunker down to survive the winter. Virtually every culture in the Heart celebrates some form of the harvest festival. The Ichetai is its equivalent."

Eridani offered no response. She observed the merriment and good cheer around her but her thoughts were far to the south. Would her army manage to delay the invaders long enough? Could Sana keep the unrest in the capital in check? And when would the snowfall come?

THE ELDERS LISTENED to Eridani, their wrinkled faces betraying no emotion. It was on the eve of the third day of the Ichetai that they gathered in the largest yurt and invited her to join them. No assistants or servants were allowed inside. Not even Chezan, despite his being welcomed at the gathering of the elders in the past. Now that his superior had arrived, he could no longer act as a stand-in for the authority of Skond.

She recited the proposal fully realizing that they heard it all before from Chezan. Her words held no new revelations for them. Still, she had to follow form. The man she focused on was Ul Kelai, an elder among elders. She briefly thought it his name but, as was custom among the nomads, it was only a title. According to Chezan, age was greatly respected in their culture. Although the Ul Kelai's tribe wasn't the largest or most powerful, the ancient nomad was the de facto leader of their tribal council.

"It is known that you do not hold our gods captive," Ul Kelai said softly, after she delivered her speech. "Their essence is strong across the land. You have but the renderings of them carved out of tree trunks by imperfect mortals."

Eridani was certain they wanted the totems back. Was this a negotiating tactic? "Honored elder," she said, "it is known that a totem is merely an idealized symbol of a god, just as a crown is a symbol of a monarch, or a sword"—she glanced at her scabbard—"a symbol of a legend. A symbol is not the thing itself but it can be important nevertheless."

"It is known that the free people have lived without these…symbols…for a long time." The elder spoke the word as though his tongue was sampling an exotic piece of candy. "If we are to assemble the war bands as we have done in the time of the great lord of Gan, we need something more."

The other elders nodded their assent.

Ah, now we are getting somewhere, Eridani thought. "What is it that the Queen Mother of Skond can offer the free people in order to entice them to once again ride against our mutual enemies?"

"It is known that the great lord of Gan generously provided a tenth share of all plunder to the brave warriors of the tribes."

Eridani considered his words. The history books she read hinted at such an arrangement although they didn't describe it outright. "We're defending the North," she said. "There will be no looting of my subjects." The tribes' history of raids against their southern neighbors was precisely the reason why the rulers in Skond decided to withhold the totems. She was prepared to unleash the trapped beast, but there were limits to what she'd accept.

The Ul Kelai nodded sagely. "It is known that the free tribes do not exact tribute from allies. We will chase the invaders back to their sweltering homeland and annex their wealth."

Eridani thought it over. She was not opposed to sharing the loot if such a rosy scenario were to ever come to pass. "I agree to that," she said. "A tenth of the plunder."

"It is known that our warriors are fierce and numerous," said the elder of elders. "We want twice that."

Eridani crossed her arms. "Kalatar paid you ten percent!"

There was a murmur among the elders. Belatedly Eridani realized that she used the legendary warlord's proper name. The Ul Kelai beckoned her and she approached. He motioned for her to lean closer, then closer yet. When her ear was only a palm's length from his face the elder whispered, low enough that no one else could hear.

"You're no Kalatar."

Eridani drew back, her face flushed, ready to issue a retort, but the old man waved his index and middle fingers in a motion that she earlier learned meant absolution. The other elders repeated the motion, indicating that her error in etiquette had been forgiven. In light of this, any rash words would have sounded doubly foolish. Eridani swallowed her pride and prepared to bargain.

In the end, they settled on fifteen percent.

ERIDANI'S SOLDIERS RODE south under the ethereal lights of the aurora. The bargain was struck. The elders would assemble the war bands by early spring. They pledged to provide twenty thousand men on horseback, an army large enough to swing the balance decidedly in her favor. She was quietly thankful that she had moved against the patriarch when she did. Otherwise, these nomad warriors would have been Kozhad-bound in the spring instead.

Now she needed to hold the Haldovans at bay for the next several months. When she explained her plan to the elders they nodded and chattered in their usual way. "It is known that our shamans can call the snow," they said. "You wish for wet, heavy snow, dense enough to make the roads impassable." They clucked their tongues as though evaluating the quality of fruit at a market stall. "It will require many healthy horses to be sacrificed at altars, but you will have your snow."

Their casual promises of sorcerous weather control sounded almost convincing inside the horsehide yurt in the middle of Glimmerholm. Now that she had spent some time with her thoughts on the open road, her usual skepticism had returned. The snow would come, or it would not. She had to set the events in motion and hope that weather would cooperate.

By the time the aurora was only a glimmer on the horizon the first snowflakes began to fall.

CHAPTER 19

THE GATEBREAKER

eo stared at his father defiantly. "I'm going. Help me or not, I'm going."

His father, Kai, stood in the middle of the workshop, calf hides drying by the wall behind him, more being cured with salt on the benches to his side. He had been a tanner for nearly forty years, apprenticed at the age of seven. He never could understand why his firstborn son would have any ambition other than to take up the family business. "Why do you want to risk your life for her? The lords of Shallowpond have capitulated to the Haldovans. Soon the rest of the North will follow."

"The lords of Shallowpond are cowards and traitors." Teo clenched his fists. "The Queen Mother is the true ruler of the North. It's our duty to help her repel this invasion."

"You're young and passionate, which is good," said Kai. "But trust my experience. It doesn't really matter who rules in Shallowpond or in Skond. We're beneath their notice, except when they need us to provide coin or muscle." He pointed at the animal skins in different stages of preparation. "We're no better than these beasts to them, only worth as much as their meat and hide."

"Eridani is different! She cares for people like us. She fights to make the lives of commoners better." Teo trailed off, realizing that he was rehashing an argument they had had many times over. "Don't you see? This is my chance to make something of myself."

His father winced. "You do that through hard work, not by killing people who only differ from you in that they carry another master's banner."

"I'm going," Teo said again. "Word has been sent for those loyal to the queen to gather in Felstown, where the baron has balls enough to stand with his liege. If you won't give me the money to buy provisions and a sword, I will go anyway, armed with a club. I'll live off the land."

Kai sighed, then reached into a small box under one of the tables and offered his son a handful of coins. "This will devastate your mother," he said.

"She'll understand," said Teo. "I will return a veteran. An officer, perhaps. I'll bring home a purse full of dragon scales. Enough so that neither of you has to work another day."

"Be safe. Please." Kai called after Teo, whose mind was already far away from Shallowpond. The tanner's son dreamt of righteous glory.

"HIS NAME IS Liodan the Gatebreaker," Caer said. "He was a legendary general even back in my mercenary days. He earned his nickname because there was no fortress that could stand before his army. I wished to fight for him, like most of my peers, but his campaigns were too far to the west." Caer sounded almost wistful. "He's a master bato player as well."

Eridani stroked her chin. "I read about his exploits. The man must be in his late seventies now. Why is he here?"

Her advisors had no answers to offer.

"No matter," she said. "Let him in. He'll tell us himself."

General Liodan walked into the council chamber alone. He was thin and tall, and his back was straight despite his advanced years. His hair and beard were both long, thin wisps of gray reaching his solar plexus in the front and below his shoulder blades in the back. His eyes were jet-black and alert. He seemed aware of everything around him, like a cautious traveler in a cheap tavern filled with thieves. He had come straight to the palace upon arriving in Skond; Eridani could see road dust on his cloak.

"Queen Eridani." He nodded rather than bowed, which irritated her slightly. She squashed the emotion. "Well met."

"Well met, General Liodan." She pointed at the seat across from her. "Please, sit. You have traveled farther than any visitor I've had the pleasure to entertain at this court. May we offer you food or wine?"

"Water, please." The general lowered himself gingerly into the chair. "I no longer partake of spirits."

Eridani motioned to a servant. "A general who doesn't drink is like a poet who seeks no similes," she said.

Caer and Sana both smiled, and Liodan chuckled. "We all grow and change with age. I no longer drink, or eat meat, or lead men in battle."

"How unfortunate," Eridani said. "We dared hope you've traveled all this way to help us win the war."

"I've come to help," said Liodan, "but not to fight battles. I wish to save lives."

"How do you propose to do that without fighting?" asked Sana. "Will you ask the Haldovans nicely to turn around and go home?"

Liodan nodded thanks to the servant as he accepted a goblet filled with water. He drank deeply, placed it onto the table and leaned contentedly against the back of his chair. "That is precisely what I intend to do."

THREE WEEKS LATER, word of Liodan's arrival reached the company Teo had been assigned to upon arriving in Felstown. He and other fresh recruits received an accelerated course of training from the veterans even as news of the southern armies gaining territory arrived daily.

"A welcome development indeed," declared Tem, one of the oldest veterans in the company. He was a man of few words except when a mug or two of beer loosened his lips. Then he became a fount of tall tales and war stories. "Liodan the Gatebreaker is a leader of great renown. They say he never lost a battle, and I bet he didn't come all this way north to learn what losing feels like."

"His fighting days are behind him," said Clyde, the company commander who was only a few years Tem's junior. "The man is a pacifist now."

"Whazzat?" asked one of the youngsters gathered around the table where the officers were drinking.

Teo elbowed the curious recruit in the ribs. One didn't interrupt the officers, or they might suddenly find errands and chores for the onlookers to complete.

Clyde must've been in an especially good mood, because he didn't so much as frown at the soldiers. He even answered the question. "A man who doesn't believe in killing other men," he said.

"Not even enemy soldiers?" asked another fresh recruit, emboldened by his superior's response.

"No one," said Clyde. He gulped his beer. "They say he spent the last decade going around, preventing wars."

Now it was Tem's turn to question his commander. "How does a single man, even a venerated general, prevent a war?"

Clyde handed his empty mug to one of the soldiers behind him at random. The man ran to the keg to refill it. "They say he walks right in to a king's court and tells them there's no sense in laying siege to the enemy capital because he already taught those enemies how to make it impregnable. Even against a larger force." He accepted the refilled mug and blew on the foam. "He then proves it to the king through war games or logic or what-have-you. Proves it definitively, especially given his reputation. And to make sure the king doesn't decide to remove the obstacle by lopping off the general's head, Liodan explains to 'em how he first visited the opposing side's castle and taught them all those defense strategies already." He drank from the refill. "So far, he managed to avert several wars and broker peace in a few more that were already goin'. The man may be bad for the mercenary business, but he saved more lives than every doctor and lekar in the Heart combined."

The men sitting around the table all drank a toast to Liodan the Gatebreaker while Teo and others watched.

"His stratagem can work when two city-states go to war," said Teo. "But how can he hope to stop the Haldovans? It's not a matter of a single castle or walled city. Even if he teaches Queen Eridani how to defend Skond against an onslaught by the gods themselves, our enemies could still blockade it and take the rest of the North."

Everyone was silent for a moment, contemplating his logic. Then Tem slammed his mug onto the pine table and belched. "This's what we're for, innit?" he declared. The men laughed and drank again.

ERIDANI PLACED TWO beads onto the bato board. The complex configuration featured dozens of blue and yellow beads as the two players vied for control.

Liodan stroked his beard as he contemplated her move. "Excellent," he said. "You're a natural at this. I'm surprised you haven't played much in the past."

Eridani shrugged. "Caer got me to play on occasion. I don't enjoy the game all that much. The abstraction of it bores me, and there are always important things to do."

"Patience is among the many skills bato teaches," said Liodan. "There's no better way to train your mind for tactics. I promised to teach you how to best defend your people. This is a part of the lesson." He methodically placed several of his beads. "Looks like I'll be able to rout you in another five moves. Still, an impressive effort."

Eridani remained silent. Then she grabbed a handful of her remaining beads and clustered them near the top of the board.

Liodan pondered the configuration. "An overly risky move. You force the confrontation, giving yourself no more than a one-in-six chance of winning."

"You said I will lose in five turns and I'm inclined to believe you," said Eridani. "You're the stronger player with more experience. If I make safer plays, my odds will only decrease."

Liodan picked up a pair of dice carved from the bone of an extinct beast, with pips hand-drawn by an artist in gold paint. "A thoughtful leader might elect to lose while preserving most of their pieces." He rolled for the first confrontation. "Your move ensures the board will be half-empty, whoever wins."

"I wouldn't be sitting here today were it not for my willingness to take chances and make risky moves," said Eridani.

"So long as you remember our agreement when the time comes," said Liodan.

"Yes, I will accept a peace treaty if the Haldovans pick up and leave," Eridani said. She rolled the dice and took one of Liodan's beads off the board. "But we're sitting here playing games while their armies encroach deeper north."

"You must be prepared," said Liodan. "The only way to avert a war is for the enemy to think they cannot defeat you."

"I disagree," said Eridani. "Greed and lust for power are human nature. As long as there are innumerable kings and princelings, all seeking glory and coveting the lands of their neighbors, wars will be endless." She rolled again. "You stand here with a bucket trying to empty out the river."

"I may not be able to end all war," said Liodan. "No one can. But every conflict I prevent, every life I save is a victory. It is a moral and correct choice to empty what little of the river my bucket can hold."

"A war can be ended, but only if a single ruler controls the Heart. A strong central government would mean no more war, no more vast armies—only a militia to hunt bandits and to keep any upstarts from having ideas. No longer expending countless treasure on war means prosperity and a better life for everyone."

Liodan rolled again. "It's a fine dream," he said. "But those kings and princelings won't surrender their power. Were another Kalatar to rise and conquer the Heart, tens of thousands would die on the battlefields."

"It would be worth it," Eridani said. "A gambit, like in bato. Tens of thousands lost to save millions of lives over time."

They continued rolling. Liodan won, but it was a close game.

TEO'S COMPANY LOST a third of its soldiers in the first battle after he joined.

The plan was to attack a supply caravan. To destroy provisions and capture weapons and horses Prince Ajelogn was sending to the army units stationed at Shallowpond. They moved silently through the forest, their footprints quickly covered by a fresh coat of snow as they moved deep into the Haldovan-controlled territory. They anticipated only a small force to guard the caravan. So long as they hit hard and fast and retreated before reinforcements could be summoned, they should have been fine.

But the intelligence was wrong. Instead of a herd of horses corralled by a handful of men, they encountered three dozen cavalrymen: experienced, battle-tested troops.

Although Teo's company of just over a hundred soldiers outnumbered the enemy, they were on foot. Cavalrymen cut into them with their curved sabers. As he fought, Teo thanked all the gods he knew of that the riders did not carry lances.

A rider galloped toward Teo and swung, decapitating the soldier next to him. Teo ducked and sliced with his shortsword at the charging stallion, inflicting a long shallow wound to the cannon of its hind leg. The horse screamed, tumbled, and rolled, crushing the rider under its weight.

The rider crawled out from under the thrashing animal. He tried to get up but his leg was twisted at an impossible angle, the bone clearly broken. Teo approached cautiously. The man saw him and crawled toward his saber, lying several steps away. He grunted in pain as he pulled his broken body toward the weapon.

Teo closed the distance in several long steps. He hesitated a moment, but the saber was almost within his enemy's reach. Teo stabbed at the back of the Haldovan's neck, then pulled the blood-covered blade out of the rider's flesh it and stepped back. Making his first kill and watching the man die by his hand felt surreal. Strangely, he felt like a child who got into his mother's cupboard and ate the sugar lumps, and was now waiting for the inevitable punishment. Although Teo thought he was mentally prepared for this, his gut clenched and for a moment he wanted nothing more than to be away from the battle, back home, in the workshop that smelled of chemicals and animal hides. He pushed those thoughts away. The battle was raging around him and he couldn't afford to be distracted.

The company lost a third of its men but accomplished its objective. They killed most of the cavalrymen and destroyed any supplies they couldn't scavenge. As they prepared to head back toward Felstown, Teo wanted to check on the man he had slain, to see if his strike was lethal or if the cavalryman was still moving, dark-red blood gushing from his wound onto the snow-covered earth, but Teo resisted the temptation. He was a soldier in the middle of a war. He'd have to get used to killing, or soon he'd be the one rotting in the middle of a forest.

A MAP WAS drawn in chalk on the floor. It depicted a castle surrounded by a wall and a moat. Special markings Liodan had taught her indicated watchtowers and food stores, the location and numbers of defenders as well as civilians—farmers and smiths and tanners and traders and children, those useful in time of war and those not—who had to be either fed or forced outside, to take their chances beyond the gates.

A few steps away from the drawing, hundreds of bato beads were laid out on the stone floor. They represented the attacking force. More arcane symbols drawn in chalk identified their siege weaponry and supply lines, livestock, and other details Eridani might not have known to pay attention to before the Gatebreaker's lessons.

"I enjoy this game a great deal more," said Eridani.

The old general smiled into his beard. "I thought you might. Your mind tends toward the practical rather than the abstract." He pointed toward the tray that held a rag and several pieces of chalk. "Deploy your troops."

Eridani hovered over the setup. Each castle was unique, each scenario more complex than the previous one, taking into account details they had ignored when they first began playing these war games. Each was a puzzle to solve, whether Eridani was in control of the defending forces or the attackers. She drank deeply of Liodan's military wisdom and couldn't help noticing how pleased the old general was with her progress.

Having considered all the variables, she reached for the chalk. "Here's what I'll do."

THE NEW OFFICER arrived in Felstown all the way from Skond. He carried orders from the queen mother, and those orders were for the troops to retreat toward the capital.

"This ain't right," Tem said, when the commanders relayed the news to the troops. "We won't stick around to defend this fine place against the southern scum? I like it here." He slammed his mug onto the table.

"It's not the town he likes," said another soldier. "It's the special friend he made. She seems to like him, too, for some reason, even though she doesn't appear to be blind or dumb."

"They're looking for volunteers to form a special company," said Teo. "To stay behind and harass the enemy troops the way we did on our last mission. That way you could stick around Felstown."

Tem stared into his half-empty mug. "Son, when you do this job long enough you learn never to volunteer for anything."

Teo didn't heed Tem's warning. If the queen mother needed him behind enemy lines, that's where he'd go. He didn't join the army to sit around, drink beer, and avoid action.

The officer from Skond was a man named Kief. He was stocky, muscular, and looked tough enough to take on a company of southerners armed with nothing but a kitchen knife. He examined each of the over a dozen volunteers appraisingly—all younger recruits, Teo noticed. Then he rolled out the map of the North.

"Any of you from these parts?" Kief pointed at a large swath of land north of Shallowpond and northwest of Felstown. To the best of Teo's knowledge, there were no towns there, only farms and a handful of small villages.

The recruits studied the map. One of them didn't know how to read maps and the approximate location of the region in question had to be described to him. There were two soldiers among them who knew the area: one was raised on a farm there and another, a city boy from Shallowpond, visited with his cousins there every summer while growing up.

"You two, report to Clyde," said Kief. "We have another mission that will require your expertise."

The next morning, Teo and the rest said good-bye to their company mates and rode the horses their new commander provided to an isolated house on the outskirts of town, where several seamstresses were sewing red-and-brown jackets.

Kief pointed at the rack of finished garments. "Find ones that suit you."

"But...those are Haldovan uniforms!" said one of the men.

Kief bared his teeth in a feral grin. "Precisely."

"I LIKE YOUR solution to this scenario," said Liodan, "but you can still do better."

"Better how?" Eridani eyed the battle lines drawn in chalk and beads. "I routed the invaders with minimal casualties."

"Minimal casualties among your soldiers," said Liodan. "You left the townsfolk to be slaughtered by the invaders. In fact, your plan relied on some of the enemy units splintering to loot the town."

Eridani studied the configuration of her hypothetical castle and its hypothetical defenders. "The only other solution I see would carry more risk."

Liodan nodded. "Real warfare isn't abstract," he said. "You're not merely a general, you're a monarch. It falls to you to take risks if the upside means defending and saving your subjects."

"And if I lose, who will defend my subjects in all the other castles?" Eridani retorted.

Liodan frowned into his beard.

"You always have the advantage in our war games," said Eridani. "Because you come up with the scenarios. Perhaps you fought these battles yourself, or used them to teach siege warfare to others. Either way, you've had a lot more time to think about them than I do."

"A certain imbalance is generally expected in a student-teacher relationship," said Liodan.

"True," said Eridani. "But for a student to surpass her master, she must eventually be given leave to design her own scenarios."

"I see," said Liodan. "Fine. Let's try it your way."

"I've been thinking about this for a few days," Eridani said. "An entire campaign, so that supply lines and attrition can be tracked more accurately. You control the invaders and I'd like to see if I can stop you from taking over my cities and castles."

Liodan stroked his long wispy hair. "All right, let's give it a try."

He watched as Eridani labored to sketch out the first engagement. "Interesting. You've given me a large cavalry force but virtually no siege weaponry." He eyed the castle she was outlining in chalk. "How much do I know about the defenders' capabilities and numbers?"

For the next several days, Liodan the Gatebreaker led his imaginary army in the war of conquest while Eridani tried her best to stop him. She was a fast learner, but the old general's nickname was well-earned.

"THERE," KIEF POINTED at the farm that lay ahead. It was a sorry enterprise—the small log house was overdue for repair. Next to it was a dilapidated barn, and a patch of snowed-over garden small enough to suggest no more than a few pairs of hands worked this land. "The rules are simple," he reiterated. "Take what supplies you can carry. Burn the rest. Don't hurt the people unless you have to."

"I still don't understand," said a recruit. "These are our people. We're supposed to defend them against the Haldovans."

"In war, sacrifices must be made," Kief repeated the words he had said so many times before. "We must destroy any food the enemy troops might find ahead of them and harass the supply lines behind them. Soldiers can't fight or march on an empty stomach."

And the blame will fall squarely on the Haldovans, thought Teo. That's why Kief sent away those with ties to this area: he wanted to lessen the possibility of any soldiers refusing to loot folks here, as well as any chance of the locals recognizing the soldiers. The family who owned this farm would hate the Haldovans and support the queen, if they managed to survive this raid and the subsequent hungry winter.

Whoever thought up this plan was a clever and devious son of a bitch.

It proved to be the coldest winter in living memory. Piles of snow high as a tall man covered roads and fields, and the white stuff kept on falling. Many of the Haldovan soldiers who hailed from the warmer climes were at a considerable disadvantage against the hardened northerners. It was rumored that Prince Ajelogn lost as many men to frostbite and desertion as he did in occasional skirmishes with Eridani's forces.

Instead of engaging the Haldovans in large-scale battles, the northerners surrendered vast swaths of territory. They operated in small bands, circling the superior Haldovan companies at a safe distance like a pack of jackals, intercepting their caravans and stealing or destroying food and supplies.

The invaders could forage precious little in winter. They found few farms that hadn't already been looted or burned. The food stores of the towns in their path had already been emptied. Their generals were forced to advance ever more slowly and commit a large portion of their troops to combing the forests for northern partisans and guarding the food wagons.

Rumors swarmed among the northerners of special Haldovan units that robbed farmers and minor nobles alike of their food supplies, leaving their families with nothing. Starving refugees trickled into towns controlled by either side and confirmed such rumors. Faced with the evidence of Prince Ajelogn's cruelty, some of the nobles that pledged their loyalty to him at the onset of the war reconsidered their decisions, and demonstrated their renewed patriotism by slaughtering the detachments of foreign troops posted in their domains.

Overextended and undersupplied, the Haldovans ceased their advance toward Skond and focused on pacification of the territories they already held.

Both sides waited for spring, when the war could resume in earnest.

CHAPTER 20
SPRING

nly learned scholars, skilled in tracking the positions of stars and phases of the moon could say for certain when spring came to Skond. According to their calendars the seasons had changed, but the view outside the palace windows told a different story. The streets were covered in so much snow that the townspeople sometimes had to wade chest-deep through the pile-ups. Many roofs had collapsed from the weight of snow and ice, and the price of bread and meat at the market, which was already scandalously high because of the war, inched upward with each passing day.

"You bragged that you'd stop this war by springtime," Eridani told Liodan. "It seems nature deigned to grant you a few extra days."

"My letters to the court of Prince Ajelogn have gone unanswered," admitted the old general. "Now that you're ready, I shall travel to Haldova myself and convince them to cease the hostilities."

"Ah, so you finally admit I'm ready?" The corners of Eridani's mouth quirked up. "You still beat me at your war games more often than not."

"You're the most astute student I've ever taught," said Liodan. "By now I believe you could hold Skond against Kalatar himself." Eridani's grin widened at the high praise the usually reserved general heaped upon her. "Now I just have to convince the emperor and his son of this fact. They'll see the wisdom in negotiating terms."

"The roads remain nigh impassable," said Eridani. "Perhaps a few more lessons before you're able to travel south? You may think me ready, but there's still plenty you could teach me."

THE SNOW WAS beginning to melt when the nomads arrived at the walls of Skond.

When their banners were sighted approaching the city, there was a brief panic among the civilians and the soldiers alike. Rumors spread of the Haldovan advance, of the barbarian tribes riding against Skond, of gods and monsters meddling with humankind in ways that screwed over the fine and innocent residents of the jewel of the north. It wasn't until the city gates were opened and admitted a handful of riders instead of a rampaging horde bent on destroying everything in its path that the citizenry dared to hope the newcomers were a blessing rather than a curse.

Eridani received the Met Kelai at the council chamber. His title meant "fist of the elders." As per nomad custom, he didn't offer his name. Back in Glimmerholm, the elders had pledged twenty thousand men on horseback. They'd managed to raise over twenty-two thousand.

"This is a double-edged sword," Caer told Eridani, Sana, and an assortment of the top military commanders and members of the Council of the North who remained in Skond. The news of Eridani's alliance with the barbarians was quite a shock to them all. "We now have parity with the Haldovans in terms of pure numbers, and a considerable advantage in maneuverability; their cavalry is now half the size of ours."

The gathered all smiled and nodded as they stared at the Met Kelai. He stood unmoving at Eridani's side, like an exotic statue, and looked back impassively.

"However," Caer added, "such a large force is an enormous strain on our resources. Extra mouths to feed, human and equine both."

He went on with a litany of logistical problems until Sana cut him off. "The nomads are like an arrow trained on our enemies," she summarized. "Once loosed it is a dangerous, lethal weapon. But one can only hold the bow at the ready for a while before their arm begins to shake from the strain and the aim is no longer true."

Caer glared at Sana but didn't contradict her, whereas she ignored the old mercenary, having diverted the flow of discussion. Eridani watched the interplay—which had likely gone unnoticed by most of the others at the table—with great interest. Sana had command of the skirt army, then the army of Kozhad, and eventually the army of Skond. She was granted titles and responsibilities that would otherwise likely be Caer's. Caer never expressed his frustration or dissatisfaction with being surpassed by a younger, less experienced commander, but Eridani knew him well enough to realize his pride was wounded. The queen's favor didn't endear him to her top general. Eridani rewarded him plenty—he was a simple mercenary who rose to become the mayor of Skond and a close advisor to the Queen Mother—but she couldn't help keeping him at arm's length. The prophecy had come true with Lady Voriana and Gavron and even Pel; Eridani was convinced the Ugly Unicorn, loyal and reliable as he seemed, would one day turn against her. And when he did, it wouldn't do to have him command her armies.

The conversation flowed, with the consensus being that Eridani's forces should move against the Haldovans immediately. The arrow needed to be loosed before Prince Ajelogn found a way to counter the new threat. Before he was even aware of it. One of the commanders was proposing a plan of attack when there was a disturbance outside the hall. Muffled voices could be heard through closed doors.

With a nod, Eridani sent an adjutant to investigate. She returned shortly and whispered her report. Eridani excused herself.

In the hall, Liodan the Gatebreaker stared down a pair of guards, their swords drawn. Although he was an old man and unarmed, they shuffled from foot to foot and clutched their weapons tightly, like a pair of jackals summoning the courage to menace a lion.

"At ease," Eridani told them, and the two sheathed their weapons with looks of obvious relief on their faces. "Do not presume to order my guards around," she told Liodan. "That's well beyond your privilege as a guest."

"They wouldn't let me through," Liodan said. His wrinkled face was flushed red, his lips trembling.

"As well they shouldn't have," said Eridani. "I was handling affairs of state. But since I'm here now, perhaps you can explain why it is you're here, disparaging my name in front of my men. I'm told you called me a devious liar."

Her tone didn't make Liodan flinch. "Are those not the nomadic tribes outside city gates? Allies you've summoned in secret to fight in your war? Is their leader not behind those doors now, planning an attack on the Haldovans alongside your generals? It takes time to raise such a force. You must've known all winter long, lied to me all winter long. You never had any intention of allowing me to negotiate a peace treaty, did you?"

Eridani shook her head. "No." Liodan was perceptive and not prone to self-delusion; he understood her intentions as soon as the nomads had arrived. She would not lie to him unnecessarily in turn.

The fight went out of Liodan and suddenly he was only a slouched old man, crushed under the weight of his years. "Oh, what a fool I've been."

"Not a fool. An idealist," Eridani said softly. "The world would be a better place had it been populated by more people of your conviction." She sighed. "It's not, though. There are wolves howling at our gates and we must kill them. One doesn't negotiate with wolves."

"That cavalry campaign from our war games... that was you preparing to go on the offensive, to take back the strongholds occupied by the Haldovans. I was so enamored by your talent, so thrilled by the challenge of playing against a worthy tactician, I never questioned your motives. I showed you exactly how to beat them."

Eridani nodded again. "Thanks to you I have a pretty good idea how to take every defensive fortification from here to the southern border of Haldova itself. In our war games some of the castles managed to persevere against the siege, but I don't believe the Haldovans have anyone in charge of their defenses as good at this as either one of us."

"What will you do with me?"

Once again the tactician was ahead by several steps and would not lie to himself about his own prospects. She shuddered to think what he and the deposed patriarch might've accomplished together.

"You're to remain an honored guest at Skond," she said. "Can't have you teaching our enemies how to defend *their* strongholds, can I?"

Liodan stared at her. In his eyes, Eridani saw sadness rather than fear. "The path you're choosing will lead to suffering and countless deaths," he said. "You're much too smart not to realize this. Is that really what you want? All those hours of studying philosophy, of discussing passive resistance and ways to use one's influence to alleviate suffering... were you pretending to agree with me so I'd teach you the art of war?"

"Your vision is fine in theory, but it relies on the basic assumption of human goodness," Eridani said. "In a perfect world populated by perfect people these ideals would work fine. In my life, I've encountered precious few perfect people. Perhaps only you. And even you aren't truly perfect because your idealism blinds you to subterfuge by mere mortals like me."

Eridani admitted to herself that she actually enjoyed exploring Liodan's worldview. His pacifist ways were interesting hypotheticals, like the war games or matches of bato. But she lived in the real world where enemies didn't lay down their arms because a kind old man asked them nicely.

"Even if your acquiescence was an act, surely you care about your subjects. Many thousands will die."

Eridani thought about the women of the skirt army she'd lost in the battle against the forces of the Duke of Buzzards. Where would she be now if not for their sacrifices? "People die all the time," she said. "It's better to die young on the battlefield ensuring the safety of your homeland than of old age in bed, having accomplished nothing."

She knew Liodan wouldn't agree. He would plead and argue and lecture for as long as she was willing to listen. So she turned around and headed back into the chamber where practical matters were being discussed.

TEO BOTH LIKED and hated being in charge.

He didn't hate it as much as the stretch of several weeks their company spent wearing the Haldovan uniforms. So much damage and death, all directed against innocent bystanders who never pledged loyalty to the enemy. Although Kief honestly tried to keep human casualties to a minimum, many of the people they encountered were tough farmers who would rather fight and die for their property than face the prospect of slow death by starvation.

Teo was greatly relieved by the news that the Haldovans had pulled back somewhat and settled in for the winter. The company ditched the despised red-and-brown uniform jackets, but it was kept intact. Men hardened by their unenviable task were ready to inflict maximum possible damage on the enemy.

In the following weeks, Kief led several incursions deep into the Haldovan-controlled territory to poison wells, assassinate commanders, and otherwise harass the enemy in ways Teo never considered when he dreamed of honorable warfare and battlefield glory. Instead of glory, he earned only blood: blood of the enemies who died—directly or indirectly—by his hands, and blood of his comrades, who didn't survive the incursions.

One such mission saw the company crossing a shallow spring on foot. They cursed under their breaths as splashes of ice-cold water stung through their trousers above their high boots. That's when they ran into a Haldovan patrol.

The Haldovans saw them from the opposite shore of the spring. There were eight foot soldiers and a cavalryman. The rider galloped off immediately, presumably to alert more troops of the incursion. The soldiers brandished their swords and waited at water's edge where they had an advantage in both height and footing. Kief gave the command to advance. It was ten against eight and none of the enemy were archers, or else several of the men would have likely died before reaching the shore.

Teo put his sword to use, slashing and parrying, his feet planted firmly in the muck. The soldier he fought against was younger than him and not overly experienced with a sword. Teo wasn't a master himself, but Kief had kept them practicing regularly and those lessons were paying off. Despite the disadvantages in both high ground and reach, Teo was holding his own.

Both Kief and Clyde before him had taught the men that the worst enemy in hand to hand combat wasn't the opponent holding the sword; it was exhaustion. Swinging a heavy chunk of steel was hard work. Apparently the young soldier hadn't learned the same lesson. While Teo conserved his strength and moved judiciously in the water, the soldier danced on the ground above him and swung his broadsword with both hands, relying on strength rather than tactics.

It wasn't long before the enemy soldier was breathing heavily, moving more slowly, swinging less frequently. Teo thrust and connected, managing a wound below the soldier's hip. His opponent stumbled back and Teo advanced onto dry ground. Before he could finish the soldier off, two of the man's friends advanced on Teo's flank. Teo retreated back into the chilly water of the spring and chanced a quick look around. His side wasn't doing well. It seemed the other foes were better versed in swordplay than the young soldier Teo engaged. They used their advantage well. Five of them were still fighting while only three among Teo's company remained on their feet. He saw Kief floating face down in the water, blood seeping from the exit wound below his shoulder. With their commander dead, Teo took it upon himself to sound the retreat.

The Haldovans didn't give chase as Teo and his surviving compatriots fled. They seemed hesitant to give up the advantage of high ground and wade into the water. Their numbers were not so great as to justify the risk. Teo and the others made it to safety, forced to abandon the bodies of their dead friends.

Instead of assigning a new commander to the decimated company, his superiors placed Teo in charge. They even replenished his company with several recent recruits for him to mold and train for the difficult missions ahead. Teo was stunned to receive such a battlefield promotion after only a few months in the army. He was told there were few experienced men, and that Teo was well-liked by his unit mates and had already been suggested for possible advancement by the late Kief.

As Teo had promised his father, he was now an officer. He still didn't have any dragon scales, though, nor could he ride triumphantly into an enemy-controlled Shallowpond. But it was a step in the right direction.

He enjoyed the perks and the power, but he hated the uncertainty. He doubted every decision he made, every command he issued. How could he send men toward danger and possible death? He was certain to make mistakes, and even the successful missions had him lying awake at night wondering if he might have avoided losing a man, or having one of his soldiers become wounded. He wondered whether Kief had been plagued by such doubts.

Teo was thrilled when a messenger arrived with news that all companies were to converge and reform into traditional, large companies over the coming days. It meant his small unit would be answerable to real commanders, people more experienced than himself. It also meant that Eridani's forces were finally going on the offensive.

IT WAS THE largest battle in the history of the North. Over one hundred thousand combatants converged in the lightly forested, sparsely populated region halfway between Shallowpond and Skond.

After the snow melted and the roads became passable, Prince Ajelogn's army marched toward Skond. An enormous tide of men, horses, and siege machinery moved inexorably toward Eridani's stronghold, like an iron-tipped spear piercing flesh on its way to the enemy's heart. The Haldovans counted on Eridani's forces, spread across the North, not being able to gather in time and in sufficient numbers to mount a successful defense.

The Northern commanders threw what troops they had available in the way of the advancing army while orders were sent for all units to converge at Skond. Although the defenders fought bravely, they were barely a nuisance to fifty thousand well-armed, well-trained, and well-rested soldiers.

The Haldovans' plan was simple but effective, and it would have probably worked if not for an unusually late cold snap that brought with it the winter's last blizzard. For three days the angry sky dumped enough snow onto the ground that men had to wade through it waist-deep. Although it slowed the Northern foot soldiers and cavalry as much as the Haldovans, it made the roads virtually impassable for the heavy siege engines they'd need to penetrate the city walls.

Historians who studied the Winter War would later argue as to whether the spring blizzard was the result of luck or magic, summoned perhaps by the nomad shamans chanting ancient incantations in smoke-filled yurts under the aurora. Regardless of its origin, the blizzard changed the course of the war.

Prince Ajelogn had to choose. He could abandon the machinery and press forward, splitting his forces, while leaving enough men behind to protect the valuable siege engines. Or his entire army could slow down and count on the strength and experience of his troops to win the day, even if this gave the Northerners more time to gather their forces. Given the disadvantage the Haldovans faced moving and fighting in the snow, he chose the latter.

Partisan companies like Teo's and oath-sworn bodyguards of minor nobles, western mercenaries and Gannian fanatics: all manner of fighters under Eridani's banner gathered from across the North. They were like springs that fed into tributaries that fed into a mighty river. Many small groups that, combined with the nomad cavalry, matched the Haldovan army in their numbers.

On the morning of the battle, both monarchs rallied their troops. Prince Ajelogn addressed his men from atop a siege engine tall as a two-story house. "You're not facing an army today," he told them, "but a mob of barbarians and fanatics and women led by an incompetent pretender. They stand no chance against our disciplined and well-trained professional army. Tonight we shall dine victorious as their remnants scatter to the four winds." His words were spread by messengers to ensure they'd reach his entire fighting force.

Eridani walked among her troops for several hours, starting well before dawn. "They're fighting for profit and conquest. You're fighting to defend your homes," she told the Skond regulars. "The enemy underestimates you. Before the day is out, they will learn not to," she assured the skirt army. "The spirit of Kalatar fights with us today," she declared in front of the Gannian recruits as she pointed the tip of the Bloodsword in the direction of the Haldovans. At Eridani's urging, all her top officers were doing the same, encouraging their troops and boosting morale.

At first light, the two sides clashed.

It wasn't long until Teo became disabused of the notion that a massive battle like this was a noble enterprise. The sky was dark with arrows, the air foul with the smell of blood and gore. The cries of the dying were drowned out by the neighing of horses and the clangs of steel against steel. He was lost in a sea of men, both northern and Haldovan, killing each other. There was no order, no logic to it, only raw violence. He hacked and slashed for hours. His arms and his soul were both numb. Men engaged each other one-on-one, until one of them was bleeding on the ground or they got separated somehow in the chaos of the battle. While focusing on the enemy in front of him, a man was likely as not to be stabbed in the back by another.

There were horns in the distance, signaling attack or retreat, but Teo couldn't see how soldiers on either side could follow any of those orders. They were too deeply mired in the fight; one simply couldn't disengage in order to move to where the generals wanted them. He thought the battle would go on forever, until only a single soldier remained standing. He had no illusions about that soldier being him.

Something changed by the time the sun rose to its zenith. There seemed to be fewer Haldovans on the battlefield. The balance shifted; two or three northerners were accosting each enemy. Then the invaders were fleeing. Some of the northern fighters displayed amazing constitution in that they were able to give chase. Others, Teo among them, collapsed on the ground exhausted, lying among the wounded and the dead.

Contrary to Prince Ajelogn's boasts, the Haldovans didn't celebrate with a victorious feast that evening. The last of their battalions turned and ran by late afternoon. And while as many as twenty thousand Haldovans managed to retreat alive from the battlefield, the rest were either dead or captured, including the prince himself.

Despite bone-weary tiredness, despite caked blood on her chainmail and aching in her bruised ribs, Sana felt elated. The crucial battle was won and the North's freedom assured. Chasing the bands of enemy troops, mopping up the few remaining nobles disloyal to Eridani—those tasks seemed hardly challenging in comparison to the odds they'd been facing for years. It would take weeks, months maybe. And then their real work could begin: eliminating corvée once and for all, empowering women across the North the way they'd done in Kozhad. All the things Eridani and she had spent late evenings talking about over the years. She walked across the battlefield with a smile on her face and a spring in her step, barely hindered by a slight limp. She issued orders, overseeing the treatment of the wounded and the interment of prisoners. Then she saw him.

Prince Ajelogn sat leaning against a tree. His hands were tied behind his back, his feet chained. His left eye was swollen, his blond hair matted with sweat and clumps of dirt. He hadn't changed much since she last saw him pretending to be the ambassador's son in Kozhad, but even if he had, she would recognize his eyes. Calculating, cold, and betraying nothing, they were the eyes of a man who believed the world was his for the taking. They were the eyes of the man who raped and murdered Genna. How could she not have seen it back in Kozhad? How could she have believed Gavron's lies? At least the gods were kind enough to grant her a second chance.

"You!" She marched toward the prisoner. "Before you die, I want you to know it won't be for invading our homeland or the many other crimes you have surely committed." She unsheathed her sword. "It will be vengeance for the life of a young woman you smothered in Kozhad."

The prince looked up at her, his expression perfectly neutral, as though they were engaged in a game of cards and he didn't want to betray the strength of his hand. Then his mouth stretched into a half-smile. "I remember you. You're the skirt army *general*." He said the last word in a tone that left no doubt as to what he thought of her title. He raised his voice. "I killed that bitch because she played at being a warrior. But she was weak. You're weak, too." He turned his head, exposing more of his neck to her blade. "Go on, then, kill a tied-up prisoner. It's the only way someone like you could manage a kill. You'd stand no chance against me if even one of my arms was untied."

Sana gritted her teeth. She knew he was goading her, but she had trouble enough exercising authority over some of the men under her command. To kill a prisoner in plain view, in front of the other captive Haldovan nobles, and in front of her own subordinates might not be wise.

She gave him another appraising look. He seemed every bit a useless royal, coddled from birth. His hands were soft, his body slightly overweight. He was dressed in silks while she wore chainmail.

"I will kill you on your terms," she told him. "Cut him loose," she said, to the soldiers guarding the prisoners. She watched as they untied him and gave him back his weapon—a rapier with a fancy hilt encrusted with gemstones that looked like it would break on first contact with real steel. She knew that no matter how good the odds seemed she was still taking a chance, but years spent at Eridani's court taught her the value of a good performance.

Ajelogn stretched, then massaged his feet. He waved his rapier around like it was a baton and he was preparing to conduct an orchestra performance. He then sheathed it, approached her and bowed theatrically.

"A big mistake," he whispered, so only she could hear. "Half-witted serfs like you are so easily manipulated."

Sana growled and lifted her sword. Ajelogn took several quick steps back, drew his rapier and pointed it at her. His hand and gaze were both steady. She swung and he dodged out of the way with a fluid grace and speed she didn't expect. Then he counterattacked with a flurry of jabs she struggled to parry. ERIDANI RUSHED TOWARD the duel as soon as word of it reached her. How could Sana be so stupid? To pick a fight with their most valuable prisoner, to release and arm him ... it was the sort of thing Danchu would have done, but she thought she had taught Sana better over the years. Sure the prince would die, but not before his usefulness to them was at an end. She had already let Sana have Gavron—was that not enough?

Eridani's tent wasn't far from where the prisoners were held, and she was alerted to the upcoming duel right away. Even so, by the time she arrived it was too late. Sana lay on the ground, the slender blade of the rapier protruding from her right eye socket. Ajelogn stood calmly nearby, a few steps away so as not to give his captors the impression that he was about to reach for his sword.

Eridani stifled the scream of frustration. This was supposed to be a good day, a day of victory and celebration. And now her best general, one of her closest allies, a woman who had never betrayed her unlike so many others, lay dead because she made a stupid, unforced mistake.

Eridani approached slowly, as though in a daze, and stood over the body of her friend. All she could think of was the memory of Danchu's death, the manner of Sana's demise painfully similar to his.

"It was a fair challenge. She died well." Ajelogn's words oozed of poisoned honey.

"Kill him," Eridani said to Toval and her bodyguards.

"Wait, surely that's not what your general would have wanted," said Ajelogn. "It was a fair challenge," he repeated. He stared into her eyes and for the first time there was fear in his voice. "My father will pay an enormous—"

She nodded to Toval. He drew his sword and severed the prince's head in one smooth, swift motion.

THREE WEEKS LATER Eridani was in the grand palace of Shallowpond. Most of the local troops had turned on their disloyal masters once word of Eridani's victory reached their barracks. It was trivial to sweep aside the remaining rebels. Heads of the traitorous lords occupied many prominent spikes along city walls.

"I'm making preparations for when we'll be crossing the border into Haldova," Eridani told Caer. They were alone in the executed duke's study, surrounded by books and tapestries. It reminded her of Gavron's old home. "I intend to leave the comfort of this palace in one week's time."

"I still think that's a bad idea," said Caer. "Their army is broken and they won't be bothering us any time soon. The Haldovan king is old. When he passes, there will be chaos. They will keep busy fighting among themselves for years, and remain weakened for decades more before they can become a threat again."

With Sana gone, Caer was the only one to challenge her, to openly contradict her when it came to strategy. Her other commanders were far more reserved, and Toval, her only remaining friend who felt at ease enough to speak his mind, knew his limitations and didn't attempt to play at strategist.

"The old bastard could live another decade or more," she said. "We just killed his favorite son. You better believe he'll remain a threat." She tapped a knickknack made of semi-precious jewels that sat atop the duke's desk and it jingled softly. "They will always come for us, be it Emperor Llewell of Haldova, or whoever ascends his throne next. The only way to be truly safe is to come after them first, to bring both lands under the control of one strong ruler ..." She caught herself repeating the same argument they'd had numerous times before. Her voice hardened. "The decision has been made."

Caer nodded, his tightly woven bun of hair bobbing above his forehead.

"I've decided to leave Lady Voriana in charge of the council. She is to rule the north in my name as governor. She'll be named a Right Hand of the Queen Mother, or some other appropriately pompous title."

She half-expected, no, perhaps *wanted* Caer to argue with her over this. To say that Lady Voriana was a traitor who only recently regained some semblance of favor with the queen. That she was complicit in Danchu's death. *Everyone you know and trust will come to betray you.* She'd struggled with this decision, made these same arguments to herself. Voriana could not be trusted, exactly. But she could be relied upon to behave rationally for as long as it suited her interests, and to govern well besides. Yet again, when it came to the Dowager Councilor, vengeance would have to defer to need.

Caer mulled it over but didn't raise an objection. He was intelligent enough to perform the same mental math. The Ugly Unicorn simply nodded a second time.

"I want you to take charge of the third battalion," she told Caer. The battalion's previous commander was retired by way of an arrow through the skull in the final battle of the Winter War.

"I understand." Although Caer's self-control was impressive as always, he didn't manage to hide his disappointment.

"I know you were hoping for more," said Eridani. "I passed you over when I handed the command of my army to Sana, and now I'm doing it again, placing General Kalib in charge." Kalib had been in charge of Skond's army under the patriarch's rule. Had Eridani not been able to gain control of the council, he would have led the Skond forces against her. But he was also an extremely able commander who inspired loyalty in his men. "Surely you understand my reasoning. You're still among my most trusted advisors."

"I do understand." Caer sounded hesitant. "And I appreciate your trust. However, I'd like your permission to return to Skond. When we set out on this adventure, I thought I wanted to relive my glory days and fight battles against long odds. I'm getting older now and I've discovered that I actually enjoy being mayor." He smiled. "I can run the city while the Dowager Councilor runs the North, and keep a careful eye on her for you."

Eridani thought it over. The Ugly Unicorn remained loyal, the only member of her original band of fugitives never to betray her. She kept him at arm's length, because she feared the day the prophecy would come true. Was that day today? Some people betrayed her outright while others, like Pel, did so by running away. Was Caer running away from her, too?

Still, other than the words of the sorceress she had no reason to suspect him. Caer had been loyal, had *been* there for her, had saved her life. She owed him. She had no reason to deny his request, and his suggestion of keeping an eye on Voriana was sound. She would miss his counsel as much as his company, but she already grew accustomed to leading a lonely life.

"So be it, Mayor Caer," she told him. She grabbed a decanter from one of the shelves and filled two glasses. "A toast. I hope this post brings you much happiness."

They shared a drink of bittersweet victory, mourning lost friends and anticipating the future. One quiet moment before the tide of events would carry them in opposite directions. Then she dismissed him; there were still a number of loose ends to tie up before she led her troops south.

BEL TALESH WALKED through the narrow stone corridors of the dungeon below the palace of Skond, followed by two hooded men in gray cloaks. At the far end of the corridor a palace guard sat on a stool in front of a locked door.

The guard scrambled to his feet, his sword arm on the hilt of his weapon. "State your business," he said. It was clear he wasn't accustomed to visitors in this part of the palace.

Bel Talesh silently showed an iron badge with an intricate design depicting a clenched gauntlet.

The guard's eyes went wide. "The Iron Fist? I thought they were disbanded after ..." He glanced at the door behind him.

"We serve the queen now," said Bel Talesh. He handed the guard a sheet of parchment with Eridani's signature and seal, then waited for him to read the note. The Iron Fist's leader was surprised to receive orders from the new queen. After all, much time had passed and she had never reached out to him before. But the orders, delivered by messenger all the way from Shallowpond, were supplemented with a heavy purse of dragon scales. The queen's gold spent as well as the patriarch's. And so, here he was.

The guard handed the letter back and unlocked the door, visibly relieved at not having to confront the hooded men. Without a word, the trio passed through.

At the end of another long corridor was a door barred by a simple deadbolt. When opened, it revealed a sparse but relatively comfortable room. A man sat on the edge of the bed reading a book. Bel Talesh drew back his hood.

"Ah, my favorite assassin!" The patriarch smiled at him. "Well, don't keep me in suspense. Are you here to rescue me or to kill me?"

"I've always liked you, my lord. I'll make it as quick and painless as I can."

The patriarch set the book down unhurriedly on his bed. "I suppose there's a silver lining. She would only do this once the North was secure."

Bel Talesh didn't make a habit of chatting with his marks, but the patriarch wasn't crying, fighting, or begging for his life. He respected the man enough to offer him the courtesy of an answer. "The Haldovans were crushed in a decisive battle, a little over a month ago."

A smile spread across the patriarch's face. "Welcome news, indeed." He rose. "I suppose I can't persuade you, somehow ... no? Well, I'm ready then."

The assassin stepped behind the patriarch and gently put his left hand over the shoulder of his victim. He then stabbed at the neck below the ear, taking care to sever the carotid artery and pulled the blade down and forward, opening the neck wide. It was a messy kill, but one that ensured the victim would lose consciousness almost instantly as the flow of blood to the brain became cut off. It was the one mercy he was able to offer.

The three killers headed to another remote part of the palace, letting credentials rather than stealth or brawn open the necessary doors.

Bel Talesh did not know the wizened old-timer so he offered him no courtesy of a greeting. He and his associates entered the room blades in hand.

General Liodan regarded them calmly. "Young man, will you allow me to borrow your blade if I swear not to use it against you?" he asked Bel Talesh.

The request, stated so casually, startled the assassin. He didn't hand over his sword—he was no fool—but it stayed his hand. The two hooded killers waited behind him.

"Please," said Liodan. "I'm a pacifist. I don't want my death on your conscience."

There was something to the man, a quiet dignity that reminded Bel Talesh of the patriarch. Curiosity won over. The assassin drew a dagger from his boot and dropped it at the gaffer's feet. He felt somewhat foolish arming his mark, but if this ancient bag of bones could somehow defeat the three of them with a knife, he damn well deserved his victory.

"Thank you, young man." Liodan bent over, then picked up the dagger. He kept his movements steady and predictable. "Please tell your master that I'm supremely disappointed in her." He then lifted his long wispy beard and cut his own throat.

The three killers exchanged glances as they watched the old man bleed out and die on the floor. After he stopped moving, Bel Talesh leaned over and checked his pulse. Then he used the dagger to stab the old man in the heart, to make certain there wasn't some sorcerous trickery in play.

Satisfied that the mark was truly dead, he wiped the dagger on the old man's cloak and left the room with his two subordinates in tow, who never got to earn their keep that day.

Bel Talesh liked this new queen and sincerely hoped she would contact him again soon. The people she wanted dead seemed to be most interesting and unusual.

PART 4

(Year 548 of the Council Era)

CHAPTER 21

THE LEGEND OF THE WINTER SWARM

ridani and her inner circle drank wine and ate tropical fruits, packed in ice and delivered by caravan all the way from the southern shores of the Quadi Empire, as they waited for the storyteller to set up.

"She's immensely popular in this region, and increasingly favored by our troops," said Arut, the scribe who had been in her employ for nine years, since the latter days of the Haldova campaign. "A rare talent, but her tales are subversive and verging on dangerous."

The blind warlock at her side shifted. It was his job to eliminate danger, whatever form it might take. Once upon a time, Eridani didn't believe magic was real. She had occasion to be proven wrong more than once. It was quite rare, yes, but a real and potent threat. When her bodyguards proved insufficient against hexes and cursed blades, she made certain that her magic users were more skilled than those employed by her enemies. The warlock may have been blind, but he could sense magic better than anyone.

Eridani sipped the finest vintage from the wine cellar of the deposed lord who would not yield and pledge his loyalty. His body still hung at the gallows. She couldn't be bothered to recall his name. "I've heard as much. There's power in stories, and those who tell them well can wield disproportionate influence. I invited Lyn to perform for us, so that we could see and hear for ourselves." She studied the performer, who was busy behind what appeared to be a small stand built of multi-colored cloth. Pots filled with fragrant liquids boiled atop miniature hearths. The performer peeked underneath lids, occasionally sprinkling various powders into the pots or adjusting the intensity of the flames.

Lyn was heavily perfumed, tall, and rather large, her face framed with strands of straight, jet-black hair grown below her shoulder-blades. An Adam's apple betrayed that Lyn had been born a man, but she wore a stylish dress cut to the latest in Haldova fashion, and skillfully applied makeup which softened her facial features. From the assured way she carried herself, Eridani could infer she made her decision to change a long time ago.

The storyteller signaled she was ready and her assistant struck an intricately-designed bronze gong three times. A hush fell over the castle's hall. Three dozen guests invited to dine with the queen paused their conversations and set down their cups to focus on Lyn. She stood behind a row of her pots, seemingly at ease among the land's powerful and influential.

"Greeting, friends." Lyn projected her voice well. It was soft and mesmerizing, and it filled the room, permeating it like the smell of whatever she was brewing. She bowed to Eridani, a motion the queen judged exaggerated more than respectful. "Tonight I wish to honor our esteemed guest with a tale of another great northerner, whose weapon she carries."

There was a hum of approval. Kalatar was the symbol of northern strength. Hero to many of those present, a fearsome legendary warrior to the rest. The storyteller seemed to have chosen well.

At Lyn's signal, the servants extinguished some of the torches along the wall, the light of her hearths focusing the attention on her stall. Every eye was on her except, perhaps, for Eridani's bodyguards, who appeared somewhat twitchy at the reduced illumination in the room. After a quick glance toward their queen they voiced no protest.

When Lyn spoke again her voice was like poetry; Eridani suspected that the performer was capable of holding an audience's attention even if she read entries from an accounting ledger.

"The river of blood flows across the world. From the sun-parched mountain peaks in the south, it runs past the ziggurats and temples of a dozen civilizations until it terminates in the frozen wastes of the North. Kalatar of Gan—leader of the Winter Swarm, undefeated in battle, beloved by the gods, and feared by men—had followed the river his entire adult life."

As she spoke, Lyn opened and closed the lids of her pots, releasing bursts of hot steam. The steam hung in front of her, swirls of brown and green and grey representing farmland, forests, and mountains. She waved her long-sleeved hands to shape the steam into a heart, creating a highly stylized and ephemeral map of the world. Then she opened another pot and slashed through the steam, releasing a streak of red that cut across the world like a lightning bolt; like a scar. She waited for the map to dissipate, the strand of red hanging in front of her for a few seconds longer than the rest of it, before she resumed the story.

"He grew up among the savage people of the tundra, who knew twenty different words for snow but only one for blood. In the brief and spare summers he hiked to the shores of the Northern Ocean. He watched the red-tinged stream spill out into the vast cold blue. He dreamt of the distant lands whence it came."

True to the words, she released a rich, blue steam and tinged it with crimson.

Eridani knew that Kalatar grew up in Gan, he was *of* Gan as the storyteller herself had said. He bullied and bribed the northern tribes into following him after he already controlled most of the North. But truth doesn't often make for the best story.

"At seventeen, Kalatar fought for and won the right to rule Gan. By nineteen, he had united the savage northern tribes and led them against the gleaming towers of Julan, the city of alchemists. Julan had never been conquered before, but it couldn't stand against him."

With black steam, she drew an outline of city walls and towers against the dissipating blue. Another splash of red made it seem like those towers were burning.

"And as Julan was sacked, Kalatar questioned its alchemist-kings. Why was the river red? Where did it come from? And what did it mean? They told him of myriad tiny plants that lived in the water, making it appear the color of rose petals. He dismissed their lies and had them executed in the streets. Then the Swarm moved onward, following the river south."

Eridani frowned as she recalled her own conquest of the city of alchemists. It had been a bloody campaign, even when compared to a plethora of bloody campaigns she'd led over the course of the past decade. But treating the alchemists harshly cowed their neighbors and allowed her to gain control of those lands with relative ease.

"With every conquest, the Winter Swarm gained men the way an avalanche gains snow as it flows down a hill. By the time he emerged from the northern lands, Kalatar was said to command more warriors than there are snowflakes in a blizzard. In hushed tones, trembling southerners whispered about the coming horde."

To Eridani, Julan was in the far south, beyond Haldova. To the storyteller, it was in the cold north. The concept of northerner and southerner shifted as her armies marched across the Heart.

Droplets of bright-white steam moved erratically as a pair of assistants fanned at them with sheets of cloth, creating the effect of a snowstorm.

"Decades of vicious battles and glorious victories followed. Far from home, Kalatar encountered exotic peoples who worshiped strange gods. The river's waters were warmer and turned a deeper shade of red. Its mystery taunted the warlord, but each culture told a different myth of the river's origins.

"Some said that a fire rained from the sky, the opposing elements mixing to create a crimson liquid. Others thought the waters to be unholy, a discharge from some nightmarish underworld. One crazy priest swore that it was wine, spilled from his deity's chalice. Kalatar rejected their claims. He believed the red to be blood, and who knew blood better than the butcher of civilizations? He killed his enemies, indiscriminately mixing their blood into the river, and pressed upstream."

As she spoke of priests and mystics, she created swirling shapes and faux mystical symbols in the steam. Eridani winced at the "butcher of civilizations"—it was decidedly not the moniker one used for Kalatar in the north. Most of the audience, however, was too entranced by the spectacle to have noticed.

"Having conquered most of the world, Kalatar, now almost fifty, stood at the river's headwater. Red, viscous liquid that could be mistaken for nothing else oozed from the base of a mountain. An ancient temple perched on the hill above."

Lyn sketched in the steam. She drew what could have been bloody water pouring from a crack in the stone or, perhaps, a gushing wound.

"'What is the meaning of this?' Kalatar demanded once he had the monks brought to him. 'Why does the ground bleed?'

"'At the beginning of time,' said the head monk, 'there was only peace. But it wasn't long before mankind discovered violence. And when the first man was slain by the hand of another, the soil of the Heart itself tore in mourning and bled the victim's blood.'"

Lyn acted out each voice, distinct from the others yet equally undeniable. Eridani could see how this woman gained her reputation as one of the greatest storytellers in all of the Heart, even without her skill with the steam. The queen couldn't help wondering whether manipulating the steam was minor sorcery or accomplished stage magic.

Lyn continued in the priest's voice. "Ever since that time, the wounded Heart bleeds for all people who perish in violent ways. It is said that the earthwound will heal only when men learn the way of peace once again."

She then switched back to her own sing-song manner of speech. "Kalatar dismissed the monks and spent the night at the earthwound, watching the flow. There was so much blood, more than even he could imagine. He thought of the fallen, comrades and enemies, and countless faceless victims of his campaign, whose blood he had caused to be added into the torrent. He was still there at first light, when his scouts returned."

The storyteller sculpted the steam with her hands. One could almost see a man sitting on a rock deep in thought, his head in his hands, against the pale blue of an early morning light. The level of detail was astounding given the medium. Even if she couldn't tell a story, Eridani thought, her craft alone would draw crowds. The combination of the two talents was doubly impressive.

"'There is nothing south of the mountains,' the scouts told their liege, 'except the sand, and scorpions, and scorching winds. But the East—the East is another matter. There are fertile lands and teeming cities, and riches beyond measure. Our victories there will be glorious.'

"'No,' said the aging warlord. 'Like the river itself, war must have a beginning and an end. A victory matters less if it's merely a prelude to another battle. We shall take our plunder and our glory, and we shall journey home.'

"And so the Winter Swarm retreated northward, following the river's current. With time, the stream lost much of its red shade, diluted by the freshwater from its many tributaries along the way."

The storyteller painted a river whose water changed hue from red to reddish to mostly blue.

"Kalatar regarded the river's surface countless times over the course of the return journey. Each time he took note of its paler hue, he smiled a knowing smile, and pressed on toward home."

Lyn waited for the last of the steam to dissipate, then bowed deeply, first toward Eridani, then several times more toward the other tables. The audience cheered. Some clapped. Many tapped the tabletops loudly with open palms in accordance with the local custom for applause.

"This is not historically or geographically accurate in the slightest," said General Kalib. "Kalatar never traveled so far south, nor did he have any sudden change of heart later in life. There is some seasonal discoloration in some of the rivers, true, but it's—"

Eridani waved him to stop. "It's a fable and its moral is rather transparent. She wants me to turn around and go home."

"How dare she insult the queen mother," piped in Toval, who was seated at Eridani's table. He had clapped the loudest moments earlier, the subtleties of the tale lost on him.

"She is a bold one," Eridani said thoughtfully. "One does not often speak truth to power, even when it's a thinly veiled truth."

"I did say she was dangerous," said Arut. "One must assume she is not so subtle in her opinions when performing outside castle walls."

"It is perhaps best if she's silenced," said Kalib. He raised his eyebrow. "A discreet accident could be arranged?"

"That would be a shame and a waste of her talents," said Eridani. She beckoned the storyteller over.

Lyn approached the table and bowed again. "My queen," she said. "My lords and ladies. I hope the performance was to your liking." She spoke with an exotic accent of which there was no hint during the performance.

"It was an interesting exercise in revisionist history," said Eridani. "One must be careful when claiming to understand the motivation of a great monarch for leading their people in war."

"Ah, but there are only four reasons to go to war." Lyn counted on her right hand, bending fingers and showing off her pink-colored nails. "Coin, kin, faith, and fame."

"That's simplistic," said Eridani. "What of honor, love, a sworn oath? Had I imbibed less wine I'm certain I could think of a few more motivations on the spot."

"There may exist exceptions that prove the rule," admitted Lyn. "Personally, I know of no soldiers fighting in any armies for honor alone. And love? It may be universal, but only the fabulously rich can afford to go to war over it."

Eridani chuckled. "If you were as skilled with a sword as you are at verbal sparring, I'd make you one of my champions." She leaned forward and said in a conspiratorial manner, "So tell me then, why do you think I go to war?"

Eridani noted with some satisfaction that her interlocutor blanched and paused for a few moments, contemplating a response. She felt like she had scored a point against the storyteller in their verbal game of bato.

When Lyn spoke, it was slower and more deliberate than her earlier banter. "You do not fight for faith, even as you skillfully use it to draw believers to your banners." She cast a meaningful glance at Eridani's scabbard. "You do not fight for coin, or when you do it is only the means of financing your wars." The storyteller found her argument; her voice sounded more certain and regained an echo of the cadence Eridani witnessed during the performance. "It is true you once fought for kin, but the graves of those who had wronged your family are in the north, far from where you wage your battles now." She looked Eridani in the eyes. "That leaves fame. You fight for notoriety, for your name to roll off the lips of storytellers like myself many generations after we're gone."

The others at the table shifted uncomfortably but Eridani's face remained serene as she listened to the storyteller. "This is an easy conclusion to reach when you have only the broadest of facts," she said. "But it is wrong, much like assigning thoughts and motivations to Kalatar of Gan when you know the legend but not the man." She drank deeply from her goblet. "I spent years fighting against oppressors and invaders. Each time I defeated an enemy, a greater threat rose in their wake. It was only after my banners flew over all the cities in the Haldova plains that we no longer faced an immediate threat."

Eridani paused for a moment, thinking of all the battles she had fought, seeing her brother's handsome face when he led the mercenaries against the Duke of Buzzards' stronghold a decade and a half ago. How far she had gone from there. How proud Danchu would be of her.

"But for how long would my people have remained safe if I did nothing?" Eridani asked. "Another warlord, another Kalatar will always rise. Dukes and lords and kings will send their armies to clash against one another in an endless struggle for—how did you put it?—coin and fame. The meat grinder's handle will never stop unless there is only one monarch; one emperor or empress to rule the entire Heart. Yes, tens of thousands will yet die in the coming wars, but when I win, I will improve the lives of millions. A single hand reining in the nobles, ensuring that there is no further war or strife."

Her advisors listened as intently as the storyteller, even if they had heard her justifications many times before. War had become their way of life over the years, and she had had time and practice to describe her grand ambitions so clearly; to unambiguously declare war on the rest of the world. Eridani wondered if the storyteller was somehow not familiar with her propaganda, or merely wanted to hear her reasoning directly.

Lyn appeared lost in thought. "What you describe has never been done," she said. "Even the greatest conquerors in history, men like Kalatar, only managed to control swaths of the Heart, and only for a time."

Eridani laughed. "Can you imagine how many times I've been told a goal I set was unattainable over the course of my life? It is true that no man has conquered the Heart, but you should know better than most that a woman can sometimes achieve more than anyone might expect of her."

"But how can you be sure?" Lyn asked. "How can you be so certain that this new order you wish to impose upon the world, this untested experiment, will be worth the price your war extracts from the peoples of the Heart?"

"I know my heart and my mind," Eridani said. "I know what I can achieve. But even if you don't place your faith in me, ask yourself: how can it be worse? Is continuing the endless cycle of small, vicious wars truly preferable to you than embarking upon this grand, untested experiment? But I also know this." Eridani's voice softened. She sounded almost conspiratorial. "I can't do it alone. I need generals, and soldiers, and bards to eloquently spread my message to the people of the Heart. Tell me, Lyn, do storytellers yearn for coin or fame? There's no reason you can't have both."

Lyn hesitated, like a rabbit who must defy a tiger while still within the reach of its claws. "I'm a storyteller," she said. "An artist. Art is not war. There's another motivating factor, and that's telling the truth."

The people at Eridani's table tensed, anticipating a violent reaction from their queen. But she only smiled as she peered at the earnest expression on Lyn's face.

"Of course," said Eridani. "You're a dissident, an artist brave enough to risk her life in order to speak truth to power. It was a mistake to think you'd be swayed by fame or coin. But there's something else. Something only I can offer you." Eridani paused for effect. "A chance to write the foundational narrative for this experiment, as you call it, for my new world. To chronicle a new legend, one that will be copied and re-told by storytellers many generations after both of us are gone."

Eridani refilled her goblet with wine. "Would you rather rabble-rouse against yet another warlord passing through this patch of dirt—an event that historically seems to occur every decade or so—or compose an epic tale of a woman on her quest to achieve the impossible?" She filled another goblet and handed it to Lyn.

LONG AFTER THE bulk of the invading force had moved on to battles farther south and west, Lyn continued to wow the crowds with her performances. She spun tales out of steam and rhyme in taverns, theaters, and city squares across the Heart. And everywhere she went, Lyn praised Eridani the Fierce, the Benign Conqueror, Spirit of Kalatar Reborn.

CHAPTER 22

THE MAW OF ARVADON

ridani pulled the rain-soaked cloak tighter to protect herself against the chill of the creeping dusk. She leaned in close to her horse's neck and gritted her teeth. The guide was late, and patience had long since ceased to be one of her better virtues.

"I don't like this," Toval said, for what must've been the third time. The big man stood by her horse's side, the reins of his horse in one hand and the lantern in the other. He stoically ignored the rain, droplets glimmering in his beard and long hair. "We don't need a guide. We know the way to their fortress."

"They're testing our resolve," said Eridani. "Making us wait here, exposed to the elements. We must play along if we hope to be admitted."

"It may be a trap," said Toval. "Any number of enemies would pay a fortune to find us here alone, away from your army." He flicked the water out of his eyebrows. "This is a foolhardy errand."

Eridani stared him down. "You're forgetting your place, Toval."

The big man bowed. "Apologies, my Queen, but you always encourage me to speak my mind."

Her response was forestalled by the sound of an approaching rider. The horse trotted into view, carrying a man whose robes identified him as a follower of Arvadon. He ignored Toval, and rode up to Eridani until the two of them were face to face on their mounts.

"Greetings, supplicant," he spoke.

Eridani nodded slightly, her face betraying no emotion.

"You're late," growled Toval, as he climbed onto his horse.

"The might of Arvadon transcends time," said the guide, as if no further explanation were needed.

"Let's get on with it," said Eridani.

THE ENTRANCE TO the temple of Arvadon was carved into the flat side of a mountain, accessible only by a rickety rope bridge over a deep gorge. At the first sign of trouble, the attendants could cut the ropes and make the temple impossible to breach, no matter the size of the invading force. A handful of priests could defend the structure indefinitely, given a proper supply of food and water. Although Eridani never intended to lay siege to the temple, her mind couldn't help trying to seek out weaknesses and points of access. She was impressed with how thoroughly impenetrable the setup was.

Fortunately, she didn't have to fight her way in. The three of them arrived in the early dawn, riding through the settlement perched on the opposite side of the gorge. The brick houses were large and well-kept, with barns and stables attached to nearly every one. Arvadon's followers lived well, Eridani noted, grown fat off the bounty provided by the supplicants.

The rain lingered, but reduced from a downpour to a light drizzle. They dismounted and handed over the reins of the exhausted horses to the attendants, then climbed the unsteady bridge, single-file, toward the temple entrance. The wooden boards, slick from the rain, creaked under their boots.

Once inside, Eridani drew back her hood and looked around. A large chamber was lit by several dozen candles. The walls and ceiling were smooth and covered with writing in an elegant script—sacred texts reproduced with great care, using expensive dyes. This wasn't a natural cave—the temple had been carved out of solid rock by generations of worshipers.

On the other side of the chamber there was an arched door. Its edges were inlaid with enormous teeth—larger than any Eridani had seen before. Whether they belonged to dragons or other beasts long gone from the world, Eridani couldn't guess. The teeth were arranged so that the entrance looked like a snarling maw.

The only piece of furniture in this chamber was a wide cherry wood table, its surface polished and lacquered to perfection. Behind it sat a man who looked to be in his late forties, the gray only recently having gotten hold of his temples. He nodded to the guide and sized up the newcomers.

"Welcome, supplicant." The man rose from his seat. Like the guide, he ignored Toval completely. Eridani was the supplicant, she was the one to whom they granted an audience. Allowing her to bring a single bodyguard was merely a courtesy. "I'm Shodar."

Eridani adjusted her soaked cloak and nodded to the annoyingly dry man, trying to keep a careful balance between a polite greeting and reminding him that, even though she came to seek favor, they weren't equals. "Are you the high priest?"

"All who serve Arvadon are of the same status, supplicant," said Shodar. "I'm the one who will guide your journey."

Eridani said nothing, but noted that Shodar wasn't the one sent to fetch them in the rain. In her experience, those who bloviated loudest about equality were the ones pulling the strings.

Shodar continued, "Supplicant, I shall tell you about the blessing of Arvadon, and the price our god demands from those who wish to have this blessing bestowed upon them."

"We know all about the ritual," said Toval, "or we wouldn't be here now. Let's get this over with, so we can find warm food and dry clothes."

Shodar did not deign to acknowledge the interruption, but their initial guide gently rested his hand on Toval's shoulder. "Patience, friend. It wouldn't be much of a ritual if it could be shortened to fill one's belly sooner. Shodar must say the words as surely as your queen must hear them."

Toval stared the man down until he withdrew his hand, but offered no further protest.

"The Maw of Arvadon is a portal that connects our world to countless others," said Shodar. "It was entrusted to us by the god himself, in time immemorial. If deemed worthy, it bestows upon the supplicant whatever sort of item they need the most."

Shodar pointed at the large leather-bound tome that sat on the table in front of him. "This ledger keeps the record of all the wonders that arrived through the portal, over the course of centuries. There is a tale of a scribe who received a clockwork songbird that trilled foreign-tongue tunes more beautiful than anything previously heard in the world. Another record is of a warrior who was given a weapon that killed enemies at a great distance with lightning and thunder. There were many more incredible divine gifts that have shifted and turned the tides of history."

Shodar's fingers caressed the cover of the ledger as he spoke. Then his voice and posture changed subtly, his expression darkened, and he seemed to grow taller. "There are two warnings you must hear before we proceed.

First," he let go of the ledger and held up an index finger, "the gift you are given is what you truly need, not what you think you need. Often those two things aren't at all the same. Second," he held up the thumb, "you will be required to pay thrice for the privilege."

Shodar leaned on the table with both hands. "You will make a payment of wealth, and give up more than you can afford.

"Then, you will pay in truth, and reveal more than you wanted.

"Finally, you will pay in love, and give up something so precious that parting with it will break your heart.

"If Arvadon finds all three of these payments to his satisfaction, you will be allowed to receive his blessing. Only a handful of supplicants are found worthy, and fewer yet are satisfied with their bargain in the end. Now that you know all this, do you still choose to proceed?"

Eridani the Fierce, Queen Mother of the North and conqueror of the Haldova Plains, did not flinch or turn away from the priest's intent gaze. "I'm ready," she said, her voice steady and firm.

"Excellent," said Shodar. The guide bowed his head—not nearly deep enough—to Eridani, and walked outside. "We begin here, with the payment of wealth." The priest paused expectantly.

Eridani looked at Toval and nodded. The bodyguard withdrew a pouch from underneath his cloak and set it in front of the priest.

Shodar opened the pouch and emptied its contents onto the table. Rubies and diamonds, emeralds and sapphires spilled from within. Shodar pursed his lips as he examined a few of the larger gems, holding them against the light of the nearest candle.

"It's not enough," he said.

"Not enough? It's a fortune!" roared Toval.

"It's all I have," said Eridani. It was the truth. She had heard rumors that if she lied, the priests would know.

"Everything you may think of as wealth, but not everything of value," said Shodar. "You took the Pride of Haldova from the corpse of its late monarch, Emperor Llewell. It is said that you kept it as a prize."

She hesitated.

"I warned you that you would pay more dearly than you expected, all three times," said Shodar.

Eridani reached under her tunic and removed the silver necklace upon which hung a ring inlaid with an emerald. The stone wasn't larger or more valuable than some of the finer gems spread before the priest. It was a memento of her greatest military victory to date rather than merely currency, and she was loathe to surrender it. But she refused to give Shodar satisfaction by acknowledging this.

With a shrug she tossed the necklace onto the table. Behind her, Toval grunted in disapproval.

The toothy door slid open.

"Arvadon has found your payment worthy," said Shodar. "You may proceed."

She stepped toward the opening. Toval followed closely behind.

"I'll wager all the jewels on that table against a turnip that the priest opened that door with a hidden lever," he murmured.

Eridani half-turned and rewarded her bodyguard with a grin before she stepped through the doorway.

The next chamber was identical to the first in size and shape, but instead of the holy writings, the walls and the ceiling were inlaid with mirrors. Eridani paused. Countless visages of herself reflecting infinitely from all sides gave her vertigo.

She focused on the table near the identical tooth-laden doorway at the other end of the chamber. Seated behind the table was Shodar.

"How..." She spun back, in time to see Shodar walk in after Toval. The two priests appeared identical in every way.

Toval had a similar reaction. "You two twins?" he asked.

"In our humble devotion, the servants of Arvadon share everything," said Shodar Number Two. "Even a face."

The original Shodar nodded, and walked across the chamber to stand by the second door.

"This is the Hall of Reflections," said the new Shodar. "Here you must pay with the truth."

Eridani crossed her arms and stared at the priest.

"Do you believe in the power of Arvadon?" asked the priest.

Eridani tensed. The truth was almost as dangerous as the lie. But the lie would not get her closer to the Maw.

"No," she said.

"Then why are you here?" he asked.

"My army is about to challenge our greatest adversary yet. I'm willing to explore every option, seek every advantage, so that we may win."

"So the rumors are true. You would go to war against the Quadi."

"Yes," said Eridani.

"And yet, you do not believe. What can the Maw possibly offer to the one who has no faith?"

"You control a portal to other worlds through which someone sends dangerous gifts. Whether they come from some god or demons below, makes no difference to me at all."

The priest thought for a moment. "The Quadi built the greatest empire in history. They control nearly half of the known world. You are but a mosquito circling their tent. Why would you poke a sleeping dragon? What makes you think you can win?"

"I'm Eridani the Fierce and I've been at war facing overwhelming odds for most of my life. Scholars and priests have declared my demise imminent, time and again. I've proven them all wrong and I will continue to fight until I rule the entire world. The Quadi are merely next; an aging, crumbling empire that has the misfortune of being in my way."

The priest glanced at the door. "The entrance remains closed. Arvadon doesn't wish to hear bravado and bluster—he demands the truth! We'll be here for as long as it takes, so why don't I help you." He walked around the table until he was face to face with Eridani, and then he pointed at the southern wall.

"Beyond this mountain range are the lands of the Quadi. You must have sent scouts who returned with reports of cities so vast that each contains more souls than your entire army. They must have observed the legions of Quadi soldiers, so numerous and well-trained that you wanted to doubt the words of your own spies.

"Might it be that you sent more trusted observers or even traveled there yourself, wrapped in the anonymity of this simple cloak, to confirm with your own eyes the futility of your quest? Perhaps you've come to realize that you were but another minor warlord, destined to become nothing more than a footnote in some scribe's treatise on barbarian history.

"Have you come here grasping at straws, desperate to find some miracle that would give you the tiniest chance at victory? Have you come here because you're *afraid*?"

Eridani grabbed the priest by his robe and snarled, squeezing each word through gritted teeth. "No one has ever had cause to call me a coward."

The priest didn't even flinch. He leaned closer, his nose almost touching hers. "What, then? Look—the door remains closed. If you want my god's help, you have to tell me the truth. Tell me what you're holding back. What you don't want even him to hear!" The priest pointed at Toval. "*Tell me.*"

"All right!" Eridani shoved the priest back. "I forged my army, battle by battle, out of zealots, barbarians, and highwaymen, out of freed slaves and captured enemies. They fight well, but they do not know how to be at peace.

When stationed in one place for too long, they must be paid and kept busy, or soon they will turn against the locals, and then against each other, and then, finally, against me."

Eridani paced the room, watching her reflection in the mirrors. "Like a giant swell wave, my army can't merely choose to *stop*. I must unleash them on the Quadi, and soon. It will be difficult and bloody. The truth you're after is that there isn't much I can do to stop it. I must ride the wave or sink underneath it, and I will ride it to victory. I have a plan."

As she paused for breath, the second door slid open. Without uttering another word, the priest joined his twin at the doorway.

Eridani and Toval approached the entrance, but the two priests blocked the way.

"Not him," said one of the Shodars. "This is as far as he goes. Beyond this entrance is the Maw itself. Only the supplicant and the priests may enter."

Eridani hesitated. "I'll need him," she said. "For the final challenge."

The priests exchanged glances. "I see," said one of them, studying Toval closely for the first time. "A trusted bodyguard. A comrade, who has been with you from the beginning. Perhaps something more?" He arched an eyebrow. "He'll make a worthy sacrifice."

Toval had never been made privy to this part of the plan. Eridani could see his heart breaking, the pain visible on his face and in his slumped shoulders, reflected endlessly in the mirrors. He stared at her, then at the priests, and turned as if to run, to escape from the nightmare he suddenly found himself in.

The two Shodars produced long, curved daggers from beneath their robes, and held them to Toval's flesh, one at the gut and another at the neck. From their lack of hesitation and fluid movements, Eridani had to infer they were used to human sacrifice.

She stepped through the final doorway and the priests ushered Toval in behind her.

The last chamber was bare. It contained no table, no mirrors, no writing on the walls, and no candles. Instead, it was illuminated by the otherworldly light of the portal.

The Maw of Arvadon was set inside a skull of what might have been an enormous crocodile, inside its wide-open jaws. The portal was a pulsating sphere of purple and green energies, half as tall as a man. Two more priests, identical to the Shodars she had already met, stood guard at the portal's sides.

They approached the portal in silence. One of its guards stepped forward and offered his dagger to Eridani. "It must be done by your hand." The other two priests stepped back, still blocking Toval's way, but making room for Eridani to deliver a killing blow.

She smiled at the priest as she accepted the dagger from his hand, tested its edge to find it razor sharp, then with a single fluid motion slid it across the priest's throat.

Before anyone had the chance to react, before the priest's body hit the ground, she withdrew a throwing knife from the sleeve of her cloak and flung it at one of the men standing behind Toval. The man gurgled and went down, the knife imbedded deep in his neck.

Toval roared and turned as the other priest swung his dagger. Toval swiped at it with his left hand, deflecting the blade at the cost of a flesh wound as he punched the priest in the face with his right fist. The priest stumbled back, blood pouring from his nose. A second punch to the jaw brought him to his knees.

The last remaining priest came at Eridani with his dagger. He was faster and clearly skilled with the blade from the way he handled himself. But, even without the element of surprise on her side, he was no match for Eridani the Fierce, who had personally led her men into battle hundreds of times. She laughed savagely as she parried his thrusts once, twice, the clang of steel against steel echoing across the chamber. The priest stepped back and circled Eridani, searching for an opening. She waited for him to make a move, then shifted to the side as he lunged at her again, and tripped him. When he sprawled on the floor, she buried her dagger in the base of his skull.

With three priests dead, Eridani walked over to the survivor, who was on the ground, clutching at his nose to try and stem the flow of blood. She kicked him in the ribs, hard enough to hear them crack. "Is this enough slaughter to satisfy your godling of the wild beasts?"

The priest moaned in pain.

Eridani walked over to the portal and leaned in, studying the pulsating ball of energy. Toval stood next to her. "I hope you don't intend to shove me into that thing," he said.

"Don't worry," said Eridani. "The plan is what it always has been." With a grunt, she upturned the huge animal skull, yellowed with age. Beneath it was an orb the size of a child's head, which, according to her own mages, powered the portal between worlds. Eridani used the bloodstained blade of the dagger to dislodge the orb from its holding place and lifted it up. Then she tossed it into the portal.

Without a sound, the portal winked out of existence. The chamber grew dim, the light of candles from the doorway leading back to the Hall of Reflections its only remaining source of illumination.

"What have you done?" The priest sobbed, tears and snot mixing with blood on his face. "Foolish barbarian, the Maw could have granted you power beyond imagining!"

"It could offer nothing but exotic trinkets that someone on the other side was willing to toss through," said Eridani. "If the portal could deliver items of any real value, the Quadi would have taken it away from you centuries ago." She spat at where the portal had been. "And, on the off chance that I am wrong, I'm not leaving an unpredictable source of magic behind for somebody else to use against me. I've always known how to guard my flank."

"You never believed." The priest sat up, his robes stained crimson. "Why come here and visit your violence upon us?"

Eridani leaned over him and sneered. "Money, gems, and other treasure you've squirreled away. Payment from all the foolish supplicants desirous of the miraculous gifts from the other side. You will show us where it is, if you want to keep breathing."

AN HOUR LATER, Eridani and Toval were crossing the rope bridge again, each loaded with a heavy satchel full of precious stones. The rain had stopped. Eridani smiled, her face warmed by the morning sun. The Pride of Haldova once again hung around her neck. All that remained was for them to get their horses and ride off before the Arvadon worshipers suspected anything might have gone wrong at the temple. Her plan had worked perfectly, but Toval remained uncharacteristically quiet.

"Out with it," said Eridani. "What's on your mind?"

"Back there, you really meant it," said Toval. "You would have sacrificed me, if you had to. These gems are worth more to you than a loyal friend."

"I told them that I needed you for the final challenge to get both of us inside," said Eridani.

"I've known you a long time," said Toval. "We've bled together in many battles. You can't fool me with half-truths, like you did those priests." Toval sighed. "Perhaps it is I who doesn't know you as well as I thought."

Eridani hefted the satchel she was carrying. "This isn't merely wealth. It's the means to buy weapons for our soldiers, hire mercenaries, and bribe men to open city gates without having to spend months on a siege. This is our best chance to defeat the Quadi. I wouldn't be a very good queen if I wasn't willing to risk anything, much less a single life, in exchange for that."

Toval made no reply and would not meet her gaze, and they continued to traverse the rope bridge in silence.

Once they had crossed and reclaimed their horses, Toval removed his satchel and handed it to Eridani.

"Our paths diverge from here, my Queen," said Toval. "Good luck to you." Without waiting for a reply, he heaved himself up into the saddle.

Words of the prophecy played in Eridani's head. But truly, who betrayed whom? She thought back to the challenge. The priests would have detected the lie. She might have tried to tell herself it was only a diversion, but deep inside she had to have been ready to sacrifice Toval. She knew this. And, unfortunately, so did he.

"Toval," Eridani called. She half-expected him to ignore her, to ride off without looking back, but he turned, seemingly despite himself. His shoulders were stooped and his eyes forlorn.

Eridani lifted both satchels and held them over the edge of the cliff. "You are a loyal friend, worth more to me than all the treasure in this temple. Say the word, and I will drop the loot, if that will get you to stay."

They stared at each other. Eridani couldn't guess what her oldest friend was thinking as he considered her gambit. She wondered what she might do if he called her bluff.

The tension slowly bled from Toval's muscles. "Keep the treasure," he finally said. He offered no further comment, no witty retort. He simply waited while she secured the precious satchels in her saddlebags and mounted her own horse.

As they rode side by side in silence, she took one last look at the gorge and the sun-bathed valley that stretched beyond the mountains to the south.

She knew that, one day, it would all be hers.

CHAPTER 23

FORTY-SEVEN DICTUMS OF WARFARE

eo followed one of his men through the vast halls of the palace, past the defaced portraits of royals and the vacant pedestals from which vases and small trinkets had already been looted. Laughter and muffled screams could be heard from some of the rooms they passed; the fighting was over, and the soldiers were helping themselves to the spoils of war.

The youngster leading them reminded him of himself at that age; a fresh recruit who couldn't wait to make a name for himself and to earn a fortune. He thought back to the early years, to the time when he savored each victory, excitedly celebrated surviving yet another engagement.

He was an officer now, and he'd had it up to his neck with all the glory the military life had to offer. The army changed around him over the years. It seemed none of the people who fought alongside him back in the North were around anymore. They were either dead or served elsewhere across the vast territory controlled by the queen mother. The unit he commanded was all local men—boys, really—who were eager to one day return home with a bag of coins and a deed to a plot of land. Except he was getting farther away from his home with every passing year, and he suspected his men were destined to share the same fate. The ones who survived, anyway.

"She's in there." His guide pointed at the wide doorway. The youngster shifted from foot to foot impatiently, no doubt eager to join his comrades.

Teo dismissed him with a nod, and pushed the gilded double doors open.

A teenage girl dressed in fine silks stood at the center of the room, blade in hand. Half a dozen soldiers circled warily beyond her reach, their own weapons drawn. Teo approached and the men parted to let him pass. He and the girl appraised one another.

"Take another step and die," the girl warned, her voice cracking.

Teo chuckled. "Your stance and grip are all wrong. The toy you're clutching is good only for ceremonies; it would break the first time you parried. Any one of them"—he pointed at the soldiers—"could disarm you in seconds. The only thing keeping you alive is that circlet."

The girl blanched, clearly unused to being spoken to in such a frank manner. Precious stones set in the silver band atop her head glinted. She regained her courage. "Keep away! I'm Princess Elena. No commoner may spill the noble blood!"

"Dictum seventeen," said Teo. "The ancient sages proscribed harming the enemy princes, for once the commoner accepts that kings are mortal, who knows what dangerous ideas that may lead to, eh?"

"You know the dictums?" She lowered her blade a fraction.

"I'm Teo, lieutenant of the Third Company and Earl of Shallowpond."

"I've never heard of an earldom of Shallowpond."

"It's all the way in the north."

"You're too filthy to be a noble," she said. "Even for one of the barbarian queen's thugs."

He straightened his coat, its hems caked in mud and ichor. "This is what war looks like, Princess." His hand rested on the hilt of his sword. "My men can't touch you, but I'll cut you down if I must."

Her blade rose. "Do it, then. I won't forfeit my family's claim to the throne by surrendering!"

"A toothless claim, that. Your side has lost. But there's a deal to be made." He wondered if she would listen or lunge. She chose the former. "What do you think will happen if you surrender?"

"I will be ransomed," Elena said.

"Dictum forty-two. You'll be treated like an honored guest until some relative pays in gold or favors."

Teo stepped forward, nearly within her blade's thrusting range. "Do you hear those screams? Thousands will be tortured or robbed, perhaps killed, merely because their liege lost a war they never wanted." Another step. He was nose to nose with her now. "You can save them."

Her hand trembled. She didn't strike, even though the dictums allowed it. "What do you propose?"

"As per dictum twelve, my queen will need a royal signatory to the terms of surrender. You can die here to spite her, or demand better treatment for your subjects in exchange for your signature."

Elena hesitated. "How do I know you'll keep your word?"

"Dictum thirty-one. The terms offered during parley are binding."

"I thought barbarians didn't follow the dictums."

"We don't," said Teo. "But I make it a habit of studying the customs of my enemies. Some of those customs are worth adopting."

Elena's lip trembled. Reluctantly, she sheathed her blade and handed it over.

Teo's men secured the princess with proper deference due to her rank.

Teo said, "You should know that I lied. I'm an officer, but not a noble."

Elena cried out as she struggled in the grip of the soldiers.

Teo felt sorry for her. He had tricked her, claimed authority the dictums didn't grant him. But he might have saved her life—had she faced a real noble who followed this ancient code of conduct, he would have likely as not gone for the easy kill. Would she still hear reason? He had to try.

"Wait. Listen. I may only be a tanner's son, but everything else I said was true. I'll take you to my queen, who cares no more for the lives of common men than any other monarch. Of the Forty-seven Dictums of Warfare, none concern themselves with compassion for the commoners. You, at least, have the chance to exceed expectations and help your people." He signaled for the soldiers to release Elena.

Elena calmed herself somewhat. She didn't move.

Over the years, Teo's idealism had faded as Eridani failed to implement the reforms she had promised. She reversed many of her early verdicts, re-instituting corvée, raising taxes, forcing young men and women to join her army, all in the name of her ultimate goal. "When I rule the Heart," she would say, "everything will be different. Everything will be better." Teo couldn't bring himself to buy into the rhetoric any longer.

Perhaps there was a chance for Elena's people. Perhaps she was young enough, and not yet fully conditioned to see the commoners as little more than livestock. She could bargain to better their lot. He would teach her how.

Teo pressed on. "I may not have the authority to make this deal, but you do. You just have to present the idea to Queen Eridani as your own. My queen has a soft spot for fiery, outspoken women. If she sees something of herself in you, she will listen."

Elena looked at him, stone-faced, her eyes cold and calculating. He feared she'd refuse, but she simply nodded assent, a barely perceptible tilt of the chin.

She accepted the arm he offered. Then, quick as a viper, she withdrew a dagger from her sleeve and stabbed him in the heart.

She stood over Teo, watching him bleed. His stunned men surrounded them, but dictum seventeen offered her better protection against their impotent fury than a plate of armor. A corner of her lip turned upward and she dropped the bloody dagger to the floor.

"Let's go," she told them. As Teo slipped from consciousness, he heard her add nonchalantly, "I'll parley more effectively with your queen if she doesn't think me a fool swindled by a commoner."

The Forty-seventh Dictum of Warfare lauded the value of saving face over mercy.

ERIDANI HELD COURT in the summer palace of a recently-vanquished king. She dispensed orders, praise, or an occasional punishment as an endless stream of officials reported on various aspects of imperial business. The smarter among them had long since learned that she wanted brief, efficient reports with none of the pomp and groveling.

To her right sat General Kalib. Although the years had added new wrinkles to the man's face and robbed him of his remaining hair, he had proved himself a consistently competent leader of her armies; almost as ruthlessly efficient as Eridani herself.

To her left sat the blind warlock. His head was tilted as he listened to the whispers from the other planes, or whatever it was sorcerers did. Next to him was Princess Elena, the last surviving daughter of the local bloodline. Eridani was pleasantly surprised to learn that she was quite eager to collaborate in exchange for retaining her title and her head. Given how small and relatively unimportant this kingdom was, Eridani was content to have Elena act as a governor, so long as it quelled any possible unrest and so long as the princess managed to keep the tax revenues flowing steadily.

One by one, the reports came of her army's conquests. The distant lands in the far west and far east regions of the Heart were added steadily to her empire. Her thoughts weren't focused on the minor victories in the obscure corners of the map. It was on the great prize, the empire of the Quadi.

Eridani built up her armies steadily, but they remained inadequate to challenge the Quadi war machine. The Quadi training, war tactics, and fortifications were developed over the course of centuries rather than years. She hadn't come up with a strategy that might work, so she kept strengthening her control over the rest of the Heart. She kept thinking and planning.

A little stocky man in front of her droned on about tax revenues and draft rates in one of the provinces. He went into far more detail than she would have liked. The empire was too large for her to micromanage it. She had learned to rely on governors and replace them quickly if they failed to impress. She was about to interrupt and chastise the official who overstayed his welcome when her warlock tensed and half-rose from his seat, like a tomcat arching his back in the presence of a rival. The bodyguards followed suit, searching the hall for a possible threat. Eridani rested her right hand on the hilt of the Bloodsword.

"What is it?" she asked.

"I sense dark magic, my Queen," said the warlock. "An unwelcome presence."

"That's no way to speak of an old friend," sounded a female voice from behind a gaggle of officials waiting to make their reports. They parted with haste and Oshekzhothep the Seer stepped forward.

The sorceress didn't seem to have changed in the years since Eridani saw her last. She carried herself regally as she strode forward. She wore a scarlet gown this time. A fishnet headpiece of red rose petals covered her white hair.

Eridani's first instinct was to order the witch killed on sight. But she knew this not to be wise. Whatever dark power this old woman possessed was not directly hostile. And, given the warlock's apparent discomfort, she was not to be trifled with.

"Everyone out," Eridani said.

"If you've come to collect on our bargain, I have no firstborn to offer you," said Eridani, once the hall was cleared and only the two of them remained. "There isn't any time for childbearing while one leads her armies into one battle after another."

"I'm nothing but patient, dear," said the witch. "You're well along your destiny's path. My rewards for ushering you in the right direction will be numerous, in this life and the next. The Invisible God is generous with those who serve him well."

Eridani kept a sneer from showing on her face. The witch might be powerful, but she was just another fanatic, her actions rationalized by some unseen force that might or might not exist. She was like the priests of the God Under the Floorboards, or those of Arvadon: creatures of limited thinking she could manipulate to her advantage.

"Has your deity sent you to check up on me?" Eridani asked with barely contained disdain.

"Do you not remember our last conversation?" asked the Seer. "I vowed to arrive and offer help in your greatest hour of need. Here I am."

"And what is it you think I need help with?" asked Eridani.

The scarlet-clad woman smiled. "Why, defeating the Quadi, of course."

Her words struck Eridani like a crossbow bolt. Could this witch truly offer a hint that would lead to her greatest victory yet? It seemed implausible, but she remembered the accuracy of the sorceress's prophecy, and the insightful advice which ultimately led to the defeat of the Haldovans.

Eridani restrained herself from leaning forward. "Tell me," she said. "What bargain will you demand next? Will you ask for my soul?"

"The Invisible God already has possession of that, I assure you," said the sorceress. "No additional bargain is required. I promised you help as part of our previous accord."

"Then tell me." Despite wanting to play it cool, Eridani was on her feet. "Tell me how to win."

Oshekzhothep the Seer held a glass flagon the size of her fist, sealed with a wax cork. Gray liquid sloshed inside. She seemed to have snatched it out of thin air; her hands were empty the moment before and her gown did not appear to have any pockets, but Eridani was too intent on the witch's promise to care about her parlor tricks.

"What is this?" she asked.

"The essence of Blue Pestilence," said the Seer. "Alchemically preserved and lethally potent."

Eridani took an involuntary step back. The Blue Pestilence was the most virulent plague in recorded history. It had ravaged parts of the Heart on several occasions over the centuries, but hadn't recurred since before the time of Kalatar.

"You can spend a lifetime marshaling your armies and still come up short against the Quadi," said the sorceress. "Or you can travel into the heart of the empire. Go to their capital, the everlasting city of Keol. Empty this vessel into the Cetai Fountain, where thousands of pilgrims gather daily. They will spread the plague and it will ravage the Quadi Empire. It will decimate their legions and undermine their government. Only then might you have a chance of triumphing over what remains of their forces."

"That ..." Eridani stared at the sorceress wide-eyed. "I could never ..."

"Oh, please." Oshekzhothep the Seer crossed her arms, the flagon clenched by its neck in her right hand. "You've spent your entire life doing what you must to survive. To *win*. Will you stop now?"

Eridani thought back to the many difficult decisions she had been forced to make. Sacrificing allies, losing friends, hurting the innocent in the name of a greater cause—she was no stranger to being ruthless when she had to. None of those were anything like what the sorceress was proposing now. Surely, there was a matter of scale.

"It's true, I've committed some sins. But nothing like this," said Eridani. "This plague could kill millions. I'm not a monster."

The sorceress swept her arm over the empty room. "There's no one here in need of hearing justifications," she said. "Save the pretty words for your subjects. You have it in you to do this. If you deny that, you will only be lying to yourself."

"I'll find another way to beat them," Eridani said. "My own way."

"You have less time than you think." The sorceress closed the distance between them, and pressed the cool flagon into Eridani's palm. "Only the Invisible God can deliver your heart's desire. Do not ignore his generosity—and mine."

Then the sorceress walked away, resplendent in her floating crimson gown, leaving Eridani literally holding death in her hand.

SIX MONTHS LATER, a spy delivered bad news to Eridani and her council.

"The emperor in the Everlasting City has issued a decree," she told her masters. "Four legions are to gather at the Ellsheva Pass in spring. They're to march beyond the Quadi borders, across the Bela Mountains, and pacify nearby lands, creating a buffer against ..." She paused. "Forgive me, I'm quoting his words. Against the nuisance of barbarian hordes amassed on our northern border."

"The emperor finally realized the threat we represent," said Eridani. "Took him long enough."

"We have to prepare for war. Recall as many of our companies from other parts of the Heart as we can immediately," said General Kalib.

"There's time," said Eridani. "The Quadi do not move quickly. They're a lumbering giant with all the strength but none of the agility. It will be many months before their soldiers come through the Ellsheva Pass."

Princess Elena cleared her throat. She had earned Eridani's trust with both her pragmatic counsel and unwavering obedience. She seldom spoke at the council meetings, but when she did it was worth listening to. "The first among the dictums of warfare teaches that one must never give the enemy time to prepare. The Quadi appear not to be wise enough to heed this tenet, openly declaring their intentions to make war months ahead of setting foot on our soil. We should strike first, begin this war on our terms and in the place of our choosing."

"Perhaps," Eridani said, recalling the priest of Arvadon and his conjecture that she might have visited the Quadi Empire herself. "The slow-moving giant has given us time to think and plan, and still preempt them." She thought of the flagon of Blue Pestilence she kept locked in her travel chest. "I shall consider all available options."

CHAPTER 24

KEOL

ridani traveled across the Quadi Empire with Toval at her side. She left the Bloodsword behind in favor of a pair of daggers hidden within the thin, baggy peasant clothes commonly worn in the south. Toval carried a wicked-looking club as swords were proscribed to civilians within the empire. The club along with his impressive size dissuaded any troublemakers from harassing the pair of travelers.

As they made their way south toward the capital, Eridani observed and contemplated the inner workings of the ancient Quadi Empire. Although most historians agreed that it was in its decline, the Quadi had ruled large swaths of the Heart for many hundreds of years. They had been notorious conquerors in the distant past, using superior military tactics and training to dominate their neighbors. In recent generations, the succession challenges and a plethora of conflicts within its entrenched bureaucracy kept the Quadi focused inward. They retreated beyond the Bela mountain range that separated over a good third of the Heart's territory to the south from the rest of the continent and seemed content to rule over that area. They left anyone on the other side of the Bela Mountains to their own devices.

The empire appeared to be a study in what Eridani was trying to achieve as a ruler. Since their sizable territory was controlled by a strong central government, Quadi citizens lived without fear of war. Villages teemed with young men who learned trades and farmed the land instead of killing each other in pointless conflicts over which noble might claim ownership of the patch of dirt their families farmed. The Quadi maintained wide, stone-paved roads and the strategic deployment of their legions deterred bandits.

Although initially impressed, Eridani discovered plenty of blemishes on the ancient empire's shiny veneer. She saw a tax collector order the legionnaires he traveled with to beat a fisherman half to death because he failed to pay. Legionnaires upturned the man's tiny boat and kicked his supplies into the lake, then left him bleeding on the shore. None of the other villagers dared help him until the tax collector and his enforcers were well out of sight.

She listened to the storytellers in inns tell of debauchery and madness when they described some of the recent monarchs of the Quadi. Inbreeding had taken a heavy toll on the ruling families. There had been emperors who hunted children for sport and emperors who lay with animals, those who lost their minds studying black sorcery and those who were born insane. The empire's rigid bureaucracy ensured that it had survived them all.

And then there were the slaves. Although the practices of feudalism and corvée were the norm in the north, outright slavery was condoned in the south. Over ten percent of the population on the outskirts of the empire lived as slaves, and that number doubled closer to the capital. Eridani noted that slave labor was the economic force that kept the enormous empire afloat. They were treated worse than pack animals, and uprisings were brutally put down. At one point, Eridani and Toval traveled past a long row of wooden poles set along the side of the road. The headless corpse of a rebellious slave hung upside down by the feet on each pole, covered with buzzing flies.

The Quadi were no better than any other government in the Heart, Eridani concluded with some relief. They only happened to be the strongest, and she would continue to search for a way to defeat them in a manner she could stomach. The flagon filled with death was in her saddlebag, but she hadn't decided yet if she could bring herself to use it.

THEY ARRIVED IN Keol, the ancient capital of the Quadi Empire, after a month's travel. They rented rooms at an inexpensive inn on the outskirts, and Eridani left Toval to rest there while she ventured toward the center of town on foot the next morning, marveling at its size and majesty along the way. Wide, paved streets were kept clean. Most houses were hundreds of years old but were kept up by experienced masons and carpenters. She saw many such tradesmen plying their trade on various roofs and walls in the early hours of the morning, before the sun reached its zenith and the heat forced them to break for the afternoon.

Having traversed the city, Eridani stood in front of the Cetai Fountain. It was located at the center of a large plaza which extended far in every direction. Half of her hometown of Kozhad could have fit comfortably on the land it occupied. The plaza was surrounded by two- and three-story buildings of limestone, freshly coated in bright-colored paint of various colors. She had been told they were occupied by government officials; few among even the wealthiest private citizens could afford to live there.

The domed shape of the Quadi palace loomed over the plaza. It was a thirty-minute walk away, but the hill it stood upon ensured that the structure was visible from almost anywhere in Keol.

Eridani bought a candied fruit from one of the many vendors so as not to seem conspicuous as she stood there, observing. A teeming mass of people moved past her, most of them pilgrims who arrived from all corners of the empire to pay their respects to a varied and strange pantheon of southern gods. Dozens of their likenesses were carved into the columns that stood in the center of the fountain: impossibly young and beautiful men and women dressed in robes, wizened elders in elaborate helmets, beings that were part human and part animal. Eridani felt as though one would need to be a scholar to keep track of the lore and the complicated relationships between all of these deities.

The pilgrims gawked at the columns, circumnavigating the shallow body of water. Each of them tossed a coin into the fountain—from where she stood Eridani could see a fortune in copper coins and even an occasional silver piece under the clear water. She was told the priests cleared the pool every night, and the money was used to finance the many temples in Keol. After their coin sunk to the bottom of the fountain, each pilgrim would say a few words—a prayer or a request they made of the gods—then scoop a handful of water into their palm and use it to wash their brow.

Ever since the meddling sorceress had reappeared in her life proffering a flagon full of the plague, Eridani struggled with what to do next. Was she prepared to kill all these innocent people? She told herself that she needn't decide then. That personally scouting in the Quadi territory, and especially their capital city, was a worthwhile mission of its own. That another solution, another path to victory might occur to her along the way.

But now she had reached her intended destination and no alternate strategy had entered her mind. And despite her inner conflict and indecision, as she stood there and watched the smiling pilgrims enjoy their rite on a gorgeous morning, a wave of peace and calm had washed over her.

The emotion was foreign to her. For years, she had been driven by a sort of manic energy that pushed her—nay, *required* her to win. Her mind was always racing, her thoughts focused, even her sleep consistently uneasy. All of it washed away, allowing her to remember what it felt like to be content.

Eridani the Fierce, the renowned warlord and Queen Mother of the North stood in the midst of thousands of pilgrims, shrouded in the anonymity of the crowd, a candied pear forgotten in her hand. She briefly wondered what her future might be like if she chose to disappear, to build a new life somewhere on the outskirts of the Everlasting City.

She heard shouting from a few stalls over. It focused her again, bringing her back to reality.

"Stop! Thief!" A pilgrim woman was screaming at the top of her lungs. Eridani's gaze followed the commotion. She saw a street urchin weave his way through the throng of pilgrims as he clutched something in his hands.

Another pilgrim grabbed the child, lifted him up by the torso. The boy must've been nine or ten years old; his scrawny arms and legs flailed as he tried to wrestle himself free, but the man held him firm until a pair of legionnaires reached them a few heartbeats later.

Eridani joined the growing crowd of curious onlookers as they formed a circle around the child. The woman who screamed earlier pushed her way past the others. "He has my coin purse!" she announced.

One of the legionnaires took the child from the man who was holding him. He pushed the boy to the ground and twisted his arm hard enough to make the child scream. He applied enough pressure so that the urchin couldn't move without risking a broken bone. The other legionnaire picked up a cheap, slim leather coin purse from the ground and hefted it.

"I saw the boy drop this," said the man who captured the street urchin.

"How much money is inside?" the legionnaire asked the woman.

"Two silver and six copper coins," she said, without hesitation.

The legionnaire pulled the string and dumped the coins into his hand. He then counted them, thus confirming the woman's claim to the purse. "It checks out," he said. He dropped the coins back into the purse and tossed it to the original owner. The crowd around Eridani murmured excitedly.

The legionnaire who was holding the child pushed him even harder into the ground, while his partner stepped on the urchin's forearm, his leather boot pinning the young thief's arm to the ground just above the wrist. The child howled in fear and pain.

Eridani cringed as one of the legionnaires drew his short sword. Were they going to kill this poor child over a pittance? There was no judge, no due process of any kind. She looked around at the pilgrims, men and women who seemed so happy moments ago. They were now focused on the spectacle in front of them, watching with a sickening combination of excitement and anticipation. She wanted to speak up but hesitated for fear of being recognized, of revealing that she didn't know the rules and traditions of this foreign land. Before she could make up her mind, the legionnaire swung his sword in a practiced motion severing the child's right hand.

The boy screamed and flailed on the ground. He was bleeding profusely from the stump. The legionnaire who was holding him let go as soon as the punishment had been meted out and the two men walked off, the crowd parting to let them pass. The entire incident lasted only a few dozen heartbeats.

Eridani forced herself to look away and focused again on the pilgrims surrounding her. Some watched the child with sick fascination, the way someone might stare at a cat run over by a wagon wheel and dying in the street. Others were already dispersing, returning their attention to the Cetai Fountain or the nearby vendors. Not a single one of them attempted to help the maimed child who was as likely to bleed out as to have his wound become infected.

The contentment Eridani felt only moments ago was gone. It was replaced with seething rage. This was a corrupt society that didn't value life. Every one of these people deserved what was coming to them; Eridani would use the Blue Pestilence to cleanse this immoral empire and then reshape it and the rest of the world into something better.

Before she could change her mind, she stepped toward the Cetai Fountain, broke the wax that kept the cork secure in the small flagon she carried, and emptied its contents into the clear water. She glanced around to see if anyone had noticed what she'd done, but those around her were too engrossed in their supplications to pay attention to her actions.

Eridani walked over to a tent where a handful of fleet-footed youngsters were waiting. They were there to deliver messages, fetch items, or perform other simple errands for a handful of coins. Eridani sized them up and nodded to a girl who looked marginally more trustworthy than the rest. The girl, who must've been only two or three years older than the thief, eagerly rushed to Eridani's side. Her eyes went wide when Eridani handed her a stack of silver coins.

"Take that boy to a healer," Eridani said. "Pay them to cauterize and disinfect his wound. The leftover money is yours to keep." Eridani thought about it for a moment, weighing the girl's perceived honesty against her likely greed. "Meet me here at this time tomorrow," she added. "If the boy lives there's a dragon scale in it for you."

The girl nodded enthusiastically. A dragon scale was close to a year's wages for an errand runner like her, and while northern currency may have been relatively uncommon this far south, it spent well enough across the Heart.

Eridani wasn't planning to return the next day, but she felt the leftover silver was enough to pay for the girl's time. The promise of an additional reward would keep her from pocketing the silver and dumping the little thief once they were out of sight. She watched the errand runner approach the boy and help him up. Then she headed away from the city center, back toward the inn where Toval was waiting.

SHE ARRIVED AT the inn by mid-afternoon and woke Toval, who was always eager to catch an extra nap when he didn't have other duties. She told him that they were heading straight back for the Ellsheva Pass. As usual, he asked no questions but merely stretched, collected their travel satchels, and went to fetch their horses.

By evening, half a day on the road, Eridani felt feverish, as though she were fighting off a nasty winter flu. They paid for a room in a small roadside inn and she managed to sleep through much of the night, but by morning she felt too weak to move.

"What can I do?" Toval sounded concerned. Given his expression, Eridani realized she must look even worse than she felt.

"I think this might be Blue Pestilence," she admitted to Toval as much as to herself. She hadn't considered the possibility that she might become one of its victims. She never touched the fountain after upending the alchemical brew into its water and thought they'd be long gone from Keol before the outbreak started.

"I'm sure it's nothing like that," said Toval. He was blissfully unaware of what she'd done, and Eridani wasn't about to enlighten him.

"I'm serious," she said. "You should stay away from me or you might become sick as well." She hoped it wasn't too late for Toval, realizing she had no idea how quickly an afflicted person might become sick enough to infect others.

"Nonsense," he said. "I'll boil herbs that should provide you some relief, then I'll go look for a healer."

True to his word, Toval fetched a village doctor. Like every healer alive, he had never treated a patient afflicted by the Blue Pestilence. While he may have heard of it, it wouldn't have occurred to him to consider a plague that hadn't resurfaced in several centuries as a possible diagnosis. He provided them with some more herbs and ointments that he claimed would reduce the fever and lessen the pain.

By the time the doctor had left, Toval was coming down with a fever. At Eridani's urging, he sent messengers to nearby towns, offering a king's ransom to a healer who might cure them.

By the following morning, Eridani lacked the strength to get out of bed. Toval took care of her for two full days, and then he too succumbed to the plague. As they lay side by side on the narrow cots in the cheap inn, Eridani tried to apologize to her oldest friend, but her throat was too inflamed to let her form the words.

CHAPTER 25

THE LEKAR'S FORTUNE

t took Eridani a moment to notice that the pain was gone. It had been relentless: the ache deep in her bones, the migraine holding her head in a vice-like grip, the constriction in her throat, and the sharp pangs in her chest, felt with each heartbeat. The pain had become her world, edging out every thought and anything from her befuddled senses. And then it was simply gone along with any other sensation. She felt neither warm nor cold, neither angry nor afraid. Even her usual wanderlust, the deep and undefined yearning that drove her forward for years, was absent.

Then she saw her brother, and emotions broke through like a spring river swell overpowering a makeshift dam. Danchu stood there in his finest Skond clothes from the carefree days before they were thrust into the deadly politics of the North. He looked as she remembered him: so very young, his blond hair curling from under a stylish hat, his shoulders wide and his back straight. He was the perfect visage of the young king he could've been if not for the cruel twist of fate.

"Brother?" she whispered, her voice breaking. Although she was now twice his age, she still thought of him as her older brother and was comforted by his presence.

Danchu wore an inscrutable expression on his face. "It's time you and I had a talk," he said.

Something in his voice gave her pause. Eridani looked around. She seemed to be standing in midair, even though her feet felt solid ground. There were no walls, no ceiling. A thick fog surrounded them in every direction, obstructing her gaze beyond a handful of steps. And somewhere below them she could make out a cot where her body lay motionless, covered up to the neck with a wool blanket.

239

"Am I ... dead?" she asked.

"Not yet," said Danchu. "It's a near thing. For now, you're still fighting. You've always been a fighter, little sister."

Eridani stared at her body, its forehead covered in sweat, its eyes shut. "Then ... how?"

"You're hallucinating," he said. "A fever dream. The last-ditch effort of a dying brain to summon the visage of me from some deep recess of your troubled mind." His lips stretched into a humorless smile. "Under better circumstances I might have been flattered."

Eridani took a measure of the ghost her mind seemed to have conjured. Danchu was always a gregarious man but not a deep thinker. This brooding, analytical version of him was rather jarring.

"Better circumstances?" she repeated.

The smile fled Danchu's face. "You've committed terrible sins in my name," he said. "And now that your fevered mind has constructed some shadow version of me, I finally get the chance to tell you how deeply disappointed I am in what you've become."

Eridani blanched. "Disappointed? I was left with almost nothing when the Duke of Buzzards cut you down, but I went on to avenge you and dethrone your enemies. Pieter Hingen, the duke, the patriarch—they're all dead. I reclaimed Kozhad and went on to rule the North and much of the Heart. How could you possibly be disappointed in me?"

Danchu stared at her with pity. "You almost believe this, don't you? You've been lying to yourself for so long that the events and motivations in your memory shapeshift to fit the mold you've created for them. But the truth can't be eradicated. You know it, or you couldn't have created a version of me to verbalize it."

Eridani felt frustrated. She wasn't a sorceress. How and why could she have conjured a lifelike version of her brother, of the person she loved most in this world, to throw her accomplishments in her face? Something else must be happening. Some dark sorcery. Perhaps she was dead after all, and this was a version of the underworld where she was meant to be tormented?

"Do you remember our conversations?" asked Danchu. "You repeatedly tried to convince me to flee the North, so we could live out our days in exile. To find a minor court in Haldova or beyond that might be generous enough to provide for a pair of refugees of noble blood. How I wish I had listened! But we were both young, and I was so foolish."

"I avenged you," Eridani said again. "I couldn't save you, but at least I avenged you. I accomplished great feats in your name."

Danchu's sullen face flushed red. "That is precisely what I wish to confront you about. You've committed terrible atrocities in my name, killed tens of thousands, and made millions more suffer. Do not for a moment think that I approve!"

Eridani was speechless. How could Danchu, of all people, not appreciate her success?

"The stress of so many deaths broke you somehow, little sister," Danchu said. "You've become obsessed with victory, trading empathy for ruthlessness. Winning is the only thing that matters to you, regardless of what it takes."

"How could I not be ruthless and still triumph over ruthless enemies?" Eridani asked. "I thought of you so many times, and always imagined you would be so pleased ..."

"Revenge is a selective thing with you, then," said Danchu. "Lady Voriana's betrayal is directly responsible for my death, and yet you've elevated her to rule the North in your name. You sent poor Dewynn to certain death by ordering him to assassinate Turo, but when you wrestled control of Skond from the patriarch you couldn't be bothered to even find out what happened to either of those men."

Eridani felt herself blush. It was true that, weighed down with the responsibilities of wielding power, she completely forgot about Turo and Dewynn.

"But it's not your vengeance or lack thereof that perturbs me," said Danchu. "It's the wars you've waged beyond the North's borders. You've become a conqueror, another Kalatar. Your armies leave death and misery in their wake. First you became like the patriarch in order to defeat him, and then you became like Prince Ajelogn, covetous of others' lands. Do you even know why you're still fighting, after all these long years?"

"You know the answer to that," said Eridani. "You're in my head. You know the mental math: if I win, millions of lives will be improved. With no competing monarchs there will be no wars to be fought in the Heart. I will save more lives than—"

"Nonsense," Danchu roared. "This was a tenuous argument to begin with. But now? Now that you've proven yourself willing to infect half the world with the Blue Pestilence? In the coming months it will burn through the lands of the Quadi like wildfire, claiming the lives of millions. It will kill innocent people, not only soldiers who oppose you. Congratulations. Live or die, you've become the greatest mass murderer in the history of the Heart."

"They're terrible people living under the heel of an empire so rotten from the inside, the only sane choice is to topple it. What they've done to that boy—"

"Do you think you've saved him? You left him, weakened from his wound, in a city about to become ravaged by the plague. What are the odds he might survive?" Danchu glared at her. "The way they treated him was shameful, yes, and you jumped at the opportunity to use it as an excuse for a far greater crime."

"What else could have I done?" Eridani whispered. "I spent so many years fighting against more powerful foes that I've learned to make hard choices. To do whatever it takes to bring them down."

"But to what end? Why do it? If you followed in Kalatar's footsteps and returned to the North, the Quadi would never bother to pursue you. You could have lived out your days ruling a sprawling empire beyond their borders. And don't feed me the line about bettering the lives of future generations. That's only rhetoric. I'm in your head and I know the truth. There's no one here but us, so why don't you admit it?"

"Legacy," Eridani said, so quietly she could barely hear herself even in the silence of the ephemeral place the two of them inhabited.

Danchu must've heard her. He appeared both pleased and saddened by her response. "And what does 'legacy' mean to you?"

Eridani looked Danchu in the eye. "A legacy of achieving something no one ever had. If I conquer all of the Heart, I won't be remembered merely as Eridani the Fierce, one of many successful warlords and kings. I will be written of forever in the annals of history as Eridani the Great."

Danchu sighed. "Little sister, don't you realize that no one whose name was appended with 'the Great' epithet was ever a good person? Throughout history, those are always people like Kalatar. Savage killers who wreaked havoc on parts of the Heart. As centuries pass, their crimes and the pain they caused, the mounds of skulls they left behind, become forgotten or glossed over. Yet people remember and even celebrate their successful conquests. Is *that* the sort of legacy you seek?"

Eridani thought about it for a long time. Then she simply said, "Yes."

It was Danchu's turn to stare at her, speechless.

"Some time ago, I met a storyteller who insisted that all war is waged for four reasons: coin, kin, faith, and fame," Eridani said. "She was right. I have no family left, no close friends, no one in this world that I love. That leaves only fame." She thought she saw her body in the bed below twitch. "If I fail to conquer the Heart or simply give up trying, then most of my adult life will have been wasted," she added. "I couldn't bear that."

"I understand," said Danchu. "This has become your nature. You're a villain now. A conqueror and a tyrant."

"I'm no villain," Eridani protested.

"No villain ever thinks of themselves as such," said Danchu. "Consider the people around you. We started out in the company of good individuals: Caer, Gavron, even Pel. You shed them, one by one, as you morphed from a good person to a blackguard. You replaced them with bloodthirsty henchmen, sycophants, and a warlock. You even had Gavron *killed* in an effort to placate the Skond mob!"

Eridani tried to speak, to offer some sort of defense, but Danchu waved her off.

"History will remember you, all right. When historians write about your life, they'll no doubt argue about the exact moment Eridani the Fierce turned into a monster. Surely none of them will argue you were still a good person when you poured liquid death into the Cetai Fountain. I'm guessing there will be many events, many decision points for them to cite earlier on, too." Danchu fell silent for a moment, then added: "You've chosen your path and you will continue to pursue it, if you live. But I don't want you, for even a moment, to think that I would have approved." Then he turned his back to her and walked toward the fog.

Eridani wanted to call after him, but found that she couldn't speak. She felt the pain and the fever again, and only a gurgle came out when she attempted to say Danchu's name. She watched him go, tears welling in her eyes.

Someone was squeezing Eridani's shoulder, calling her name. The female voice sounded like it was a day's journey away. It took enormous effort for Eridani to open her eyes. Her vision was somewhat blurry, but she saw a middle-aged woman hovering over her. The woman smiled.

"Good," the woman said. "You're awake."

Eridani thought of Danchu, of all the disdain and condemnation in his voice, of how he left her behind a second time. *Everyone you know and trust will come to betray you.* Surely the witch did not mean Danchu. Hadn't she even said so, all those years ago? But she said nothing of Eridani betraying herself. After all, it was her fevered mind that invented this nightmarish version of her brother.

The strange woman gently stopped her when Eridani tried to sit up. "Easy, easy. Don't push yourself. You're still near death's door."

Eridani's instinct was to disobey this woman, whoever she was, but her body was not up to the challenge. She collapsed onto the sheets which were damp with her sweat.

"I can heal you," said the woman. "But the price is steep. I will take away your affliction, but you must relieve the burden of mine in return."

Eridani's eyes focused on the woman. She must be a lekar, Eridani realized. Her brand of sorcerer traded in diseases as if they were rare gems, swapping one for another like merchants at a bazaar. And like the merchants, they always got the better end of the trade.

Eridani struggled to speak, coughing the words as much as saying them. "What affliction?"

"Please allow me to share a memory with you," said the lekar. "So that you can understand."

The pain was returning, even if it wasn't overwhelming as it had been earlier. Eridani managed a tiny nod.

The lekar touched Eridani's forehead with cool, slender fingers. She whispered an incantation, and Eridani's mind filled with strange memories.

UNATHI IS MAKING house calls.

"Thank you for coming, lekar." The man's voice is both tired and hopeful.

The lekar notes the cheaply made furniture and bare walls of the small home. A woman sits on the couch, her eyes red and puffy. She stares into space and makes no move to acknowledge Unathi. Her husband looks grim and determined. His hands tremble slightly as he offers her a bundle of banknotes.

Unathi glances at the notes. It isn't much, but there is more than one way to pay for her services.

"You understand how this works?" Unathi asks.

Both of them nod. Neither will look her in the eye, nor each other.

"Lead me to him," she says.

The man shows her to the next room, where a four-year-old boy is lying in bed. Unathi walks in and shakes her head when the father tries to follow. She shuts the door behind her.

The boy is burning up with a fever. She lays her hand on the child's forehead and focuses on his illness. It's merely pneumonia—a disease that should have been treated with herbs and mixtures instead of magic. The family was too lax, or too poor, to seek such treatment in time. The sickness lingered and grew. It had taken firm hold of the child's lungs. It's too late for the healers, she realizes, as she studies his small, sweat-drenched frame. Without her help, the child will be dead within a day.

Unathi closes her eyes and readies herself. She focuses on the prison within her mind which holds a thousand deaths. She wills the tiniest opening into existence, taking great care not to permit any of her wards to escape. She begins to hum softly, using her magic to draw the pneumonia out of the boy. She traps the malady, contains it within a mental cell. A few minutes later the boy's fever is gone, his breathing steady.

The lekar feels bloated like a balloon overfilled with water, stretched to its limits and ready to burst. She exhales slowly, forces herself to focus again, and begins humming a different tune. She grabs hold of another sickness, one that is more potent, more dangerous. One that takes up far more space in her prison. She pours it into the boy.

She feels instantly lighter, as if an enormous pressure is lifted off her temples. The malignant tumor she expelled had been a challenging prisoner to contain, a burden that required vigilance and fortitude; one that she bore for far too long. It nestles in the child's brain now. Unathi exits the room without looking at the boy again.

"I bought you a decade," she tells his father. "Perhaps longer. Then he will need another lekar." But she knows that this family will never save up enough to pay for a lekar to take on this tumor by the time it has fully grown.

The man thanks her profusely, but his wife stares daggers at Unathi until finally she can hold back no more. "Don't," she tells her husband. "Don't thank her. The witch has done us no favors."

Unathi has heard it all before, but she can't help responding. "Your son will live longer. He has a chance now; without my ministration he would've had none."

The woman stares her directly in the eye. "You're a usurious merchant, not a healer. You trade death for worse death and profit from the exchange. I don't know how you lekars live with yourselves." Then she spits on the ground at Unathi's feet.

Unathi pities the woman's lack of facility for logic. This forlorn creature knows nothing of the burden she bears, of the strain of containing so many deaths for so long. She thinks back to her years of training; to her mentor's patient guidance. *It takes a special mind to become a lekar. And special strength.* His words reassure her just as they had back when he lived.

Without another word she turns to leave. The father trails her, tries to apologize for his wife's discourtesy. Unathi ignores him and walks away.

Back in her home, Unathi gradually releases the pneumonia into her own body. Her adult immune system would be able to handle it, and she cannot afford to hang on to every sickness she captures. Her prison is nearly full as it is, replete with much worse things. It isn't often that she can unburden

246

herself the way she did with the tumor, and even with it gone she can feel the rest of her deaths constantly pushing, probing against the prison's walls.

Four days later she is coughing, nauseous, and feverish, when her steward arrives with news.

"Go away," she croaks. "I won't see any clients for another week."

"This can't wait," he insists. "I found a vessel."

The news jolts Unathi. If true, this is a rare, once-in-a-lifetime find. A vessel is a healthy living body of someone with the talent for magic, which also lacks a conscious mind. Her mentor searched desperately for one late in life, when he felt himself becoming too weak to contain his captive deaths, but didn't succeed. The steward, who served her mentor before her, was well-trained to never cease searching. She has to hurry before other lekars find out about the vessel too; some would spend all their treasure to possess such a prize.

Unathi chants the pneumonia back into the mental cell. She needs to be in her best form for this.

She arrives at a house in the prosperous part of town and is ushered to a young woman's bedside.

The girl fell and hit her temple on a sharp edge. Or, so her widowed father claims. There are tell-tale signs that insinuate a different story. Her body is perfectly healthy though, beside a few bruises. Her mind is gone. She will never wake up from her coma. Unathi can sense the magic within the girl. She is indeed a vessel, the greatest fortune a mature lekar could hope to possess.

What's more, the father, eager to keep the circumstances of the girl's injuries discreet, demands only a small fortune. The word of the vessel hasn't spread, sparing Unathi the necessity of a bidding war against other lekars. She hands over the money, and is alone with the vessel at last.

The girl's magic is strong. It takes a special mind to become a lekar. Had things turned out differently, she could have made a fine one. Unathi wonders briefly if her magic could overcome the girl's death, wake her from the coma. But even attempting this would be ludicrous, akin to a diver using a mallet to shatter the finest, largest pearl she found in her lifetime, just to learn if it would break.

Unathi places her hands on the vessel's warm forehead and opens the gates of her prison, wider than ever before. She chants. Cancers and plagues, heart disease and strokes, schizophrenia and smallpox pour into the vessel until, for the first time in decades, Unathi's prison is vacant.

The lekar staggers out of the house, lightheaded and weak. She can't think, can't focus. Is this what she's supposed to feel like? She lets her steward help her into the carriage and drive her home. Moments after she crawls into bed and permits herself to lower her eyelids, sleep claims her.

In the morning, she wakes with a feeling of anguish. Guilt and revulsion at the things she's done, the way she is, her calling as a lekar, hit her all at once. She has never felt this way, not before her apprenticeship to become a lekar nor since. It is infinitely worse than corralling a multitude of deaths within her mind, and she can't bear it.

Unathi remembers with perfect clarity her calm demeanor, her ability to survive and even flourish while plying her trade. The detached, clinical manner she can no longer muster. It takes a special mind to become a lekar, but perhaps what makes it special is a flaw rather than a gift. She comes to believe that whatever depression or mental block had allowed her to function must've somehow been poured into the vessel along with all the other sickness. Whatever thing both made her broken and allowed her to live with herself, she must have it back.

She rushes over to the vessel's home, but she's too late. The young woman passed away overnight, extinguished by one of the many deaths meant for others. The body has already been burned.

Unathi leaves the vessel's house, its darkened windows staring at her with censure. She picks up the pace as she struggles to cope with the guilt in her heart, the weight of decisions she made feeling much heavier than her mind's prison ever had. Her feet hit the cobblestones faster, until she is running down the streets of her city, her eyes stung by sweat, her lungs burning in agony.

She is an expert lekar, able to capture any sickness, contain any disease. But she doesn't know how to outrun her humanity.

"MY PAST TORMENTS me," said Unathi. "I quit my practice; shut myself away from the world. I would have taken my own life, were I less of a coward." She held Eridani's hand with both of hers. "A fortune teller once told me that I would meet a queen afflicted with a deadly ancient plague. She told me about you. Told me that you're possessed of the same indifference that allowed me to survive." She stared at Eridani like a cat at a saucer of milk. "Give it to me! The woman said you have it in spades. Give it to me, and I will cure you of the plague."

Eridani considered her situation. This woman didn't seem interested in the coins Toval had offered when seeking healers. Whatever the exchange this lekar had planned might do to her, it was better than dying. She wasn't done yet; her legacy was not secured.

"Do it," she croaked.

Unathi exhaled a sigh of relief, a sigh of a woman dying of thirst in a desert who had reached an oasis. Then she touched Eridani's forehead again and began to hum.

The procedure took less than a thousand heartbeats. Eridani felt the pain draining from her until it was gone entirely, trapped in the prison of the lekar's mind. By the time Unathi finished humming, Eridani felt considerably better but could barely move.

"You're going to be weak for the next few days," said Unathi. Her voice was detached, as though she was thinking of something more important. Her facial expression was calm but lifeless, like some important unidentifiable quality had gone missing. It reminded Eridani of the woman who she had seen in the memories the lekar had shared. "It appears to have worked. I'm feeling like myself again."

Eridani wondered what it must be like to be impervious to emotion. How could the lekar gain such an ability from *her*? It took her all her strength to utter the words: "What did you take from me?"

Unathi looked at her with that peculiar expression from her shared memories. "It's difficult to explain. A way to cope? An antidote to empathy? You had an overabundance of it." She crossed her arms and added defensively, "I needed it more."

Eridani searched her emotions. She didn't feel the kind of despair Unathi experienced after she lost whatever made her unique to the vessel. She still felt guilt and shame over releasing the plague, disappointment and confusion about her encounter with the imaginary Danchu. Were those feelings hers, or were they artifacts of the way she had been changed by the lekar's magic? Eridani forced the thought out of her head. It didn't matter. She wouldn't allow yet another source of doubt to take up residence within her mind.

"Your immune system is weakened from the plague," said Unathi. "Try to rest as much as you can in the coming weeks. You will make a full recovery, except for one thing." The lekar hesitated.

"What's that?"

"A side effect of the plague that my power couldn't mend. You will never be able to bear children. I'm sorry."

Eridani thought back to her bargain with the sorceress and began to cackle. She laughed heartily and as loud as her enervated body would permit.

Unathi observed this reaction with clinical interest. "Rest now," she said. "You need to recover your strength."

"Wait," Eridani glanced at the cot next to hers. Toval lay there, unmoving. His breathing was shallow and irregular. "Heal him, too. I'll give you whatever you want."

Unathi sized Toval up. "I'm sorry," she said. "Even if I wanted to, I'm not powerful enough to contain two instances of the Blue Pestilence."

Eridani hadn't the strength to argue. She closed her eyes and fell into deep, troubled sleep. By the time she woke up, nearly a full day later, Unathi was gone. Toval's cold body lay unmoving an arm's reach away.

AFTER RESTING FOR several days, Eridani traveled across the Quadi Empire and away from the center of the Blue Pestilence epidemic. The plague was spreading quickly despite the emperor's decrees and his government's best efforts to contain it. When Eridani made it through the Ellsheva Pass, she ordered every road and pass blockaded by archers, and anyone attempting to cross over to be shot on sight.

The plague ravaged the Quadi Empire for over two years. Several small pockets of the Blue Pestilence afflicted villages outside of the Quadi borders. Eridani had every such village surrounded and burned, no person allowed to escape alive.

By the time the outbreak died out, it was estimated that one in every four men, women, and children in the Quadi Empire died of the plague. Eridani waited several more months to ensure there were no reports of new outbreaks. Then she ordered her armies to cross over the Bela Mountains.

Even weakened by the plague, the well-trained and well-disciplined legions of the Quadi presented the most difficult challenge Eridani's armies ever had to face on the battlefield. They retreated grudgingly, making the invaders pay in wounds and lives for every village, every town, every patch of farmland. Even after the rest of the empire had fallen, the legionnaires defended the Grand Palace of the Quadi to their last man. Ultimately though, the Queen Mother took Keol and moved her court into its palace, the Heart's most recognized seat of power.

The war of conquest against the Quadi Empire lasted eleven years.

CHAPTER 26
ERIDANI'S CROWN

ridani the Fierce, Queen Mother of the North, Sovereign of the Haldova Plains, and as of recently, Empress of the Quadi, studied the silver crown. She twisted it this way and that in her hands as she reclined on the throne. She caressed the time-worn runes etched on the outer rim with her callused fingers, and squinted at the secret inscriptions that encircled the inner rim. Then she shrugged, and tossed it aside.

The crown clanged as it rolled down the steps of the dais and past the small group of Eridani's most loyal advisors, generals, and mages. It came to rest at the feet of Arut, a gnarled old scribe who had remained in her service despite his advanced years.

"My Queen?" Arut grunted as he labored against his arthritic joints to pick up the discarded headgear.

"It's insufficient," said Eridani.

Her advisors turned to each other, trying to decipher their ruler's meaning. Arut's hands shook as he clutched the priceless artifact.

"The Quadi emperors have worn the silver crown for over six hundred years," said Arut. "It is the best-recognized symbol of power in the Heart. And now it's yours by the right of conquest, my Queen."

Eridani got up from the throne, descended the three steps from the dais. "It is an ugly chunk of metal," she said. "Heavy and crude, like the ruling hand of the Quadi." She towered over Arut, a head taller and wider-shouldered than the scribe. "If I wear this, I might be looked upon as nothing more than a northern usurper who managed to bring the world's greatest empire to its knees. Is that what you wish for me?"

Arut wouldn't meet her gaze. He stared down, past the crown, at his feet, and remained silent.

Eridani turned to her advisors, steel in her voice. "I am the first to unite all the kingdoms of the Heart under a single banner. None of the dead emperors who wore this crown managed this feat. My accomplishments are greater than those of the Quadi." She turned back to Arut. "Send word to the best jewelers and goldsmiths. There's a handsome reward for whoever will design a crown worthy of me."

SIX MONTHS LATER, Eridani sat on the same throne. Its soft cushions had grown familiar but not comfortable.

She half-listened to the reports of her navy hunting down pirates in the west, her armies quelling rebellions in the east, and her laborers paving roads across her vast empire. None of these projects were interesting; concerns barely worthy of her attention. She nodded absent-mindedly after each messenger delivered their report. The unending stream of interchangeable minions prostrated themselves before her and retreated, bowing, only to make room for more.

She remembered wistfully the days of conquest, hardships and wounds and hunger, sores from weeks spent on horseback, rare defeats and countless victories. Her army swelled and her empire grew, until she ruled it all. And what had it gained her? She wished for a worthy enemy. She financed fleets of sailing ships and dispatched them in all directions from the Heart in search of new lands to conquer, but the ships that managed to make it back reported finding nothing more than tiny, uninhabited islands.

A messenger from the governor of Haldova stepped forward. The governor reported that the road construction was progressing ahead of schedule, ever since he ordered citizens to perform an additional day of corvée labor per month, at times proscribed by their religion as days of rest. The governor humbly requested additional funds from the treasury, to erect a statue of Eridani, and to build an infirmary for the poor.

Eridani approved the funds for the statue, but not for the infirmary. "The statue will stand for a thousand years," she said. "Two generations from now, no one will recall whether we tended to some peasant's sore foot."

At last, the messengers and advisors had completed their reports. The royal hall was filled with the favored nobles, and a trio of musicians thrummed their stringed instruments in the back. It was time to receive the emissaries from her various domains.

The delegation of three women from the Far Isles came first. They spoke flowery praises in an exotic accent, and they brought a gift of a coronet inlaid with amber. Eridani wasn't impressed.

She looked into the women's eyes and failed to find the fire of ambition, the steel of resolve, or the arrogance of nobility. The true leaders of the islanders had sent these women because she herself was a woman, and they must've thought this would please her. Eridani dismissed them with a wave. She nodded to a servant, who carried their gift off to a room where hundreds of crowns from every corner of the Heart gathered dust. None of them were deemed worthy by Eridani the Fierce.

Other groups came and went, delivering hollow tidings and forgettable gifts, until it was the turn of the Artificer's Guild of Elod. Two wizened old men pushed a small carriage, upon which rested the strangest of crowns.

Atop a platinum base sat a miniature replica of the Everlasting City, with the palace of the Quadi towering over the other structures. Powered by golden gears, dozens of tiny carriages, soldiers, and townsfolk moved around the finely crafted streets in a mesmerizing dance of constant activity.

"Glorious One," spoke one of the old men, "the greatest machinists of Elod labored for months to construct a clockwork crown like no other, fit for the Queen of the World." He bowed deep. "Will you do us a great honor by trying it on?"

Eridani was pleased to see such an innovative design, but something in the artificer's body language, in the way he was looking at her, gave her pause. She looked to the warlock, who sat at the feet of her dais, motionless as a statue day after day. He shifted, crawling toward her on all fours like a great ape. The warlock whispered into her ear, and as she listened, her expression hardened.

"Guards!" Eridani called. "Seize them. Place the crown atop that one's head."

Armed warriors, veterans of a thousand campaigns, were upon the artificers before anyone else could react, their curved blades pressing against the old men's throats. Two guards held each of the artificers while the third picked up the clockwork crown and placed it atop the head of the man who spoke the greeting.

He stood there, head bent under the weight of the artifact.

The warlock whispered in Eridani's ear again.

"Unwind it," she said, pointing at the small gear located near the base of the crown's right side.

The crowd watched in absolute silence—even the musicians had ceased their playing when the commotion had begun—as the guard rotated the gear counterclockwise, to emulate the passage of time. Each complete rotation culminated in a loud click. The old man's face turned white, but he stared at Eridani in defiant silence.

After five clicks the guard looked to his queen for guidance.

"Keep unwinding it," said Eridani.

The guard swiveled the gear and the crown kept clicking. On the fourteenth click, a hidden compartment opened, and a tightly wound spring forced a needle deep into the old man's left temple. He died instantly and without a sound, his body hanging limp in the hands of the two guards.

"The needle is dipped in poison," said Eridani. "The traitors designed the trap to spring long after they had gone, to save their worthless hides."

"We do not fear death, despot," said the remaining artificer. "My brother and I are too old. Our hands shook and we could no longer craft fine clockwork." He pointed at the clockwork crown, which fell to the ground next to his brother's body. "Fourteen revolutions, one for each day your butchers spent savaging Elod. Burning our homes and workshops, murdering our sons at the walls. We judged this a fitting end for you."

"It was war," said Eridani, staring down the artificer. "The moment your leaders had the good sense to surrender, the killing stopped. There was no rape or murder in the streets, no retaliation against the defenders. Elod, like every other city, is allowed to prosper under my rule. I imposed peace upon the world."

The old man didn't flinch. "Tell that to the million ghosts of those who died in your war."

"Take him away," said Eridani. "Watch him day and night. I want him to live to see his punishment." She turned to one of her generals. "Lead your army to Elod. Evacuate the city. Then burn it to the ground." She scowled at the artificer. "Before you let its citizens go, I want you to find every machinist, clockmaker, and gearsmith, from grand masters who run the city down to the lowest apprentice. Cut off the right hand of every last one."

Only then did the old artificer scream.

TWO YEARS INTO her reign at the palace of the Quadi, there was still no crown good enough for Eridani.

Two rooms of the palace were now filled with rejected crowns. Each room contained more wealth in gold, silver, and precious stones than an average kingdom's treasury. Over time, the number of gifts she received dried from a flood to a trickle.

Have they given up because I keep rejecting their offerings, thought Eridani bitterly, *or because they hate me so?*

When she'd run out of enemies to fight, Eridani had set out to build the greatest empire in history, a legacy that would last long after she was gone. She'd ordered roads and aqueducts built, trade routes protected, and tariffs reduced. All she'd asked for in return was loyalty and obedience. All she got instead was insurrection.

The first open rebellion against her rule was led by Elena. It was a pathetic thing, a few thousand fighters against the might of the Heart-spanning empire. Eridani sent an overwhelming force. Her generals razed the rebel stronghold and executed the rebels in ways that made the Quadi upside-down hangings seem tame by comparison. Elena drank poison rather than be captured.

Eridani was distraught. She had elevated Elena, made her a provincial governor. She saw much of herself in the young woman. She even considered her as a possible eventual successor.

In retrospect, perhaps that should have been a warning sign. Like Eridani, she had too much ambition.

More rebellions sprung like weeds across the empire, two new uprisings for every quelled revolt, no matter how brutally the rebels were crushed. Eridani's enemies refused to learn. She pursued her agenda, loath to allow dissidents to thwart her.

It was during another routine audience session that she had noticed the ring. The fat man who wore it was among a group of representatives from the merchants' guild in the northeast. They seemed genuinely appreciative of the good job her soldiers had done clearing out the bandits and making the routes safer for the guild to move their goods. The crown they brought was a tasteless hat made of fur-lined gold, and she spared it no more than a glance. But the ring—the ring was exquisite, complex patterns of spun silver woven around a perfectly cut amethyst.

"You there," Eridani beckoned to the portly trader. "Let me see that."

The man took a few steps forward, uncertain as to whether he should climb the steps of the dais. Eridani rose from her throne and descended toward him. She unceremoniously grabbed his hand and examined the ring.

"Who made this?" she asked.

"I...I don't know," stammered the merchant. "I bought it at market."

"Where?" asked Eridani. She held out her hand.

The merchant struggled to liberate the ring from his finger, then pressed it into her palm.

"It was a small town along my trade route. There were several baubles of similar design, but the purple hue of the stone had caught my fancy. If it pleases Your Majesty, I shall purchase the rest of them the next time I pass through there, and send them to you by courier."

"You will take my men to this market and show them the stall." She turned to her generals. "I want this jeweler found and brought to me, along with his tools, and every trinket he ever made. Spare no effort and no cost."

ERIDANI NEVER TOLD anyone about the origin of the plague, but she had charged her most trusted spies, her most deadly assassins, and her most learned sorcerers with tracking down Oshekzhothep the Seer.

Her troops searched the witch's home in Skond but it appeared abandoned long ago. For years there had been no sign of her, despite Eridani spending a fortune on bounty hunters and fortune tellers. She began to suspect that the old sorceress had passed on to the next world. But finally, all those years later, Bel Talesh's secret police managed to find her and bring her in, having suffered considerable losses in the process.

For the first time in well over a decade, Eridani was face to face with the witch of Skond. The old woman wore blood-soaked rags instead of her usual flowing gowns. Her feet were chained to the wall of the torture chamber, her arms tied behind her back. Her ribs were broken and she bled from numerous wounds. Bel Talesh's assassins weren't the only ones to be hurt during her capture. An array of knives, saws, and other sinister-looking tools were laid out on a stone slab along the wall.

"You nearly killed me," Eridani said. "The Blue Pestilence ravaged my body and your damned prophecy tortured my mind. But now I'm queen of the Heart and you're a condemned prisoner, moments away from execution. You have failed, sorceress."

The old woman drew herself upright, a glimpse of her power and confidence resurfacing in her broken body. Despite her injuries she was still beautiful, her skin unnaturally smooth, her white hair long and straight. She stared at Eridani for a long moment and then she cackled.

"Failed? I have succeeded beyond imagining," she declared. "Do what you will with my body. The Invisible God will reward me richly in the afterlife."

"You must've lost your mind from the stress and the pain, old woman," Eridani said.

"You still don't understand, do you?" The witch's eyes shone. "Pain is what the Invisible God craves. It's why he created this world! We live and we die, and we suffer. It is inevitable, like the sun rising in the morning and setting at night. We're merely cattle, existing to generate pain same as sheep live to provide the shepherd with wool and milk and meat."

Eridani gritted her teeth. "If your god likes pain, he'll be sure to enjoy yours."

"My pain is too insignificant for him to notice," said the witch. "I've already given him a much greater offering. I've given him you—the most terrible monster in history. You've caused enough pain for the Invisible God to gorge upon for millennia." The old woman cackled again, then broke into a coughing fit, spitting up blood.

An image of the river of blood as conjured by Lyn the storyteller came unbidden into Eridani's mind. She thought of it often as she got older. Sometimes she dreamt of it. She came to realize that Kalatar's retreat in that parable was ultimately a sign of his weakness. Faced with the prospect of managing the affairs of a vast empire, he fled home instead. The pain he caused turned out to be for nothing, whereas any suffering she had caused was a means to an end. She wasn't merely a successor of Kalatar. She had surpassed him.

"Are you attempting to take credit for my accomplishments?" Eridani asked, her voice dangerously calm.

"I'm taking credit for *you*," said the witch. "I made you what you are. Without me, you would have most likely died in obscurity at the hands of your enemies in the North. But no, I forged you like a fine blade." The old woman coughed again. "My prophecy made you paranoid and mean, and set you on the path of vengeance you would have abandoned had I let your brother die of poison. Then I made you exile your one true love. That man was too decent. He might have made you a better person had he been allowed to remain in your life."

Eridani thought of Pel. She had hoped he would return to her once the wars were over, but he never resurfaced. She consoled herself by imagining the life he led away from her was a good one. Whatever her other claims, the sorceress deprived them of a lifetime together. Eridani punched the old hag hard in the solar plexus. The witch twisted as much as her restraints would allow and retched bile onto the floor.

"I'm not some plaything of the Invisible God or a puppet of yours," said Eridani. "I made my choices and I own the consequences, good and bad. You were merely a resource, another fanatic whose religious fervor served my goals. You never got the best of our bargains. I granted you no favors, didn't surrender Pel, and certainly never had any intention of giving you my firstborn."

"I forced you into a bargain from an old wives' tale, and it ensured that you'd bear no children," the sorceress spoke again, once she regained her breath. "No lover and no heir meant no reason to strive for the world to be better."

Eridani punched her again and she hung there, limp. Eridani used a bit of smelling salt from her torturer's arsenal to force the old woman back into consciousness.

"Why did you manipulate me into releasing the plague?" Eridani demanded. "You could have easily done it yourself."

"Ah, my greatest achievement." The witch's lips spread into a pained grin. "Anyone could have released it," she said. "But you doing so simultaneously broke you and steeled you against the world. It prepared you for all the atrocities to come." She cackled again, a pitiful sound. "You have killed and hurt so many more people since then. Why else do you think I sent that lekar, Unathi, to save you?"

Her words felt like a slap. Eridani's cheeks flushed with anger and shame at allowing this chained, tortured creature to get to her. She took several deep breaths and regained her composure.

"Enjoy your so-called victory," she said. "You and your god will both be forgotten, but the memories of my reign will last for millennia. My legend will grow with every passing generation. People will recall my victories, whereas any death and suffering associated with my wars will become an abstraction, the losses in any given battle merely numbers on the page of a historical treatise. In time, my name will become synonymous with both wisdom and valor."

"Yes," whispered the sorceress. "Just so. More is the reason for future despots to emulate you." She smiled weakly. "The Invisible God rewards those who serve him."

Eridani picked out a large knife from an array of blades set out on the slab and stabbed the witch in the heart.

The lifeless body hung there, mocking. In her mind's eye, Eridani imagined whatever enchantment the witch had cast breaking once her heart stopped, and the corpse showing her true age: her skin wrinkled, her hair wispy and matted, her teeth yellow and rotten. None of that happened. In death, the sorceress remained defiant, a superior smirk on her motionless lips.

Eridani ordered the body burned, but the witch's words would not stop haunting her dreams.

ERIDANI SAT IN her private chamber in front of a large mirror. She used a pair of iron tweezers to pluck the gray hairs from her head. She wore her hair short in the front, but flowing down to her shoulders in the back. When she'd led her troops on horseback, she'd tied her jet-black locks into a braid to keep them out of her face during the charge. There'd been no gray hairs then.

She sifted through her hair, hunting down any traces of gray and pulling them out without wincing. Much like the uprisings by her disloyal subjects, this was now a constant and never-ending battle.

There was a knock at the door. Arut shuffled in after she voiced assent. "She is here, my Queen," he said.

"Who?" Eridani asked, without turning from the mirror.

"The craftswoman from the North." Arut pointed at the amethyst ring that had sat on Eridani's desk ever since her encounter with the merchant. "The one who made that."

"Have they collected her other designs?"

"All that they could find, my Queen."

"I wish to see them first." Eridani put away the tweezers and the brush.

Arut led her to the room where several wooden boxes were stored. Eridani refused to wait for the servants to unpack them. She rummaged through them herself, dumping the hay padding on the floor and pulling out various rings, necklaces, and bracelets.

Each piece was marvelous. They were made with copper and silver and semi-precious stones, but the design and craftsmanship were beyond anything available in the finest shops of the capital.

Eridani rejoiced. This obscure genius would do perfectly. "Lead me to her," she told Arut.

The scribe shuffled uncomfortably. "There is something you should know first, my queen." Eridani stared at Arut until he continued. "The craftswoman...She is not a loyal subject. She refused to come; the soldiers had to put her in chains."

Eridani felt as if she was kicked by a horse. She was used to having enemies—but how could someone capable of creating such beauty be among them? "In that case, I wish to speak to the men who brought her first," she said.

ERIDANI WALKED TO a small room at the far end of the palace. The two guards bowed to her and unlocked the door. Inside, a woman in her fifties sat in a teak chair. She was dressed in thick wool peasant clothes and wore no makeup or jewelry. She made no move to get up.

"Hello, Dahlia," said Eridani. "Do you know who I am?"

The craftswoman nodded. "I recognize you from the new coins." She looked the queen up and down. "The engraver flatters you."

"You don't like me much, do you?" asked Eridani.

Dahlia's mouth was set in a hard line. She did not speak.

"Explain," said Eridani. "I wish to understand why you feel the way you do."

Dahlia looked at the floor and steepled her long, slender fingers. It was only after an awkward pause that she spoke. "You are a very bad woman. You wanted power, so you killed countless people to get it. And to keep this power, you have your soldiers kill many people more." Dahlia's voice gained some confidence as she spoke. She raised her head and looked into the queen's eyes. "During my journey here I saw villages burned, rebels hanged. Thousands forced against their will to clear and pave your roads. Fear in the eyes of honest farmers. Do you not know this, hidden away in the palace? Must you abduct a simple old woman to tell you these things?"

Anger welled within Eridani. No one had dared speak to her in this fashion for many years.

"You don't understand," said Eridani. "You don't see the bigger picture. For the first time in history, the world can be at peace. There are no borders, no petty rivalries between princelings. We are on the verge of the era of lawfulness and prosperity. Only a handful of dissidents who stand in the way of progress are burned and hanged, for the greater good of the many. For every life lost in the war, a multitude will be saved if the empire I built outlives me. If the peace lasts."

Eridani stepped closer and bent down until she was face to face with the craftswoman. "I didn't abduct you. I brought you here to make you a part of history. To honor you, by letting you design a crown for me. To elevate you above your station, like I've elevated all of the Heart."

Eridani put her hand on Dahlia's shoulder. "I talked to my men about you, and was struck by how much you and I are alike, in certain ways. We're each the best at what we do. We both have no families, no children, no close attachments. Our lives are dedicated to our craft. You bring beauty into the world, and I bring order. Surely, we're well-suited to understand each other. To become friends?"

Dahlia rose from her stool and took a step back, freeing her shoulder from the queen's grasp. "I never learned to talk pretty, but I do know that we're nothing alike. The only blood staining my hands is my own, from when I prick myself with a carving tool."

The queen's face turned red and she opened her mouth to speak, to shout at the ignorant commoner before her, but she thought better of it. If she could convince this one woman, could she not find a way to convince all of her enemies? Her legacy demanded it. "We shall talk again," she said, and left the room.

Arut was waiting for her outside. "I want her placed in the finest guest room of the palace," Eridani told him. "Bring her the best food and drink. Dress her in the softest silks. And I want our most silver-tongued diplomats to tutor her daily, and explain in plain language the grandeur and the necessity of my reign. Do whatever you have to, but by the time you're done, she's to become a convert."

ERIDANI THOUGHT OF the craftswoman often, but she remained patient. It was several weeks later that she came to visit her captive for the second time.

She barely recognized Dahlia. The craftswoman's hair was cut and styled in the latest fashion. She was finely dressed, and smelled of lavender soap. The only thing that hadn't changed was the expression in her eyes.

"Have you not learned to love me?" asked Eridani.

"You can't gain a caged tiger's loyalty, no matter how well you feed him," said Dahlia.

THE SEASONS HAD changed twice before Eridani came to see Dahlia again. She was kept busy by the affairs of empire. The insurrections kept getting worse. Entire regions foolishly tried to secede. Her armies dealt accordingly with each revolution, but her soldiers and her resources were being stretched thin. The taxes had to be raised again, and the grandiose irrigation and construction projects across the empire were put on hold.

Eridani took one look at Dahlia and knew that the commoner hadn't changed her mind.

"I'm tired of waiting," said Eridani. "It's time for you to get to work. A workshop has been set up, filled with every jeweler's tool and instrument known to exist. There are hundreds of crowns stored there. Melt them down, scavenge the gems, request anything else you might need, but I will have from you a crown unlike any that came before it."

"No," said Dahlia, and folded her arms across her chest. "Do to me what you will. I'm not afraid to die, and I've got no family for you to threaten."

"Look out the window," said Eridani.

The two of them stepped toward the wide glass window of the second-story chamber and looked at the lawn below. There, shackled together in rows of ten, forced into formation by the spears of the guards, stood one hundred children.

"These are the sons and daughters of traitors, none of them older than ten," said Eridani. "You will deliver a wondrous crown, the best you can create—and I'll know, for I've seen your other works—in three months' time, or I will have their throats cut and force you to watch."

Dahlia's eyes grew wide and her voice trembled. "Surely, even you aren't capable of such evil?"

Eridani grabbed hold of the craftswoman's collar, pulling her face close. "There is nothing I won't do to build and protect my legacy," she whispered. "I will kill whomever I must to achieve my goals. In the end, history will vindicate me. Look at me, woman. Do you doubt my words?"

Dahlia shook her head, tears streaming down her cheeks.

THREE MONTHS LATER, Eridani and her retinue came to the workshop. "Show me," the queen told the craftswoman.

Dahlia removed the cloth that covered her workbench. Eridani's heart raced at the sight. She heard several of her advisors gasp behind her.

The crown was the most beautiful thing she had ever seen.

Atop an elegant circlet, strands of gleaming metal interconnected in ways that were both surprising and inevitable. The intricate mesh formed a semi-sphere, covering an ensemble of diamonds and rubies and emeralds, hung suspended in perfect harmony, arranged to display a detailed map of the Heart. The crown drew one's gaze and held it as if by magic, making it impossible to look away.

Eridani took a step toward it, but stopped herself. She looked to her blind warlock. "Is it safe?"

The warlock crawled toward the crown, sniffed at it, then returned to his queen and whispered to her. Eridani smiled and stepped forward. She picked up her crown—which was surprisingly light, yet sturdy—and placed it atop her head.

"Satisfied?" asked Dahlia, hands on her hips.

"You have done well," said Eridani. "It is everything I had hoped for."

Then Dahlia stepped up to the queen and spat in her face.

The guards were on her in an instant, holding her back, their curved blades in hand. Eridani wiped the saliva from her cheek with a sleeve.

"You shouldn't have done that," she said. "I was going to reward you by making you part of history. Hundreds of years from now, you would've been revered alongside me, as the world's greatest artisan to the world's greatest monarch. But, no more. I will order all of your other designs melted down, and your name struck from the records. No one will remember that you ever existed."

Eridani stepped forward until she was face to face with the craftswoman again. "You are right. The caged tiger can't be tamed. And when it bites, it must be put down." She withdrew a dagger from her belt, sunk it deep into Dahlia's belly, and twisted.

ERIDANI'S CROWN WAS the talk of the capital. Artists begged to make drawings of it, and poets wrote verses inspired by its beauty. For a short while, Eridani was happy. Then things took a turn for the worse.

Rebellions sprung across her vast empire with renewed vigor. Her armies were no longer sufficient to control the entire world. Her diplomats were forced to sue for peace by allowing various warlords to carve out swaths of land for their own. There was talk of armies being raised to march against the ancient Quadi capital itself. And, worst of all, the map inside the crown began to break apart.

Eridani first noticed it when a small ruby fell out of its place and landed at the base of the mesh. Out of reach, it rolled and rattled underneath the jeweled map whenever she moved her head.

Experts were summoned to the palace. By the time the capital's best jewelers arrived, two more gems dislodged from their settings on the map.

They scrutinized the crown with bits of magnifying glass, and conversed in hushed tones, cowed by Eridani's presence.

"I'm terribly sorry, Your Majesty," said the lead jeweler. "It seems that whoever created this crown used cheap glue instead of solder to hold the gems in place. An inconceivable error, given their obvious level of craft."

Eridani gritted her teeth. She knew that Dahlia's choice of material was no error. "The map will continue to fall apart, then?"

The jeweler nodded. He trembled with fear at delivering the bad news. "It is impossible to reach the gems without cutting open the platinum mesh."

"I will pay their weight in gold to anyone who finds a way to repair my crown!"

"None of us," said the jeweler, "and no craftsman in the world that we know of, possesses the skill to recreate the design. If the crown was pried apart to get at the gems, it could not be put together again in the same way."

The wily commoner deprived me of my prize, when she manipulated me into killing her. Eridani slammed her fist against the armrest of her throne, which prompted another small gem to fall from the map within the crown. She growled and waved, dismissing everyone from the room.

Jewelers and advisors alike rushed for the doors, jostling each other to get out before their ruler's infamous temper might erupt.

ERIDANI LOCKED HERSELF away from the world and spent days gazing into the crown. She no longer wore it. It sat in a sturdy display case in her throne room. Even so, the map continued to come apart.

There was a knock on the door and Arut entered, a sour expression on his face.

"More bad news?" Eridani asked.

"I'm afraid so, my Queen." The scribe shifted his weight from foot to foot.

"Out with it," she ordered.

"The North has rebelled," he said.

"Which city?"

"All of it," he said.

Eridani gritted her teeth. "I always knew Lady Voriana could only be trusted while things were going well," she said. "I should have replaced her a long time ago."

"It wasn't her," said Arut. "The mayor of Skond denounced you and had Voriana beheaded. The rest of the North appears to have followed suit. They claimed independence and declared this mayor, an old mercenary named Caer, their leader."

Eridani said nothing. *Everyone you know and trust will come to betray you.* Even from beyond the grave, the sorceress of Skond was haunting her with her prophecy.

"What are your orders?" asked Arut. "Shall we send the legions to pacify the North? Dispatch Bel Talesh's assassins to eliminate this Caer?"

Eridani's thoughts turned to the river of blood, and to Kalatar's journey home. She thought of Sana and Gavron, Toval and Liodan. All the friends and allies, whose life blood filled the river of her own journey. She always felt like she swam against the currents of fate. She thought of Danchu, of his smile when they shared evening meals during the siege of Woodcastle, and of the way his apparition looked at her when she was dying of the plague. She knew that, unlike Kalatar, she could never go home again.

"You will do nothing," said Eridani wearily.

She motioned for Arut to leave and watched as he shut the door behind him. Then she retrieved the crown from its display case and hugged it to her chest.

Eridani the Fierce, Queen Mother of the North, Sovereign of the Haldova Plains, Empress of the Quadi, sat alone in the throne room of her crumbling empire holding her crumbling crown, and pondered her legacy.

CHE END

ACKNOWLEDGMENTS

Writing may be a solitary pursuit, but publishing is a team effort. I'm deeply thankful to everyone who helped usher this book toward publication and only regret that I can list but a few of them below.

My wife and son, for putting up with me spending so many hours holed up in front of the keyboard.

Editor extraordinaire Elektra Hammond for making my writing look good and fixing my misconceptions about horses, archery, armor, and all sorts of other medieval things. Accurate descriptions herein are partly her doing; any remaining errors are due solely to my bullheaded refusal to adopt *all* of her suggestions.

Tomasz Maronski, for creating the best cover I could possibly hope for; as well as Melissa Neely and Jay O'Connell for making the book look great.

Nicola Chapman for lending her mesmerizing voice to Eridani and the gang in the audiobook.

The many beta readers who helped me polish the manuscript, including but not limited to Ken Liu, Andrea G. Stewart, Ali Nouraei, Zach Shephard, Tarryn Thomas, and Daniel Chulsky.

And last but not least, to you, dear reader, for picking up this book. You've read far enough into the credits that, were this a superhero movie, you'd earn an end scene. Given the limits of the medium, best I can offer you is another story. Join my mailing list at alexshvartsman.com to automatically receive my award-winning short story and be notified of future releases.

ABOUT THE AUTHOR
ALEX SHVARTSMAN

Alex Shvartsman is a writer, anthologist, translator, and game designer from Brooklyn, NY. He's the winner of the 2014 WSFA Small Press Award for Short Fiction and a two-time finalist (2015 and 2017) for the Canopus Award for Excellence in Interstellar Writing.

His short stories have appeared in *Analog, Nature, Strange Horizons, Intergalactic Medicine Show,* and a variety of other magazines and anthologies. His previously published books include collections *Explaining Cthulhu to Grandma* and *The Golem of Deneb Seven,* as well as his steampunk humor novella *H. G. Wells, Secret Agent.*

In addition to the UFO series, he has edited the *The Cackle of Cthulhu, Humanity 2.0, Funny Science Fiction, Coffee: 14 Caffeinated Tales of the Fantastic,* and *Dark Expanse: Surviving the Collapse* anthologies. His website is www.alexshvartsman.com.

CPSIA information can be obtained
at www.ICGtesting.com
Printed in the USA
LVHW031942111219
640174LV00013B/1138/P